W9-AWP-451

REQUIEM
FOR A SUMMER
COTTAGE

REQUIEM
for a SUMMER COTTAGE

A Novel by

Barbara Lockhart

SOUTHERN METHODIST
UNIVERSITY PRESS
Dallas

This novel is a work of fiction.
Names, characters, places, and incidents are either
the product of the author's imagination or are used fictitiously.

Cover art: "Coming Storm" by Lynne Lockhart.
From the collection of Karen and Daniel Prengaman.

Jacket design: Tom Dawson and Kellye Sanford
Text design: Kellye Sanford

Library of Congress Cataloging-in-Publication Data

Lockhart, Barbara M.
  Requiem for a summer cottage : a novel / by Barbara Lockhart. — 1st ed.
    p. cm.
  ISBN 0-87074-476-3 (acid-free paper)
    1. Eastern Shore (Md. and Va.) — Fiction. 2. Manic-depressive persons — Fiction.
  3. Father and child — Fiction. 4. Rural families — Fiction. 5. Farm life — Fiction.
  6. Maryland — Fiction. I. Title.

PS3562.O256 R4 2002
813'.54 — dc21   2002029238

Printed in the United States of America on acid-free paper
10   9   8   7   6   5   4   3   2   1

To Dorothy Marie Elbert Strayer, the youngest,
and to the memory of Spring Thorpe,
née Dorothea Helena Spring Peele, 1965-1999

ACKNOWLEDGMENTS

I would like to thank the following people, without whose knowledge and support this novel could not have been written: the many writers who influenced and guided me by their superb work; the Maryland State Arts Council for an Individual Artist Award; Chris Noel, Phyllis Barber, and Walter Wetherell for their generous readings, teachings, and words of wisdom; Richard Elman for helping me see characters had their own destiny; Fran Lewis and Mark Treanor for encouragement when the book was in its infant stages; Dorothy Strayer and Elizabeth Marion for their readings and comments in the later stages; John Logis for technical support with the computer; Michael Waters for his inspiration and friendship through the years; Kathryn Lang, whose unbelievable faith and wisdom helped make this a far better book than it was; and my daughter, Lynne Lockhart, who generously provided the painting on the cover. My greatest debt is to my family, whose enduring patience, humor, and love steady me.

CONTENTS

Thus sailing with sealed orders, we ourselves are the repositories of the secret packet, whose mysterious contents we long to learn. There are no mysteries out of ourselves.

HERMAN MELVILLE
White Jacket or The World in a Man-of-War

PROLOGUE: BOAT PATH, 1970

~✗~

The sunburst on the chrome of the boat's windshield beckoned to Justin as he entered the water. He waded slowly and without a ripple, as though weights were attached to each foot, a man surrendered as he held the boat cushions over his head. There were no signs of life yet along the string of cottages yawning piers out into the river, and the boats lay still and white and silent, the mooring ropes relaxed into hammock lines as the early tide ebbed. On the nearby bulkhead, a heron stretched great wings and Justin noticed it for the first time. A second later the bird lifted toward flight trailing spindly legs, then rose higher and higher with wings broad and sure into the windless morning air.

Justin was about to bring the boat in from the mooring pole and guide it to the bulkhead so Rosemary could board. As he unhooked the line and tossed it to rest on top of the pole, he held the boat by the bow rail and turned to face the sun. With the heat of midsummer on his face, he shaded his eyes from the low angle of light and looked back on his land—the narrow beach with clumps of swamp grass, the long curve of seawall extending into the river, and the summer cottage with its windows open to the June air. The cottage, far from his complicated life in the city, every board and nail marked with the sweat of his own hands, had withstood two hurricanes so far, the cedar weathered to a soft gray—like his dreams. He worried about his dreams. Sometimes he lost steam. Then the dreams pricked him as they did now in this expectant stillness. All he could think

about was fleeing—toward open water, open sky. Away. He pulled the boat
along behind him as he headed for the bulkhead and listened to the quiet
slap of water along the hull.

Water slick as oil this morning. Perfect for skiing. His kids loved to ski
and weren't afraid to try anything. Got it from their old man. When he was
sixteen, he raced the boat he'd built, *Miss Behave*. Ah, those were the days!
He and the boat against the mood of the water, the roar of motors tearing
around him, the rush and thrill of shooting ahead of the others—the pay-
off for months of planning and practice, the elation of winning—nothing
else called to him so loudly or satisfied him so well. The race. The tension
before, the release after. Yeah, those were the days. Now the pull of the ski
rope on the boat reminded him how family anchored him and tugged at
his freedom.

Maybe he should look into flying. Sell the boat, keep the twelve-foot-
er, *Greenfly*, for fishing and get a small plane. Once he asked Newland,
the pilot of the local crop duster, to take him and Rosemary up for her
birthday. He remembered the river from above—like a blue vein on a
long arm, contained and etched into the land, and the dot of a cruiser
speeding its way downriver with the long, white V behind it—its course
as predetermined as anything else in life. But take flying—there was infinite distance and unbounded dimension to fool around in. He squinted
at the forever of space and focused on the speck which could be the
heron.

He was up on the bulkhead tying the boat fore and aft, its sides gently
rubbing the poles, when the screened door banged. Davey, just six, leaped
toward the beach. Whooping, flailing his arms, he splashed into the water
and in another instant disappeared. Justin watched and mumbled, "Son of
a gun. Never know where he'll turn up," and continued watching for what
seemed like five minutes for Davey to emerge. "Damn kid," he said and
bit his lip. He crouched and peered into the water. Maybe Davey hit a
rock or something. Then Davey's head popped up swinging left to right,
looking for direction.

"Davey!" Justin called but Davey was under again before he could finish saying his name. "Hell with 'im," he said under his breath, realizing
there was nothing he could do or would want to do about the reflection of

himself he saw in his youngest son, the kid who somehow stayed out of reach. Justin waded toward the beach.

"Michael!" he called out instead.

Michael, eleven, appeared alongside the cottage carrying the anchor. He raised it in answer to his father's call.

"Yeah, that's right." Pain in the ass having only one anchor. One day they'd go off without it. A real sinking feeling—watching that other anchor drop into the water and the whole line go with it, the end jerking like a cat's tail and disappearing into the deep. Never did find out who untied it, but he could guess. He was anxious to be off now. Right now. Darting away from the shore. Only Michael was ready. Where the hell was Rosemary? Water like a mirror. Perfect for skiing. God, what a day!

Underwater, Davey listened to water rush by his head, hoping the breath that filled his chest lasted so he could see how long he was able to stay under this time. Should've counted. Next time, by fives. He followed the silver dashes of the minnows. His legs were powerful, Superman legs. He felt a cape of water flutter over his back as his arms reached out. His body parted the water. The world stayed like this for eons, hairy stones and nails and old bottles, the water connecting them. He was connected to everything too, just by seeing.

His chest was going to burst. Up through the skin of water—a splash of sun, air, a gasp, the other world waiting, vigilant—down again—five, ten, fifteen, twenty—his father's legs just ahead, knees like big knots, minnows nibbling at the hairs—ankle bones like bolts hinging giant flippers plodded through the water. The minnows flashed away. He'd follow them but his father might be ready to go. A quick look. It was okay. Dad was heading toward the cottage to get Mom and she always took a long time. He had the whole river to himself. He could swim straight across to Cheetam Point if he wanted to. Underwater all the way. He'd come up for air like a turtle. Nobody would know where he was. Hey! He forgot to count! He stood up but ducked in the water again: Michael was coming after him. Bet he could stay under long enough for the *Guinness Book of World Records*. Michael would never get him.

Michael laid the fishing rods on the grass and stepped down into the boat. Taking care not to knock the anchor on the fiberglass hull, he placed it on one of the boat cushions and began tying the anchor rope to the fitting. A clove hitch. He'd never forget to do that again. He reached for the rods, put them in their places and checked the spinners. Davey should get his own rod, which could be anywhere on the point. It wasn't in any of the places Michael had looked. *Phough!* He peered over the side of the boat at the sound. "Davey," he called, but Davey was under again. Michael jumped in and swam after him. "Wait a minute. Where's your rod? Go get your rod!" he yelled to the water. Then he heard his father calling, "Never mind the rods. We can't fit all that stuff on board at once. Just the skis, Michael, just the skis."

He loved showing off on skis. He put the tow bar behind his head, *Look Ma, no hands!* That made her crazy. She started screaming, *Stop, you'll break your neck!* But his father liked it and took off his hat and waved it around in a wide circle over his head, *Ha ha hey!* he yelled. It was better than a good report card, which he didn't get too many of.

He'd never carry Davey on his shoulders again, though. He thought he'd killed him, and sickened at the thought of Davey slumped in his life jacket, his face white and his eyes closed. He never forgot how Davey looked, how it felt to think he might have harmed his brother. The image of Davey hurt kept him from taking a whack at him whenever he felt like it. Getting up on skis, he'd come out of the water with Davey slippery as an eel on his back and he prayed his brother wouldn't fall even though his father began whooping it up in the boat and laughing.

Davey, in panic, had grabbed Michael's ears and hair and finally held onto his head without realizing his hands were over Michael's eyes. So there they were skimming over the water with Michael blind, although he could still hear his mother's screams and his father's whoops. He could only hang on, feel his brother slipping and slipping, the crazy shift and wobble of his brother's weight, the bar in his hands the only thing he could count on. He'd had to let go when his feet slipped out from under him and then he felt the rush of water through his legs, Davey's weight lighten, heard the ski smack Davey in the head—tough little Davey who could take anything Michael dished out to him. Davey, the human sacrifice. Everybody said he'd saved Davey, "You pushed him toward the boat, Michael—if it weren't for you—" his mother said with tears in her eyes, but Michael didn't feel any better. He didn't know what made him so mad at Davey sometimes. It just flared up. Wham.

In the distance, he heard his father yelling at the door of the cottage, "Throw me some towels, will ya? Hey, anybody? You girls ready yet? C'mon! Let's go!" The sun burned his shoulders as he sat on the transom and squinted out over water so smooth he could try it on one ski this morning. A greenfly sat on his arm. He watched its iridescence until he felt the bite and slapped it off.

Jeez, women took a long time.

Finally, Anne slipped out of the house and ran toward the bulkhead. Justin called, "Where's your mother, skinny Annie? Hey, c'mere," he said without giving her time to answer. "'Member the turtle you made in the sand yesterday? Look."

In the same spot where she and Davey made a giant turtle the day before, Justin pointed to a mound in the sand, and to tracks from the mound to the river.

"She laid eggs and took off."

"Nu-uh!" She looked up at him with almond-shaped eyes green as his own. He could tell she was torn between pretending and knowing better and for a moment he hated the passing of time, the planting of logic into childhood. What he wanted most for his kids was that they would always be able to imagine, to dream.

He uncovered a white ball. "Feel. It's got a paper-thin shell."

She stooped, enthralled with the eggs like smooth golf balls, then stood again, saying, "But I made a he," as her small, quiet face lit up at her joke. She was everything he would want in a daughter, spirited, keeping up with the boys, and there was an astuteness, a spark he adored. She was already nine, he thought with dismay, watching her run to tell Davey.

Rosemary, ski belts draped over her arm and a large cooler in her hands, descended the narrow, wooden steps of the cottage and walked toward the boat, a signal to the others, even Davey, who swam out from behind the pier, where he was probably planning to splash Michael in the stern of the boat. Michael, who patiently waited where he was supposed to, suddenly straightened up and whirled around toward Davey, water

running down his back. "Get you later," he hissed as he reached out to
Rosemary to steady her boarding.

"Never mind, Michael," she said. "It's only water."

Signs of life appeared from other cottages—doors slammed, flags
went up, a dog barked. Rosemary guessed they had awakened everyone,
voices carried so easily here on the river. Even inside the cottage sounds
bounced off the cedar and resonated. She was constantly shushing kids,
but sometimes there was no hushing this crowd and, of course, she didn't
really want to. Next door, white-haired Mr. Phillips walked along his pier,
carefully picking up his bare feet to avoid splinters. He leaned over the
water and pulled up his crab pot, which contained a dead turtle. Standing
unsteadily in the boat, Rosemary caught the look of horror on Anne's face.
She waved a good morning at Mr. Phillips, feeling secure, maybe even a
little smug with her family contained in the boat. She was proud of their
uniqueness and of her busyness, her clear purpose in nurturing them, yet
in Mr. Phillips she saw a glimpse of life without mate or children, of what
was to come, and for a second was chilled despite the heat of the sun. She
had time—she was only thirty-two. She settled herself before the windshield in one of the built-in seats on either side of the bow, legs outstretched. Justin stood at the helm; he could see above her, his eyes disappearing in the shadow of his visor, his long, lean fingers around the wheel,
his shoulders stooped to reach it.

"This okay?" she asked although she knew this was where he wanted
her. "Want me to drive—to practice for when you ski?"

He nodded without looking at her. "Later," he said, his eyes scanning
the water. He left the controls to undo the bowline while Michael pushed
the boat away from the bulkhead. With the motor idling, they drifted
toward open river. Then Justin moved the throttle forward and the boat
leapt through the water. Once again he imagined the view from the air,
the tree shadows along the fields, the long rectangles of green edged by the
river and his boat slipping away as the river widened and joined the bay
and other boats. Just for the hell of it, in case anyone in that plane up there
should be watching, he turned the wheel to the left and in a giant, magnificent sweep to the right and to the left again and to the right, so that his
path was different from all other paths.

Rosemary turned and looked up at him while she hung onto the bow rail with one arm and forced a smile. "Careful, Justin!" she warned, listening to the kids laugh and squeal as they hung on. She saw how they trusted him and kept their eyes on the horizon that skimmed and swirled around them. Beginning to relax, she enjoyed the brilliant flashes of sun bursting on the water, the rainbows in the wake, and the osprey startled from its poled nest, but returned to the children to watch their pleasure, to feel the certainty of her purpose in their brown, slender bodies as they anticipated the turns. Leaning in rhythm to their father's playful passage, they screamed at the fun. She hoped they would always have each other. A ski belt slid across the deck and Michael caught it with his foot. He stooped to retrieve it to its proper place under the seat. She nodded at him in thanks.

Suddenly, the boat slowed. "Aw, Dad! Do it some more!" Davey said, but Justin waved his hand and motioned toward the bow. He moved the throttle to idle. The boat lurched and began to dance in its own wake. Something big was in the water—dark, like a piece of the woods broken off, branches bleached and dead. Floating? No. Coming toward them. Against the flow of the tide with a will of its own. Swimming. As they watched, the branch turned into a buck with a huge rack that was paddling across the path of the boat. Justin shut off the engine and in the abrupt silence they heard the weighted breaths of the deer pulsing in the still air.

Davey whispered, "Gaw!" Michael shushed him. How can a deer swim? His legs are sticks! Four, six, eight points. The rack must be heavy, unsupported by water, not like the rest of him. Would he make it? What would happen if the deer started to flounder, drown? What should they do? It wouldn't, though. It was moving steadily through the water.

Anne leaned over the bow. For one grand instant the deer was directly in front of her. She could see its nostrils drawing in and puffing out with each breath, and its black globe of an eye in which she saw, or thought she saw, the glimmer of the bow rail and herself peering into it, distorted like the mirrors in the Fun House at Ocean City. What did that eye see? And the eye on the other side? Two different scenes that it must put together in its head? Did it see everywhere at once? The sky, the water, the boat, the beach, upriver, downriver, the gulls, the herons, her in her blue and white bathing suit leaning, wishing she could touch it? Were they all the same to the deer, all things equal? Unless they moved. She understood. If she moved she would panic the deer. Some things you just know. Nobody tells you. Too quickly, the deer was past.

With his eyes on the rack, Justin breathed hard. That's life for you. Like going down the road and running into a goddamn deer. A thousand dollars worth of damage to the car. What if he'd hit it with the boat? They all should have their life jackets on. He saw the path on the river from the air again. The white wake cut into the blue in a wavy line, and the deer's swim line drawn across. An omen. Something always in his way. He had only begun, with a thirst that would not let him waste a minute. Monday morning in less than twenty-four hours. Thirty-five years old already. His father gone at forty-four. Were his own arteries filling up with plaque? Believing in sneak attacks, he took off his cap and studied the cork he had tied in its peak, a flotation device in case it flew off when he was in the boat. Maybe he could patent the idea.

Rosemary hugged her knees. They were privileged to have seen the deer, fortunate for all the things that brought them to this precise moment, the cottage, the boat, the day, Justin. She scanned the woods to the left from where the deer had come, and imagined the dark, moist, decaying floor from which it rose that morning, the smell of the black acidic earth warmed by its body, the dew gathered along the hairs of its hide as it made its way slowly toward the water.

The kids would tell their cousins on the next visit, "Bet you've never seen a deer swim across the river. We did. We even saw its eye-balls, and its nostrils pushing in and out—that's how close we were!" The deer would be a part of the repertoire with which they storied the world and they wouldn't forget, reminding each other through the years. It would be among the things that girded them as family, a moment to measure all other moments by, a kind of forever. She glanced from face to face and hoped she would remember them like this, still and rapt as they watched the buck rise slowly from the water, its hind flanks glinting in the sun as it pranced quickly through the shallows to the sand and disappeared between the rows of newly tasseled corn.

She heard Justin call out, "Life jackets, everybody. We're not moving till everybody's got one on. Who wants to ski first?"

Part One

UNQUIET EDEN

PURCHASE, 1965

⌣

Byte. Megabyte. Funny words, Rosemary said, when he tried to explain them. "Don't laugh, Baby. They butter your bread," he told her back when he was fresh out of college. The new language included words like *per diem* and *all expenses paid.* They'd moved cross country eight times like prospectors in a gold rush on the first breaths of computer technology. Three kids later, they settled in suburbia outside of D.C. All hail to NASA.

Time to think about investments. A vacation home. On the last visit to his mother—he still wondered how she ever wound up in a town called Pucam, a far cry from Long Island—they drove to a place called Sulley's Point. "Justin," she'd said, adjusting her glasses. "Talk about possibilities! Taxes and expenses are low here. Waterfront everywhere. Pay attention!"

Good old Evelyn. She was right. The river, trafficked only by local watermen and lined with cornfields, lay like a safely guarded secret accessible in only a few places along its shore. Barring a waterfront farm, there was only one place he knew for a vacation spot and that was Sulley's Point, a precarious and shifting sandbar stretching between river and marsh where local elites vacationed along with people from the city in cottages quietly passed from generation to generation. Through one of her bridge-playing friends, Evelyn arranged the rental of one of the cottages for two weeks. She had filled the refrigerator with food and tacked a note on its rounded front: *See you tomorrow afternoon for a swim. Hope you find what you like inside.*

The smell of the city dropped away. Rosemary, worried about being surrounded by water that first week, insisted the kids wear life jackets wherever they went. By the second week, she had relaxed. Anne and Michael stood on the pier with fishing rods for longer than Justin ever thought they could, and he listened to their excited calls every time they added another small perch to the bucket. Davey, a year old, knew what to do with his arms and legs in the water. "Instinctual," said Rosemary grinning, her hand supporting his slippery, round, brown body. When she looked up to see if Justin was watching, he was happy to see her smile. Her vulnerability made him feel a grave responsibility. And pride, too. He was, after all, a man with a man's responsibility. He'd always *been* responsible, hadn't he? Started delivering newspapers at eleven. Never had to ask his parents for money for even a haircut from then on.

Evelyn, delighted to have them close by, came every afternoon for a swim. "I understand," she said one afternoon, "that the Marshall place is for sale and with it, odd sections of waterfront that may be too narrow to build on. Brought you a number to call."

But Marshall's was too run down. It needed more than a coat of paint. There was a hole in the roof the size of a basketball on the slope facing the water and plenty of rotted wood below as a result. On an adjacent lot was a small storage shed. Although the lot was too narrow to allow additions to the shed, he could line the walls with bunk beds, sink, stove—or they could set up a tent. Another lot, barely forty feet wide, mostly marsh—he'd have to get tons of fill dirt—had a shoreline that stretched sixty feet out into the river in a crescent. Bent itself around into a little harbor and a small beach. Could build the house right there. Kids would love it. They could roll out of bed in the morning right onto the beach. He'd always wanted waterfront. One might measure success by a piece of waterfront. Besides, it was what fathers did for family. Didn't his own father and mother bring him and his brother, George, up to Lake Placid every year? For two weeks they'd be wild with the pleasure of it, diving off the pier and dunking each other, swimming races with his mother joining in. It was the only time he saw his father laughing and playing, his serious lawyer face lighting up for the duration.

"Relax, will you! One more week and it's back to the grind," said Rosemary.

He couldn't. He was revved up. He had extraordinary energy. It was that sparkling, beckoning river and its possibilities. His ambition flowed from the same fountain that caused greatness in men and incredible feats, he was sure. Trucking through marsh grass and slapping mosquitoes, he took measurements with the children scampering after him. At night, he sketched and planned, five bunk beds for the storage shed, two and two, one swung up during the day to allow use of the sink and stove underneath. He dreamed. He ruled out nothing. He could make anything happen. He was alive with fire and nerve—he had both—that was what separated him from the rest—always had. *Anything! Hear me, Rosemary? Anything is possible.*

In the morning he showed her his plans, but what he saw was panic. "I don't even want to think about spending summers in a shed lined with bunk beds," she said wearily. She put up with his ideas but never took them seriously, waiting patiently for him to go on to something else, change his mind, *flit*, which he did at times, he admitted. But it was all part of the process, the grand gathering of sparks out of which would come *something*. What was she so afraid of? Coming from that tight little house in Queens from parents who worked and saved and rarely enjoyed, she didn't understand it was only the beginning. Once he got a foothold on waterfront down here, no telling what it might lead to. She had no vision of her own but would resolutely cancel his.

He didn't have to call the real estate agent. The guy called him. "Mr. Wells, heah," in a voice that sounded smooth and confident with just enough down-home in it to call him buddy. "I understand you might be interested in a good deal, buddy," he said in a slow, rumbling drawl. Word got around. He had a feeling he was being watched during all that measuring. "I've got an island for sale, a whole island with a view of the Chesapeake Bay, one hundert and seventy-five acres. Could take you on down there if you're interested." His voice had a silky easiness. He was a man who'd probably put his feet up on your coffee table and never think a thing of it.

Bringing Rosemary and the kids was probably a mistake, but if he included her in decision-making maybe she wouldn't object so much. Mr. Wells sighed as they piled into this yellow Buick with Davey in Rosemary's arms in the backseat along with Michael and Anne. They drove for an hour through scattered towns of thirty houses, then towns of ten houses, a town of six, then out where marshland stretched along both sides of the road into patches of mud and reflections of blue sky in a maze of brown, blue, and green, where red-winged blackbirds teetered on thin blades of marsh grass and herons rose from the water, wings stretched, aawking at the intrusion. An incredible place. And there was no one, not even a work-boat along the horizon, when the macadam ceased. Then the dirt road narrowed, a tunnel with eight-foot-tall marsh grass on both sides, till finally white sand slowed the Buick.

"Now I would suggest, Ma'am, that you and the kiddies stay here while we go on foot. Got to cross a few muddy places, see what I mean? We won't be long," said Mr. Wells, running plump fingers along his brow.

When they got back, Rosemary was furious. The baby cried like he was never going to stop and Michael and Anne whined about hamburgers and French fries. The four doors of the Buick were open wide like wings on a dragonfly and sand covered the red carpeting. "You've been gone two hours," she snarled. "Two goddamn hours in this mosquito-infested heat." It was rare to see her so worked up, her face flushed, her eyes small.

Truth was, he forgot about them. There was a path at first, then they had to make their way through marsh grass and a thick pine forest with nearly impenetrable briars and although Mr. Wells, now "C.J.," was ready to go back, he kept talking about the view of the Chesapeake with such fervor that Justin plowed on one more mile and then another, excited as a kid, heart racing, intoxicated with blue sky and wilderness he'd never seen before. They spotted a herd of eleven deer leaping across a stretch of marsh grass, enough to stir any man to an appreciation of grace and valor in the struggle to live. An owl on the ground, puffed up to twice its size, stared at them with ringed eyes and guarded mystery, while two bald eagles circled the white, stark limbs of a dead loblolly. And that cloudless sky—he'd never seen so much of it all at once. He'd been born in the wrong time, he thought, gazing at the horizon unmarred by anything man-made. Here he would make his mark, in this piece of wilderness. He had so much energy, so much strength—and he had only tapped the surface of his inner resources. He was more alive than others; he had a gift. But he needed opportunity. He needed expansion. He could own an island—think of it!—put in a bridge across the marsh, maybe an airstrip, dredge a harbor, build a huge bulwark of a house.

At one point, C.J. said, "I do believe I'll turn 'round now," and mopped his brow while huge patches of dark blue sagged under his armpits and across his chest.

"Suit yourself, man, but I've got to see the water and the shoreline before I can make a decision." The pine forest should provide wood for the house—he could build his own sawmill—some of the pines were sixty or seventy years old and ought to be harvested anyway. Still he'd preserve as much of the woods as he could.

Then suddenly there it was around the bend, luminous between the pines. The bay. A vibrant, tremulous blue, opening possibilities as infinite as a body could stand, as deep as the water itself and as wide as that uninterrupted sky. Off in the distance, he saw a container ship riding high, slowly tracking its course to Singapore or Iceland. Here, on this bay-washed shore, was his link to the rest of the world, too. With his own dock, his own airstrip, *Justin Williams Enterprises*, maybe.

But—there were fallen trees along the shore that reached out into the water, upturned roots half buried in land seared off by stormy seas. Hmmm.

"Looks like there might be considerable erosion along here," he said to C.J.

"Well, yessir. There is. But the government will help pay for the bulkhead to cut down erosion, and at a foot a year you've got a long way to go even if you don't seawall it, ay?" C.J. looked up at Justin with an old buddy smile, beads of sweat on his upper lip.

He'd heard of islands disappearing into the bay, but that took a while. There was plenty left of this one. Besides, he'd have the shoreline built up and protected before long. Thing was to get started. Grab it while he could. There were just so many islands, just so much waterfront. At his feet the water lapped quietly, small gushes of bay nudged at the toes of his muddied tennis shoes.

On the way back, thoughts galloped through his head. *Riprap. Cheap. Broken-up highways, old buildings, could ship blocks of the stuff out here and line the shore. Cost like hell. Maybe not. Old tires. Corrugated sheeting. A hundred and seventy-five acres—a lot of seawall.*

A red-winged blackbird swayed on a thin reed. He watched, sensing his life as an island owner was about as tenuous because here was Rosemary who couldn't see farther than the kids' creature needs as she leaned on the side of the car, the tendons in her neck taut, her face steamed. She was all blown up like a toad as she slapped mosquitoes off Davey's legs and her own.

"C'mon," he said to Michael and Annie, "first one in the car gets two hamburgers," not ready to tell Rosemary anything.

In the end it was not the island but the ferry that let him know he'd gone too far. He felt her mounting anger, watched her slap bacon in the pan and whip eggs with a vengeance. He knew she wanted to harness him, make him pay attention to her instead of his grandiose ideas. Pushed him away in bed again. But he couldn't concede anything. She'd be glad in the end. And proud. It was always like this. A little game, a little prancing around they must do. But he wouldn't let her cloud his vision.

Then he heard of a deal that held the advantage of a partnership with someone who shared a vision as great as his own. A friend of C.J.'s called. Olie Patchett. Word got around. *Here comes a guy with money.* Yeah. If they only knew, but he wouldn't mind laying down their savings with the promise of excellent returns. Patchett said he had, stored at this very moment along rails installed on his beach for that very purpose, a now obsolete Hampton Roads–Norfolk Ferry. The idea was to plant it west of the Choptank River Bridge and convert it into a restaurant.

"I'm looking for a partner," Patchett said over the phone. "Why don't you and your wife and kids come sailing with us on Thursday? We can talk over details. I'll take you down to the site I have in mind."

They stood on the beach looking up at the rusting hull, the deck that tilted crazily as the tide ebbed, the now nostalgic proclamation of

Hampton Roads–Norfolk in green letters across its bow. He knew all Rosemary saw were the gray-white sides bleeding rust from every bolt. But it could be fixed up—sandblasted, repainted, returned to former glory.

"Sturdy little ship, don't you think, Rosemary?" he said in a voice he hoped appealed to her sense of the romance of the sea (which he planned to market for the tourist trade). Maybe he'd do both the ferry and the island, develop a settlement of vacation homes and use the ferry to make runs between the Western Shore and his island.

"You're not going to do this, Justin," she said between clenched teeth so Patchett couldn't hear.

"But it could be a real moneymaker."

"No. No way. We haven't got money to spare and that thing will soak up whatever we do have."

He could tell its grandness frightened her. It was too big a digression. She thought she was some kind of compass for him as to where the path should be, but it was the beaten one. He wanted to go the other way, whatever way that was. He sure as hell didn't want to be like everybody else— afraid. Yet he didn't like to upset her. He hated confrontation.

That was why they'd been back in the city for two weeks before he told her. He sat on the edge of the bed, yanking off his socks with his back to her when he said he bought the waterfront on the point. The one with the harbor.

"The *island?*"

"No, the lot at Sulley's Point."

"Is it big enough to build on?" she said, walking over to his side of the bed to look him in the eye.

"Just barely."

"It's just a piece of swamp!" Her hands were on her hips and it crossed his mind to grab her while she was still dressed and tear some buttons, surprise her, hear her shriek—he loved it when she lost her calm—but he was afraid she'd fight him off just now.

"I'll fill it in. You'll see, Babe. He only wanted a thousand for it. I've ordered a house, too."

"What? How can you order a house, just like that?"

"Comes in a kit. Just the shell. Need to get some fill dirt first, though."

"Can we afford it?"

"I got a loan."

"Why didn't you tell me?"

"What do you think I'm doing now?"

In the end, she didn't seem to mind that he hadn't discussed it with her. He overheard her talking to her friend Hannah on the phone. "Well, we had an opportunity to buy an entire island," she said, "but we settled for a smaller piece with a wonderful little harbor."

Later, when the kids were in bed and he was reading the paper, she said, "You have so many zany ideas you scare me. I don't know whether you're brave or crazy. I'm always worried about what you might do."

"You exaggerate," he told her. "You want me to be like all the other husbands on this block, just grinding away?"

"Of course not," she said smiling at him, and in those three words he heard her pride in the grandness of his ideas. She believed he was going to make his mark someday and she depended on him to do just that. He returned to the paper. He'd done it. No regrets. He was going to build a cottage by the river and they'd have access to the whole bay. He planned to use it as the model home for a franchise on vacation homes. Offer people a day on the river if they'd make the trek across the Bay Bridge to the model home—maybe feature a line of sailboats as well—maybe rent a booth at the boat show, build the cottage in the fall, do sales promotions on the franchises in the winter—who knows?—maybe buy the island yet, all in his spare time. Laughter bubbled up but he suppressed it into a wheeze behind the paper, his first million on the way.

He ordered forty truckloads of sand—an invasion of yellow on the black marsh mud that interrupted the peace of the neighboring clapboard cottages built early in the century. The following weekend he set the cinder block pilings just high enough to escape a good tide, and on the next Friday the lumber arrived, all fresh and sweet smelling, the newly hewn Michigan cedar boards bound together by size, precut and stacked against the clear, blue autumn sky.

Each weekend he worked alone and relished laying the first plank and then another, and another across the pilings in the sharpness of the October wind sweeping off-river. He glanced at the clouds of dust from harvesting corn on the opposite shore, listened to the honking of thousands of Canada geese as they gathered in the harbor downriver, breathed in the sea breezes and thought how grand it was to be working outdoors like his forefathers who had built ships on the shores of Long Island long ago. Suddenly he knew them, and how they must have felt with their hands on new wood as he looked down at his own hands raising plank after plank in a kind of celebration, fitting them tongue in groove like a giant jigsaw puzzle until the four walls stood. He imagined the wood weathering in the years to come, the house withstanding storm after storm. With it, he had a place in the world, a permanence that was rare in his life since he was fifteen and his dad died. The world seemed to take a plunge then. He'd worked to help his mother as much as he could, and his brother, George, four years younger than he. He had learned never to count on anything except his own two hands. This cottage was his ship, his handprint the masthead.

The four trusses presented a problem. Each consisted of three logs bolted together in a triangle, the base of which would rest on the outer walls while the other two sides supported the roof. He needed help lifting them into place, and so after breakfast at his mother's on Saturday morning, he drove to the colored side of town down along the railroad tracks and stopped at the small gathering of men at Duke's Gas Station.

"Anybody here want to earn a few bucks?" he called from his car.

Two of them strolled over while he waited, engine running, coffee mug in hand.

"What you got?" said the taller one, his flannel shirt buttoned up to his neck, hair in a mild bush.

"I'm building a house—down Sulley's Point? Need some help lifting the trusses."

"Oh, yeah. You the one what had it come in a truck."

Word got around. "I figure it'll take a couple hours. Twenty-five bucks apiece and I'll buy lunch."

Buttoned-up looked at his chum whose okay was no more than a flicker of his eyelid.

"When?"

"Now." Just standing around on a Saturday morning, chewing the breeze, nothing else to do, strong, healthy young men—he wondered why, yet he envied their camaraderie. Once they were in the car, he introduced himself and asked for their names, but after brief utterances of "Tyrone" and "Jim," they looked down and didn't seem to want to say much, uncomfortable in a white man's car.

Tyrone, to whom he'd spoken first, said, "You not from around here."

"Western Shore, D.C. area," said Justin. "But my mother lives here. She was married to Miller, the guy who owned the big farm next to the pickle factory."

"Yeah. Yeah! I worked for him haulin' 'maters."

Talk went easier after that as did the rest of the morning and by noon, the four cedar triangles pointed skyward. Wiping their foreheads on their sleeves, the men sat laughing and talking down by the water, feet hanging from the neighboring bulkhead, when he suggested they get some lunch. Both men looked down again, and he took their silence for shyness.

Down the road, idle gas pumps from the twenties stood on cement islands lonesome and plainspoken in front of the place everybody called Muskie's. The screen door flapped and a dozen flies came in with them. The chrome bar stools were occupied by watermen dropping by for a short one after the first good catch of the oyster season. Justin guessed it was Muskie himself who came toward them across the checkered floor and said, "Turn yourself right around, boy. You got company we don't let in here."

He looked behind him. The men hung back, hands in pockets.

"What the hell," he heard himself say. "What are you saying?"

"You know what I mean. We don't allow them in here." Muskie nodded at the men now backing out the door.

"But they work for me. We just want a sandwich."

"Look now, they know better than that. You're the one what doesn't know so it's time you did. Get your ass out of here—hanging with them—you're no better than they are."

There was no answer, none that he could think of in the face of such idiocy. He understood now the silence of the men but hated their defeat, their hangdog look, and wondered why grown men would accept such indignity, never revealing to a stranger they weren't allowed in a place like Muskie's, as if the shame was theirs.

Why do they take it? It had nothing to do with him even though he knew he'd surely be branded the foreigner now, here on these quiet shores along this pristine river. But he *was* a foreigner and glad of it. For a moment he felt disgust with them all, with Muskie as well as the men who met the world cringing. A man made his own destiny.

Before getting back in the car, he tried to look them in the eye. "Any other place we can go?" he said, but their eyes never met his as they shook their heads, so he apologized for the mishap, thanked them for their help, and when he placed the bills in their hands, gave them a little extra to get lunch. He went back to study his house and think about his next move. Yet he thought of them throughout the afternoon with an odd heaviness in the pit of his stomach, how they'd backed out the door, shoulders hunched. Men so beaten had nothing to do with him, but the look in their eyes frightened him.

He showed her pictures he took of the broad beams laid on the pilings, and she imagined him standing, feet apart, a cigar hanging from his lips, his nose pressed into the Kodak. Alone on the weekends and often during the week, she felt left out as if he had a lover. He was so absorbed he forgot her, and she didn't see the cottage till it was finished. She depended on his words, but he was sparse with those, and asking questions only got her vague replies.

He left for the Eastern Shore on Friday evenings and returned late on Sunday nights when she greeted him through a drowsy fog of sleep. *Walls are up*, he'd say, or *Weather held out*, and pull off his work boots. Seconds later, he'd brush his teeth furiously and slip into bed without bothering her. She wanted to be bothered and worried he was losing interest. But his interest always had been sporadic, she told herself as she lay awake listening to him snore. Remember when you were married only a year and he didn't want to bother for a good six months? Turned his face to the wall and said he'd hit his sexual peak at sixteen? She thought he was kidding. He wasn't. He had no interest. But now, she was certain it was only that he was absorbed in every board, every nail, every angle, and using up all his energy on hammering and sawing. During the week, he was often away on business trips. Snappy and smart as he left the house on Monday morning in a suit and tie, you'd never know it was the same person. He lived in two different worlds; she wasn't in either one. But he was a gifted man. He could do anything. She *was* proud of him. He'd make his mark.

In the meantime, she took the kids for long walks and made trails through the suburban sprawl in different directions from the house—to the park, the Seven-Eleven, the swings at the school with Davey in the stroller and Michael and Annie hanging on each side. "He's building a house on the water," she'd say to the neighbors, or "He's off to California this week." He was *so* ambitious, her husband. She waited for him with a patience only wives distracted by young children can muster.

One Sunday night he didn't come home. She woke up at two-thirty with Davey crying and realized Justin wasn't next to her. Comforting the baby, she waited for a while but in the end decided to call Evelyn.

"I don't want to worry you," she said, "but he's not here and I thought maybe he was too tired to drive home. Thought maybe he decided to stay with you."

Evelyn said, "I'll ride down to the point and check. Knowing Justin, he's okay. He's a bit compulsive about some things, you know. Try not to worry." But there was a tremor in her voice, and Rosemary was sorry she'd called.

Forty-five minutes later, Evelyn called back, her voice firm and sweet. "Rosemary? He's fine. He's on the roof hammering away. He's in his glory. Believe it or not, the moon is so bright here he has enough light to hammer shingles. He won't come down. God knows what the neighbors must think. Anyway, he stood right up there on the roof. 'Careful,' I yelled, 'don't slip!'—but he just laughed like he owned the world. It was a grand sight to see, him under the stars wielding that hammer, grinning ear to ear as if he was in some sort of spotlight. He's okay. Just like his father—doesn't know when to stop. Says he'll finish tonight and go to work from there. He'll see you tomorrow night. Go to sleep, dear."

In the spring, when the shell of the house was up and he began to work on the rooms, Justin took Michael, who was seven now and big enough to hold ends of boards and fetch nails and tools. He told her, "It's so cool, Mom, wait'll you see. We got the bedroom walls up for Davey and me, and there's a room for Annie and one for you and Dad. And sliding closet doors. And big windows so we can see the river from anywhere in the house except the bedroom for Davey and me. But we can see the marina from our window and the crab boats and the rail they use to pull up the boats to paint their bottoms. We even bought a boat. A green rowboat. We're going to get a motor for it. Dad wrote out the check, sixty dollars, just like that. The boat fit right on top of the car so we brought it to our beach. I thought of a name for the boat—we have to get the letters, one G, one R, two E's, one N . . ."

"Just tell me its name, Michael."

"Greenfly!" he shouted. Standing behind Michael, Justin grinned. "Next weekend," he said, "come on over. Measure for curtains," and he reached around and pulled her to him as though he just remembered she was there. He was a genius, her husband, with all the signs of greatness—talent, determination, self-reliance—he could do anything.

PATCH OF SKY

⌁

Annie and Michael said it was the summer of the swimming deer, but Davey thought of it as his first summer on the top bunk. He couldn't remember a time when they didn't have the cottage, but Annie told him that when they moved in, he was still in a crib. After that he had to sleep in the bottom bunk, which he hated. He figured he'd already had years in the bottom bunk and was entitled to sleep on the top for a long time instead of switching every week. He hated the saggy place in the mattress where Michael's big butt was going to break through one of these days and he, Davey, would be like a whopped fly on the window. *Smushed.* Purple guts dripping down the sides of the bed. They'd all be sorry then they made him sleep there.

Not like their house in the city where he had his own room. At the cottage he not only had to take turns with Michael for the top bunk, but he had to listen to Michael snore. Not that he really minded. There were so many other things to listen to if he couldn't sleep — the halyards on the masts when the wind picked up, the slap of water on the pier, the crowds of crickets in the marsh.

Last night, Michael fought for the top bunk, and didn't wake during the storm so he got rained on, but Davey stayed dry because the window didn't reach down to the bottom bunk. Still, it was like sleeping in a grave on a rainy night with the earth pushing down on a coffin, rotting the wood, trying to get into the only air space you had left, ready to get you. Worms too. That was why Michael hated the bottom bunk—he had dreams about blood pies and someone knifing him. When Michael told him, Davey was afraid it might come true. Maybe that was why Michael woke up mean some days. Maybe Davey had to be Michael's age, which was almost eleven, to get bad dreams, and maybe when he did, he'd know he was finally growing up.

But tonight he'd be on the top bunk, and he wasn't going to trade any-thing for it. Or else he'd escape again to his favorite place—the lounge chair on the beach—so he could watch the shooting stars which he count-ed to thirteen last time and woke up with the tide coming in and swishing around the legs of the lounge chair and his mother all frantic like she got, looking for him. But maybe not. He never planned things—they just hap-pened. It was like the ching, ching sound of the halyards against the masts of the catamarans—like a bell calling in the distance for you to come that way—not all of you but just your thoughts, and your thoughts left your body and flew anywhere so even if you were on the bottom bunk you could still have a good time. He never told Michael about it but some-times if your thoughts were strong enough, they'd come back for your body and your body just went along. You couldn't always help it.

Now he watched his brother sort through the Lego pieces on the rug. Axles and wheels were in a pile between Michael's legs. Anne was making a house, which was her way of saying she didn't care about making trucks anyway because Davey had hidden the rest of the axles and wheels under the couch to trick his brother. He said, "Michael, you got all the best parts. C'mon, gimme some."

"Give you four axles for the top bunk tonight."

"No."

"Forget it, then."

"Mom, Michael won't share," he sang out. But there wasn't any answer as his mother washed dishes with her back to them. Sometimes her thoughts dragged her away, too. Just as he reached for the axles under the couch, she said, "Look. The wind chimes are quiet, and that means this rain will last all day. How about going to *Treasures and Trash?*"

"Yah-ha-ha-ha-ha-ha!" exploded Davey, producing the stash. Did he win for once? Michael's face told him he did.

"You twerp!" said Michael, but he grinned and didn't punch him so it was going to be a good day. Davey stuffed the axles and wheels in his pockets. The pieces were his till bedtime. Those were the rules. And he was going to get the top bunk, too. Way to go, Davey, he said to himself, heading toward the bathroom. They could pick up.

When he came out he said to his mother, "Do we hafta?" just because he always did.

"Not right away," she said, meaning as soon as she combed her hair and put on lipstick and stood for a minute real close to the mirror inspecting her skin and smiling at herself—a smile that disappeared as soon as she turned from the mirror like she had a secret.

They drove to the shop on Route 50 with a long aluminum shed in the rear where things spilled out the sliding doors, blocking two of the entrances. *Grandma's Attic—Treasures and Trash* was written in script on the cinder block side of the shop and Jesse Howard, owner, stood at the one entrance that was clear, watching the rain as if he expected them to appear since it *was* a rainy day. Davey thought he heard Mr. Howard sigh as they walked by him, which puzzled Davey because they always bought something, things that were a quarter or fifty cents, books or buttons for which Mr. Howard's place was famous. Mr. Howard would follow them around sometimes and tell that story again about the time, who was it?— Elvis? Robert Mitchum?—somebody famous—stopped by to sort through his button collection.

"See anything you want, Davey? A mounted deer foot?" his mother said. He put it back after carrying it around for a while. "Wait a minute. A 1953 Studebaker hubcap! Your father had a green Studebaker when we got married. We went across the country in it reading all the Burma Shave signs to each other: *All his love, all best wishes, don't smooth out his durn ol' whiskers. Give him . . .*"

He grinned at her. She loved to tell how Dad made her laugh all the time when they were young. He could see them, his mother and father before they had kids, laughing in the Studebaker. He'd heard the story before; he knew what to do. "Burma Shave!" he shouted and she laughed on cue.

"It had red leather seats. Before your time. Yeah, Davey, get that. Your father'll love it."

He carried the hubcap around for a while but put it down when he spotted the *National Geographics*. He pulled one down from the shelf and started looking at tiger pictures, white tigers, zebra coats. Twenty-five cents. Overhead were two Red Flyer sleds, a long one and a short one hanging up on nails hammered into the beams—too high for him to look at close. He didn't want to ask for them to be taken down so he could see if they were wobbly. Michael would laugh. "It's the middle of summer," he'd say. "Jerko."

There was a box of soiled stuffed animals with a camera on top, a Brownie. Michael had one. Maybe it was under a dollar. He turned it over in his hands, inspected the insides, and then peered through the viewfinder. He saw a flash of light, a mirror, and Michael and his mother standing in front of something big. He pressed down and heard the familiar click. Too bad there wasn't any film. Real pictures were when people weren't posing, giving you their cheese-smiles.

Anne found a copy of *The Yearling* with pictures by somebody called N. C. Wyeth for thirty-five cents. "He painted good pictures," she said. "I love it when they put nice pictures in thick books. They forget kids never stop liking pictures. The old books have pictures all through them. Look at this, Davey. This boy has a deer for a pet." Her almond-shaped eyes peered at him. "And there's a kid who dies, too. There's his coffin." He looked over her arm at the picture of willows sweeping dark shadows to the edge of the page and the small wooden box hoisted up on a bearded man's shoulder in the sunlight.

"Who's the kid with the deer? How does he get him?"

"Wait," she said and flipped the pages with her long, thin fingers. "Here. See? He has hair just like yours. Yellow-white. The deer is just a fawn when he gets him, but he has to give him up when he gets big."

"If I had one, I'd never give him up. I'd go in the woods and live with him if I had to."

"You would, wouldn't you, Davey." She gave him a quick nudge with her bony shoulder. "Here," she said, giving him the book. "You can look at it but give it back because I'm getting it, okay?" She always trusted him.

When he found his mother so he could ask about the camera, she was inspecting a big old organ and Michael was pressing the keys with one finger. Nothing happened.

"How does it play, Mom? Does it have to be plugged in?" said Michael.

"You have to pump it. See those pedals?" She bent over and pointed to two carpeted pedals at the bottom of the organ and when she straightened up Davey could tell she was going to buy it by the way she studied the dark oak finish and the decals of the gold-tinted mandolins on the compartment doors, the bright square of beveled mirror, the crown of spindles high overhead.

Jesse Howard appeared at their side so quickly and quietly his mother thought she was only talking to Michael when she said, "I wonder what he wants for it." She jumped a little when Mr. Howard said, "Picked that up last Saturday at a auction in Ridgely. A lady had that in her parlor since the turn of the centry. Bellows is still good. Got to sell her cheap because I need the space. If you got room there ain't nothing nicer than a organ, know what I mean?" His narrow blue eyes were set close to his nose and his false teeth whistled. At his throat, his string tie gathered up his sagging skin. He must be very old, thought Davey.

Every summer his mother took them to auctions. That was where she bought the bunk beds and that old wooden clipper ship that stood on his dresser. It had cost twenty-five cents. He remembered because Mr. Howard only bought what came in boxes and that clipper ship was in a box with some jelly glasses and old records nobody wanted. The auctioneer went into his song, "Hey! Surprise package, now! Never know what you'll find in these goody boxes. Who'll gimme-me-a-quarter-gimme-a-quarter-gimme-a-quarter-now?" and looked around the crowd. He went into the roll again with sounds let loose so that the words disappeared, talking as if his tongue slipped around his mouth till his breath gave out, then finally, "All right, Dorsey," he said in plain English to the man at his side—"Throw in that mop too and those hangers—now that's a real bargain, folks. Who'll gimme a quarter now?" He sang about the quarter until Davey heard him say, "Sold to the man with the money. Thank you, Jesse," he said, nodding toward Mr. Howard. But the best part was when his mother walked over to Mr. Howard and offered a quarter for the clipper ship. It had a little gold anchor on a chain and nine canvas sails. "Sure," he said. "Only wanted them records anyhow."

Mr. Howard used to care how he displayed things because a lot of jelly glasses were in rows on the shelves and a lot of books were in categories, faded labels written in pencil: *Mysteries, Classics, Novels,* and *Reader's Digest Condensed Books.* But he'd given up. Now the boxes of stuff he bought were just stacked along the narrow aisle of the shed and spilled out the door. You had to climb over piles to get in. There were old radios and boxes of 78's, old-timey seven-foot skis, saucers without cups. Davey loved *Treasures and Trash.* It was like the bottom of the river where things settled and stories waited.

"Seventy-five dollars," Mr. Howard said, nodding at the organ.

"Bet he bought it for a dollar," Anne whispered to Davey when he handed over her book.

Before them the organ stood high and dark, scaly skinned, a little ominous, like something from a spooky movie, a thing too big and gawky to settle anywhere.

"It won't be hard to move," Mr. Howard reassured his mother. "Just tell your husband to bring a screwdriver and we'll take off the top portion—see right above the keyboard?—it comes off. Do you play? Could you play a song right now?"

"No, or rather, I haven't played in years. I'd have to practice," she said and shrugged her shoulders.

"Oh," said Mr. Howard, looking disappointed. Michael crawled under the keyboard and began to push on the carpeted pedals with his hands. "Go ahead, Mom," he said. "Try it." But Davey jumped in and picked out "Frère Jacques." It was so easy.

His mother said, "When did you learn to play that?" He couldn't remember. It was as if he always knew. From the minute he heard the song the notes hung off the ends of his fingers. He could start "Frère Jacques" anywhere on the piano at school, fooling around after hours so he could practice. On the organ, some of the notes were missing on the *Dormez vous* part.

Mr. Howard whistled through his teeth. "Needs a little cleaning— blow out the pipes—she'll be good as new," he said, smiling, his lips stretched back over his false teeth. Davey thought it was the song that pleased him and took a bow.

"One dollar for the camera," said Mr. Howard, extending a yellowish palm.

On Saturday, his father got Pete, the waterman who lived across the way, to help him lug the two massive pieces of the organ up the narrow steps of the cottage. They shuffled by Davey, grunting and sweating, and placed it against the back wall of the big front room. Hot, steamy air breezed in off the river and swirled around the pores of the old oak, filling the room with a musty smell. Anne gathered tiger lilies and sweet pea vines from the edge of the marsh and put them in a vase on the organ and Davey put his favorite rock there. Michael told both Anne and Davey to get down on their knees and pump for him. "Faster!" he commanded when the organ wheezed as if it were out of breath.

"You pump for us, Michael," said Anne, standing up, hands on hips. Miraculously he did and Davey got to play not only "Frère Jacques" but "Chopsticks" too, and then a song he made up when he was in the tub last night although just now he forgot some of the words, which was okay since Michael would only laugh.

In the beveled mirror, the bright square of sky lit up the dark end of the big room. When Davey walked by he saw his mother or father or Anne and Michael, but never himself. He wasn't tall enough. His father was only there on weekends. Mostly it was his mother in the mirror, vacuuming up the sand or dusting shelves, doing the dishes. He wondered about the silence of her face when no one was looking, how she kept inside herself except when he or Anne or Michael showed her something they made. He wished he had film for his new camera so he could take her picture when she wasn't looking.

When they were in bed that night, he heard her play the organ, old Methodist hymns and "O Solo Mio." He called out to her from the top bunk, "Play that Schubert one, Mom. Play it three times, okay?" It was his favorite. She always made a mistake in the same place, but he was used to it. She played the piece again and again and was in the middle of the fourth go-round when he heard the ching, ching of the halyards beating on the masts—the stronger the wind the faster the beat. A squall—coming off the bay. Curtains fluttered, bedroom doors slammed, the wind chimes jangled. He heard his mother shut the front door as he, Michael, and Anne scrambled out of bed to pull *Greenfly* and the catamaran in from the waves. His mother, her arms full of life jackets and towels, shouted into the wind, "I just saw lightning! Inside! C'mon!" He and Anne folded the lawn chairs and threw them down under the house. Again he heard his mother, louder, "You hear me? In the house, quick!" But he and Anne ran to the other end of the yard, toward the washline and jumped up to yank the bathing suits that had been thrown over the line without clothespins. He looked up to see the boats in Pete's marina straining their ropes, lit by a diagonal yellow gash in the sky. "I'm going in the house!" he shouted. "And so are you!" He panicked: Anne wasn't running. She just stood there for way too long and stared at the sky as if she were waiting for something.

"C'mon, Annie," he screamed. His pajamas felt heavy, plastered to his skin by the pelting rain, and Anne's braids were stuck to her shoulders like thick snakes. Shivering in the cool rain, he wouldn't leave her even if they'd be zapped by the next bolt—a single black thread singeing through them both at once, singeing them to that black sky and the black earth and each other forever. The lightning came again and she was lit up, a tinseled ghost, her eyes enormous. She wasn't even flinching—she was grinning, her front teeth lit up like two—*Chicklets!*—he sang out, making fun of her to bring her around. He ran behind her and pushed, butting-goat fashion till she started to flail at him, the spell broken, and they ran toward the shelter of the lighted doorway.

"I told you to come right in! Where were you?" his mother yelled, taking the wet things from their arms. "Saving Annie," he told her.

"You two," she said, and lightly smacked their behinds. "You come when I call, hear?" He giggled, prancing in place and shaking. She didn't look too annoyed. Soon their wet pajamas and bathing suits hung from the exposed beams in the big room and he was warm again and dry. He listened to the sound of pelting rain on the roof against the swishing of rainy sheets outside his window, short and long sounds together in a song, the smell of earth and shingles and fishy creatures mixed together. He climbed up to the top bunk. The window was open but that was okay because the wind came from the river side of the house. Now he listened to the sound of the halyards against the pelting and the swishing, and Schubert, too, as his mother began exactly where she'd left off, and this time, she played it perfectly. Michael, down below, already started to breathe in the slow, into-sleep way. Davey got on his knees and peeked over the partition.

"Annie?" he whispered.

Her sheet-covered shape shifted. "Why'd you take so long? You scared me."

"I just didn't want to miss it, Davey. The lightning was far away. I counted."

He lay down on his pillow, listening. He couldn't sleep because of the music. It wasn't like the boat sounds. It didn't let his thoughts fly away. He had to listen. Even after he fell asleep, part of him listened.

CATAMARAN

By two o'clock in the afternoon the breeze was up. Along the point, flags sprang to life. Rosemary, basking on the lawn chair, watched as Justin released the spring on the screen door so it would stay open and knew this meant he was going sailing. He stood on a kitchen chair and reached for the mast of the catamaran that rested on the trusses, passing it hand over hand until the Styrofoam ball attached to the top end appeared through the doorway just as Anne was going up the steps. She caught the ball and held it.

"Atta girl, Annie! But grab the mast, not the ball. There you go. Lay it over the canvas," he said as they walked in tandem toward the bright yellow hulls. Once the mast was resting on the deck, he began to connect the cotter pin at the center of the huge triangle supporting it. Seconds later he raised the mast and the white ball bobbed on its perch at the top. He secured the mast at the lower end with another pin and undid the cord that bound the sail.

The sound of the released sail snapping back and forth in the wind was Rosemary's favorite, and her favorite sight was Justin getting ready to sail, the way he looked over his shoulder every few seconds to size up the water, the tide, the motion of the waves, the wind direction, as if in the seconds between, everything might change or drop away while he wasn't looking. His hands were busy at the cotter pins and a faint smile played around his mouth under the long peak of his cap. Rosemary focused on the blue bathing trunks that drooped on his hips, his long sinewy feet half-buried in sand.

"Ready for a sail?" he asked.

"Right now? Davey fell asleep."

"Perfect time."

"Never know what he'll take it in his head to do when he wakes up. I'll wait for Evelyn."

"Well, I'll come back for you in a while." She heard him gasp at the chill of the water as he pushed the pontoons afloat. The boat danced and almost got away as he walked it out. When he was waist deep, he jumped up onto the canvas deck with a deluge of water falling away from him. The loose trunks slipped lower. She laughed but he couldn't hear her as he hoisted the trunks up with one hand and rushed to command the sail and tiller all at once. At the immense push of the wind, the catamaran shot from shore, the pontoons cutting into the sea like knives—away, away. She watched how he studied the wind and leaned into it, and waited with him for the giant swell of sail knowing he'd throw the tiller suddenly so the boat would head into the wind. The huge black and orange sail luffed, rippling against itself, then filled again with a loud snap. He was off to his own world, beyond her reach, the diminishing orange triangle marking his spot. She wished she'd been able to go. She could feel the tug of the rope, the spray against her skin, hear the hum of vibration between the ropes and the sail, feel his decisiveness and skill—he said he'd come back for her.

The sun burned her forearms and legs as she sat back on the lounge chair and picked up her knitting. They were all knitters on her side of the family—all five of her aunts and her mother. It was the thing women did while they waited. Only her knitting was more labored. She had to pick the wool up and around the needle for each stitch where she'd seen her aunts and her mother loop the wool around one finger and pull the wool into the stitch all in one easy motion, clicking needles furiously as they talked, hardly looking down. She tried their way again but dropped a stitch, then laid the knitting in her lap and caught sight of Evelyn coming around the corner of the cottage with her green terry cloth beach jacket draped over one arm and a bag of pretzels in the other. Gentle, unintrusive, her opening comments were usually about the weather.

"Tide's high. Nice breeze!" she said and settled in the lawn chair by the shade of the hedge. "Good to see you're getting some rest, Rosemary." Rosemary smiled. Her mother-in-law always looked out for her. Evelyn began untying her sneakers and asked, "Where are the kids?" But there was no need: Anne and Michael appeared out of nowhere.

"Where have you two been?" Rosemary asked.

"Over at Pete's pier, checking for doublers," said Michael, putting on the face he saved for explanations. "Grandma, that means there's a male and a female together and when the female crab is gonna shed her shell, the male stays with her. See, she's real helpless when she sheds and he brings her to the pilings and climbs on top of her to protect her. But you can get a soft crab and a hard crab at the same time that way and we got two of each." He held up the bucket for her.

Anne called out, "Grandma brought pretzels! Yay, Grandma!"

"Well good," said Evelyn, handing the bag to Anne. "You can cook me up a soft crab for dinner. But what I want to know is what happens when the male sheds? Who protects him?"

Michael looked up at her. "Maybe he's braver . . . maybe he just goes off by himself." He peered into the bucket. "I have to check 'em. Sometimes they're on the way to getting hard again and then they get a paper shell and then they're only good for bait. I'll show you." He ran to get the tongs as Evelyn winked at Rosemary.

"Doesn't miss a trick, does he? Annie, share those with your brothers now, will you?"

Anne took two pretzels and handed the bag back.

"See, Grandma?" Michael came back holding a limp crab. "It's a good soft one. You can have that one."

"But what will you have?"

"I don't even like 'em. I just like to catch 'em."

"Well, who's going swimming?" said Evelyn, standing up, hands on her hips, her white hair done up in a French roll fresh from the hair-dresser's.

"Me—me—me," Davey called from the screen door tugging his bathing suit up over his white bottom.

"Coming, Rosemary?" Evelyn said to her.

"If you don't mind, I'm waiting for a sail. Justin said he'd come for me. Will you stay with the kids?"

"Of course," and she advanced with the three of them squealing behind her as the sea engulfed her ankles, shins, knees, hips at every step—"Now, don't you splash Grandma, Davey," though she knew he would—"Huh!" she grunted—until finally she sat down while the children dove and splashed around her, "Where did Davey go to? OOPS! There he is!"—and the sea claimed her shoulders—"Careful of Grandma's hair, thank you!" She began to paddle lazily, drifting, and waved her arms like two graceful oars and laughed again and again.

Rosemary hoped she would be like Evelyn when she grew older, still slender, handsome, never complaining, enjoying everything, even though she seemed a bit detached from Rosemary and Justin, never wanting to discuss things much. Which was where Justin got it, Rosemary supposed. She wanted to know what Justin's father was like, if he darted from one idea to the next, if he had as much energy and drive, and if there were other times when he was completely passive. Justin was such a puzzle. Once she thought she heard him crying. She went into the bedroom and found him sitting on the edge of the bed, his head in his hands. "What is it?" she said and put her hand on his shoulder. He looked childlike crying to himself like that. He looked up but quickly turned away. "Nothing," he said. The incident passed into the chasm of silence that seemed to contain more and more of them as time went on. Rosemary wanted to ask Evelyn about it, but it was the kind of thing one couldn't ask her. The only time she mentioned Justin's father was the comment she'd made about being furious that her beautiful wedding crystal lasted longer than her husband. She said little about the time after he died, too, except that she'd had to sell the house he'd built and move to a smaller, older one that needed repair. "Justin jumped right in to fill his father's place," she said. "He took it on himself at the age of eighteen to remodel the kitchen, put in new cabinets and counters—I was amazed that he knew how to go about it. His talent with wood came directly from his father." Evelyn surprised Rosemary with her next comment. "Boys are easy to raise. They don't require much. They're independent early."

Rosemary took up her knitting again but before beginning the tedious stitches, she looked out at Evelyn, the kids bobbing in and out of the water around her, and at the catamaran's Styrofoam ball bouncing crazily in the wind. Justin had only one pontoon in the water, the other up dangerously high with the mast at a precarious angle to the water so that the cat looked like a beginning skier, stiff and awkward, tottering in the wind. The mast tilted crazily on the edge of imbalance and upheaval while Justin flirted with the elements. If she had gone sailing, she'd be sitting on the high side of the canvas deck trying to steady the boat, the water splashing her back, Justin laughing and calling for her to *lean out, lean out for Christ's sake.*

She felt the sun burn her legs and shoulders and thought about how she mostly waited—waited for Justin's return, waited for the children, waited for four o'clock so she could start dinner, waited to wash the last dish. She wondered if this was the best way to spend what was left of her youth as she closed her eyes to slits through which she could see the children and the white Styrofoam ball, which maniacally bobbed to the rhythm of the waves. Yes, of course it was the best way. (Where were her sunglasses?) She woke to slap a mosquito off her thigh. The knitting rested in her lap. She had everything. Her mother said so on her last visit, speaking with her chin in the air, her perpetual knitting bag at her side, and in her forthright manner that bore only a trace of New York, she said, "Rosemary, you have it all, don't you? Two houses, three boats, two cars, a piano, an ambitious husband, three beautiful kids and summers away. Now let me show you one more time how you pull the wool into the stitch. It'll save you time."

"He's over! Dad's turned over!" Michael shouted, pointing to a pontoon high above the water as the boat lay on its side. The white ball bobbed to the right of the floating sail and prevented the boat from turning completely upside down. They all strained to catch sight of Justin hanging onto a pontoon, strained to see his dark head, a glistening arm. Nothing. Maybe he got caught under the sail and was knocked out, although she doubted he'd allow that to happen. He'd done this same maneuver many times before.

"He's all I have," she blurted out loud, not in the sense that he was all she had but that everything depended on him. She looked to him as a musician looks to the conductor. Frozen to her chair she stared momentarily at life without Justin. Justin swallowed by the sea. Watching the scene before her, she felt strangely detached as if she simply had to wait for everything to right itself. The upturned catamaran began to shift, then slip across the horizon. She should, she thought with tantalizing dullness, get the binoculars and see if he was all right. But then, of course he was all right. He was competent and smart. He was impervious, capable, one who moved through the world with confidence and grace. He always knew what to do. He probably had the whole thing planned. She didn't move though the sun stung her shins and burned deep into her bones, like worry.

Evelyn stood looking out to the river with her hands at her waist. The river flared out from her buttocks like a huge skirt. Michael stood with her but called out to his mother, "Should I get *Greenfly* and go out to him?"

"Wait a minute, Michael. He'll be all right," said Evelyn.

Davey dove underwater again and Anne watched for his head to appear so she could chase him. Rosemary told herself Justin and the boat were going to drift to Cheetam Point on the opposite shore and she would pick him up in the car. Nothing terrible was going to happen. Yet, she should do something. What should she do? She'd never started the motor-boat herself, and by the time she waded out to where it was moored— Justin always handled everything. Ah. Mr. Phillips, next door, was starting up his boat. He'd come back and reassure her. The scene before her was a painting with a little disturbance. A few brush strokes would right it.

Suddenly, Justin was balanced on the surface pontoon and reaching up to the airborne one. With his legs swung free, he hoisted himself to the high pontoon and as his weight pulled it back into the water, the sail scooped up river water and shook itself free. The boat jerked, stiff and unyielding, upright now and the white ball danced again along the line of trees beyond. Mr. Phillips circled the catamaran and waved to Justin who waved back. Rosemary knew Justin wouldn't be in for a long while. With the incoming tide, the water was rougher and the wind fresh. He'd ride on one pontoon again and again.

The neighbors had gathered along the seawall, watching. Rosemary felt a secret pride—he had more life and daring in him than most people ever experienced. His joy was more deeply felt—why, he *allowed* himself joy, that was it!—and it was what she loved most about him. She waited.

Soon the children would come in from the water shivering and reaching for towels. Then they'd dig peacefully in the sand. Evelyn would share the pretzels and Rosemary would get them drinks. The afternoon would breeze itself out and before she knew it she'd hear the flap of the sail near shore and the catamaran would skid across their harbor and scuff at their beach. Justin would say, "I'll start the coals for hamburgers." What more could she want? She picked up the needles and began to twist the blue wool around her index finger.

Justin thrilled to the cat's speed. There was nothing like the sudden catch of the wind, the snap of the sail, the simplicity of hull slicing the water, the clouds stately and serene, puffing up magically in all that blue. He was powerful, ready to inhale the day. Alive, so goddamned alive—he identified with the fullness of the sail. Immortality came in increments, moments seized. This was one. This day. What a day! Wild as it got, he was ready.

He heard the wires sing as the hulls shot ahead. The sail strained. He imagined it stretching way behind the pontoons, scooping up all the wind it could find. The boat charged right into the teeth of it—might just as well be Cape Horn. He loved it. Cottages, flags, piers, screened porches, the brief beaches bearing seaweedy clumps, the assembly of neighbors in lawn chairs—all flitted by. Ducks scattered. He came about swiftly— almost unbalanced the boat, which made him chuckle. It bounced free a moment before the wind caught the sail again and he was off. Flying. Right into the clouds.

Those other guys on shore who stood watching him, what did they know? Old fogies. Only this morning, J. B. Phillips said to him with his stomach hanging way out to here, "We don't cotton much to guys with beards around here. What are you, a hippie or something?"

He threw back his head and laughed and as the sound left him, he looked up at the silhouette of the black cat leaning forward on two pontoons with the word *Aquacat* printed underneath. In the distance he heard laughing gulls and he laughed again in answer and at the ball at the top of the mast, at the ingenuity of its position and purpose riding on top of the world like that, laughed at the challenge of everything oddball and un-Methodist about his tiny hold on Sulley's Point. The foreigner. Bet they were saying it among themselves at this very moment. *The furrener. Bought that piece nobody thought was big enough to build on. Squeezed hisself right in there. Builds hisself a house. Up there at two in the morning hammering on the roof.* They just didn't know what to make of him. Neither did Rosemary. He was alone. But irrepressible. He laughed out loud again.

"What you going to do about that stretch of marsh up your way?" J.B. had asked him, holding onto a bag of ice with his thick fingers as they stood outside the IGA in Pucam. "See, my land being next to yours, tide comes in behind my bulkhead, eats away all that fill I put in. You figuring on building a seawall anytime soon? Hooking up to my bulkhead?"

"Thinking about it. Want to help?"

"Lord, nobody could do a job like that on his own! You got to call Taylor—he'll fix you up with pilings, a nice pier, bulkhead—the works." The bag of ice dripped into a puddle on the sidewalk.

"Yeah, for a nice pile of money. Well, I'll give you a call when I'm ready to start," Justin told him with a smile. Actually he had the whole thing planned. No problem. Well, maybe one or two.

He glanced back at his children splashing near the shore and calling against the wind; their sounds carried in the opposite direction as he darted away. His kids. He hoped they'd never lose their playfulness, the in-touch-with-themselves feeling that he loved. He watched the bows dip and rise. Whitecaps. But happiness was fragile, a skittish thing, especially with the world the way it was, against playfulness, against anything out of the ordinary. Sometimes he got wrapped just as tight as the rope that dug across his knuckles. Sometimes that feeling stayed for a while—like the year he graduated college, trying to pass his exams, in a slump so bad he could hardly move the pen across the paper. He didn't know how he got through it. All he had to hold onto was the faith that his real self would come back. He guessed it was his real self but he didn't know. He only knew happiness had a limit, so he better live all he could while it hung around. He eased the tension and listened to the hum of the guide wires delicate as a violin string dragged across by catgut, or was it horsehair? Rosemary would know.

Corrugated sheeting. Nothing like it on the point. Way cheaper than wood. Combination asbestos and cement. Corrugated for strength. One hundred pounds a sheet. Only problem was lifting them.

The wind—strong enough to ride on one now—pay attention—see how much lean she can take. Ride on the edge, top lip of pontoon on the lip of the water—it's all in the tiller and the pull of the sail, a flick of the wrist, *Noel Coward?*—a blink of the eye, or down you go. When a pontoon went under—shot through the water with the speed of a torpedo—he had to watch it—loosen the sail—or tighten it. Rosemary would be screaming by now, leaning way out to save them, arms all goose-bumped from the spray and the wind, worried something was going to happen. More. More. More. Farther over. Yeah. It was all about balance—of wind, water, rope, tiller. When you find it, don't move, just listen. Boat sings to you then. Listen to it sing. What if the sail ripped? That'd be good. That's next. Be paddling with the centerboard then. Calm down. Calm down. Down. Sliding down. Dumped—into the brink. Water warm as dishwater—warmer than air. Rope around a foot. Somebody else's foot. Couldn't be his.

The water enveloped him. Bubbling around his ears, it accented his singularity—he was more alone than he'd ever been. The water had an orange glow; the sail canopied the surface. He swam away from it into the tentacles of a sea nettle and felt the sting across his shoulder. Did the rope anchor him or he anchor the boat? He looped around and tried to loosen the tangle, his one purpose—*un-do-the-um-bi-li-cal*—lungs bursting—more he moved—tighter it bound—he'd swim home, drag the damn boat with him. Now toward the orange glow—the rope—caught at the other end by the centerboard. He was dangling. He thought about a knife—they tell you to carry a knife. He followed the rope hand over hand for a few more feet until he broke through the skin of the water. He did it. The rope loosened. He ducked down, tore it from his foot—and came up with his head poking the sail. He was free.

He rested a moment with the sail floating around him and listened to his own hard breathing, felt his shoulder sting and realized there wasn't enough air under the sail. He dove down again—into the murky orange-green—toward the hull—grabbed on with his arms and legs and pulled himself up. Standing now on the bottom pontoon and hanging from the one in the air, he pulled it down to the water with his weight and the sail rose, the boat righted. He got dunked again, and heard his own, *hah, hah hee* as he went under which sounded fiendish to him and he wondered if he was mad. He was, he decided, mad about life. Full of it. A second later, he hoisted himself to the deck. With tiller in hand and the sail snapping above him, he was off once more.

J.B. was on his way. People did look out for one another here. Knew exactly what was going on. No sooner done than said. Conducting a lifetime of research into other people's lives, they fed on people like him. He glanced toward shore where the neighbors were gathered, waved his thank you as J.B. circled the catamaran in his cabin cruiser, busied himself with the ropes and tightened the sail to tell J.B., *I'm going around again*—as he listened for the guide wires' whine and turned to fly into those welcoming clouds.

CRAB FEAST

～

Just he and Dad were in the boat this morning. He loved it without
Davey or Anne around, when Dad talked to him about things he was planning—and he was always planning something big.

Greenfly felt like his boat. His father never actually said it was, but
ever since last summer he was allowed to take it downriver alone to the red
buoy where he'd watch the gulls circling, telling him where the fish were.
For his eleventh birthday just last week, he got a Mitchell Garcia reel,
Model 301, the model for left-handers, from his dad and a Shakespeare rod
from his mom (she said she liked the name), both of which he kept in his
room next to the beds.

From the first time his father rigged up a roller for the trotline—
Michael was nine then—it had been his job to tie bait on Friday mornings. He'd reach into the bucket of salted bull lips (which stung if he had
a cut on his hands but were good to dangle in his sister's face and gross her
out) and knot them on the line every foot and a half. He never tangled the
line and was careful to drop it round and round in the bucket ready for his
father to use on Saturday.

You could lay half a mile of line without having to get a license, Pete
told him, and he ought to know, being a waterman. During the week,
Michael went out with Pete in his workboat, the *Miss Linda. Time I need
a new boat, it'll be time to git a new wife,* said Pete, winking at him,
although Michael's ears got stuck on the sound of the word *time,* which

seemed to come out of Pete's nose, *toim*. Not that he got to dip for crabs, but he did cull them while Pete dipped, and the best part was Pete was a storyteller. When he was young, he had sailed skipjacks on the bay, *seen squalls come up so fast they could put a boat down in two minutes*. But it wasn't the stories so much as the way Pete told them, his voice a singsong of strangely pronounced words and his eyes slits in his sunburned face as he squinted out over the water. Michael thought Pete was like a mooring pole, thick and gray, and always the same no matter what the weather was. Michael didn't have to *be* anything when he was with Pete; he just tied up to the mooring pole and did what he was told. Got paid for it, too. Secretly he hoped one day he'd have biceps as big as Pete's, which were thick around as Michael's waist was now.

On Saturdays, he crabbed with his dad. Just before sunup, he listened through his sleep for his father to stir and whisper, *Michael!* They'd pull on their clothes in the dark and sneak out the door into the dead quiet. Except for the *Miss Linda*, they had the river to themselves.

When he was a little kid their house seemed gigantic. But now, from the water, it looked small, the roof lower than those of the other cottages as though it had sneaked in like a cat on the prowl. He thought of the sleeping shapes of his mother, brother, and sister, and of the privilege to be out with his father alone, the two of them taking turns as they aimed the boat along the line and scooped up crabs in the wire net, the air so still and quiet that the putt-putt of the motor and the swish of the net as he plunged it into the bright water seemed loud enough to wake Davey back in the cottage, something Michael didn't want happening. The sun was just rising; its rays bounced off the tin roof of the barn across river blinding him for a second, just long enough to make him miss a big one. His heart sank. *Awww.* The crab was saved by the glance of sun on the water and he by his father's quiet, *That's okay.*

Sometimes he was not so lucky. Sometimes he couldn't do anything right. "Bring the boat farther up on the beach, Michael, for chrissake! Can't you see the tide's coming in?" or, "Put the crab tongs on the hook in the hallway—How many times do I hafta tell you!" or, "How about the boat cushions you left out?"

"Well, nobody's perfect," his mother said and told him a story. "When you three were little, Michael—you might remember this—we had a sail-boat called *Flying Tern*. Your father forgot to tie it up one day—this was back when we rented a place down here before the cottage was built—and we were eating lunch when Dad said, 'Looks like someone else has a yellow *Flying Tern* just like ours.' The boat was way out in the middle of the river and Dad turned to me with a dumb look on his face, and said, 'Where's ours?' Mr. Phillips had to take Dad out in his boat and tow the tern in. Your dad's just trying to give you the benefit of his experience, see?"

He laughed but he shouldn't have. His dad could figure out anything. Theirs was the first new house on the point in fifty years, and he'd built it on a lot everybody thought was too small and swampy to build on.

They finished the line and his father leaned over the edge of the boat, the peak of his hat shielding his face. Steadying himself with one leg against the boat's side, he lifted the line from the roller with the net handle and gently dropped it back into the water. The river took it with a soft sucking sound. His father never missed, although Michael missed a lot, and they'd get hung up in the line and have to stop the boat. He was glad his father was dipping this time although dipping was his favorite job. You had to concentrate hard especially if they came steady on the line. Then you didn't even have time to turn around to empty the net into the bushel basket because you had to hold it tight against the flow of water or you'd lose what you already had.

"Hungry?" his dad asked as Michael culled the crabs that were too small and flung them into the river. He nodded. He was always hungry. "We'd best go in then. Let 'em get on the line good for the next run."

"When do we start the bulkhead, Dad?"

"Soon as they deliver the cement sheets. We have to get a tractor too, some fill dirt, couple hoses."

He had gone with his father to order the gigantic sheets of corrugated cement at Robbins and Robbins. The sheets lay stacked on the ground, gray and stiff, rippled like the water when the wind starts up. They were longer than his father was tall and just wide enough for him to pick one up with his arms outstretched. They were so heavy his father had to bend down, lift one end to shoulder height and then walk his hands down the sheet in order to stand it on end.

"Cement and asbestos. Something new," he panted as he lay the sheet back down. "Pretty soon everybody'll be wanting corrugated cement for seawalls. And this is what we'll do. We'll get a long hose, see, and I'll shoot water down where we want the sheet to go and the water pressure'll dig a trench for us down on the river bottom. When we get the sheet in place, you sit on top and rock it side to side while I keep shooting water down there to loosen up the bottom. Okay? Think you can do it? It'll be like riding bareback till you toughen up a little." Green eyes looked at him, man to man. "Then when the sheet is down two, three feet and holding steady, we'll go on to the next one and when they're all in place and we've got a wall, we'll use the tractor to push the fill dirt up to it and pack that in on the land side. Guess we'll have to prop it up on the river side till everything settles. I've still got to figure something out for the top edge, though, to steady it. Especially where it curves around." His father narrowed his eyes and squinted. Creases ran from his eyes down toward the sides of his long nose. "Unless we just take those two-by-eights and bolt them on and gradually tighten the bolts to conform to the shape of the wall. Yeah, that might do it. Are you with me?"

You bet. He loved it when Dad was excited like this. Every meal he sat with one knee sticking out from under the table, a knee which had a life of its own like a wind-up toy. Up and down it bounced, up and down like a spring gone wild. The floor vibrated and the dishes rattled until his mother said, "Justin, can you stop that? It's driving me crazy." He'd stop but start up again in a few seconds. Then his mother would roll her eyes and get that blank look like she'd gone off somewhere else even though she'd keep nodding at him while he went on planning.

Now, quick, before his father revved up the motor for the ride back, Michael put into words what he was worrying about. "What about the beach part, Dad? It won't be as much fun as it is now if we build a wall across it."

"No, uh huh! You're right! We're going to leave the beach alone and end the bulkhead right where the beach begins. We'll build a stone wall from the bulkhead to where the beach starts to slope down to the water. You're right—we want the beach! Glad you're thinking about it. Here. Take us in." He moved from the stern and allowed

Michael to take his place. Michael thought things just couldn't be better.

The motor was out as far as it would go and he made a smooth arc toward the cottage. He saw Davey run from the house and splash into the water. His father pointed and turned around to warn Michael and Michael at the same time began to slow the motor. He knew what to do: cut the motor and pull on its back end to tip it forward before the prop hit the sand. In the sudden silence, he heard Davey call out, "How many?" Next it'd be Davey's turn, and then Anne's, but Michael wished they could have stayed out all morning, just him and Dad.

They could sleep fourteen with the three bedrooms and the great room. Bunk beds lined the back bedrooms, some built right into the wall like people shelves. Trundle beds slept two; couches pulled out into double beds. Rosemary recounted the spaces, linens, loaves of bread, iced tea, ice, butter and brownies she'd need. There were droves of people coming to visit on the weekends now, and more than once she'd dream that the huge log truss that ran the width of their bedroom had fallen, pinning her to the bed, and she'd lie there, worrying about all those people to feed. "Keep it simple," Justin would say, bustling into the great room with pot after pot of crabs. "Where's the Old Bay? The vinegar? Got enough butter? Newspapers?"

She was wide awake. She listened to Justin snore and wished she could be as satisfied with the day as he seemed to be. Churned up about her helplessness when the catamaran overturned, she fought the voices that said she was of no account, useless, dependent, a nobody. Frightened, she got up and answered his muffled "Where are you going?" with, "I'm going to read for a while." But she knew she would look out at the indefinable blackness and think.

The lights across the river intrigued her. There was talk among the neighbors of a drug run upriver, but she didn't believe it. Not here. Not in this place run by wind and tides. She heard laughter, a high cackle and a deeper hum, and imagined an affair, love aboard a rocking boat. Tender words. Then wildness. Heat. An undoing of buttons, an impatience. She watched the still water, the moonless sky, glad for the time alone, the only time she was free.

She could walk up the road if she wanted to, watch the shadows from the lights of the cottages spread across the road, listen for the high-pitched tremor of crickets in the marsh, or walk down to the marina and read the names of the workboats moored there, wives' names, all of them. At least they had something to mark their spot on this earth, those women. But she would have to dress again, or slip into the bedroom and get her robe and chance waking Justin. So she stayed, staring at the water, watching the stillness of the boats. Nothing stirred.

In the day, the children absorbed her. She answered their calls as well as Justin's. She laughed at their capers and jokes—Justin's too—worked to feed them, keep them safe and satisfied, together—but *who was she?* The gnats swarmed around the light. In the morning there would be a pile of them to sweep up, a gathering of light, dry bodies to sweep into the dustpan. Tomorrow night there would be more. And so on. But she had just so many sweeps in her. How many? One day they would be used up. And then what? Was it only a matter of pointing to Justin and the children, saying, *That's how I spent my life!*

The night lay quiet. The gentle breathing of her children should give her purpose enough, and the boundless pursuits of her ambitious husband. Things were as they should be. From the bedroom she heard, "Rosemary?" When she slipped into bed, his back was to her. He turned and reached for her breast. She lay still hoping he'd begin to snore again and waited, her breathing shallow as she could make it, shrinking her further.

Company came in the heat of day. Car doors burst open, floats and coolers were pulled out of the backs of station wagons, kids leaped from car to back step to beach having changed their minds about entering the house. The Wurtzes, Hannah and Giles, were neighbors from the city, but Rosemary didn't know the Lesters, Truman Lester a co-worker at the new computer firm Justin had just joined. His wife, Nancy, was perfect in her green miniskirt and yellow sandals. Her blonde hair swung smooth, a gold fluid mass that changed shape with every step. Each family had three children around the ages of Michael, Anne, and Davey.

Soon the big room held food offerings on every flat surface—

Tupperware containers filled with potato salad, brown bags of tomatoes and corn, plastic bags of potato chips, six-packs of Coke and beer. Tennis shoes, towels, T-shirts, life jackets, shorts and duffel bags littered the floor. Hannah, Rosemary's friend, marched in with two huge loaves of bread she had baked in the shape of fish. Her wide cheeks pushed up her glasses when she smiled and she was constantly readjusting them. Built like a football player, thick in the back and chest, rolled waist and narrow hips, her weight was the one thing she seemed powerless to conquer although if her boys were built like her she'd have pigskin stars. Rosemary guessed Hannah already disliked Nancy's perfection and Nancy, too, and became uneasy at the disparity of her guests.

Everything was a bustle of running feet, splashing water and shouts from the women to the children, from child to child. Hannah's husband, Giles, round as Hannah, offered cigars to Justin and Truman and the men clustered around the crabfloat to survey the cottage.

"Comes in a kit, every piece precut, just the shell, of course," Justin was saying. They scanned the boats, puffed away on the cigars, pulled a foot up onto a step or a cooler to lean on a knee with one elbow. They talked about investments and vacation homes. Justin's done it, they agreed. He was way ahead of them, although they were "looking around."

Truman and Giles decided to take out the catamaran and pushed it out gingerly, way past the harbor before even attempting to get on board. When they did, they lingered around the mooring pole and the catamaran bumped into the side of the cruiser moored there. The sail luffed. A puff of wind came up and the catamaran moved backward toward shore. Justin swam out to them and called out instructions. Finally they were off with the wind slipping off the sail. "Let it out a little," Justin yelled, cupping his hands around his mouth. The catamaran bobbed on an incoming wake, then eased on out.

The boys gathered on the neighboring pier and took turns jumping into one of the tractor tire tubes while the three girls, Anne, Amy, and Nancy's daughter, Lisa, hung onto the other tube. Two of them climbed up, straddled it and giggled as Lisa pulled herself up, but then all three slipped off into the water. They tried again and again, shrieking at each dunking while Hannah settled on one of the lawn chairs and took out her knitting, one eye on the children. Rosemary joined her while Nancy disappeared into the house to change into her bathing suit. Evelyn arrived. She sat down briefly and called to the kids. A minute later, she waded into the water with her bathing cap stretched over her newly coiffured hair. She preferred to be with the kids. Widowed twice, she mostly listened to the chatter of young mothers and didn't say much. The kids, at least, made her laugh and she had a genuine appreciation for them. "Grandma's here," they yelled.

Justin started up the motor to the rowboat and invited Steve, Hannah's boy, to dip for crabs. Motioning and laughing, he promised to come back for each of the kids in turn. Misinterpreting, Chris, Hannah's youngest, just Davey's age, jumped in the boat. "Michael, pass me another life jacket, will ya?" Justin called.

Rosemary watched, counted kids, listened to Hannah, wondered lazily what was keeping Nancy so long. She watched Evelyn and admired her graceful swimming stroke as she felt the sun burn her legs and wondered dully where the Coppertone was. "Michael," she called, "put on some of this!" Suddenly self-conscious at the thought of Nancy in a bathing suit, she pulled in her stomach and wondered if she would ever again wear a bikini. Lying back in the chaise, she caught sight of Evelyn stretched across one of the tire tubes, paddling and kicking her legs.

Hannah was knitting like Rosemary's aunts. Her motions were smooth, and the wool gently flowed through each loop on the needle to a new loop in easy progression. Rosemary studied her fingers for a moment and thought about getting her own knitting, then decided against it.

"I think I'm going to take some courses, Hannah, in the fall, I mean—at night."

Hannah glanced sideways at her but her hands went on. "What kind of courses?"

"English—literature, poetry—kind of pick up where I left off." She surprised herself but saying it out loud established something. "I had some college before we got married."

Without enthusiasm, Hannah said, "Sounds neat. You don't have enough to do? With three kids?"

Rosemary shrugged. Hannah seemed much more content than she.

She felt the afternoon breeze begin like an afterthought, rolling those fluffy cumulus clouds along with it. A picture postcard day. She closed her eyes and listened to the children splash and squeal, listened to Hannah's talk, the flags flap, the pages of Nancy's *Redbook* magazine flutter. This is nice, she told herself. Everyone's having a good time. All because of Justin. When she opened her eyes, colors swirled around her. Nancy came out of the house in a scant bright yellow bikini, her face made up with fresh lipstick and mascara, her blonde hair shining. The children sparkled, never still, a perpetual round of wet, brown bodies in red and orange and green suits, diving, jumping, shouting, laughing, wet, bare feet slapping against the old, gray wood of the pier which splintered the nearly cobalt blue of the water and sky. Flags rippled American red, white and blue, Maryland gold, red and black; towels sprawled with Disney characters in purple and pink lay draped over striped lawn chairs; the huge orange and black sail slid across the horizon, the sleek, white boats bobbed alongside mooring poles all along the point catching blinding flashes of sun in windshields; and Nancy's brilliant red toenails bloomed at the end of the green and yellow webbed lawn chair—the whole great rush of life, of summer, of every blade of grass, of their very own beach and the boats, her children, like all of her hope, strong, promising, churning about her. The other cottages lay sleepily along the narrow shore, but theirs was teeming with life. She drifted in and out of listening to Hannah tell about the Pillsbury Bakeoff she'd entered, watched her hands shape her words as she told about the men in tuxedos who lifted the finished breads high above their heads as they carried them to the judging table, watched her laugh through the exaggerated movements of her huge arms, the graceful sweep of her knowledgeable hands, the bright red half-finished sweater in her lap, her reddish-brown hair in wisps around her face and thought, *Hannah is beautiful in a way I hadn't noticed before.* She laughed with her not just because of the story, but because of everything she saw, everything that filled her. At all this happiness. And at Justin now coming toward her—but too hurriedly, the tendons in his neck strained as he said, "Where's Mom?"

She looked out over the water for the black inner tubes, and could only account for the one the boys were using. Justin ran into the house, calling, and Rosemary called to the children, "Where's Grandma?"

"Maybe she went for a walk," they answered. "She was in the tire tube, Mommy," Anne said, and they both looked out to the river. There was something mid-river. Could it be the tube? Pushed upriver by the tide and wind? Panicked, Rosemary screamed for Justin.

"Look! Way out!" Seeing only a small black dot now, they couldn't tell whether there was anybody on it. Suddenly Anne dove off the pier and began swimming out to deeper water.

"No, Annie, come back! It's too far! Anne!" Rosemary shouted, but Anne's slim golden arms paddled crazily while her head stayed underwater. Justin ran toward the rowboat. In seconds, he pushed the boat to deeper water, tipped the motor forward and down, and yanked on the cord. It started right up, thank God. He caught up with Anne now in water over her head, put the boat in neutral and reached for her arm. After he pulled her in, he revved the motor and headed out.

Rosemary stared hard at the black dot. "Please, please," she said to the air. The kids had gathered on the beach. "Everything will be all right," she said and reached out for Davey. Hannah began throwing towels around her shivering children. Nancy stayed on the lawn chair, her legs still crossed, her ankles slender and smooth, toenails sticking up like little red flags. Rosemary ran for the binoculars. The screen door slammed behind her as if to shut her off from hearing or knowing anything she didn't want to know. She could not believe harm would come to Evelyn or any of them. Evelyn was an excellent swimmer. The afternoon was hot and sunny and the flags flapped gently as if to reassure her, but in her mind she saw dark clouds, whitecaps rolling in any minute, complicating everything. That's how it was—in the midst of a good time—when you least expected it . . .

She searched the horizon with the binoculars, but in her fright she couldn't even find the boat. She took the glasses from her eyes and put them back again, trying to aim better. The boat was slowly coming toward her and she couldn't see whether or not Justin was towing the tube. He probably was, and Evelyn would surely be on it, annoyed that Justin had spoiled her ride.

There she was—drooped across the inner tube, her head lying on its side in a helpless aspect that brought tears to Rosemary's eyes. There was no one she felt closer to than Evelyn despite Evelyn's reluctance to talk about her life with Justin's father or maybe because of it. The dignity Evelyn carried Rosemary emulated. She'd known acceptance and love from Evelyn unlike any other in her life, even from her own mother. Evelyn wasn't moving—she must be resting, and horribly frightened. Oh, the terror of underwater space. Unseen depths. Unimaginable quietness, on the surface so beautiful—glancing rays, mirroring skies, expanding sunsets—below, so deadly, so dark.

The boat danced in place for a while, Evelyn probably refusing to get aboard. She never could manage that first unsteadiness of putting a foot in the rowboat. The boat headed towards shore now, slowly, carefully towing the tube. The children were back diving off the pier. Nancy remained on the lawn chair browsing through her *Redbook*, and Hannah took up her knitting again. Truman and Giles were still out on the catamaran. Rosemary paced on the shore. When Justin pulled the boat onto the beach, she reached out for Evelyn, whose legs wouldn't support her. Her face was as white as her hair and Rosemary felt her tremble as they staggered together toward the sand, Evelyn's weight against her.

"Well," Evelyn said, trying to make little of it with a faint smile, "I didn't want to let go of the tube, you know—swim back without it—the children enjoy it so. But once I began drifting, the current was swifter than I thought. I just couldn't paddle hard enough to steer the darn thing," she said. "I'm okay. Just let me sit awhile. My arms are a little achy." She was shaking. Justin brought her a bit of vodka and orange juice and she asked for her beach jacket as she sat in the nearest lawn chair. Rosemary covered Evelyn's legs with a towel and looked up to see Justin pass by Nancy's lawn chair, trailing his hand across Nancy's neck, sweeping her hair to one side, an action so fleeting Rosemary wasn't sure she was seeing it at all. She must be mistaken.

He disappeared around the side of the house and came back carrying the enameled steamer pot, a signal the kids did not miss. In a second he was surrounded by dripping children. Davey said, "Let me, let me," but Michael already had the tongs down in the crabfloat. "Aw, you get to do everything, Michael," he said as Michael pulled the crabs out one by one and Anne slammed the lid on the pot after each crab. One hung on to another and let go just before Michael got it in the pot. The crab scrambled sideways toward the water. Kids jumped out of its way, screeching.

"Give Davey a turn, Michael. Just let him try it once," said Rosemary, but it was Anne, dutifully helping Michael, never asking for attention, who Rosemary saw clearly in this moment. The sight of her diving off the pier and swimming toward her grandmother, taking things in her own hands at such a young age—she was the valiant one. Rosemary, close to tears now at the relief of seeing Evelyn in the lawn chair chatting away to Nancy, bent over to whisper in Anne's ear, "Anybody ever tell you what a good kid you are?" Anne smiled back and shrugged as if no one ever had.

With the children following, Justin hosed off the crabs at the outside spigot and water poured out of the bottom of the steamer. The crabs, subdued, bubbled quietly in the pot.

"Watch out now," Justin said to the kids. "Annie, hold that door open for me, will ya?" He disappeared into the house with the pot.

Rosemary followed. She just wanted him to look at her, reassure her in some way, help her ward off the doubt she felt. Would he, did he, do more than look at other women? He did spend Monday through Thursday alone in the city. She'd never had cause to suspect anything. She would not wreck the status quo with suspicions and accusations. He would enjoy it too much. It was an ego thing with men, she decided and said instead, "Do you think your mother is okay? She looks awfully pale."

He nodded. "Oh, sure."

Then there was a rush of kids between them—"C'mon," Davey called. "This is the best part." He meant the crabs scratching the side of the pot as they cooked. Usually he covered his ears, but today, the others would be as horrified at the sound as he.

"Eew!" said Kevin, Nancy's boy, about Michael's size, his nose screwed up. "You cook 'em alive?" He looked at Justin and then at Rosemary and back again as if they were murderers. "Eating a crab that's dead before you cook it will make you sick," Rosemary explained.

"Timer's on," Justin announced, a fact she could see for herself. "Who wants to go for a swim?" But the children listened to the pot as Rosemary began laying newspaper on the table. Then Davey gave a yell. The crabs, escaping down the side of the pot, dropped off the stove and onto the floor.

Eight of them scratched across the linoleum before she got the lid back on and laid a heavy bowl on top. The crabs' claws clacked midair across the rug like they were playing castanets. The other kids yelled and danced in exaggerated leg lifts but her kids tried to catch the crabs with bare hands. They knew how to do it. Michael had taught them.

"Okay, okay," said Justin, bursting back into the room. "So we forgot to tie the lid on. Maybe they deserve to be let go, warriors that they are. Open the door! Down to the sea in victory! Step aside you tender earthlings before they sink a claw in you!" He leaped toward the door and swept a folded newspaper at the crabs, funneling them to freedom. The kids squealed and giggled, stood on couches and chairs, looked at Justin and looked away and then back again not knowing whether to trust him or not, eager to join in the game if there was one. Kevin shouted, "Here's one; here's one!" Michael pinned down the claws with a broom handle, then picked up the crab with forefinger and thumb around the back end behind the swimmer fins. He ran out the door and flung it out into the river as far as he could. He turned around to face them with a big grin on his face. The hero.

"Look out!" cried Justin, bending to grab Amy's toes. She yelped and jumped, her round face red with heat, but looked up at Justin with a grin. She began to follow him around for the next hour or so, while he brought the next batches of crabs for steaming—in and out, trailing him to the rowboat until he took her out to dip crabs. Twice more the pot was filled.

Rosemary slid the red crabs sprinkled with seasoning onto trays and set them on the newspaper-covered table while the smell of crab overpowered all other smells. It filled the room, lay on her damp skin and permeated her hair as she marched back and forth through the crab steam with trays of crabs, mallets, steak knives, rolls of paper towels, cups of melted butter, a bottle of vinegar, platters of potato salad and sliced tomato and Hannah's bread.

Steam rose from the heaped crabs. Outside, flags drooped at the poles. The air was suffocating. Even the fans didn't help much. The kids jumped in the river before coming to the table and when they did come in, their hair plastered to their heads, sniffling, eyes bloodshot, they dripped puddles on the floor despite the wet towels wrapped around their middles.

Before they took their places, Rosemary put dry folded towels on the assort-ment of chairs. Justin passed around cans of beer. There was never enough ice for the tea; the lemonade quickly warmed in sweating juice glasses.

They reached for the crabs and began pulling off claws, putting the larger ones in piles to crack later and sucking sweet bits out of the smaller ones. The crabs lay burnished and plump on the trays and Giles acknowl-edged their glory like a grace, "Nothing prettier than a pile of hot, steamed crabs!" Justin showed Nancy the best way to break off the hard shell while Rosemary sat with a huge crab before her on the newspaper, the crab red-ugly and angry in its final revenge. She picked it up and pulled off the shell. With her eyes on Justin, she yanked its appendages vehemently—as if crabs had testicles. Sex seemed to get in everyone's way, Nancy's way, and Justin's way, and hers, she thought, as the juice ran down her arms, sex being the thing she least understood. Furious, she watched as Justin drenched a piece of back fin in vinegar while Nancy opened her mouth wide to receive it. *Fooling around,* he'd say. He'd make light of it, maybe even laugh at her. The chunk of meat in her mouth wouldn't be swal-lowed. She looked down, afraid of revealing anything like need or hurt, or her plainness in the face of blonde competition, and broke open the crab's body to the bittersweet smell of the mustard-yellow butter inside. She stole a glance at Truman, deep into his crab claw, sucking out the meat, ham-mering the tip to get out the last bit. Maybe he was right to absorb him-self. Maybe he was stupid or didn't care, or maybe small flirtations were acceptable and she was being foolish. *Why make a big thing of it?* she thought, as she listened to the chatter, the hammering, the drone of the fans, felt the heat melt her as she glanced up at the sweating, flushed faces around her.

No, she said to herself. *This is it—this day, this gathering, this feast, our children. Didn't he build the cottage for us?—so much effort for us? This is it. The forever people reach for.* Besides, Justin was looking at her now if only to see if she was watching him, conscious she might be offended, but that was all she really wanted—to have him look at her as though she mat-tered. All too quickly he was telling Giles what he thought of the presi-dent's war on poverty. Evelyn, engrossed in her crab, pulled the meat with fingers that looked too small and delicate for the task. She was silent, still pale, with a new seriousness in her demeanor. Her cheeks wobbled, something Rosemary had never noticed before, as she refused Rosemary's offer of more tea.

"Anything I can get you, Evelyn?" she asked, to which Evelyn raised eyes that said, *Am I like a child now? Do I have to be looked after like one of the kids? Counted, kept track of? I saw myself helpless today. Dependent on you to save me.*

"No, thank you, Rosemary, deah," she said softly.

Hannah picked the crabmeat quickly and gathered it in three small dishes for her children, who were happily eating her bread and waiting, trusting mother would provide. We are all dependent on each other, Rosemary thought, in such close and distant communion, so trusting in the tight web of family, feelings, and words that create an aura of safety. For her it was Justin and the children. For Evelyn, it was having them live close by now that she was alone again. For them all, these were good times, the ones that would be the good old days someday. She breathed deep, feeling satisfied and strong. They were so fortunate. Don't worry, she wanted to tell Evelyn, *I'll always love you, look out for you.* She thought about the word *always* then, as she concentrated on the lavish bounty on the table before her, listened to the hammering, the shells cracking open to reveal mysterious innards, and knew time was as measured as the diminishing pile of crab, the voices around her but a momentary distraction.

Soon the children lost interest and found their way back to the water, trailed by parental warnings to stay in the harbor where it was shallow. Occasionally they ran in to check on the circle of families and complain of a splinter from the pier or a mosquito bite. The table was heaped with mountains of crab skeleton while hands reached out to push back the debris to make room for picking the last crab. Finally, Evelyn raised herself stiffly from the table and washed her hands at the sink, then drifted to the couch, lit a cigarette, and stared out across the water beyond the children to watch the sunset.

Rosemary turned on the hanging lamp over the table; the gnats gathered and flurried overhead. The youngest of the children, Lisa, came in crying and would not be comforted. Events run their course, lose momentum, become memory, Rosemary thought. Change sneaks up on us. Something, something is different. Justin spends four nights a week in the city alone or not alone. She lit a citronella candle and heard the whispered hiss of something caught too close to the flame.

Maybe she was staging dramas again, she told herself. They would talk it over some afternoon when they were out on the catamaran and she was calmer. Justin would wind up laughing about it and then they'd both laugh, but not now. Now she had guests to see to. She needed to straighten the room, wash the dishes, bunk the kids, and help her husband, who was rolling up the newspaper around the crab hulls, his face still flushed, his eyes bright as he swept everything into the trash bag, gathering the top in his fist and spinning the bag as if it were a partner in a dance she could not know.

HOLDING BACK THE SEA

He and Dad planned to start the bulkhead on Saturday. Early Friday afternoon, instead of coming into the house and calling, *Hey, where is everybody?* Dad went to the waterfront and stared at the mountains of fill dirt and stacks of corrugated cement that had been delivered while he was gone. He dropped his briefcase—something usually so important to him that he wouldn't let any of the kids go near it—right in the dirt and left it there. In fact, he walked away from it. Then he took off his tie and threw it in the dirt, too. And then his white button-down-collar shirt. He bent over and took off his shoes, those hard brown lace-up jobs he only went to work in and hated because they hurt his feet no matter what kind he got, and kicked them away. Then his socks, hopping around on one leg because the left one was stuck on him, and when it was free he flung it behind him. He rolled up his pant legs, too. And climbed right up the mountain of dirt.

"Dad, hey Dad," Michael yelled as he ran out of the house. "What're you doing, huh?" He was thinking maybe his father was going to run down the hill on the other side and dive into the water. It was low tide—Dad could see that for himself—but maybe he hadn't noticed. Michael was afraid for a minute that something was weird, too weird; that his dad was going to hurt himself, but then, he should know how his father was always coming up with something great, some kind of surprise.

His mom stood in the front yard with her hands on her hips, and

Davey and Anne ran up the hill giggling and it was okay because his father ran down toward them laughing his *hah, haaa hee* laugh, his whole face wrinkled up and all of his teeth showing.

"Rosemary!" his dad called, and then stifled a laugh as if he was stifling a sneeze and said, "I got canned! Can you believe it? I got canned, and while Jack's telling me, I'm trying to look like I'm taking a beating but I can't wait to get outside and start shouting! It couldn't have come at a better time. Now I can get the bulkhead done. I got all summer!"

He made it sound like good news, but Mom just stood there looking scared and said, "Justin, what're we going to do?"

"Aw, it'll be okay. Space program's been drying up, you know, but in the fall, things'll pick up again. I'll find something. I'm not worried. I can't believe it," he said, laughing. "I haven't had a summer off since I was a kid!"

She laughed, too. "You," she said, and shook her head. Then Michael knew it was okay.

What he wondered was whether his dad liked computers. Maybe he'd rather be a house or seawall builder, or a farmer, because when he rented a tractor and drove it down along Sulley's Point Road from the farm across the way with Michael sitting on the fender and holding onto his shoulder, he was laughing and singing.

"Hot damn, Michael!" he said, his voice deep and loud as he sang over and over, "Bringing in the sheaves, bringing in the sheaves," a song which must have had some other words, too, but Michael didn't know them.

None of the neighbors thought he could build a bulkhead, but they didn't know him. Pete said one morning when he and Michael were on the *Miss Linda*, "Your dad's not gettin' Taylor to put in his bulkhead?" Michael shook his head and Pete just went, "Hmmph."

And when he went out in the *Greenfly* one afternoon, he saw one of the neighbors down at the end of the point looking at the dirt piles through binoculars. He was with Mr. Abbott, another neighbor, and they passed the binoculars back and forth. Mr. Phillips, next door, sat on his porch and watched his dad all day and then he went over to the next porch, to the Dublins', and they talked and laughed and then he came back and watched some more. Now maybe the neighbors weren't talking about them, but when that big kid Marty, who was thirteen and lived in the big house next to the marsh, met Michael on Pete's pier looking for doublers, he came over and said, "Your father's crazy. He can't put in a good seawall without a pile driver. That seawall will be busted up come the first storm." He said it like it was something his father said, not him. He didn't have brains enough to come up with that on his own. *Reetard.*

When Michael asked his father about driving piles to hold up the cement sheets, his dad said, "I don't think we can do that. You need a piece of heavy equipment that comes in on a barge and costs a fortune. But what we want to do is increase the water pressure in the hose so what we do is attach a pipe and flatten the end of it a bit. Lessen the area the water has to come through and the pressure increases. Savvy? We'll be able to get the sheets in deep enough that way and we'll support them midway and top with two-by-eights."

Michael knew he'd have it all figured out. "Anything's possible, Michael," his dad said. "Just takes some thinking."

When they began on the section farthest out in the water, they could only work at low tide. The first few days were good because low tide was in the morning before the mosquitoes got too bad. They were out at sunup just like on days they went crabbing. Davey and Anne played in the dirt piles and sat on top of the tractor pretending to drive it and his mother took pictures of them. Davey waved and smiled. Then she turned and with the wind blowing her hair across the camera lens, she took a picture of Michael sitting sidesaddle on top of one of the sheets. He grinned at her and stopped rocking for a moment, glad to give his bottom a rest, shifted his weight a little and then heard his father say, "Okay, start rockin'!" Michael held on, his body used to the motion. The muscles in his arms tightened as he braced himself; the muscles in his thighs as his legs clenched the sides were bulging and burning. His father could do anything, and if he paid attention, he'd be able to, too. He didn't know he was this strong, that he weighed enough to help drive a hundred-twenty-pound cement sheet into the river bottom. He sat high looking out over the water, and pretended he was on the rigging of an old pirate ship.

After a while, he mostly watched his dad. Even when he'd built the cottage, he didn't work this hard—all the mud and stirred-up river water, the mosquitoes, his soaked sneakers sucking along in the marsh grass, his muddied T-shirt and shorts that were slung low on his hips, the old leather work gloves on his hands, his not-so-big-around arms that seemed like the puniest things to jiggle those sheets with, the puniest things to hold back a river with as they stretched across the panels. He looked almost like he was nailed to each one as he lifted it into place, grunting and sweating.

While his feet held the hose in place, he started jiggling the sheet and when he got it started a little, let it lean on his shoulder while he boosted Michael up. He had to hold the slab and Michael and the hose all at once. The cigar in his teeth looked like it would set the peak of his cap on fire, and so did his steamy-looking face. He was not big like Pete, but he was strong. *Wiry,* his mother said once, and Michael thought of wires running through his father, electric wires humming with energy.

By the end of the week, they had eight sheets in place. They had ordered twenty-four altogether. They even worked in high tide, because they were coming closer toward the house where the water was shallow. Michael could hoist himself up on the panels from *Greenfly,* and when it was low tide, they dug a trench with the shovel instead of the hose.

"We'll saw them off even, once we get the two-by-eights to do what they're supposed to," his father said at the dinner table. His legs jumped and vibrated the floor. He looked out at the bulkhead, sheets sticking up out of the water at different heights, two-by-eights bolted to them but stuck straight out instead of following the curve of the wall. "A little rain would help those boards bend," his father said. "Maybe I'll hose 'em down."

Each day he tightened the bolts. Miraculously, the boards began to bend into a curve, and once the tops of the sheets were sawed off at the level of the two-by-eights, the shape of the seawall became apparent. It was like a huge question mark and they were coming toward the straight part at the bottom, toward their own harbor.

Michael had gone through every one of his jean shorts; his father through two boxes of panatela cigars and was on his third. There was enough seawall now to hold back the fill dirt, and his father, high on the tractor seat with Michael sitting on the fender, graded the earth. Michael thought about the river being held back, mountains being moved, the geography of Sulley's Point being changed forever. He thought, too, about forever, about their hold on this one spot, how far down in the earth they owned, a cone shape reaching down till it was a tiny dot at the center, the cone rising in the opposite direction, up into the sky, reaching up into forever. He wondered how far out into the water they owned, and too, how this piece of land put here by his father and him would go down through the family, to his kids someday, and their kids. The tractor growled beneath them. The pole to the purple martin house looked much shorter and would have to be extended. The land they made was as high as the piece where the cottage stood.

He had watched his father work the gears on the tractor enough to know how to shift. "Can I, Dad? Just run it back and forth to level it some more? Can I do the topsoil, Dad, before we put down the grass seed? Huh?"

For the first few turns his father watched him, smiled and nodded in approval, and when he was sure Michael could manage, he turned and went into the cottage. The putt-putt of this baby was a lot louder than the Evinrude. The wheels could grind over anything. He hoped that kid, Marty, was watching. He smelled oil from the engine and turned to watch puffs of smoke rise out of the exhaust just behind him. Maybe he'd be a farmer. He liked changing the face of the earth. He lowered the scraper blade and moved earth toward the seawall. Stopping, he raised the blade to back up for another load of the light brown soil. Claylike, it broke up in stiff chunks. The topsoil was darker, looser. He'd smooth sandy soil first. Forward again, right to the edge, almost to the seawall. He put his foot on the clutch, pushed the throttle and turned around in the seat to see where he was going as he backed up. He released the clutch. The tractor didn't move. He jiggled the throttle and felt the tractor move forward instead of reverse. He had shifted into third instead of reverse! Panicked, he rose from the seat and stood on the brake as the tractor hung on its belly over the edge of the seawall. He looked out high over the water and his heart leapt out of his chest like some old discarded sook crab flung out on the river, its swimmer fins fanning the air. He turned off the ignition and heard the bang of the cottage door and his father yell, "Jesus Christ,

Michael! Take it easy!" He thought about diving into the river and wondered if he could clear the scraper blade that rose above the seawall like the blade of a giant ax. He thought he wanted to swim till dark.

"You okay?" his father shouted, running toward him. He jumped down from the tractor.

"Yeah." Depends. No broken bones or anything. No bruises. But inside he was a pile of oatmeal.

"I think it'll be all right," his father said, hand on his shoulder. "I think you can just put it in first gear and drive it on over. Then turn right and go on up the beach. Knew leaving that beach alone was the sensible thing to do for emergencies like this."

He searched his father's face. Not a smile or a wrinkle anywhere, but his eyes were laughing down under the shadow of his cap.

"Yeah," he said. "I could."

"Well, get back up on 'er. You got 'er there. Let's see you undo 'er. Just make sure you hit reverse this time."

But in the end his father did it. "Don't want you flinging yourself out in the water, Michael." He got up on her and threw her in reverse. The back wheels dug in as the belly scraped up the two-by-eights a little, but not too bad, and when the tractor was free, his father let him do the topsoil. "Figure you'll never lose reverse again, Michael," was all he said.

When the bulkhead was finished and the rocks were cemented in the wall where the beach sloped down to the river, his mother said they should celebrate. She bought sixteen candles and folded down the edges of sixteen brown grocery bags. Then Anne and Davey filled the bags a quarter of the way with sand—about two sand bucketsful each—and put them along the bulkhead. Michael placed a candle in each bag, down into the sand so they'd stand firm without tipping over, and lighted them in the long August dusk. They burned far into the night while he and his mother kept watch. Anne and Davey fell asleep. When his father turned in early and his mother dozed over a book in the front room, Michael went out to check the candles. As he turned on the top step of the cottage, he saw the difficult curve, the gentle slope back to their own beach, the giant, fluid luminescent question mark at the edge of the dark water and the freshly seeded earth. It was the most beautiful thing he'd ever seen and although his father was already snoring in the middle bedroom, he thought he heard him whisper, *Anything is possible, Michael. Anything.*

That Rosemary was uneasy about his unemployment was plain to see. She began picking berries on the side of the road as if they were going to starve. "It'll be all right," he told her. "I'll pick up another job in the fall. No sweat."

He wasn't in any hurry. He liked wearing his old khaki shirt from Army days as he lay back on the couch not worried about Monday morning. When he looked in the mirror, he couldn't believe he'd become what he'd always wanted to be, a free spirit, in tune with the times and all those flower children. They ate crabs from the river and fish Michael caught, and they stopped having tribes of company on the weekend. *It's a good, slow time,* he thought. *A reprieve. Nobody's suffering.*

There was a feeling of pulling together. Rosemary didn't spend a dime extra. They joked about how the only essential things they needed to buy were flour, sugar, coffee, and condoms. They'd disconnected themselves from the world and simplified their life. They bought crab bait from Pete, eel, at first, and then bull lips, and let the bills go for the time being. The ease of living off the river sang to Justin and he was listening. He felt misplaced in time, knew he would have been good at living a hundred years before—no paycheck, no boss, only one's own intuition and gumption and that river out there, silent and opulent. But it was the sky's fault, so much of it in this flat place, an openness that seduced him into enlarging his vision. Nagging at him was the idea he no longer fit into his other life. A job identified a man. He could see how men might jump off buildings without one. What a man does was the first thing people asked. He thought about how much he'd had to do to maintain a family. Not that he could wish them away. He had never thought about kids too much figuring they were inevitable, but all this scrambling—acquiring things—first a wife, then kids, then houses, cars, boats, tennis shoes and jeans, gallons of milk—it never stopped and all he ever really wanted to do was make his mark, figure out ways to play the game and win. But in all those figurings, he was always alone.

His joblessness was only an interim. Meanwhile, they crabbed all day and picked the meat out at night to put in the freezer. Just he and Rosemary talking quietly as they picked, the kids drifting off to bed when they wanted to—all rules out the window. A candle stuck in an empty bottle of Chianti dripped multicolored layers of wax, a measure of the hours they sat. Rosemary laughed easily and the talk was as comfortable and eager as it was before the kids came. He had a real thirst for her, more like a constant ache, and he grabbed her hand and licked the crab juice off her fingers just to let her know they could do the rest tomorrow and take care of something more urgent just now. It got to be a habit, and he enjoyed the way she looked at him sideways, laughing at everything he said. It was the joke about Henry that started it. About this guy named Henry who said he had sex with his wife once a year and when they asked him why he looked so happy, he said, "Tonight's the night!"

He told her things between them just kept getting better and better. "Yeah," she said, sounding as though she didn't mean it. She would often agree and keep her thoughts to herself. Once, after they made love, she said, "It's just that you're silent so often, I feel as though I'm out in space— on hold till you need me again—and I get lonesome." He couldn't sleep after that. The fact that she had a complaint and he never knew. He just got busy, that's all, holding everything up. It would be good for her to go back to school, have something of her own. She'd always wanted to. He lay listening to her breathe deep. When she stirred, he felt her back turn to him like a shield. The only thing was to start planning where to buy zoysia grass plugs—terrific root system and not affected by brackish water—figure out what kind of business he could start so he wouldn't have to answer to anybody. There were franchises to investigate. Restaurants. Aquacats. Maybe he should look into a real estate license. Worlds to conquer. All of it easier than women, he thought in the darkness.

Two good things in one day. A kitty, snow white, *Snow White,* Anne thought, small enough to fit in the cup of her hands. Fuzzy fur, like the down on a chick. Blue eyes. It was hers. They had a dog, Chessie, but he was mostly Michael's. He only came when Michael called.

She'd found the kitten creeping across the road as if it'd been wondering where it belonged, and she scooped it up. "You belong to me," she said. Her mother made her ask around—the next-door neighbors, the people renting the cottage two doors down, and finally Pete's wife, Miss Linda, standing at the hauling-up motor for a boat being pulled along the rails to have its bottom scraped. Her hand on the motor switch was lined with the blue blood of her veins just like on the chart at school.

"Yeah," said Miss Linda, her lips in a bright red smile this morning. "We had six in the last litter and you can have that'un if you'd like or choose another." No. This one. The kitten had come looking for her.

The other good thing was the berry farm. "Gather up the baskets and put on shoes," her mother said with her eyes on the table she was wiping. "But you'll have to leave the kitten. It can't stay in a hot car."

"What if I brought it in a basket?" Anne said.

"It might jump out and get lost."

"I'll be careful," Anne said in her quiet voice, which made her mother look at her.

"It'll be safer here," she said. And that sounded final.

So she left it in a carton box, curled up on an old towel with a saucer of milk close by—right under the window where the breeze came off the water with the water sounds for comfort. She gave it one last kiss on the nose before she left, holding it under its armpits, staring into its eyes—slits now, when she kissed it and laid it down. Sleeping in another second. Curled up on the towel. She stroked the white fur.

There were rows and rows of blackberries—the seeds-sticking-between-your-teeth kind, and raspberries—the don't-eat-so-many-till-I-pay-for-them kind, and currants hanging green and bitter—the *don't-get-them* kind, and blueberries—lots of different kinds. They each had to pick one quart basket full till Mom said, "Go on. I'll do the rest. Now remember, behave yourselves."

Which was what they'd been waiting for, all of them. Davey and Michael had their favorite places, and hers was the little bench near the lily pond filled with goldfish, where the willow bent over and skimmed its branches across the water. Michael grabbed the rope swing and tossed himself far out over the pond in the cool shade and swung and swung and wouldn't give either Davey or her a turn, but she and Davey reached for the tire swings and stayed in them for a while, acting like they didn't care, and when they got tired, they ran for the platform swing and listened to its creak-creak against the sound of swishing leaves, the birds calling and the cicadas.

The garden path trailed in and out of itself like a French knot and just when she thought she'd found all the trails with Davey chasing her, there was another path she hadn't noticed before, where bunches of tiny flowers grew—those bright blue elephant ears with the yellow part shaped like a trunk. She named them Baby Blue Elephants. There was so much to look at—she could spend all of her summer here and never get tired, never see it all. She came upon a rock garden with water trickling down to a stream. Above, there were birdhouses. One, an apartment house for purple martins, rose high on a pole. She could hear the babies chattering inside.

She followed the stream and watched the dragonflies skitter, stooping once to swish her hands in the water while Davey went back to the swing and Michael flew through the air, back and forth, back and forth, all quiet. As if this were a church. She came again to the pond where lilies floated in the shallow water, yellow, pink, and white, and resting on a lily pad was a frog. She never believed frogs did that—a leaf couldn't hold a frog, she'd thought. It took a while to learn all there was—you'd never run out of things to learn. She'd have a garden like this one day (Snow White would love it), and people could come and rest and look. Looking was the most important thing. People could come and pick berries and when they were tired and hot they could look at her garden—she'd make them look—by making it so pretty they couldn't *not* look. Maybe this was her garden and she was already grown-up, floating by as her grown-up self. She could own the garden as long as she was in it. Take it home with her even. In her head. She stared hard at small, shady places, collecting them, and then closed her eyes remembering. It was like taking pictures again and again. She'd always remember. Where do you put all the things you remember? Your head must have many, many places for everything. Maybe that was why older people didn't pay any attention sometimes. They ran out of places to put things.

Michael found a snake. It was yellow and green. He started shouting, then he picked it up and it wrapped around his arm. He held the head between two fingers. She knew he'd shove the face at her. She tried not to flinch. "Stop it, Michael," she said, in a calm voice because he'd only get meaner if she acted scared. Then her mother said it was time to leave and told Michael to put down the snake, while Davey started whining, "No!" and since he was the only one she gave in to, they stayed longer. Her mother sat on the platform swing next to her and pushed with her feet on the wood while Michael and Davey sat across from them. "I've already paid Mr. Harding," she said. "The berries are at the end of the first row and everybody has to carry a basket to the car in five minutes, okay?" That sounded final.

And so was something else. When they got back home she ran to Snow White's box and reached out to pet it but she could tell it wasn't alive the minute she saw the mussed up fur and its head twisted around. Mom said the kitten would be safe, but she was wrong. She'd forgotten about the dog—somebody let the dog in at the last minute—and Anne hated the dog now and couldn't think what it must have been like to be picked up by a great big mouth and crunched to death or whipped till your neck snapped. She hated the dog—hated him hated him hated him, and Michael, too, while she was at it, and her mother—everybody, as a matter of fact. Now the only good thing she could remember about that day was finding Snow White—the little warm, white kitten body it hurt to remember. She cried a long time because remembering was stuck in her brain all through dinner and after she went to bed and even a little the next day. She wouldn't ever get it unstuck, she thought, even if there was another kitten from Miss Linda.

"I'm sorry, Annie," said her mother, holding her. "I'm so sorry." But that made it worse because her mother made a mistake and even though she was sorry, Annie knew she, Annie Williams, was not in control of anything.

TRANSITIONS

THE WALL

～

September, they were back in the city. The impatiens by the back door had grown tall, blooming red and fuchsia against the green shingles of their suburban, white-shuttered Cape Cod house. Inside, the cluttered rooms had grown musty-smelling and lonesome in their absence. To Rosemary's relief, there was not a lipstick stain on any of the glasses or a stray blonde hair in the bathroom. On the first morning, she peered out the kitchen window down the long, green tunnel of trees and watched the kids set off to school. Davey scurried ahead, surprisingly eager, and Anne, who had dropped her sweater, yelled, "Wait up!" Michael walked alone to the corner where he waited for the bus to middle school, eyeing the neighbors' new Chevelle, a car he yearned to drive one day.

The chain-link fence around the yard suddenly irked Rosemary. She closed her eyes to retrieve the scene in front of the cottage, the small waves on the narrow beach, the horizon line across the water that divided earth and sky, a view from which she always knew where she stood, where she could see the children playing in the river and Justin sailing—not like the small pieces of sky peeking through the trees here, her family disappearing among the shadows.

Justin, with old enthusiasms, marched down the walk in those uncomfortable brown oxfords, snapping the catch on his leather briefcase. He was hired as East Coast sales manager for a new line of computer software in a fledgling company. Home each night in time for dinner with only an occasional business trip on the month's schedule, he could be counted on to watch the kids the evenings she attended classes. His beard was gone, giving his face a boyish nakedness, revealing a vulnerability that startled her. He was cheerful and playful, teasing her again. She loved the attention and answered with laughter. "Keep smiling, Babe," he said. "You look good when you smile." Saturday he showed up with a new car, a Caprice. "A boss has to show up in a good car," he said. He'd bought two new suits, too. Amazing how easily he could slip into any role. She envied his confidence.

"You gotta play, too, Babe," he said one night, spitting around the toothbrush and foam in his mouth.

"What do you mean?"

He scooped up water from the faucet in his hands and rinsed. "You know, be the wife of somebody on the way up, support the effort, be part of a team."

"Like what?"

"Like — get your hair done once in a while, get a couple of sexy outfits — you know, play the part of the executive's wife, greet me with a martini in your hand when I come home, maybe wrap yourself in Saran Wrap when you bring my slippers." He grinned into the mirror and winked at her.

She threw a pillow at him. "Actually, Justin, a bigger house was what I had in mind."

"In good time, Babe. All in good time," he said as if he already had a plan. Lately he'd taken to holding her all night. With his body cupped around her, she woke up in the charcoal gray of early morning to his steady breathing and sweaty hands, feeling contentment like a full stomach. Her doubts faded; she'd been right not to make a big thing of his flirtation with Nancy. It was an impulse. Something as easily forgotten as yesterday's shopping list.

This morning, with the kids off to school, the dog fed, dishes done — Rosemary walked out onto the back step. It had rained the night before and the geraniums and impatiens were as lush as they'd ever be. The bank between their yard and the next had silted down badly. They were losing ground and should do something about it. Build a retaining wall of some sort.

She walked through the yard listening to the hum of traffic on the highway, the cars speeding to assigned places and paychecks. The other sound, the brook at the back edge of their yard gurgling with the rush of new water, drew her, and she began to study the rocks along the embankment. Across the gully, two women played tennis in the park and she heard the steady pong, pong and calling out of scores, but her thoughts were centered on rocks, which ones were easy to reach and which were the right size as they lay tumbled about on the bank. Minutes later, she found herself pulling the wheelbarrow out of the shed.

She chose the rocks carefully. Dropping them into the wheelbarrow, she listened to the ring of stone on its metal basin, and when she delivered them at the foot of the slope where the soil had eroded, she felt the vibration of their stifled thud reverberating to her feet. Again and again she went down to the creek, gathering; soon there was a rut in the lawn where she'd wheeled back and forth. She placed the first row of stones in a line about fifteen feet long, eyeing them to see if they were straight. These she half-buried with the trowel. A wall needed firm footing, she guessed, although she'd never built one before. Lost in rock thought, she regarded the stones in terms of opposing grade, how they'd fit together without slipping.

Hannah, driving by, beeped and waved, and Rosemary waved back. The mailman said, "See you got yourself a project there," but other than that, it was as if she were the only one in the world. Hours passed, shadows moved around her. Where she had been in shade, she now worked in full sun, the armpits of her shirt turning damp. She supposed she should look for a pair of work gloves, but hated to take the time. A rock slipped; her fourth finger split. The pain made her hand feel big. Blood dripped to the rock and trickled to the wall's edge. Holding up her hand to stop the bleeding, she stepped back and took in the whole of her work, the wall three layers high now, and was amazed she was doing such a thing. It seemed daring, and assumptive. She'd asked no one's permission, hadn't thought Justin might have had a plan for this spot. She couldn't even be sure the wall was on the property line, but her doubts were fleeting, her finger demanding attention. In the bathroom, she ran cold water over it. Tearing off a piece of paper towel, she folded it small and secured it to her finger with masking tape. Her nails torn and every crease on her hands accented by mud, she was about to return to the wall when the phone rang. Justin.

"Tell Michael I'll go with him to the game tonight. I forgot to mention it this morning and I figure he's probably wondering."

"Good. He'll love that."

"How's it going?"

"Okay. Everything's fine."

"Couple of the guys here and their wives are getting together for dinner Friday so see if you can get a sitter—other phone's ringing—see you later."

She'd have to do something with her hair and keep her hands under the table, but Friday dropped off the end of the week as the screen door banged behind her. The smell of wet earth beckoned. Everything was a little harder now with a finger out of commission. As the rock layers grew, she had to fill in the space between the slope and the wall with soil, packing the earth down with her feet. Mid-afternoon, she wandered down to the creek to rest. Ball sounds from the tennis court were suddenly interrupted by laughter as a ball came over the fence and dropped into the water in front of her.

"I got it!" she called and waded among the rocks, sneakers and all, for the ball. Throwing it back, she realized how much her muscles ached. The women waved and shouted, "Thanks!" Another load of rocks, and another. Her shoes squished. She pulled them off and put them on the steps to dry. Looking back at the wall, she eyed the top of the slope and the top of the wall to see if they were even. One more layer.

When the kids came home from school, dragging backpacks and sweaters, they all wanted to help. "Not this time," she told them. "It's my wall." Anne and Davey nodded and watched her for a while before drifting off to play with Hannah's kids. Michael lingered and said, "I could get a load of rocks for you, Mom."

She relented. "Okay. Just one load."

It felt late. She should start dinner, take a shower, run a comb through her hair—but she was almost done. She heard quick steps coming up the walk, the sound of oxfords. Justin. Attaché case in hand, he stopped with a look of dismay, his finger snapping the catch in his impatience.

"Jesus Christ, Rosemary" was all he said as he turned to go in the house.

He never looked at the wall. Suddenly self-conscious, she looked down and saw what Justin saw, a drudge—barefoot, muddy, sweaty, bloody bandage and all. Returning to her work, she chunked a few more rocks in place just to let herself know it was a good wall and needed to be finished. He was disappointed in her. She'd never be what he wanted. But he, of all people, should understand how marvelous it was to build something. It's the best thing I've ever done, she thought.

Friday, they returned home to a quiet house after dinner with Justin's salesmen and their wives. The children had long been in bed. The baby-sitter, Beth Anne, lived a few doors down. Justin walked her home, saying as they went out the door, "And what's a pretty girl like you doing baby-sitting on a Friday night?" Rosemary sat in the living room thinking about the evening and how difficult it had been trying to fit into conversations since both of the other wives had office jobs and did not have children. Justin had had a lot to drink which he didn't normally do, and by the end of the evening he'd kept everyone laughing, the women responding in shrieks. But he was silent on the drive home, his lips set in a straight line. When he returned from walking Beth Anne home, Rosemary got up to go into the bedroom. He grabbed her arm and pulled her to him.

"I'm awfully tired, Justin," she said, uncomfortable with his rough-ness. But he kept at her, laying his hands on the back of her neck and slip-ping his fingers inside the neck of her dress; he yanked so that the back seam along the zipper tore down to her waist. It was so unlike anything he'd ever done before—did he think it was sexy? Fun? He kept ripping as she fought him, realizing she should just shut up and succumb, pacify him—because he'd become a stranger. The more he tore at her, the angri-er she got till there was nothing but anger and pulling and ripping and her pleading, "Stop, for God's sake!" Then fear silenced her—for herself, for the children who might wake up, and no protection either, dear God— would she get pregnant? and guilt because she had brought him to this, hadn't she? If only she hadn't said she was tired! It was her fault. For all the things she wasn't. She hadn't seen how badly he needed her or someone right then, anyone—that was it, of course, she could have been any-one—or maybe there was someone else he thought about—and there now—he'd relieved himself—that was the only way she could think of it—as he lay spent in a heap on the floor. And vomited. And didn't bother to get up—or move—or care.

Who, in God's name, was he?

"Justin. Come on. Get up. Don't let the kids find you like this."

He rolled away from her and stayed there, eyes closed. She cleaned up around him. The dress had been new, violet—her favorite color. Never wanting to see it again, she stuffed it in a trash bag. And covered herself with her bathrobe. Shaking. Trying not to cry. Remembering how her father had frightened her, how before he struck, he held his mouth the same way Justin had. Although he never touched her sexually. No, he never touched her at all except to hit. She and her mother had spent their lives tiptoeing around him.

She thought she'd married someone the opposite of her father. Justin used to make her laugh. He did this very evening. He'd made them all laugh. And now this. She'd seen that expression before. She should have recognized it. Looking down at him, torn between anger and feeling sorry, she wiped his face. What was it she had seen in that face when she was nineteen? Someone breezy and cool, sharp, witty as hell, a brilliant light. He had a willingness to be irreverent and he was always thinking about things in new ways. He had a thirst for life that was seductive. But his was a passion for things and ideas, not so much for her. His feelings were directed elsewhere. Anyway, she knew how to build a wall now.

There was no use talking about it. Everything right was on her side. What he didn't remember she told him, tearfully, and Justin couldn't stand it when she cried. She had a certain smell about her then as though all of her had turned sour as week-old milk and once she started, it seemed she'd never stop. At those times, she was Miss Exaggeration, just like she was now about what had happened the night before.

"It felt like rape," she said.

"I just had a little too much to drink, for Christ's sake. And—well—I don't like it when you turn me down."

Her eyes narrowed; he was getting nowhere. He reached for her but she didn't respond. Sometimes the ground shuddered beneath him and when he felt like that, all he needed was for her to turn him down. It triggered something in him close to hate. Although he didn't hate her. He didn't hate anyone. Only himself, sometimes. But he couldn't say any of it out loud. He thought of his mother and father. They always held each other. He'd come upon them and there they'd be, heads together, talking in their private world. They often played golf, riding off in the convertible his father surprised his mother with on her birthday. Justin supposed he and George had more freedom than most kids their age.

He wished he was as good with words as his father had been. A lawyer who made friends easily, he ran for public office and won. But memories of that time were vague. Everything happened quickly toward the end of his father's life, the election, the building of the grand house in Hewlitt—they'd only lived in it a year when his father took to bed, the tin toy cricket on the nightstand he pressed when he needed something—events occurring in such rapid succession their sequence had been lost to him except for the last, the week-long silence about his father's illness, a secret between his mother and his father he dared not question, and then the massive heart attack one afternoon in November and the doctor's car parked in front of the house. When he came home from school earlier than George that day and tossed his books on the davenport, his mother came trembling and white from the hall and, putting her hand on his arm which she never did, said, "Before you go in—Justin dear—he's gone. He's gone! Whatever will we do?" reaching up to cover her face with her hands. He'd never seen her cry before. It sent an icy fear to his middle that had never melted, because he, at fifteen, had been playing ball and working his paper route when he could have helped his father build the house. He hadn't known his father's heart had been damaged as a child by rheumatic fever. Secrets had power. They were the ultimate sneak attack. He felt an anger he could never reveal, and because dark things had a way of bubbling up in the light of day, he concentrated on getting people to laugh. He was good at it. He kept a notebook with jokes for every occasion and he could be outrageous, to the delight of those around him, but he wasn't good at the serious, mushy things women wanted to hear.

Now, with Rosemary glaring at him, he thought he better pay some attention to her. He loved looking at other women, which he hadn't done anything about yet—but he might. It was one way to fit in. He wheezed out a laugh. Ah, shit.

"What's so funny?" she demanded.

"Nothing, Babe. I don't want to fight. I'm not good at it."

He wondered if his father had ever been unsure about anything. He must have been that last week, with the toy cricket in his hand, click-clicking for his mother.

DREAM HOUSE

～✦～

The kids running in and out on a bitter cold Saturday afternoon set her on a campaign for a larger house. Whenever the front door opened, she tensed in the frigid air that swept into the small L-shaped kitchen–living room, and dreamed about a foyer, a separate dining room, maybe a family room where the kids could spread out.

"Let's just see," she said to Justin, "it doesn't hurt to look." Taking heart from his silence, she studied the advertisements in the Sunday paper.

"A split-level clearance," she said to his back as he pondered monthly sales reports, "over in Crofton." Next thing, she was on the phone with Hannah, who said she had an hour to spare and could take Michael, Anne, and Davey to play with her three.

In the Caprice, she looked at him and waited for a sign—it was rare for them to be alone together in the middle of the day—but he was distant, busy with the keys, adjusting the radio and the heater. She glanced back at the house and tried to imagine life in a different neighborhood. The bright yellow curtains in the kitchen window made her suddenly nostalgic. A house was an outer coating, an extension of themselves, and they were moving on. It was inevitable. Just look at how well Justin was doing in his new position. His hands on the steering wheel had lost all the roughness of the summer. Anyone would think this was someone else, this man in the gray felt hat, the black-and-white-checked car coat with the fur collar and matching dark gray trousers. He looked every bit the computer firm executive although he did look pale, and he was unusually quiet and spiritless.

"So what do you think, Justin?" she said. "Can we afford to do this? I mean it will take me a while to get my degree—before we have two salaries."

He shrugged, tilted his head to one side and glanced out the window on the driver's side. The unsaid words might not be the ones she wanted to hear anyway so she sat back to watch the scenery change from their tightly woven neighborhood to the rolling countryside, the openness of narrowed roads where traffic lights fell behind. Soon there were billboards announcing *Pulte Homes, Models Open,* and smaller signs, cardboard tacked to sticks that wavered in the wind: *Enter Here, Model Open till 4 on Sunday.* Around the bend, before the gentle sweep of new, black macadam, four dazzling model homes sat at the foot of a hill, variations on a single theme of bigger and better. Inside the model with the narrow front porch, the light blue one with the gray roof and compelling sign on the front lawn, *The Crescent,* $69,999, she was charmed by the emerald green wall-to-wall carpeting. And the huge foyer. And the mud room. The four bedrooms. The house unfolded into more and more rooms, each one more sparkling than the last, with metallic wallpaper, swirls of green and silver that went perfectly with the carpeting.

In the sales office, they puzzled over blueprints under glass. The salesman, bustling through stacks of papers, seemed too busy to talk to them; however, he invited them to walk up the hill and see Lot 102 on the cul-de-sac. He pointed to the area outlined in blue with his pen, land that curved out into a big tongue and was sliced into numbered sections. There were three lots left, but 102 was the only one on a cul-de-sac. If they didn't make the decision today, they might have to wait a year for the new section to open up. They could drive along the paved road and, where it ended, follow the dirt road on foot.

Justin didn't like the salesman's attitude. "A salesman's spiel should be like a symphony," he once said. "You get 'em in the palm of your hand, move to a crescendo, and sweep 'em away." Justin loved a good salesman. He'd invite them into the house as if this were a pleasure he didn't think he'd have cross his path that day—insurance salesmen, vacuum cleaner salesmen, Bible salesmen, and aluminum siding salesmen. He'd sit them down, watch their delivery, and smile with a kind of glee she could only describe as his one form of camaraderie. But this guy, this guy was a hack, he would tell her as soon as they got out of there. Still, maybe this was the bargain of the decade and most of the sales had been easy, the model and the lot speaking for themselves. She wasn't about to have her hopes dimmed by some salesman's attitude.

"Guy's a hack," Justin said as they left the model home.

They parked the car at the bottom of a steep hill. The unfinished road was staked with little orange flags marking where it would be on ground scraped into deep ridges. They followed the lane of bare earth up the hill, the brim on Justin's felt hat turned down against the wind. Her brown tweed coat flapped open and gusts of glacial wind whirled around her hips. She tried to keep the coat closed in front, one arm tight around her waist as she hooked her other arm in the crook of Justin's.

She'd pictured trees. But the wooded lots had already been bought up. They climbed the hill to a wide vista of rolling countryside. Rosemary looked back at the deep ruts in the outline of the new road. It must be fun to decide where a road should go and then actually bulldoze the way, she thought. But it did open the earth like a wound, changing things forever. They could see for a long way in the distance, the knots of woods, the highway below snaking itself through neat clumps of housing developments and the patchwork of empty fields waiting to be developed. They would be in the new megalopolis between Washington, Baltimore, and Philadelphia, opportunity galore—the best educational system for the kids, close to Justin's new company, and a university for Rosemary. But it was cold and bare up here. The earth was frozen, cut into by the blade of the plow and lying in chunks like miniature boulders at her feet. She twisted her ankle trying to step through it. Why hadn't she worn her jeans and a thick sweater under this thin coat instead of a skirt, trying to look like the wife of an executive?

She looked at him as he braced himself against the wind, the cold stinging her cheeks. She tried to get him to return the look, but he was off in his own thoughts. Maybe it was too much stress, pressure at work he never talked about, wife clamoring for a new house, the thought of moving. She shouldn't have asked anything more of him. This wasn't a good time.

"Hey," she said. But he just said, "Hmmm?" and watched his feet. She looked at the gray sky, heavy and menacing, pressing down. A few thin snowflakes swirled around them. Justin turned up his collar. They were at the top now and Justin silently walked around what might be the perimeter of the lot. Watching him plod through the dirt clods, she thought how separate he could be from her, keeping his thoughts behind his green eyes where he seemed to live another life entirely. She had said to Hannah the other morning when she'd stopped by for coffee with the kids in tow, "Well, he might not say much but he always comes home to me." She shivered. At the time that sounded like enough. Hannah nodded and agreed that was *something*.

"What do you think?" she called to him. He shrugged and looked out over the march of orange flags up and down the hill. She imagined the model with the emerald carpeting right in the middle of the lot facing the cul-de-sac, its narrow, bricked front porch and pillars, the blue-shuttered windows grandly and rhythmically spaced across its front. She could see the matching blue porch benches she would have, the window boxes overflowing with geraniums. Inside, that thick, lush carpet would absorb the sounds of stomping feet; they'd gather in the family room with the fireplace ablaze every night and in the huge dining room there'd be a table large enough for teenagers and their guests as they came home from college. That the children would go to college, that they would have opportunity she hadn't, was one of the givens. Of course. She could see it all as she looked around her at the bare, frozen earth, a light layer of snow gathered now in the crevices. She would remember this moment when she and Justin stood on the top of this barren hill. She would think of it on cozy nights in front of the fireplace, the house brimming with life, with kids, with the velvety green carpet.

She could never find her gloves. Her hands felt like they would crack and shatter if she moved them. She crossed her arms and tucked her hands deep against her. Her short hair allowed the snow to prick her neck. Justin was always at her to grow her hair long. It would be useful now. She tugged at the collar of her coat, pulled her head in like a turtle and peered out at her still-silent husband who was looking down at the highway, farther away than ever. In that moment, she realized she was as ephemeral as a snowflake. If she were blown away by the wind's choice, swept off this hill and tossed into the woods below, no one would notice. What she wanted for the family and herself was all beside the point. The knowledge was bitter. Emptiness, the longing for closeness, the feeling all the choices were his, had suddenly gathered on this unembellished hill of her dreams. Must she follow him no matter what he decided? Of course. She had children. It may turn out all right, she told herself, yet she saw her helplessness, felt it in the biting wind and in the empty green eyes that looked at her now, the thin lips that said, "Let's go."

In the model house once again, in the enveloping warmth of that green carpeting where she stood rubbing her hands together, he wrote out a check for two thousand dollars' deposit, just like that. And yet, her heart didn't soar like she thought it would. It was his indifference as he tucked the checkbook into the inside chest pocket of his overcoat, the way he picked up his gloves from the salesman's desk and walked out not even holding the door for her that made her distrust the moment she'd hoped for. She followed him through the maze of metallic swirls, out the double door entrance, down the white brick steps, and hurried behind him to the car. Then, in her hand, the cold chrome door handle.

"There's a party at Stan Feldman's," he said. "A costume party. We have to think of something good." Stan was his top salesman and his name was mentioned often over dinner, his house, his sales reports, his wife. Justin even made reference to the fact that Stan's wife "liked to get serviced regularly," as if it was some sort of standard. For them to share that kind of talk, Rosemary thought, Justin's relationship with Stan might be the closest thing he had to friendship. It made her wonder what Justin would say about her. He'd probably tell his old "Tonight's the night" joke.

Stan's house was a palace with a serious-looking gray stone exterior. On the second story a series of brown French doors with brass handles led out to a narrow, wisteria-laden deck, and the large brass front door knocker glittered in their headlights. The house spelled grandeur. Through the window she saw a crystal chandelier and *knew* there would be people in there she wouldn't be able to think of a thing to say to. We look ridiculous, Justin and I, she thought. Flower children. She had sewn her outfit out of a turquoise and gold flower print from Woolworth. Justin had on a pair of orange corduroy bell bottoms. On the large round belt buckle he'd cut out of cardboard, he had carefully measured and marked out a peace sign with magic marker, his tongue licking his top lip as he concentrated. On his head he wore a stringy orange mop, also from Woolworth, and he couldn't stop *he heeing* in anticipation of the entrance he'd make. Elation poured out of the fingertips tapping the steering wheel, and the jitters in his knees and elbows seemed exaggerated. God help us, thought Rosemary.

He left her as soon as they got in the door. She roamed among the leopards, lions, gypsies, and Roman orators—she wouldn't have recognized anyone even if they weren't in costume. At first, faces appeared for a quick hello, "You must be Justin's wife—make yourself at home"—but she remained a vague presence, wanting only to blend in with the wallpaper. She busied herself looking for Justin. She kept a hand down at her side to cover the tear she'd discovered in the seam of her homemade bell bottoms and carefully held a drink in the other, sipping it slowly, just wetting her lips. Gradually people paired off and became oddly absorbed in each other, tiptoeing upstairs, fleeing around corners, becoming shadows as doors closed behind them. Somewhere there ought to be someone who wasn't paired off to whom she could talk. Then, to her horror, there was Justin in a corner of the kitchen with someone dressed as a black cat with a cute little black-tipped nose and charcoal whiskers, a boa wrapped around her slinky, black-leotard-clad body. He was kissing her, one of those long drawn-out hold-your-breath-forever-kisses, and his hands were on her backside.

"Justin!"

He turned to her, but only the bottom half of him because he still stared into the cat's eyes as if directing the peace sign at his waist towards Rosemary, as if he were flashing her a signal to accept what she saw along with this world of his about which she knew nothing. It seemed so separate an act, so much beyond husband and wife, and children safely sleeping at home with a bag of potato chips and a soda left for the sitter and picking crabs late at night in the quiet of lit candles, so separate from giving birth and hospital stays and pressing his shirts and him with his motor leg vibrating at the table, his planning and his exuberance that tended to explode and was now so dangerous an assault on their lives.

"Justin. I want to go home now."

He mumbled, "A few more minutes."

"No, now."

He reached in his pocket and threw her the keys. It was worse than a stinging smack across her cheek, and she couldn't duck, couldn't get away because she was tied to him, entangled and tied. She'd been raised to live with sudden attacks, knew what to do, could do it again if she had to. If she left, he might spend the night with this woman despite that *other* side of him, the responsible father, the wraparound husband. He was two people, maybe three, maybe many.

But it must be her fault too. If he was satisfied with her this wouldn't be happening. Love was a membrane around a set of furniture, toys, cars, and meals—a set of kids. And now there was a tear in it. She couldn't imagine that he didn't love her. Which is why she stooped to pick up the keys. What he'd just done was to give her the power to stay or go without him. But it was her choice to go home with him in tow, no matter what.

Someone with a toothy grin appeared at her side. He had dark hair and a red cummerbund around his middle—what was *he* supposed to be?—and he grabbed her by the shoulders and tried to steer her away. She wrenched free.

"You should join in the fun," he said. "Lighten up." She stepped close enough to him to deliver a smack, a hand-stinging whop across his cheek, the one she'd been intending to deliver to her husband. She steeled herself—he might hit back—but she didn't retreat and for the first time didn't cower. Her reaction would have sent her father into a killing rage, but the toothy-grinned one just allowed himself a weak, stunned, laughable "He-ey!" which strangely satisfied her. She considered making a wild dash for the Caprice and letting the gravel in the circular drive make shotgun holes through the windows as she drove off. But instead she went back into the kitchen and said, "Hey!" herself. Not "Justin" but only "Hey!" loud, and again, louder, until he looked at her and let go of the cat, his face smeared red and black and gray, indefinable and ludicrous.

"Now," she said, and threw him his jacket, hating this image of herself as a woman demanding her man back as if loyalty could be commanded, as if her show of wanting him was an admission he was worth it, which this minute he wasn't. But he was otherwise, or the children were—their life together—oh, the hell with it. Everything was out of kilter.

She waited till he put on his jacket, glaring at him while his eyes darted around the kitchen. Then she turned toward the door.

The next day, Hannah asked, "How was the party?"

When Rosemary told her, Hannah said, "Hang in there. It'll pass. They all try it. It's called swinging, Rosemary. He wants to be a swinger. He just doesn't know who he is and he has to be *something*."

Maybe that was all it was, but new knowledge coursed through her veins and settled in her stomach: he was as precarious as a rock loosened from the side of a mountain.

"It isn't anything," he insisted the next morning. "She's just like me, looking for a little thrill. Nothing happened. Don't make a big thing of it."

"You've got to be kidding. What if I acted that way?"

"Go ahead. Nobody's stopping you. Do a little fooling around." He shrugged his shoulders. His eyes darted about again. He looked unsettled, even frightened. He feigned detachment as though it had nothing to do with her or him and nothing to do with their marriage, which confused her.

There was a knock on the bedroom door. "Mom? Dad?"

It was Saturday and Michael had ball practice and a game.

"We'll be right out, Michael." She turned to Justin and said quietly between clenched teeth, "You take him. In fact, take them all. Spend the day with your kids and think about what you're doing—how it would hurt them if they knew. As for me, I have to get away from you. I can't even look at you! But I'll be back tonight—because of the kids."

He held out his arms, palms up, like *so what* and *suit yourself.*

She drove without having to think where to. The Bay Bridge swung high over the water as if flinging her to the sky, connecting the two lands that separated Maryland into two distinctly different lifestyles, perhaps as much as the opposites that defined Justin, if he could be defined at all, and their marriage that contained such incongruities. From the second bridge, the Kent Island, the scene held the jagged banks and swamps of the flat miracle of the Eastern Shore, where land and water intermingled, exchanging shape and jurisdiction depending on the time of day, where you could see laid out before you the definition of peace. And balance. Her hands relaxed on the steering wheel while her eyes searched the openness that had been missing in the seasons beyond summer, those long, difficult, nameless seasons that now washed away as easily as the bridge eased her down to the road bordered by swamp grass.

She realized now it wasn't the cottage she wanted to see, the summer house standing cold and unwelcoming in the bitter winds. Without the shouts of her children or Justin to bring it to life, its lonesomeness would be too much to bear today. She wanted to see Evelyn—Evelyn in the substantial brick house on the edge of Pucam with the Bavarian china and good silverware and New England maple furniture, where the staunchness of upper-middle-class Boston and refinement sat in the middle of Eastern Shore rural like graceful insistence. One husband had brought her to Long Island and another to Maryland, but she was still imperturbably Boston.

"Rosemary! Whatever are you doing on the Shore? How nice of you to surprise me," she said at the door, although Rosemary felt Evelyn studying her and quickly looking away out of politeness, the white hair coiffured into the familiar French roll. Soon her small, delicate fingers rested on the arms of her chair as the sun streamed in the bay window, warming them both. "Are you all right, Rosemary, deah?"

Yes, she was. Of course. Thank you.

"A cup of tea?"

There was nothing to say and everything. There was Justin's new job and the burgeoning social life. And then there was school and the courses she was taking, and the kids and the new house they'd put a deposit on and the party they went to last night—the costumes. She chatted on and on.

"I admire you, Rosemary," Evelyn said suddenly.

"What for?"

"For going back to school. For handling everything so beautifully with the children and Justin. You spoil him, you know. He's always been such a loner, a whirlwind, so focused on himself and his projects. But I know he loves you."

Rosemary left that last comment alone, her mouth full of cliché. "Never a dull moment."

"No." Evelyn was studying her again. "And thank you for not telling me—whatever it is. I know a Saturday morning visit is highly unusual. But it will be all right. Whatever it is, my dear, it will pass. In marriage, the only unrectifiable thing is death."

Rosemary looked down at the silver spoon in her hand. 1903, the date of Evelyn's birth. Each spoon in the collection was dated. As a child, Evelyn had been given a spoon with a different design every year on her birthday. "I love these spoons," Rosemary said, looking deep into the lilies molded into the handle of the one she held.

"They'll be yours one day," said Evelyn.

Embarrassed, she said, "I didn't mean . . ."

"They will be. And it is my pleasure to think about you having them."

The message was silence. Things to be borne for the sake of the children, for solidarity, for sparing a mother, and for the passing of silver spoons. She understood, and blinked away tears. Maybe she shouldn't have come. Did she expect to tell Evelyn anything? No, it wasn't that she needed to tell on him. She just needed to see some form of sensibility and reason, to be reminded of things that didn't shift.

He didn't know how it started. Or when, exactly. He was slipping even before the head honcho hinted the company was in trouble. Was it that or something else? Paralysis set in. And pain. There was no fighting it. A veil dropped over him. Darkness. He dreamed of standing in an elevator with a broken cable. It was crashing to the basement. Down, down, the terror of going down—he both dreaded the landing and welcomed it.

Beside him Rosemary was like a bird, chirping away. *This comes next. Then that.* He knew, dammit, he knew. She was still tuned in to one program and he was in another. He didn't let her know. Not her fault. It wasn't easy to admit doom and failure and death out loud.

The cars hummed along the highway—everybody going to work. Computer firms all over the place. Money poured out the beltway, overflowed all the exits. The blood of the economy—rich and red—and he was jaundiced. How could that be? Some mornings, it was all he could do to get out of bed, even with all the props, the briefcase, oxfords, suit, tie, new car. He just went through the motions. What was it? Somebody cut his goddamn heart out when he wasn't looking?

They went for a walk. The kids were watching TV. He tried to tell her there was a change in him, that he felt sick, although he wasn't *physically* sick. "Know what I mean?" he said. She looked up at him, worry lines around her eyes. He hated that look. Like maybe she could help him do something he couldn't do himself. As if he needed her. *Together-we-can-make-it crap.* No, she had no idea what he meant.

"Whatever it is, Justin, we can take *care* of it," she said. "If you feel you need to get help—see a psychiatrist—we'll do that. If it's the job—too much stress—change it. I know you have a lot on you. Maybe *I* should get a job."

He couldn't tell her anything more. He didn't *know* any more. He didn't even want to take another step *walking,* let alone call a shrink or change jobs. He didn't want to look at her again—just stared straight ahead for now—stared down a long, dark tunnel even though the day was so crisp and clear it hurt to breathe. He heard her steps alongside his, felt her arm nudge him. He wanted to cry. It wasn't the job, or the house, or her, he wanted to say. It was *inside* him. But he couldn't get up enough energy to say that much. The elevator was going down, every cell in his body drained.

The two black guys backing out of Muskie's flashed through his mind, how their shoulders were hunched, how they couldn't help themselves. How they couldn't look up.

Her advisor at the university was to outline the courses she needed. She'd waited an hour in the hallway for Dr. Hollingsworth, reading everything on the bulletin board about studying abroad in Oxford, England, and Greece. Choices were luxuries. Although hers were limited, she could tiptoe steadily towards a goal. She would have something of her own. After the children were in bed, she filled the long, quiet nights reading Emerson, Thoreau, and Faulkner. Knowing things made her feel strong.

The door opened and a small woman in her mid-fifties appeared— plaid skirt, sweater with a string of pearls, stacks of textbooks behind her. Rosemary got a whiff of that safe life and could picture the woman pledging for a sorority years ago, getting ready for the homecoming dance. Daddy footing the bill. "There's Methods and Materials, Reading Methods, and Math Methods, all of which you need before you do your student teaching," Dr. Hollingsworth was saying as her pencil pointed to the list of requirements. Orders Rosemary could carry out. An outcome she could count on. Teaching was safe. She'd have the same days off as the children.

She tried to concentrate, but between her and Dr. Hollingsworth was the face that peered at her across the breakfast table this morning. Justin, his green eyes lackluster and murky, fear written in the lines that seemed to have appeared overnight—he only nodded at her chatter about registering for school today, his upper torso flaccid as he leaned on his elbows. Rosemary listened to the precision of Dr. Hollingsworth's words, looked at her pink fingernails, perfect and uniform as they fluttered over the well-organized desktop where freshly sharpened pencils in the pencil holder pointed upward. But upward was for other people, thought Rosemary. Justin's company had folded.

"That's it," Stan said. "Space Program's out. We're out." But Stan wasn't worried. He could sell anything, close any deal, and within a few weeks, he had a job with a company selling mutual funds and heading the branch office.

"Guy's incredible. I don't know how he does it. The jobs just aren't there, Babe," Justin said after sending out résumés to answer twenty ads listed in the *Post*, disbelief in his eyes, his shoulders in a helpless shrug.

"Don't worry, Justin," she'd told him. "Something will turn up; it always has. We'll just tighten our belts and keep going." He began to apply for everything: a job as a shoe salesman, a Sears appliance repairman, an Utz Potato Chip delivery man. "They keep saying I'm overqualified," he murmured one night.

"What did you say, Justin?"

"I'm fucking overqualified!" he shouted and banged his fist on the table.

Now she stared at Dr. Hollingsworth thinking she'd been an idiot to expect the world to right itself. "Thank you," she said as she stood. She could no longer brush aside the frightened look on Justin's face, the face she tried to be cheerful for—she'd have to get a job immediately and forego her courses. But give me a minute here in this hallway, flanked with news of scholarships and pictures of cathedrals and Swiss meadows, she thought. Let me recover my patience and subdue the desire for a degree as if it were some sort of license to be.

They let go the deposit on the house. It couldn't be helped. She found a job typing numbers into a computer and lasted three days. "Speed will come," said the instructor, numbers rolling off his tongue and boredom breathing from his thick, loose lips. She tried, but the numbers got jumbled within the first five minutes. When she returned from work, Justin was sitting in the yellow armchair watching her open the door as if he'd been waiting for her.

"I thought you were coming home to have lunch with me," he said in a monotone, his hands still and limp on the arms of the chair. Of course he was depressed, he was out of work. Of course she was frightened, this wasn't part of their plan. But she wouldn't allow him to fold. She knew him. He had fire and imagination. This was only temporary.

"I'm quitting," she said. "You'll have to find something. You'll just have to, Justin."

They were on unemployment again, a disgrace they both felt and left unspoken. They sold the Caprice. Rosemary found a job as a Dictaphone typist transcribing case histories for a group of social workers. Her days were filled with listening to other people's problems. She came home and repeated some of the stories to Justin. "See, there's always somebody worse off than we are," she said. He had a way of looking past her and nodding absentmindedly.

She changed the ending on one of the stories, afraid it might upset him, although the image of a couple dressed as Raggedy Ann and Andy shouting at each other on Halloween night before going to a party had entertained her for the afternoon. On the tape, the social worker droned on about the number of children, jobs the couple held, their sibling place-ment in the family—when suddenly she was describing them dressed as Raggedy Ann and Andy in red wool wigs and striped stockings. Andy, shout-ing obscenities at his wife, stalked to their dresser, pulled out a pistol and fired it at the ceiling. While the social worker pursued the couple's feelings at this point, Rosemary, in earphones and with her foot pausing on the pedal, laughed silently. But on the drive home, the story seemed less funny when she thought about the masks she and Justin wore these days, and the possibility of Justin taking out a pistol if he had one and using it on him-self. But when he came home that evening with a lunch box, the black kind with the rounded top where the thermos lay in its small wire catch, she felt enormous relief. He'd also bought insulated coveralls and work boots. He would be okay; they would be okay. She knew it all along. So it *was* the job then. He had good reason to be down. He'd been worried.

He said he told the plumber nothing about himself. He wore his worn-out jeans and an old flannel shirt, took his wrenches, stained his hands with motor oil and became Justin, the plumber's helper. Justin, who went out whistling each morning at five with coffee in the thermos, was on his way up again. Not the career-wise Justin, but the laughing, joking, playing-with-the-kids-again Justin. Jovial Justin was back. He bought a white Volkswagen and put yellow daisy decals on its doors. Took guitar les-sons. Learned to play "Sparkling Stellar" and laughed when he realized it was "Twinkle, Twinkle, Little Star."

"I'll be damned," he said, laughing *Hah haaaa!* "That was the only thing I could play on the trumpet when I was a kid."

Rosemary loved it, his plunking on the guitar. There was a sense of them both rolling up their sleeves. They would be all right.

Then there was this: a newfound courage to move ahead. Was it courage? Hannah and Giles thought it madness. "How can you make a change like that?" they said, shaking their heads. "Aren't you scared, Rosemary?" asked Hannah.

No, she wasn't. The change was already set in motion as if they were riding the tail of a shooting star. She was used to such rides. She came home from work one day to Justin taking apart the old rusted swing set in the yard. He sawed off a three-foot section of pipe, flattened it at both ends and nailed it to a rectangular wooden box he'd hammered together out of scrap wood. His new toolbox. Home improvement. He'd start his own business and stay with Evelyn for a while, trying his luck on the Eastern Shore in the area near the cottage. When he'd gotten things under way, they'd sell this house and move over.

"It's no good here," he said, the rims of his eyes burned red. "I feel like I'm always on the outside looking in. Nothing fits. Things will be simpler on the Shore. Are you with me?"

Of course she was. She'd follow him anywhere. He'd been so unhappy and so had she, the pressures too great, the disappointments too cutting. They'd start over. She trusted him to do what he had to. He was giving up his career, but he'd be working with his real talent, his hands. Of course she was with him. She watched with great, wild hope as he traded the Volkswagen for a van and hung ladders horizontally along its side. When he rolled down the street turning to wave at them between the shifting of gears and the clanging of ladders, she felt a sense of adventure. They'd recapture the glory of summer and hold on to it all year. They'd live close to Evelyn where Rosemary could find respite if she needed to simply by staring down at the long ago dates on those silver spoons and listening to the sound of *Rosemary, deah*. Evelyn's influence on Justin would be steadying. Rosemary could picture herself in a large, solid house like Evelyn's at the edge of town somewhere, the emerald carpeting still a possibility.

In the calm that followed, the Cape Cod house, even with three kids, felt empty without Justin. She traded in her S&H Green Stamps on an aquarium for Davey for his birthday and waited. Justin, on the next visit home, brought Michael fifteen fertilized eggs and made him an incubator with a window along one side. The kids pressed their noses against the glass and anticipated wonderful things.

Justin was set on some acreage. The real estate man in Pucam, Lenny Fooks, his face shiny, pockmarked, and interrupted by bottle-bottom glasses, leaned back in the black leather desk chair—so far back one little slip and he'd be dumped white socks over head on the floor, thought Rosemary—and crossed his hands over his ample middle. "Small farm? Not much in the way of that right now. There's one over to Shiloh, but the house on it ain't much. Been vacant a few years. You'd probably not like it. It's going real cheap, though. Needs a lot of work. Like I said, you'd probably not think much of it, coming from the city and all."

Justin, hands in pockets, walked across the uneven, creaking floorboards and stared out the storefront window. "Whereabouts?"

"Well, you go down Main Street, right on out of town about three miles. When you get to the T in the road, make a right and follow that down to Dorsey Road. Make a left there—ain't nothing but a dirt road—follow that, and about a quarter of a mile down, you'll see the lane. House sits back against the woods."

"Guy's a hack," said Justin as he opened the truck door for Rosemary, but he laughed and rubbed his upper lip with his index finger, a gesture he saved for serious thinking. "Thirty-five acres, though. Most of it woods. Just seven miles from the cottage." His feet danced around the front of the truck and he leapt up to the driver's seat. The kids called from their seats on the lumber stacked in the back of the van, "Where we goin', huh, Dad?"

The house sat sideways to the road. The front door greeted the woods as if it missed something, turned the wrong way while the rest of the world went on about its business, the broad, cedar-shingled side of the house facing them like a turned shoulder. Long lane, deep ruts. The ladders on the truck banged. A high-pitched roof sloped down to a porch. Was that ivy growing out of the upstairs window? Broken panes? Broken shingles swinging by one nail? Closer now, bumping down the lane and holding onto the door handle of the truck so as not to lose her balance, Rosemary saw shingles were missing from the roof, the chimneys on either side of the peak leaned toward each other, the doweled screen door hung by one hinge and thudded gently in the breeze. The house was a ship abandoned in the reeds. It was darkness, musty old darkness, all dark brown moldy wood, dried out timber, wormed, termited, splintered, composting into earth again. She saw they'd be turned away from the main course of life here, thrown to the wayside. They'd be worn down by the elements and distance, struggling to find out what they were made of. For there was no doubt he would buy it. He'd see the trees, the grape arbor, the clouds sailing by as he sat on the front porch steps and he'd dream of woods, the long, immense fields, his hands in the soil, planting. He'd leave 1971, leave the soured world, his career, the rat race, the expectations of him. He'd escape. He would not see that the nearest store was eight miles away, the nearest super- market sixteen, the schools poor and backward. He'd not see that they would be confined to each other with nothing to distract them, not anoth- er house, a neighbor, a passing car, not a library, a university, not a movie, or a Seven-Eleven, no place to run down to for a kite or an ice cream cone or a newspaper. Nothing would include them in civilization—not a gas line, a sewer line, a water main, a beltway, a service station, garbage col- lection. They said *chimley* here, and *zink* for sink, and *war* which was *wire* and *tar* which was *tire*. And he'd decide. Yes, he would.

What he saw were deer crossing the lane. Five of them. He was enchanted, and all she knew was fear. If she told him how she felt, he'd remind her she had been anxious over the purchase of the waterfront and the cottage and that turned out all right. What she couldn't say was he went from one extreme to another. Each time there was no warning. He was like a cat with nine separate lives.

Anne knew who used to live here. She and Michael found pictures in a room on the second floor which was the tiniest bedroom she'd ever seen. They went exploring and heard the bees buzzing round the window and when they went in, half the wall was gone and in the boards behind the plaster was a huge beehive. Michael said there was honey dripping out and she said, *Nu huh*, but when she looked, sure enough, honey *was* drip- ping down the boards inside the wall. And then they found the pictures, two of them, all curled up and yellow in the corner of the room, like some- one had placed them carefully, not like they'd been dropped. In the pic- tures a mother and a father sat on the steps of the house with two boys playing in front of them on the walk. All were wearing white socks. The pictures must have been taken in the summer because the man was wear- ing a tank top and the woman had a sundress on. The boys' hair was all slicked down tight to their heads.

The glass was gone from the dormer window. Only the frame was left. From it, she could see Michael and Davey playing below on the front walk, only it was a funny front walk. It didn't go anywhere. It went for three squares and then just stopped in the middle of the lawn. When she came upstairs to look at the pictures again she heard birds flying out.

The house was like a history book. People didn't have closets a long time ago. They hung their clothes on hooks against the wall. And where chunks of wall fell down, long strands of hair were buried in the plaster. It was spooky, hanging down like there was a person caught in there, a ghost maybe. Dad said it was horsehair. They mixed horsehair and ground-up oyster shells and that white stuff together and smoothed it over the wood slats. The house was made of dead things from the sea and the land all mixed up.

In the woods, they found old bottles and pots and tiles, and an old shoe with buttons on it instead of lace holes. Maybe there was buried treasure. They needed a shovel. Mom said they'd need more than a shovel and looked gloomy, but Anne knew her father would buy the place. He was sitting on the front steps writing things down on a yellow pad while Michael and Davey ran from the sidewalk that didn't go anywhere to the old tractor trapped in the weeds at the edge of the field.

She could have a horse. Her father said so. There was even a shed where she could put one. There was another shed with a car in it—a Corvair. Michael wanted to know where the keys were and Dad laughed and said it needed an engine and *what are you worrying about keys for, Michael.* Michael got the door open and sat behind the steering wheel. His feet almost reached the pedals.

Just before the edge of the woods was an outhouse. It leaned to one side. She could see it from the bedroom window. She hoped this room would be her room. All it needed was a closet and a new window. She'd talk her father into leaving the ivy that grew on the walls. It made her feel like she was outside. She could see across the great, big field—she didn't know there was so much space in the world. And on the other side of the house were so many places to explore in those woods. And new paths to make with her horse. *Star* would be a good name, she thought. We can all have what we always wanted. A horse for me, a shop for Daddy, a motorcycle for Davey, and chickens for Michael.

She didn't know what her mom was going to do. Knit, maybe.

So that was it then. Rosemary had done everything she could to dissuade him—cried, pleaded, threatened to stay in the city alone, although she never was serious about that. He looked at her with great patience, with eyes that looked hurt but determined to go ahead, as if he had only to be patient with another whiny kid who would eventually come around. She did come around, of course, just as she was supposed to. She'd gotten caught up in the great rush to build and restore now that the decision had been made. The grape arbor, the old trees, and the long lane now signified a road less traveled, a branching out and freedom. But she was confused, too. He was possessed. What drove him? Where did this enormous force come from?

She worried about him staying in that gloomy, unheated house working through the night and returning to Evelyn's only to eat. He had lists upon lists, sketches in his head for every corner of the house. He planned to raise the roof over the front section and make two more bedrooms. Every wall had to be knocked down, reduced to oyster powder and shoveled out the windows, new wallboard nailed to old laths. Every window had to be replaced. The exterior shingles—new cedar shakes, each one nailed in place, two nails to a shingle, thousands of shingles—how many nails could one arm hammer? The kitchen, which was not much more than a back porch, was tiled with scraps worked in by the tile mason who lived there before them. Behind the tile lurked cement and chicken wire, exposed in damaged places. The rest of the wall would succumb only to a sledgehammer. The chimneys were unsafe—a new fireplace had to be built, and an upstairs bathroom constructed from a small bedroom.

He was so alone in his task. He never called when she was back in the city. It was as if he'd forgotten them. But this immense project was for them, wasn't it?

It was raining again—the rainiest February she'd ever seen. She and the children visited him like careful, expectant guests from out of town as they drove up the lane. When he strolled out to meet them, she was shocked at the change in him. He looked as though he had shrunk, as if he'd been weakened by further injuries to the house and to his dreams. He would either be able to fix the house or not—the careful balance between taking down and putting up threatened by his weariness. It was too much for one man to do. Whatever carried him to the great impetus to undertake restoration of the house was gone now. So was the front slope of the roof, a space covered with sheets of plastic in silvery, unseamed layers, drooping with the weight of the rain. Inside, water poured on the banister and the stairs like an indoor waterfall, causing the living room ceiling to sag and break into chunks of wet plaster. Clumps of horsehair hung like stalactites.

Now he was at the top of the stairs, hammer in hand, watching her climb to where he waited, the look on his face inviting her to say something, his eyes pleading for encouragement. She stared into those green eyes as if she had some kind of power to infuse hope in him. She couldn't smile although she knew he would have liked her to, because with each step, with the gush of rain at her feet, she climbed closer to his weariness, closer to the fact that he was falling apart, the house was crumbling, and that she could do nothing. She was more frightened than she'd ever been. Frightened for him. And frightened for herself. He was not invincible. When she got to the top, all she could think to do was put her arms around him. "I love you," she said. The cure-all. The catch-all, safe thing to say. And he lay his head on her shoulder and shuddered. It would have been a sob if he'd let it. What she felt was such sorrow for the abandonment of the other self, the one that accomplished miracles, that glorious strain of energy; in its wake now was only silence and doubt. He was scooped up in strange tides, bound to their coming and going, bound also to making a life and supporting a family.

All she could do was act as if she understood. She stood inside his arms, but then he pulled back and the creases were deep around his eyes. He looked away. "When the rain stops, I'll fix it," he said, meaning the roof, meaning the ceiling, meaning his life, and she nodded *yes*, but his words were lost in the sound of water rushing and the house listing.

Gone. Died a thousand times so far and here I go *again*. My hands . . . share that other person, the one I love to be and this . . . this drowned rat. Water envelopes me.

Can't breathe…don't care if I do.

Started with the rains—which came when I opened the roof. Water dripped through the house, flowed down the stairs. Walls went soggy, dropped away. Ceiling bowed, caved in. Hands slowed, moved through gelatin, no longer knowing who they were attached to.

Took the crowbar and tore out the windows. So I wouldn't drown. Let 'em shatter to the ground. Window weights shot like bullets down the walls, lay like anchors under a hull.

Twenty-eight windows. Fifteen to go.

Air—need air—but more rain comes, seeps down between the walls.

Sleeping bag's my wet cocoon while all night the house sighs and creaks. Can't sleep—yet every muscle screams for rest. When this body can't take any more, it'll drift through the weeds, on out over the flooded fields. The house can cave—waitin' for it to—set me free over the fields—or bury me.

I can only wait. If it takes too long this time, good-bye. A good place. Away from the kids, from Rosemary, from town, from eyes that criticize. Meanwhile—there's the crowbar and the sledgehammer and the shovel.

Release the house. And me. Bad scene anyway. Sinking ship.

It eases me to stare into the woods. In February, the truth of the trees turns silver some nights. Real things have seasons. Some more than others. I don't know why. God, why?

Days, the woods drip. Green wood smells good—like the cottage. Different when you start out framing the hull, shaping the contours of your own ship, which may have already come in—come to think of it. Maybe that's all she wrote. Now—it's just shoveling oyster shell and plaster out the windows. Watch the dredge return. Conform to another's framing.

Funny. How life turns out. Didn't used to believe I'd die. Now I don't believe in staying alive. Can't believe life will come again—can't remember what that's like—or if it's worth it. Can't see my way through constant mist.

The shovel scrapes the soft pine floor. There's no silence like wet dust in gray air, falling. No sound so final as its return.

Most of the chicks hatched in his bedroom. Two didn't, and two were crippled. They couldn't stand. Michael got a shoe box, lined it with crumpled tissues, and punched holes in the top so they could breathe. Then he and his mother drove to the hatchery. "They'll know what to do, Michael," she said. "They must have chicks with twisted legs hatch all the time."

There were eleven healthy chicks. One started hatching and it was as if the others got the idea because by mid-morning, they'd hatched out, wet and scraggly, except for the two eggs he left in there figuring maybe they were just a little late, and the two chicks in the tissue box.

The hatchery was out near where they almost bought a new house—out past all the traffic lights, out where there were still a few farms with big old barns. He'd been there on a field trip in second grade which made him think of it when they were trying to decide what to do with those two crippled ones. The hatchery was stale and warm, like the smell of chicken soup. He hated to see how the chicks were kept in drawers. His chickens were going to have green grass and fresh air and cluck around the yard and lay eggs wherever they wanted to.

He didn't like that lady in there, either. She had her hands on her hips and a grouchy look from the minute they opened the door. She looked just like Mrs. Greenholtz, his sixth-grade teacher, when she was telling you your answer was wrong. She just stood there with her fat lips puckered up, her mouth all dropped down into the wrinkles on her chin like she couldn't believe anyone could be so stupid as to not know what to do with crippled chicks.

He was afraid the chicks might have had a rough ride and that they might have caught cold even though he'd wrapped a bath towel around the box before he left the car. He told her his dad had given him fifteen eggs and a big incubator and that the rest of the chicks had hatched just fine. But these. And his mother said they didn't know what they were going to do with the chicks until warmer weather—keep them in the incubator for a while longer, she guessed, until his father could build a pen for them at the farm.

His mother was in the middle of telling all that when the lady picked up the chicks—not cupping her hands and scooping them up like he did but sliding her fingers around the chicks' necks so that one neck was between her first two fingers and the other was between the next two fingers and it looked as if she held them too tight. With her other hand, so quick he could hardly be sure exactly what she did, she gave their bodies a slight twist—and tossed the chicks in the trash barrel behind her. There wasn't even a peep.

"There you go. All taken care of," she said. "You want your box?"

He didn't think things could die that quick. Didn't think there could be sudden quietness. Not like in his dreams where blood dripped and knives twisted, when he screamed a long tortured scream that no one heard. He was scared to go to sleep sometimes, hated to close his eyes and let it happen over and over. He saw where death could just be a blackness and not so terrible.

"Yes," he said. "I want the box. And the chicks, too, so I can bury them." He thought she'd hate to put her hand down in the barrel, but she only laughed and said, "You got a lot to learn about farming, son." She lay the chicks in the box a lot more carefully than she first picked them up, closed the lid, and politely pushed the box across the counter. "They never would have made it," she said to his mother, who stood with her mouth open.

"That's okay," Mom said. "We'll know what to do next time." Not that she would ever do it. He'd be the one, he knew.

This was a different kind of summer than they were used to. This summer they listened to the migrant workers sing as they picked cucumbers and watched them truck up to the house in bare feet to ask for a drink from the outside spigot. This summer they slapped mosquitoes as they hammered and nailed and tore out and scraped and painted. All of them. Even Davey, who picked up the old cedar shingles she'd thrown down onto the driveway. But most of the time he wandered along the edge of the woods hunting frogs and snakes as she stood on the scaffolding nailing on new shingles, keeping an eye on him.

The summer cottage stood silent during the day, its grandness swallowed by the nearness of the farmhouse. Each night just before dusk, they went down to the river and dove in with burning muscles. The kids chased and swam in the sunsets, but she lay on top of the water with only energy enough to lose herself in the orange sky. In the darkness, she and Justin were engulfed in so deep a sleep they no longer heard the clanging of the halyards, the slap of water on boat bottoms, or held each other. Mornings, she hated to leave the river, the placid water of rosy dawns, and the echoes of across-the-water mist making her heed the stirrings of her soul, those times when she stepped back to look at the direction in which things were going, when she allowed herself to doubt and retrieve determination.

Close to finishing, she would attend the university on the Western Shore until she had her degree, doubling up on courses. She worried about the two-hour drive each way. The car sputtered and burned oil. It would have to be replaced. The children would have to spend time alone. She'd have to arrange everything; Justin could not be approached. He was not in a place where he could listen.

"Pick out a car, Rosemary. I'll get it for you," said Evelyn, her generosity bringing tears to Rosemary's eyes. She cried easily these days. She missed the lazy days of summer at the cottage and seeing Evelyn wade slowly into the river, the rubber bathing cap tight around her forehead and cheeks, the children shouting around her. Evelyn often came to the farm with baskets of food for picnic lunches, trying to lure Rosemary and the kids for a swim down at the cottage. Evelyn kept her thoughts to herself as they worked, but she watched for ways she could help and tried to ease Rosemary's mind. "Are you okay, deah?" she said gently, her eye on the stooped backs of migrants slowly moving along the rows close to the house. "Will you be ready by September?"

Justin called down from the roof, where he was nailing shingles, "Not to worry. Picked up some heaters for the cottage. We'll stay there till this is ready if it takes all winter." It sounded like an aria. He was full of plans again. Once they sold the house in the city, and Rosemary and the children had moved to the cottage, his spirits seemed to lift. Was that the reason? Or was it just time to, and not connected with anything that was happening? He was in command again, laughing and wielding his hammer as though a roof was the best place to be. It reminded her of the time he worked through the night on the cottage roof. Within a few weeks, the rooms upstairs were defined, the roof closed in, and the ceilings downstairs in place. She didn't know how he did it.

There was little left of the old house except the layers of wallpaper downstairs where all of the rooms wore the same vague green tweed. Rosemary could see her deciding on it—the old woman who'd lived here with only the distant lights from Pucam to comfort her—choosing a quiet, go-with-everything color, *what does it matter so long as it's clean and cheap,* never looking up at the muslin-colored plain paper on the ceiling, water-stained and loose at the edges. Rosemary imagined her puttering from room to room, lighting the kerosene stove in the living room, where the stovepipe reached its arm into the chimney of the old fireplace, thinking the kerosene was a luxury compared to splitting wood. Carved on the garage door Rosemary found the names of the old woman's sons, Albert and James, who would be after her to sell out and move to town while she, clinging to the old place, watched the leaves turn on the sugar maple in the front yard. She would have hated to leave, saying to herself, *just one more year.* In the ivy growing up the north wall and finding its way inside the window, Rosemary could hear her words, "Let it be. I'm eighty-five this year"—could see her on the old davenport in the living room, her bones too rickety to allow her to climb the stairs to the bedroom, and wondered how long she lay there before they found her, this house her coffin till the buzzards flew overhead, signaling someone from town or alarming one of her sons.

She could see her fingers, stained purple from picking grapes, her hands as they stirred the enameled pot on the cookstove, the September ritual, in the fifteen jars of jelly that Davey found in the cellar, the labels yellowed and scratched in black with *Concord Grape, 1966.* It would be Rosemary's ritual now. She pictured the scrolled wicker chair they found in the chicken coop set out on the porch each spring as the old woman waited for the lilacs. When was the last flock of chickens? The last blow of the ax, the last feathers plucked, the last bird made ready for Sunday dinner?

Rosemary watched Anne straddle the oil drum as if it were a pony and Michael smash demons in the cemented kitchen tiles with the sledge-hammer, glad to be destroying with permission. They brought their own dreams and nightmares to this old house, which was like a history book with whole paragraphs scratched out. What would they add? Davey held the end of a board for Justin as he leveled and nailed trim on the archway between formal living room and everyday room where sliding doors used to conserve the heat. Old traces disappeared; only the old beams and lathing were left to record the ancient mouse trails in the walls.

The chickens were ecstatic. The new roosters strutted through the yard and grew plump with Michael's care. He painted a sign for them over the small chicken coop door that led from the new pen. *Home* was what it said. The old woman would be pleased, she thought.

DECEMBER COLD

The first sound of the day was his mother tiptoeing to the door. From the top bunk, Michael watched her walk to the new car Grandma had bought and place books on the passenger seat just as the tip of the sun showed at the horizon. So much effort to finish college—something he'd never do. He couldn't wait to get out of school.

Wide awake but reluctant to leave his warm quilt, he watched for geese, feeling relief to see the day after the onslaught of nightmares he didn't want to remember. His days weren't much fun either. December cold sank into the clothes in all the drawers and inside shoes and even into the toothpaste. His father had promised it wouldn't be long before they'd be in the farmhouse. He had to earn some money, he said, and spent his days building kitchen cabinets and repairing roofs for other people while he finished walls and floors at the farm in the evenings and weekends. The furnace had been installed a few days ago and Michael liked to think about a furnace, heat at the push of the thermostat's lever instead of the kerosene stove at the cottage. There were places in the walls where the wind whistled through—after all it was only a summer cottage on cinder blocks—practically a boat anchored on the shore, ready to float away come a good high tide. Sometimes he wished it would and he with it, a fishing rod in his hand.

He missed the outside sounds of summer nights—boats slapping and the steady swish of the hoses in the peeler tanks where Pete kept soft crabs.

The sounds buoyed him through the night, let him know where he was when he was awakened by bad dreams. But now he was suspended in winter's silence, wandering through the night, sometimes running from monsters and huge flesh-eating insects, frantically trying to escape strange landscapes—where was he—and why was there always so much blood and where was home? He hated to close his eyes. He dreamed of death by explosion, an extraordinary brightness that sucked him in till he could no longer breathe and he screamed in his sleep, but never out loud. No one ever knew unless he told them. He did tell his mother once and although she looked worried and put her arm around him, she didn't seem to know what to do or say. Maybe there never was anything but he went on being troubled just before he went to sleep knowing the dreams would come again and again to terrify him. He died a little each time, devoured by the night he knew was inside his head, the worst kind of terror, insidious and secret, inexpressible when he awoke. He was weak. His dreams told him.

And it was worse now. The cottage in winter. The new school. His father never around. His mother gone off to school from early in the morning till after seven in the evening and only Anne and Davey who he watched over, or tried to. It was tough, especially on the school bus, a dangerous mixture of white and black, angry faces that exploded in torrents of words and punches, halting the school bus amid shouts from the driver. Anger everywhere. Girls' purses emptied, tampons thrown around like missiles. "What's that?" said Davey. "Later," Michael told him, "just shut up and look out the window."

At school he felt cut off—a white kid from the city, a smart white kid just moved here—though he never thought of himself as smart. He realized even on the first day he'd been exposed to more just by where he'd lived, which made him feel worldly—but *why* were they making him take Home Economics?—besides which, he was a white kid who talked to blacks and made friends with them. And he *was* careful to make friends with them because they traveled in gangs, in a camaraderie he envied, while white kids walked in quiet twos and threes. The schools had just been integrated the year before and everybody was ready for a fight. He made friends with the biggest and loudest, just to be safe. Mazie. A head taller. She made three of him. Magically, she let him in her circle. Maybe it was because he looked directly at her as she entered the bus and didn't take his glance away when she sat down in front of him and turned around to study him—he didn't know why—but her taunting lost its harshness and melted to mellow, the words like a croon: "What chew doin'," she said to him on that first day, "with hair that curly? Any worse, you'd be like us!" and grinned. Right off, she knew he was a foreigner and let him know it was a good credential. "He's okay," she said later when the black kids were blocking the entrance of the white kids onto the bus, "Let him go," which didn't help matters with the white boys in his class who stood with their backs to them.

Now he watched his breath hit the air and listened as his father stirred oatmeal on the stove. He'd call them soon—Anne already stretching and yawning, and Davey, who never could wake easily and would have to be routed out with threats, Davey on whose soft breathing he depended when fears of falling asleep kept him awake.

He jumped down from the bed onto the icy floor. In the great room his father had set the table. "Get those other two on out here, will ya?" he said. He was in a hurry. Everyone was always in a hurry now.

"What're you doing today, Dad?" Michael asked, more to sidetrack him than anything, more to bring back to his face the light it held when he was planning things, more to be in on things with his father.

"Couple cabinets," was all his father said, like maybe he was wishing he was back selling computers this morning. Like maybe he was hoping to try something he hadn't tried yet. *Then why, Dad, why are we here?* thought Michael, though he told himself he'd be able to hunt, raise chickens, have a big garden, maybe some rabbits, even learn how to drive before he was sixteen (they had the car in one of the sheds). He felt the reasons they were here were all mixed up in the fact that they *were* here and had to make the best of it. He knew what people meant when they said *there's no turning back.* It made him feel uneasy—like being carried off on that school bus to a prison seething with trouble, making him learn things he didn't care about, a place—may as well say it—he hated.

Just before sundown, Rosemary crossed the bridge over the river, noticing a high tide had covered most of the marsh. As she turned onto

Sulley's Point, the river looked closer than it should have and some of the pines stood in water. Water gushed at the wheels of the station wagon as she came around the bend, and she was startled to see what stretched before her was not road, but river, interrupted only by cottages and a few trees and bushes. And their cottage? The kids? Sensing she shouldn't go any farther by car, she stopped and pushed open the door. Water was only a few inches below the door frame. As she sank one leg down into the river, the chill that ran through her was not from the water. The kids might have been left off by the school bus because this tide could not be seen from the main road. No neighbors could have taken them in; they were gone for the season. So where? As she trudged through water now above her knees, she worried they might have waded home and taken *Greenfly* out to explore. Maybe Justin came and got them, if he knew. But how could he know working as he did on dry land? Oh, it was foolish, downright stupid to think they could make it in the cottage till the farm-house was ready. They were in jeopardy all the time—the damned old house—and now the kids, marooned in a flood for God's sake—dear God, let them be all right! How did things get so precarious?—she must have been mad to say yes to Justin's crazy ideas as if she had no will of her own. She hated the danger, the terrible effort they had to make, and for what? Because he had decided. She'd always gone along, supported him blindly. She was weary to the bone of the work, of his struggles, of her own struggle and her worry about the children. The children! Abandoned. They were abandoned and she hadn't realized. Her focus had been all wrong. Her mad distraction. She was as driven as Justin. And as guilty.

She'd seen a tide like this only once before, one August, when a full moon and weeks of rain had caused the river to swell its banks and flood the yards and road. It was fun then, the river only up to the second step of the cottage before it retreated. They rowed over the front lawn in the *Greenfly* and laughed.

The kids were safe because Justin and I were there. She waded on down along where the road should be, feeling her way, the ground uneven and sinking beneath her. She must be off the road. Leaves float-ed past, silent as the tide. With the weight of the water, her wool skirt pulled at her waist. Holding it above her knees, her hands shook with cold as she strained to see the windows of the cottage, hoping to see faces looking for her, hands waving, but the windows were dark in the gray light. She could see the whole house now, the cedar planks, dark and wet, soaking up water.

At the cottage, her foot searched for the bottom step. She reached for the screen door handle, the water an inch from the door sill, and stepping up with river water sucking off her shoes, she heard voices and then the tinny sounds of canned laughter. There they were, the three of them, faces blue-white in the light of the television, eating toast. They were all right. But were they? Apathetic like that? They glanced at her, oblivious to the danger, set off on their course together as if floating away from her, self-contained and distant. They'd been dragged out of their life in the sub-urbs; they'd had to say good-bye to childhood friends and been plunked down in this strange place, their education diminished—their lives endangered. While their parents were off. Preoccupied. *What are we doing to them?* she silently screamed as she stood dripping and cold, study-ing them as they stared into the TV screen. She felt tears brimming as she realized she hadn't really looked at them for a while. Their innocence had melted away in the difficult interim of their move to the Shore. Michael's chin had a squareness to it now, his face more angular; Anne twisted her hair around and around her fingers as she sat and stared; Davey had wrapped himself in his quilt as if it were a cocoon. She had hoped for a renewal for herself and Justin and therefore a better life for the children. They were strangers sitting there like that. Islands. She understood what their move to the farmhouse held for them in their imperturbable stares, each in his or her own place on the sofa, silently watching, waiting for things to happen.

"Hey!" she yelled. "Anybody hungry? Anybody got a hug they can spare?"

Davey came. She wrapped her arms around him. His hair needed to be trimmed and he had a sour smell. "What's for dinner, Mom?" he asked.

"Something—I haven't figured out yet," she said. "Something in town. We can't stay here. Have you looked out the window?" They'd go to Evelyn's. The haven. Or maybe she'd drive over the Bay Bridge and never come back. Nothing could be counted on, not even the cottage. Least of all the cottage. It was out of season—just like Justin when he was out of season.

December twenty-third and the wind bit through the cedar boards of the cottage walls. Ice clung to the pilings and glassed over the bulkhead. The swamp grass bloomed crystal ice showers above the drifted snow. They couldn't get warm. They left the cottage like stunned bears driven out of a cave. At the farmhouse, some of the downstairs walls still needed repair and the stairs needed mending, but the windows were in place and the furnace purred. They moved in and made the best of it.

Justin and Michael went down the logging road with a hatchet to find a Christmas tree. They came back with two thin, scraggly loblollies. "Which one?" laughed Justin, and answered himself with, "Let's tie them together," but when the tied-together trees stood in a corner of the living room, the scene set off a feeling of gloom in Rosemary. She was angry at the trees—and Justin. It would have meant so much to be able to have a beautiful Christmas tree, one that touched the ceiling, brilliant with lights, so she could keep her mind off how this house sat at the end of the corn rows, gray-brown and bleak as the soil, and how they'd soon be buried in snow which would swirl around their solitary house like ocean waves around a lighthouse. She needed a tree that would bring colors into her heart and send a message out the windows saying they were here, that despite the barrenness there was rebirth, that the struggle had been worth it. In answer, the wind howled at the windows. Despite herself, she thought about the blazing fireplace and family room in the house of her dreams while she stapled pine branches to the peeling woodwork and exposed lathing. She felt like crying. She didn't though. She had her degree now and was qualified to make it through hell and high water, literally. She stared at the cracked wall where Anne was painting two reindeer that looked like horses with wreaths around their necks. "When can we look at ponies?" Anne was saying. "Today, maybe? Huh?"

Because of the promise of a teaching job, the next day Rosemary celebrated her achievement by buying Anne a pony, a thick-coated, smallish stump of a beast, a chestnut with a white blaze. Anne fell in love with it the minute they got out of the car and watched it gallop along the fence.

Rosemary didn't know ponies had long-haired coats. "Of course, Mommy," said Annie, red-brown hair in pigtails. "It's winter!"

When it was delivered, Rosemary was amazed at Anne's ability and willingness to take on responsibility. She tied the pony to the old hitching post by the barn and brought a bucket of oats, a bag of which had been delivered along with the pony. Meanwhile, the pony stamped the ground and puffed out steam. Rosemary stood back, well clear.

"We'll fence a pasture in the spring, Annie," said Justin, enjoying his new role as farm owner. "Till then just tie her to a cement block."

"Holly, Dad," said Anne. "Her name's Holly."

One night in January, Evelyn came for dinner but she didn't eat much and Rosemary wondered about that as she watched Holly drag the cement block across the north field.

"Excuse me," said Evelyn, "but I really don't feel well. Think I'll lie down. No, don't be alarmed. I'm all right. Just a touch of stomach virus, I suppose," and she went toward the couch.

"Well then, go get her, Annie, and tie her to something else," said Justin. "Take the wheelbarrow out there and get that cement block, too," he called after her as she went out the door.

"Justin, that's a bit much for a ten-year-old," said Rosemary.

"That's how she'll learn," said Justin.

Rosemary was clearing off the table when Anne ran in crying. "I've wanted a pony for so long and now I can't ride it," she sobbed all the way to her room. "She threw me off!"

"I know how you feel, Annie," Justin said, but the words were directed toward Rosemary. She couldn't miss the derision in his voice. Now that he was up again, he couldn't get enough. He was in his wise guy mode, compulsive, impatient, cold, needing sex much more often than Rosemary did. What was it her mother said once—*A wife who turns down her husband one out of four times ain't doing so bad.* It was all she had to go by. Certainly not feelings. If she thought feelings were involved she really would go mad. When he was down, he wanted nothing to do with her for months at a time. It was peaceful. Their lives were getting stranger and stranger, a far cry from what she had envisioned. She looked down at the rough pine floor, meager as their marriage.

"Get down here and get on that pony again, Annie. Show her who's boss or you'll never be able to mount her. C'mon. I'll go out there with you this time," Justin hollered up the stairs.

He could be brazen when he was feeling good, lose all judgment and sensitivity toward others. There was no love in him then. There were only occasional glimpses of the fun-loving person she'd married. Well, hadn't they both changed? Lately, she carried resentment like a lance. She was tired. And he must be, although he didn't seem to be able to slow down.

Their bedroom door was warped and didn't close smoothly. It had an oval doorknob and a lock with a skeleton key which Justin had hung on a nail. On the nights he wanted sex he forced the door shut with a bang, took the key down from the wall and locked the door. Between the sound of the old door creaking to a loud slam and the lock which made the heavy sound of a bolt, she lay with a sick feeling knowing she mustn't, *simply mustn't*, ever let him see her growing disgust or anger. He wasn't violent, just silent, mechanical, with never a tender word.

Out the kitchen window, she watched him put his arm around Annie and look down at her with a tenderness that made her jealous. But Annie, now, Annie would learn to take control of at least some things. She'd find a life that depended on no one. She'd know *who she was.*

For Rosemary, there were dishes to do, laundry to fold, and Evelyn to see to. It was dusk; the snow geese flew just beyond the dark shapes of Justin and Anne as they headed through the field toward the pony.

Part Three

❖

THE FARM

COME, CALM CONTENT, 1973

⌒∿

He had customers from the first ad. A seemingly endless supply of old ladies in dilapidated farmhouses greeted him with their knotted gray hair and helplessness and asked him to replace rotting windowsills and falling plaster. Soon he had other projects, kitchen cabinets, additions, and new roofs. He entered houses similar to what his own had been and knew the devilish secrets that lay behind old plaster walls, leaky pipes, and beams gone soft with termites. He could fix anything. The women were always happy with his work, although more often than not they squawked about the bill. Yet, he could always get them laughing at some bit of nonsense, figuring it was attention they wanted most.

His life suited him to a T. He wondered how many men could say the same. Being his own boss, he decided when he worked and when he'd have a day off to roam his land. To the north and east were twenty acres tillable which he rented out to the neighboring farmer. "North and east," he said to his mother with a chuckle—the phrase like a grand gesture of his hand over all he owned—"we've got corn," which rose up out of the ground so fast he could hardly believe it. Only hints of green in May, the seedlings grew to a shining sea of rippling leaves within a few days. To the south and west were hundreds of acres of woods, of which he owned fifteen, a virgin forest of pine and oak that held eagle nests and owl hoots. He made a trail and discovered it connected him to another that was already there, and wandered for hours hearing nothing but birdcalls.

Mornings, the world lay so still and welcoming he couldn't wait to pull on his boots and walk across his land, dreaming what would be good planted where.

The house was finished, all but the front porch, which he would screen in. Rosemary liked to sit out there and Lord knows she deserved it. She'd begun teaching and although her salary helped pay the bills, she was continually in a panic, rushing through the house determined to finish the laundry, start dinner, sew curtains, scrub something or other. He'd grab her arm as she passed, trying to slow her down.

"Come sit with me," he'd say. Sometimes she would, but most of the time she pulled away. "I can't. I've got to—" Annoying, that. But it was just her way. He had no complaints. She worked hard. One morning when he set out to walk, she came too, stumbling behind him. The woods were eerie—was it gypsy moth? Webworms? Long threads hung from the trees. In places where the sun shone through, they were like a long curtain trailing after them, gossamer threads that clung to their clothes and hair. He turned around. "I'm glad you're first," she said, wiping the sticky silk from her face, "breaking the path. Let's turn back, Justin." She talked in a whisper, the woods too quiet for words.

"Oh come on," he told her softly. "Nothing's going to get you."

"The kids will be up soon, wanting breakfast."

"The kids. It's always something."

"You're right," she said and took his hand.

So much life in a forest going on about its business without a sound! The threads swayed in the faint breeze, silvery pink in the early light, draping from the high branches to the orange mushrooms and pale lichen underfoot. Mysteriously, they spelled a silent industry, the creature that made them far from view. Here in the open places where the dew still clung, webs gathered over the honeysuckle and drooped from patches of wisteria, covered the blackberry blossoms along the sandy path toward the state road, and lay interrupted by deer prints and possum. Nothing here could make him doubt himself. Nothing here to fear. This was life as it was meant to be lived. He turned to Rosemary. "All right?" he said as the path turned again into the shadow of trees.

"Yes." She was looking at him in a way that said yes with her whole body. He waved his arms to clear a space among the webs. He ached for her, and she for him, he could tell. He wanted to complete the puzzle that was his wife. Hear her sigh break the stillness. For a few moments, the threads held them as if they were missing pieces that had found a place, their sounds belonging.

He planted raspberry bushes along the edge of the woods, and apple and pear trees near the low place in the field where water held when it rained. He had the farmer who rented from him scoop out the earth with a bulldozer, declaring what was too low to be plowed he'd make into a pond with a nature trail around it, where he'd plant weeping willows and serviceberry trees with fruit the birds loved.

His ideas were only limited by his own back and muscle, not anyone else's approval. That's what he liked. As the pond filled with each rain, he saw deer come cautious out of the woods to drink, a sight that always startled him to pleasure. He ordered free bass from one of the government agencies. The day the fish were to be picked up, he filled the back of his truck with empty buckets and was shocked when the ranger handed him a small plastic bag with fish an inch long. "I could have held them in my mouth and spit them in the pond," he told a smiling Rosemary.

He planted a garden the size of a tennis court, carefully measuring the space between each row, and put up enough bean poles for an Indian village. The chickens had to be penned until September, he told Michael, and the guineas as well. He bought three pigs for Michael to raise, built the sty, fenced in the pony for Anne, built a pony shed, and hung a long swing from the maple in the yard.

It was a gathering, the harvest of a lifetime of secretly held wishes, this house in the country, and when an itinerant photographer showed up one day in June with an aerial view of the farm, he stared at it with a satisfaction that settled into a deep sigh. Here were the house and the drive encircling it, the orchard, the pond, the garden, the mass of woods, and the neat rows of corn. Here were the markings of his existence and vision, his tire treads on the bare earth, his shovel's turn.

"How much?" he asked the photographer. A moot question. How much would a reflection of your soul be worth?

Since then, roofs were his favorite places to work, he thought as he climbed to Miss Marguerite's roof and looked over her neatly fenced flower garden. You could learn a lot about a person by looking down from the roof. It was like studying the map of a lifetime, what cars lay abandoned in the weeds, where the family graveyards stood, whether there was an out-house or not, a shop to work in, a shed to hide behind or fill with junk, what sort of work a person did, how they planted flowers and bushes — in a row or in a way that pleased the eye — whether they kept their dog in a pen or free roaming, whether they neatly stacked extra pipes and pieces of wood which would wait for some precise and well-planned moment of cre-ation or whether they strew things about with a carelessness that spoke of fire and focus elsewhere. You could tell the worn paths where people walked, the narrow path the dog took on his nightly prowls, and whether a place was near the end of its usefulness, how tired the people were inside or if the place was bursting with life and kids, and just beginning.

You could tell, too, how people had been treated, some of the houses of the colored jerry-rigged by the ignorance of a cold heart, and he won-dered how men could close their eyes to real need when it sat so openly in the country air. What would he have seen had he stood on Stan's well-shingled, manicured roof? What would he have known of the man or the complicated undercurrents? Here ordinary life was in plain view. No illu-sions, pretenses, or anonymity. It was what it was, so that when he spoke to customers he already knew something about them. That he was curious about them surprised him — they and the landscape so plain and all. He'd been above that. And now he was content with it.

If you could see from a different angle than anyone else, you had spe-cial knowledge — an awareness of the great struggle — even when you were just a fix-it man. Yup, a roof was his favorite place. Sharpened his senses. Kept his shoulder to the wind. Exhilarated. Changed his whole attitude. Made everything a person worried about look insignificant. But then leaks were small at first, and pretty darned significant when he thought about it. They'd start at a loose shingle and soon water stains would appear on the ceiling ten, fifteen feet away. If left alone they'd cause a dip, falling plas-ter, disaster.

Now, after seeing to that leak of Miss Marguerite's, he was ready to climb down the ladder. He felt a sharp pain in his back, a paralyzing stiffening. He couldn't move one way or the other. The only thing he could move without pain was his eyeballs as he clung to the ladder, dizzy as though the thing that held him together had snapped and even his brain was loose, spinning around inside his head. He looked down at the ground—he may as well have been on top of the Empire State Building for the height, now unconquerable, each step of his descent an event of excruciating pain.

He left the ladder where it was, hobbled to his truck and went home to bed. He called the doctor. "Rest," the doctor said. "And get a door to put under the mattress. Remove the doorknob first."

He laughed. "Stop it, Doc. Jeez, stop it. It only hurts when I laugh," he said, and laughed again, taking in gulps of air, wondering how soon Rosemary would be home.

HEARTWOOD

⟡

Walnut, chestnut, holly, loblolly, black locust, red maple, persimmon, mimosa—she knew all the names. Lucifer, her cat, trailed at a safe distance. She paused. The cat sat and began to lick his paw, ignoring her. She turned and went on naming, bushes this time—rose of Sharon, yew, bridal wreath, forsythia, azalea, lilac—already showing tight green buds though it was only March. Branches wove themselves into a basket around the house. Anne imagined that even underground, the basket weaving went on as roots met each other and kept on growing. Inside the basket world were other worlds: bird nests and bug hatcheries, toads crawling sleepily out of tunnels, rabbits' holes with babies for Lucifer to sniff out.

She headed toward the giant red maple spreading its limbs to the peak of Dad's shop, the barn door, the smokehouse roof, and the windows of her parents' bedroom. Its thick trunk leaned away from the north wind, balanced by a limb as big around as any tree on the farm. It extended like a muscled arm and held the tire swing Dad made for them. He'd let her and Davey climb on his truck to catch the rope and pile on top of Michael, the three of them swinging at once while their mother shrieked from the kitchen window, "My God, Justin, they'll break their necks!" It added to the thrill. After that they got the idea to put on a circus of swing stunts while Dad took movies, puffing on his cigar while they each thought of their own trick. Dad was so much fun last year.

Anne grabbed the rope and threw her leg over the tire like she mounted

Holly. She added her weight slowly as if to test the tree, glancing up to see if the limb gave way like Dad had warned. It didn't budge. A holly bush grew in the fork of the tree. The idea of a seed's willingness to grow anywhere intrigued her. She liked to look at it.

She began her views, the spinning view and the upside-down view. That was something they didn't tell you in school—how many different views there were, each one another story. She dragged her feet and watched the world wobble, then began the seesawing view from which she caught a glimpse of the goat skull Michael had thrown on top of the chicken coop to bleach out for his collection. On the other side was the hole in the tree, the yawn of its giant mouth with lips curling around a papery gray beehive. Old man tree. When he wasn't yawning, he was shouting or singing, depending on the light and time of day. Today, in the soft, gray haze, he was spooky. He knew things that made him scared. So did she.

She, Michael, and Davey liked to join hands around the tree and with their arms stretched and cheeks pressed against the rough bark, they would measure the trunk to see if it had gotten bigger. When the trunk seemed to get smaller—or that's what Michael told Davey—Davey said, "Nu huh. Your arms got longer, Michael."

"Yours too, birdbrain," said Michael.

"Lame brain. Reetard," said Davey, breaking away from Michael's grasp and slipping behind Anne for protection. Even two against one they were no match for Michael if he got riled. She swung higher and thought she'd like to climb the rope to the first thick branch and stay there till somebody found her. They would miss her brothers before they missed her. What if they didn't ever miss her? Dad would. He'd see her from his bedroom window, which was across from the tree. Not that she spent any time looking into her parents' bedroom—they were hardly ever there— but once she saw her mother yank her arm away from her father's grasp like Anne did when Michael wanted to show her his word was the last word. He'd hold her arm tight until she yelped or broke free. Her mother didn't yelp; she didn't say anything at all. When Dad spotted Anne, he leaned out the window shouting, "Get outta the tree, goddamn it!"

She was the one who discovered the beehive no matter what Michael said. On the first warm day, she'd heard their droning and watched them crawl into the hole that grew bigger each year. The hole worried her. From it came chunks of yellow wood that littered the ground and when she picked them up they were light and airy as if everything alive had left, juice, bugs, worms. Sheets of bark lay all over the lawn, too. But it was the wind that worried Dad. When it blew hard he paced the kitchen. "That tree—knew I should've taken it down. When she goes, the house goes," he'd say. It was scary. She didn't think fathers ever got scared.

She closed her eyes and threw her head back so that she was in a combination spin and upside-down view. She heard, "I'm telling you, Anne, stay out of that swing." Dad appeared in snatches, his face blurred. He'd been so quiet, she didn't know he was around. She wished the Dad who puffed on his cigar and played tricks on them would come back. You always knew where that dad was. If he'd been in a better mood he would've called her Annie.

"C'mon. Off," he said, and stood in her way, blocking the spins. She felt the pull of his arm as he grabbed the rope. "Matter of fact, I'm taking the swing down. This tree isn't safe," he mumbled.

She jumped down. "Aw, Dad."

"Yeah, well . . . I've already called the tree man," he went on, the words sounding as if they were spoken underwater.

"Can we hang the swing in another tree?"

"Whaddya mean, 'we'?" he said angrily. She stared at him. Usually his hands would be flying around like loose springs, but now they were in his pockets. His mouth turned down. Sometimes anger howled through him like a bad wind, turning his ears bright red and his hands restless at his belt which he would unbuckle and yank out from the belt loops and swing and snap on the wall, then on whoever was nearby. Mostly Michael. It was mostly aimed at Michael. Was it the tree that upset him, or her? Maybe it was the thought of spending money on a tree man when he didn't have a job. Maybe her mother had yanked her arm away again. He must really hate that. Michael did too.

Anyway, she wished she had climbed the tree for one last look. She began imagining the yard without the tree, just as she had imagined how it would be not to see her friends in the city every day when she'd found out they were moving to the farm. Her life—anyone's life—could change in an instant. That's why it was important for her to keep all the views safe in her head. She thought about drawing the tree so she'd never forget it, but she wouldn't know where to start. It was too big.

Just like that, she thought, so quick. You grew a long time and then a lightning bolt hit and you weren't a kid anymore—she watched her father haul the extension ladder to untie the swing rope—like the lightning that struck the ground next to her when she carried the water bucket for Holly before dark one day last week. She'd heard the loud crack and thought the tree had split behind her as the wild stab of light pulled at her hair and blinded her. Dropping the bucket, she ran toward the house. There was the thrill of what could have happened told over and over at the kitchen table. Even Michael and Davey listened and her mother ran her hand through Anne's hair, tears in her eyes. The next morning she found the charred patch of grass right where the old well used to be.

Her father swung the ladder upward and banged it against the tree. It rattled as he adjusted its lean. When he stepped onto the first rung, she tried to hold the ladder steady, watching the seat of his pants, his jean legs, and then the soles of his work boots make their way up the steps.

"Atta girl, Anne," he called down. "Keep that ladder from slipping. Don't let anything happen to your old man."

She held on tight. If the ladder started to slide to one side, she doubted she could keep it from falling, but he was counting on her. She clenched her fingers tighter around the aluminum, feeling his weight sag the ladder with each step. Pushing both her feet against the ladder legs, she looked up at the mud packed in the crevices of her father's boot bottoms. The muscles in her arms began to burn.

"What about the holly bush?" she called to him when he began to tug on the swing rope.

"I'll try to save it, but I'll bet its roots are deep in the tree. Don't let go of that ladder, now," he warned and peered down at her.

She stood very still, trying to think what it must be like to die, although a tree couldn't know, of course. Would it miss the tug of the swing, feel the space where the holly bush had been like a missing tooth? Did it feel the tickle of bees inside, the bark dropping away? How was it with people? Would you feel your toes shutting down? Your fingers? Would you just lie there and wait with people staring down at you, waiting, too? Would you care or would you just be curious about feeling the shutting down? Or does most of your worry about dying happen when you're on your feet and very alive—when you care the most about everything?

The tire dropped to the ground with a bounce. She watched it dance back to being just a tire again. What would it be next? She'd seen planters made from tires with one side cut into petals and spread open, painted blue. Everything had another life somewhere. Even Dad. He tried something new a lot of times and he'd probably be something else again one of these days. Maybe a pilot. That time he took her and Michael up in his friend's plane, he held her hand tight and said, "You'll see, Annie, it's the neatest thing to go through a wide space where there aren't any roads." And it was, although Michael didn't think so. He threw up.

Now Dad reached across to the fork in the tree. She gripped the ladder even tighter as he tugged at the holly bush. Soon he was at the bottom of the ladder saying, "Some of the roots ripped off when I pulled it up— but it might be okay if you give it plenty of water," without looking at her.

"Where should I plant it?"

He shrugged and pulled the ladder toward him so it pointed skyward, dizzily, and walked his hands up the rungs. When it was low enough, he hoisted it on his shoulder. "Aaaagh!" he said. He teetered for a minute and his nostrils flared.

"Is it your back again, Dad?"

"It's okay," he said through clenched teeth.

She wanted to ask him where it was exactly that he hurt and was it pain that made him so sad. But he would never tell her. She set the holly bush down next to the pony shed and went to look for a shovel, worried about the look on her father's face when he picked up the ladder.

Soon after, Michael and Davey appeared out of the woods, muddy and scraping their boots along the graveled drive. They left the bucket by the back doorstep. She wanted to warn Michael about Dad and the bucket being left, but she was too late. He kicked it across the lawn and yelled, "Put it where you found it, lummox!" Michael scrambled to get the bucket and Davey ducked around the side of the house, but what saved Michael was the tree man, who pulled up in the yard in a rusted pickup

and yelled, "Hey! This the Williams'? Hi—I'm Willard." He had as much
hair on his head and face as she'd ever seen on a man. Red, too.

Soon her parents and Willard were standing with their arms folded
across their chests looking up at the tree. Dad thought if they pruned the
tree back maybe they could save it, even though one whole side was dead.
Her mother suggested they fill the hole with cement; she'd seen trees with
cement in them when she was a little girl.

"Or the hole painted black with creosote," said Willard helpfully.

"Do you think it can be saved?" her mother asked, searching his face.

"Well now," said Willard, "I seen them go either way. Live a few years
and then die on you or die right away. You never know. Either way. Live
or die." He rose up on his toes and down again, still looking at the tree.

Anne snickered. Her dad looked at her and winked. She was relieved
to see him smile. He was talking to her like he used to—with his eyes—
like when he'd hide her mother's fork when she got up from the table for
more milk and would catch Anne's eye with a look that said, "Talk about
something and don't let on," something the boys could never do as they
giggled and gave it away. Closer than words, Dad and her.

Dad baited Willard. "Seen 'em go either way, eh? Bet you've seen a
lot of trees in your day."

"My Lord—a mess of 'em. From the topside down. But, hey, before I
do anything you'll have to get rid of them bees. I don't fool with them
none."

So this would be another story, the way one thing leads to another like
a road you go down with adventures on either side, one after another,
where you always lose some things and gain some and in the telling make
it funny if you can so people will help you laugh instead of cry.

When Willard had gone, Dad told them all to wait in the house.

"Can I help?" Michael said.

"Nope, not this time," Dad said, waving him away.

Michael ran his fingers through his own red hair. "See that guy's
hair?" he said to Davey and Anne on the way into the house. "I'm gonna
grow mine just like that," to which Davey said, "You is gonna be just like
yo Daddy, Mickey—a little bit missin' up top."

"Yeah and you is gonna stay jest a little bit too shote if you cain't shut yo mouf," Michael said, but he was grinning, looking pleased that he might be like his father, though he's really more like Mom, Anne thought, which was maybe why Michael made her father so mad sometimes.

"I told you kids to stop talking like that," said her mother.

"Like what?"

"First thing you know, you'll forget where you are and say it in the wrong place. What's your father up to now?" she said as she pulled clothes out of the dryer. They watched him from the kitchen window. He was hopping around the yard, yanking his white beekeeper's suit on one leg and dragging the shoulders on the ground. Then he twisted his body around for the sleeves, and jumped up and down as he pulled up the zipper. It was when he pulled on the helmet and mask that Davey said, "He looks like a moonwalker."

"When did he get that?" said her mother, her brows hunched up like she did when something happened without her knowing about it. Their father spending money needlessly was one of the things she got most upset about.

"Back when he first built the beehive—the one that's out by the cucumber field that always has dead bees in it no matter how many live ones he puts in there," said Michael, fanning flames.

They watched him wrap a rag around an old broom handle and pour gasoline over it, splashing some on the ground. When he lit the rag, it flared into a torch which he jammed into the tree hole. Anne thought they would see a swarm or a beeline but the bees just trickled out, and some crawled along the ground for a while. Smoke poured from the hole and from other holes they didn't know about. It looked like the tree was on fire. "Yeah, it is!" said Michael.

"Do I call the tree man or the Fire Department?" her mother called through the kitchen window, posing with the telephone in her hand. "Nothing's ever simple around here," she mumbled to the wall.

"Don't call the Fire Department! They'll probably fine me for not getting a permit to burn a tree," he said through the mask. A bee crawled across the front netting, up, down, across, and back again. "Let's just wait on that. Maybe the fire will burn itself out."

He underestimated the tree. It smoked for three days and on the morning of the third day he stood looking up into its mouth with his hands in his pockets. He finally decided to call Willard.

"How much you charge, Willard, for a burning tree?" he laughed into the phone. "What? Jesus Christ, man! How much for just the tree and forget about chipping the stump? How much if I help instead of your crew? How much if we can get the fire out before you come?" Silence. "Yeah, I guess I haven't got a choice, have I?" He hung up and stared at the tree.

Willard began with the gigantic limb that had held their swing. He climbed the tree with his ropes and chain saw as easily as he walked the ground. Soon he was dropping branches so big they dug craters into the lawn, bouncing as they fell.

"Got to balance her jest right so when she falls, she'll go where I want her to," Willard called down to her father.

Anne strained to see each cut. Maybe there'd be another heartwood. Once when Dad cut down a small tree, there was a red-brown butterfly shape in the center of the wood—Heartwood, Annie, he told her. He cut her a slice and then another and another, but with each slice the dark shape in the center changed till finally it wasn't anything but a blob. "Imagine," he said, "picking that tree and cutting that piece in exactly the right place to find a butterfly. Makes you want to believe."

"In what?"

"Luck—magic." It was the way he said it, smiling at her as though the world was full of luck and magic.

"Can I have it?" she asked him.

"Sure! Put some varnish on it to keep it from drying out. Might work." But in a few weeks the butterfly faded, then vanished altogether, although she still kept the piece of wood on her bookshelf.

Now Willard paused at the fork in the tree to study the branches. Once he called down, "Fire hadn't gone beyond the trunk, but she's still smoldering. Wood's too green in the rest of her, but I can feel the heat clear out to here." He started up the chain saw again.

By the time he was ready to cut through the base of the trunk, the tree stood with its chopped-off arm reaching nowhere. Anne opened her sketch pad. She wanted to keep the branches somewhere, the whole tree, the swing, the yawning hole, the red buds. But where to begin? With the bark? The bee hole? The swing? She tried to sketch what was left, the trunk as it was now, then with branches extended, but she'd already forgotten the shape of the tree. The views got in her way—the upside-down view where the branches became roots buried in sky, the tree dancing as she swung high and low, the view from her parents' bedroom in the moonlight—she would never get the tree's whole story down—never. It was too late. When she looked up from her sketch pad, ropes had been tied to the branch stubs and the tree looked like a gigantic lassoed bull, rearing in panic. Dad stood out of the way and held onto a rope.

Willard cut a wedge on the far side of the tree; a shower of wood chips covered his flannel shirt and pelted his safety goggles. The tree stood solid. Then Willard sawed the side facing them and the tree shuddered. As he went deeper and deeper, it began to stir and then, with a clap that would break a heart, the wood gave way in a great, jagged splinter and the tree fell like thunder. Dad grinned at Willard.

"Right where you said she'd go."

The stump was charred. Willard was up on his toes again. Up and down, up and down.

"Should we put a hose to her?" he said.

"Naw. Let her burn. It'll be easier to chip her out," her father answered.

Lucifer sat down on the outer edge of the stump with his head turned toward the smoking blackness. Anne sketched him, and filled in the stump around him.

"Lucifer at the Gate of Hell," Michael said.

Maybe the tree would come back to her another time. She would only do trees until it came back to her. Maybe her fingers would remember the tree. But not now, not while most of it was lying on its side, smoldering. The sky outside the window was vacant, and in the kitchen, new light changed the walls to plain old yellow.

For the rest of the day, Willard cut up the limbs into fireplace-size logs while her father fed them to the cone-shaped log splitter on the tractor. In the afternoon, Michael, Anne, and Davey stacked the wood in the shed to season. In all that wood, there was not one single heartwood. Willard cut up the trunk and carefully loaded the pieces, charred side up, onto the bed of his pickup. Then he left.

Meanwhile, the stump kept on smoking, glowing red far into the night. Thinking it would help smother the fire, her father and mother covered the stump with a corrugated sheet of cement left over from the bulkhead. In the middle of the night, they all woke up to what sounded like gunshot close to the house.

"What's that, Dad?" Michael called through the upstairs hallway. "Want me to get the rifle?"

"What the hell?"

"It's coming from the stump," her mother said, and turned from the window mumbling, "Nothing's ever simple around here."

It's just that there's more to the story, Anne wanted to tell her. In the moonlight, chunks of asbestos sheeting shot into the air followed by showers of glowing cinders like the Fourth of July. She could see the fire through the jagged-edged holes in the sheeting from the upstairs window. It was red-orange now.

"Ka-pow, ka-pow," Davey said, his blond hair looking as though it had been combed by an egg beater and his arms and fingers extending in gun position.

Tugging at the belt of her green bathrobe, her mother followed her father in his blue-and-white-striped pajamas into the yard below. Anne was breathless at the danger—especially at the sight of them bending over the corrugated sheeting, struggling to pick it up—of her mother or father losing an eye or being shot in the forehead—while the chunks of asbestos and cement continued to shoot up into the air as high as the bedroom window.

"Pull it to the right, no—your left! Keep your head back!" her father shouted, but then she heard her mother's laugh, light as a bubble floating up to them at the window. Even though it was interrupted by the explosions of asbestos, their father's shouts and their mother's shrieks, her laughing made them forget any of the scarier sounds.

"Whew!" Davey said.

One last shot from the asbestos as it lay on the ground—well, one more as they went back to bed. In the morning Anne saw that the black hole in the stump had deepened and widened. The cool-edged bark was Lucifer's favorite place to sit now. He was there this morning, licking his paws, enjoying the cozy heat.

"Let her burn," Dad said at breakfast. "Who needs a chipper for two hundred bucks? I'll get this baby out myself."

"Why don't we just get Willard to come and be done with it," said her mother, her lips red with fresh lipstick, ready for her day.

But the story wasn't done yet. There was more, or at least Anne hoped there would be more. A story needs to come to its own end. The chipper would be too easy. She understood that her father thought so too, that it was more than the money, her mother, or the tree.

The stump was still warm when one morning as she, Michael, and Davey ran for the school bus, they left their father standing on one of the swells of tree root, with the ax in his hand, breaking away the blackened wood. By their return in the afternoon, he was on the stump and in it too, up to his boot tops, flinging chips into the yard. Each day he was farther down into the stump, grunting and sweating on their return home. A week went by, two weeks. By the third, it was getting harder for him to climb out at the end of the day and straighten his back as he walked to the house.

"You been in there all day, Dad?" asked Davey, bending over the rim to see how big the hole had gotten.

"Most of it." He never looked up, and kept his eye on the hammer and chisel in his hand. The days were warmer now; his flannel shirt lay in a ball where Lucifer used to lie among the exposed roots. It was as if the tree were sucking him in, until one day he peered out at them, eye level with the ground. Only the top of his head could be seen jerking in rhythm to the chipping.

"Are you past the fire, Dad?" Anne asked him. He stopped to look out at her, but beyond her too. His whole body fit inside the shell of the tree now.

"Justin, please let's call Willard," her mother said when she came home from work, her arms loaded with books and papers. "You've gotten most of it out and the chipper can probably do the rest in five minutes."

He seemed surprised to see her, as if he hadn't for a long time. In a voice so low it sounded as though it pained him to speak, he murmured, "Still burning. Can you believe it? Down in the lower roots. I'm following them, feeling the heat—more I chip, more she burns. Be a while yet. Miles of roots."

Then her mother got that stiff look on her face like she was through pretending everything was okay and marched quickly into the house. Anne watched her father disappear down the hole again and by the time she got in the house, her mother was on the telephone. She didn't sound friendly.

"What do you mean you can't chip the stump?" she said. "No, he can't come to the phone right now. I'm asking you to do it. He's not going to be calling you. I'm calling you. I'll be paying you, too. What do you mean you don't take orders from women? What if I didn't have a husband? Willard, I don't believe this!"

Her mother still had the telephone directory open to Tree Service when her father came into the kitchen. She quickly closed the book as he said, "What's for dinner?"

"Are you through out there?"

"For today. What's for dinner?"

"Justin, we need to make a decision here."

"How about hamburgers?" he said, busying himself with taking off his work boots.

"I mean about the stump."

"No need to. I got it."

"Willard could do it in five minutes with the chipper—save your back—leave you free to do other things."

"I'm taking care of it."

"But so many other things have to be done—the windows have to be caulked and painted." It was almost as if she were pleading with him, like Davey did with Michael. Aw, c'mon.

"I'll get to them."

"I know you will, Justin. I don't want to nag, but there's no need to dig down so deep when the outer rim of the stump is what needs to come out." Her voice softened. There was a tremor in her words like when she was tired, or sad, like she was taking in air to say something she didn't want to say, the words sticking in her throat. But Anne worried about the same thing her mother worried about. What did her father do, she was asked at school. She didn't know. Was it that he couldn't decide to be one thing— a beekeeper, or a pilot, or a carpenter and just keep doing it no matter what? She wished her mother would say in that taking-charge way of hers, "Justin, go get a job!"

"You telling me how to do it now?" he said. "You realize how much money I'm saving us?"

Then, what was really scary was that her mother seemed to give up on him in the same way he was giving up because she stuck her head in the refrigerator and mumbled, "Okay, hamburgers it is," as her father sat down in his easy chair. He turned the Heat and Vibrate High buttons as far as they would go and leaned back with that shutting down look in his eyes.

Yet, she did try once more. She poked her head through the kitchen door frame and said, "How about if you put an ad in the paper to wax cars till something comes up? Or maybe teach a course at the community college on heat conservation till you can get something else? Justin?"

It was amazing how many things she could come up with. Cut grass for all the old ladies in town, go back to school and pick up some credits toward a teaching certificate in math or science, After all, Justin, you did get straight A's in Physics in college, raise chickens for Perdue and get one of those long chicken houses on the farm, sell insurance, rent beehives out to the farmers in spring—had he seen the ad in the paper for carpenters to do finish work on sailboats? ending with, "You can do anything, Justin, anything. Always were good with your head and your hands."

But her father never answered, just like tonight. His eyes were closed now and his mouth open, his thin lips around the hole in him. He snored.

Her mother said, "Annie, will you set the table, please?"

Would the story be finished soon? It depended on which story was ending. For there were stories within stories, like the roots that went on weaving with other roots under the house.

The wind tracked them down that night and swirled itself around the yard as if looking for the swing and the tree with the holly bush. Anne listened to it whistling inside the stump, stirring the ashes. She was sure she heard it in her dreams, especially when she awoke the next morning and found the stump smoking again.

"Justin, Davey's got an appointment with the orthodontist at three-thirty today and I've got a meeting," her mother said at breakfast. "Can you take him?"

Anne was sure this would be the end of one of the stories. That's why she ran up the lane after the school bus dropped her and Michael off, expecting to see her mother home early. And she was. She was talking to a man who was not Willard, someone who seemed to be in a hurry because he kept looking down the lane toward the state road. As Anne got closer he was saying, "Like I said, ma'am, I wish the master of the house was home. I don't like to do anything without his okay. Know what I mean?"

"Look," her mother said. "The check's made out to you. It's got only my name on it. You won't have to worry about not being paid."

"Well, like I said, let me get this over and done with before he gets home. Man works hard. It's his castle. Like I said, I don't generally do anything 'less I talk with the husband."

"Oh, for Christ's sake." She had her hands on her hips now, warrior's stance. "Guess who makes the money around here."

He shrugged. "No need hitting a man if he's down." He eyed the check in her hand. "Well. You kids stand back a good ways."

With the roar of the chipper, there quickly grew a hill of sawdust, a soft yellow rise in the middle of the lawn.

"Abi Yoyo's grave," said Michael.

The man took the check from her mother's hand and studied it. "Where you workin?" he said.

"At the Board of Ed." She looked him right in the eye.

"Teacher?"

"Superintendent."

"What happened to what's-his-name?" He grinned at her but she had already turned to go into the house. It was the second time she'd lied in one day. But they weren't lies really. Just parts of other stories, other views.

If Anne ever told this story, she decided, she'd say she went in the house and drew that tree just like it had been, every leaf, every branch in place, even the holly bush in the fork. And the swing, with her and Michael and Davey on it all at once. With a swarm of blackbirds flying toward them. Which is the way the story should end. Like a picture book. But what she couldn't ever tell was how Dad looked when he and Davey got home, how he climbed out of the truck and leaned on the door a minute staring at the mound of sawdust, how he walked over to where the tree had been and kicked up the sawdust a little as if he thought the rim of bark must still be in there, how he never answered Davey when he said, "Will the sawdust burn now, Dad?" He just stood in the yard with his hands in his pockets and when he finally came into the kitchen, he acted as if all the caring had gone out of him. Anne looked for signs that the smoldering in the tree had become part of him somehow, that maybe he did care a little, enough to let his ears get all hot and red and pound his fist on the table. But he didn't look at any of them and laid his keys down on the counter so quietly it was as if the sound had been turned off.

"I just couldn't stand it anymore, seeing you work so hard in that hole," said her mother, trying to explain herself.

He shrugged. "I was almost finished," he said. That was all.

But as her mother turned toward the stove, she looked as though she'd just been startled by a snake hanging from the first limb of the tree and was doing her best not to let on.

But Anne knew then, as she climbed the stairs to her room, the way you know about something after it's gone, that you could only find a butterfly in the heartwood one time, and you'd always remember it had faded, that there was nothing you could do to save it. Her father knew as he handed the chunk of wood to her, his cheeks pink from the cold November afternoon, laugh wrinkles spreading from the corners of his eyes, his hands restless for the pull of the chain saw and eager for work, waving the cigar at her as he grinned, piercing her with green eyes like her own, as he said, "Luck—magic! Might work," planting yesses in her heart.

She raised the window, feeling the wind that stirred everything now stir her hair and rustle the pictures tacked to her wall as she dropped the heartwood into the yews below, remembering the curve of her father's back and bowed head, his words, *I was almost finished*, that tightened her throat.

THE SIXTEEN BY TWENTY, 1976

Each Sunday, Evelyn came for dinner. The sight of her yellow Buick making its way slowly up the lane signaled the end of the weekend to Rosemary, a preface to the whirlwind of work that faced her each week. Rosemary hoped Evelyn did not have a sense of this—didn't read signs of being unwelcome in Rosemary's busyness. Tonight Evelyn held onto the door frame as she came in, swaying a little as she made her way to the kitchen chair. She landed with a thud. The kitchen smelled of meat loaf and garlic, but Evelyn didn't comment on dinner as she usually did.

"Been reading about Justin in the papers," she said. "How did he get himself involved with the nuclear power plant issue?"

"I don't know, really," said Rosemary. "Remember when he started attending PTA meetings a couple of months ago and was elected president? People were impressed with his ability to speak before a group. Next thing I knew he was appointed to a committee. Now the phone never stops ringing. He's rallied a lot of opposition. It may even go to referendum in the next election. He's off now to a meeting—but Evelyn," Rosemary added, "isn't it wonderful to see him like this? He's found his niche, I think."

"He has a bit of the lawyer in him, like his father. You know—" Evelyn stopped to look at her hand which shook on the table before her and, covering it with her other hand, she said, "I'm not the sort of mother who wastes energy on self-recrimination about where I went wrong, but I've been blaming myself for Justin's inability to find a job that pleased him."

"You can't blame yourself for anything," Rosemary said, thinking this wasn't at all like Evelyn.

"When he first went to college, he wanted to go to some expensive nautical design school and I thought he should get his engineering degree instead. I figured if he still wanted to go to design school after he graduated he could pay for it but I would rather he get a basic degree and then specialize. I don't think he was ever happy in engineering. Flunked out that first year and went into the service." She waved her hand and adjusted her glasses. "He finally got serious about his education after that, but by that time, you and he were married. Maybe boat design was his true calling, you know? Did you know his forebears were boat builders? Schooners. From Maine to Long Island, they built some of the best ships in the Atlantic. It's in his blood from his father's side. Did he ever tell you that, Rosemary?" Evelyn took off her glasses and wiped them with a napkin.

He had, one evening as they sat on the porch swing and looked up at a full moon shining through the trees and lighting pathways through the wild growth, limbs and leaves silvered and shadowed by bright moon, dreamlike—she remembered thinking—the kind of night that would make you talk about what might have been, what was yet to come, the kind of night that took you out of yourself. She remembered feeling removed from the scene as if the whole fabric and context of their lives lay out on the ground. An immense feeling of well-being surrounded her as Justin put his arm around her. She remembered how she'd relaxed and nestled against him.

"Maybe I could go to design school now," Justin had said. "Leave you and the kids for a while and just do it. Maybe it's not too late." She loved hearing that. He could do it.

He said, "They all built ships—my uncles. We spent weekends on a sixty-foot yacht when I was a kid—my Uncle Arthur built it—all wood, varnished mahogany, like furniture, smooth as silk. That damn wood glowed like nothing I've ever seen before or since. *Lady Luck*, he called the boat. Every inch of it he did himself."

She remembered thinking, *Anything, Justin, anything.* Maybe he'd been through some kind of midlife crisis. Maybe he was coming into a good time, his goals clear to him at last.

Now Rosemary watched Evelyn's flushed face, the sweat gathering and dripping off the end of her nose. "Anything I can get you, Evelyn?" she said. "Dinner's almost ready."

"Actually, dear, I cannot even tolerate the smell of food these days. Some sort of bug, I think. I probably should not have come, but I get tired of the four walls and the quiet." It was not like Evelyn to complain, either.

"He's brilliant," she went on. "I don't have to tell you that, I suppose. But complicated. When he was little, he would turn his face to the wall when he was sick—said he wanted to be left alone. Always so independent. When his father died, he never shed a tear. He was just fifteen. The only thing he said was he wished he'd known his father was sick, he would have helped more around the house. He always had a million interests— ambitious, resourceful—remarkable really, in everything he touched, but very involved in his own doings. He felt guilty about not helping more, but he was a good son. His father's death was sudden. A bolt of lightning."

Evelyn had never said so much in one sitting as long as Rosemary had known her. She looked tired, her hair in clumps around her ears, hair that used to flair into the beautiful French roll that Rosemary loved. "Drive me home, will you, Rosemary? Stay with me for a little while?"

"Of course, Evelyn," Rosemary said. She had a feeling she would remember these words at the kitchen table like the first wrap of a shroud. There she was, dramatizing again or, on the other hand, seeing clearly. Moments later when Davey came in the door and called, "When's dinner?" Rosemary told him to slice off some meat loaf, and help himself to a baked potato.

"Where are you going?" he said.

"To take Grandma home. She's not feeling well."

"Oh, Grandma," he said, putting his arms around her, his head on her shoulder.

"Someday—someday, Davey, you're going to break a lot of hearts," Evelyn said. She looked over at Rosemary and whispered, "Cutey."

It was cancer. In the large intestine. The doctor said he got it all. They always say that, thought Rosemary, staring at his glowing forehead under the fluorescent light of the hospital hallway and avoiding his eyes. Evelyn lay in the hospital bed with her thin arms sticking out of the sleeves of that green gown and grew weaker. The doctor said he dared not release her. Perhaps they ought to find a nursing home for a few weeks. "You work, don't you, Rosemary?" he said.

Meanwhile, Justin was busy writing articles about the long life of nuclear waste and the need for energy conservation. He was full of ideas, spending long hours into the night drawing up strategies for his role as spokesman against the government's plan to build a nuclear power plant in their midst. The change in Justin was remarkable and Rosemary was proud. She knew he had it in him. A person with his capabilities and global insight was badly needed in this rural community. He was gone again but in a different way. She understood. It took a tremendous effort to dig yourself out of the doldrums and begin anew. He liked to come into the kitchen and put his arms around her waist, kiss her on the neck, then wave his clipboard and his finger in the air as if she'd just given him inspiration for another new tactic in his war against the government.

To cheer Evelyn, she reported each of his triumphs on her visits to the nursing home after work. "He's going before the state legislature next week," she told her. If Justin seemed a bit too jovial at times, his light-heartedness was a relief from the sorrow Rosemary was feeling over Evelyn.

Evelyn said, "I want to go home, Rosemary. Will you drive me? I only want to sit in my own chair for a few hours."

"Of course," said Rosemary, as she pushed Evelyn's wheelchair through the gardens and wept as she looked down at her white hair stirring in the vague breeze.

Justin heard an itinerant photographer would visit the local firehouse. "We should get a family photo," he said to Rosemary. "Mom would like it. Besides, it's important to record the family," he said, "not only for her but for us, too." They went down one evening after school and work, Rosemary wishing she'd had the time to do something with her hair, while the photographer moved them into place: *Stand here—and here—that's it, here. You sit here, and you here. Smile, turn slightly, put your hand on her shoulder, move over a bit, behind Mother. Dad, put your hand over hers, move closer. Everyone smile now, no, don't laugh. Hold it!*

Michael, though, didn't laugh. He was looking but not seeing, aware his skin held everything in, aware that a picture was forever even though he was not, a fact that filled him with terror for he could see how easily one was erased though how could that be? It made him ask where did a person go? Where did the telephone numbers stored in a brain go, the recipes, and the favorite sayings? Why did we have to die? He hoped his father would say yes to the gun safety class although he didn't know if he could actually kill anything. That would be one thing that would make him feel safe—if he had a gun. His fist clenched and his teeth ground like they did in his sleep because it took fierce strength to be a man and what he didn't know was whether he could or not, would or not, find his way or not, and he was already sixteen. One more year of school and he had to decide what to do. Still, he would like to hunt. See if he could. He held a gun once and it felt good in his hands like he was complete and ready and not afraid. The woods would be his then, and deer—he saw one yesterday, a buck at the edge of the pond, drinking, hooves buried in leafy muck. He'd get meat to put on the table, but only to eat, never to waste, and he didn't want to smile thinking about killing and feeling the jump his stomach made when he thought about it because it also made him think about how he was devoured in his dreams. At the last minute, he put his arm around Davey.

Davey hated that and squirmed, but stopped because it was only for a second and this was for Grandma. It was all they could do, Mom said. Grandma might never get to hear him play trombone in the school band. Anyway, he wanted to play drums which he'd have been better at if they'd let him but someone else was already playing drums, which pretty much was the way things went, being the youngest. Dad was saying, "Show your Chicklets now—the ones we paid good money for,"—but Davey kept his mouth closed—*metal mouth* his brother called him. Dad laughed and said, *Baa, baa,* and Davey pulled himself up on tiptoe wishing he were as tall as Michael or taller, even though he wasn't afraid like Michael was. He came up to Michael's chin and he could see the hair on the back of his father's neck and heard him wheezing, stifling a laugh. Davey loved when that happened. "Davey's like his dad," Grandma said, but he knew he was not like anybody, and besides, his father was many people, depending on which day.

The photographer took Justin's hand and placed it over Rosemary's—
why was it so cold? thought Justin. Sons and daughter and wife around
him, he got up to look at them and check the arrangement—he hadn't
done too badly, had he?—as he moved Davey a little to the left, saving
room for himself between his sons, coming into his own now, living the
other half of his half-life, the up side, making hay while the sun—you
know—belonging. He was connected now. What took him so long?—
well, he knew the answer to that one—little detours, you might say. Told
his mother once. She wrote him a check. Get help, she said. Did the only
thing she knew. *Talk about it,* said the shrink. Yeah. *What birth order were
you in the family? Oldest? Explains your deep sense of responsibility,
depression when you can't provide.* Horse shit. Forget it. The down side
never was because of anything. Just was. This time, though, the phone
never stopped ringing. The community wanted him. They just discovered
a Pied Piper in their midst. He'd take that nuclear business all the way to
the legislature. Maybe run for office. The politician and his family. It was
so easy. So easy. *You can charm a snake,* Rosemary said, going along for
the ride.

She could feel his hot hand over hers—he had to be told to do that,
of course, because he'd forgotten her and she could get on a bus and not
tell anyone where she was going, tend to this wild hair, wild hare inside
her, find someone dark and mysterious, not bothering to know his whole
name. Would Justin miss her, except for supper being late? She had to
believe she could go astray and the family would still be all right. People
do, women do, except they didn't look like she did, haggard, with this
crummy hair, and bags under her eyes. And Evelyn dying. And when will
he work for pay?—although she mustn't complain. He would find himself
and maybe something would come of this new turn of events, fame in the
county, another aspect, a new dimension, even though she often wished
he would take the truck and keep on going down the road. She was so distracted, he, so distracting, with Evelyn dying and nothing to be done about
it and the kids all becoming adults so fast and she out of breath in the
flood, only trying to swim to shore each night to rest—the days so crazy
with fifty-two five-year-olds in the classroom and her three, and a husband
starting a new career every five minutes and Evelyn dying. *Hurry up and*

take the damn picture, why don't you? She felt Anne's hand lightly resting on her shoulder, a warm, undemanding touch.

Anne, standing behind her parents, one hand on her mother and one on her father, joked, "Now you two, behave!" She looked into the lens that reminded her of the deer's eye she'd seen up close that summer so long ago, with a sudden awareness of her family in the way that death made people aware, she supposed—of that odd assemblage, imagining she was seeing them in a reverse, out-of-proportion, convex view that only added to the strangeness—her plaid and Michael's plaid clashing with her mother's flowered print, splotches of color and skin and hair looking in on itself, and herself in the center, standing erect with her shoulders back like Mom had taught her, and dressed in her favorite Western shirt, sleeves rolled. *A dress,* her mother had said, *how about a dress?*

Yuk!

And click . . .

So there they were in a sixteen-by-twenty color photo—Justin, robust, full-bearded, his face flushed and looking as though a belly laugh was about to burst forth, and Davey, twelve now, grinning dimples and wearing an expression close to his father's—what was it Justin said just before the photo was taken to make them all laugh? Rosemary couldn't remember. And Anne, fifteen, with braces and red-brown hair down to her shoulders, her almond-shaped eyes and high cheekbones giving an expression of openness and friendliness that was magnetic, and Michael, sixteen and unsmiling, with a seriousness about his eyes that never left him, his red hair wild and curly despite his best efforts to straighten it, and Rosemary, waxen, pale, the sinews in her neck taut as she attempted to smile, but instead produced something close to a grimace. When she and Justin presented the picture to Evelyn as she lay in the nursing home, her face jaundiced and shriveled, her only comment was, "Oh, Rosemary, this doesn't do you justice."

One day when Rosemary took Evelyn back to her room after one of their walks, Evelyn insisted on standing at the sink, carefully washing her face, and then, lifting her nightgown, scrubbed her crotch, her eyes never leaving the stranger in the mirror, forgetting Rosemary's presence in the room. It was an action so remote from the dignity Evelyn always carried that it broke Rosemary. Evelyn had shut her out, as the dying do in their isolation. Rosemary already missed Evelyn's kindness to her, the way she enjoyed the kids, the way she always called her *daughter, meet my daughter*, she'd say, never *daughter-in-law*.

She died the next day with Justin at her side. He called Rosemary from the nursing home and said, "It's over." He called George, his quiet, gentle brother, who had none of Justin's verve and was considered by Justin to be quite bland, and his wife, Maude, always ready for a bit of gossip, high drama, and a new diet. It was Maude and Rosemary who outwardly grieved, Justin and George who took care of things. On the day of Evelyn's burial, her sons and Maude drove to New York with Evelyn's ashes in a wooden urn. Justin brandished a cigar in the front seat with George, and talked for the whole five-hour trip to Long Island, Maude told her later.

"Watch your ashes, you two," Maude said, "I don't want them to mix with Evelyn's," and they all chuckled at the strangeness of everything while Justin told the story of the nuclear power plant and his strategies to fight it. Maude said she was impressed at first, but then fell asleep with the urn planted carefully between her feet while Justin's voice blended with the sound of the engine. "Amazing," she said. "Not one word of sorrow, that is until we got to the grave site and George broke down. Justin got real quiet for once."

Rosemary stayed home with the children, including the cousins, Thomas and Parker, and listened to their exuberant cries as they chased frogs down at the pond, their bare feet slipping in the mud. Evelyn would have had a good laugh over them. Evelyn. Rosemary found solace in the children's remembrances of her. Michael asked if Grandma had died a noisy death or a quiet one. "It was quiet, Michael. She was in a coma," Rosemary told him. He cried then, and took off for the woods alone, wiping his eyes with the back of his hand.

Justin was silent. He was like a sound that wanted to happen but didn't. She tried to imagine what sound he would make if he could. She thought it might be a long, low mournful moan, a coming together of all the sounds of a lifetime poured like colors into a ribbon of brown, for when a mother dies, a world dies, a whole childhood, and time perches on one's shoulder like a hungry hawk. But all he said one evening when they were sitting on the porch in a still-warm October dusk, was, "She was a good mom, but she never said much. I think she loved you more than me."

"Oh, Justin, I'm sure that's not true."

Ignoring her protest, he said, "Because you could talk to her, and I couldn't. She never knew what to make of me." He got up quickly and faced the north field where combines droned in the dark distance, their headlights beaming across the tall stands of dried corn as they harvested before the next rain. They'd work all night, and in the morning the landscape would be empty.

"The dust," he said, "chokes me," and he coughed into his hands and wiped his eyes on his sleeve.

DARK SOUP, WHITE ICE

～✖～

Shaped like a boomerang, the pond lay west of the house covering about an acre. A ring of trees, branches bent low, shaded its banks. Davey kept watch from his bedroom window for the white edge of ice that would soon form. In summer when there hadn't been much rain, only the deep end of the pond held water, while in the shallow end saplings sprung up. Heavy rains in fall had filled the pond. Despite the persistence of the saplings, there would be plenty of clear ice to skate on. And besides, skating through the trees and under tree tunnels along the edge would be fun.

Earlier in the week a skin of ice had formed, and two days later it turned milky and dense so that by Saturday, Davey could stand on it, timidly at first, listening for cracking sounds. "Pond's frozen," he announced at breakfast. Their skates hung on nails along the basement beams so the mice couldn't nest in them. Michael wore Dad's skates and passed his old ones to Annie which left Davey with a white pair, but Davey didn't mind as he didn't mind most things that would have bothered Michael.

His mother thumped her biggest pot on the stove and asked him to go to the freezer in Dad's workshop for bags of corn, tomato, peppers, and zucchini. He did, dropping the slippery bags of frozen vegetables on his way in. When he opened the kitchen door, the hamburger meat and onions were already browning on the stove. Dumping water and the vegetable rocks into the pot, his mother said, "You want to call some friends?"

They each took turns calling kids from school and soon they were down at the pond lacing up skates.

Michael went first. The ice cracked, but held. He skated slowly, testing the ice, seeing where it was thickest and where the best spot for a hockey game would be, and by the time Davey, Anne, and some of the others were stepping gingerly onto the edge of the pond, Michael had etched long arcs along the entire acre of pond, swinging his arms wide, his chin forward, racing against himself with a smoothness Davey envied. He thought he'd never skate as well as his brother, as his skates stumbled on a rough spot, but he caught himself and went on with baby steps and short slides while Michael slid easily through the trees.

They could hear the ice break in dull thuds, but Michael said it was okay, so they started a game of hockey, the main purpose of which seemed to be to get the girls to trip over the rough patches. Annie played as well as any of the boys while some of the other girls hung back. She fell a few times, one time flat on her back, but laughed as she got up and skated off. Annie was better than any of the girls at just about anything, and Michael was the best skater of them all and he, Davey, wondered if he was going to be best at anything, ever, although he was skating a whole lot smoother now and able to whack the puck back. He loved the sound of the hockey sticks on the ice and against each other and the krisp-krisp of the skates, the echo of their shouts returning from the woods—he was a sound collector mostly.

When he and some of the other kids got chilled, they went up to the house, where his mother stood at the stove, stirring and laughing as the kids giggled and jostled each other. She dipped dark soup into brown bowls and shoved wet gloves in the dryer, warning them about getting too cold and watching out for cracks in the ice. "Davey, another bag of tomatoes, please?" she said and added more water to the pot, but the kids didn't linger and spilled out of the house as soon as their bowls were empty. Down to the pond again. "Come back," she said, "whenever you need to warm up." She liked having kids around. She said once the clock that ticked on the mantel was too loud when they were not in the house.

By late afternoon most of the kids had gone home, but Davey and Michael took turns whipping each other across the ice on the old Flexible

Flyer. The sled spun round and round and the ice cracked menacingly. Michael let go of the rope and the sled slid to a dead halt, caught in tall grass. In the silence, Davey listened to his brother's blades across the pond, a sound singular and curious like a strange animal in the woods, and watched Michael's red hat in a blurry line through the trees, not believing his speed. He watched Michael in the open space at the deep end lean back with his knees bent and his feet turned out in a heel-to-heel position, bringing his body lower and lower to the ice. Now he lay on his heels and leaned so far back his hat brushed the ice. Losing momentum, he jumped up, gathered speed and began it again with his feet heel-to-heel. Davey had never seen anybody do that, not even in the Olympics. He admired Michael's thick thighs, how he could speed, crouch low and lean into the wall of numbing cold as if he would crash it down. Davey loved the flush of happiness on Michael's face, and the way he spoke triumph with his whole body, turning his mittens palms up in victory. When the ice gave way with a loud crack, Michael leaped forward to safety easily, and laughed as the ice behind him dipped underwater.

"Will you skate like that tomorrow, Michael? I want to get a picture," said Davey.

"Sure!" Michael coughed up and spit on the ground just like Dad. Davey did too, to see what it felt like, as if it were some sort of manful right. They both coughed up and spit again as far as they could, satisfied.

Justin watched the kids through the window as they skated, the swirling colors of their jackets among the gray trees. He was glad for them. And maybe a little jealous. At Davey's age, he'd been working and providing for himself. Between the summer cottage and the farm, he had given his kids a good childhood, an easy one. He suddenly felt a stab of sorrow too, for what was ahead of them, for himself, and for the awful passing of time.

The clock ticked; his foot tapped; the floor vibrated; the lamp shook. He was really percolating now, Baby. He might not have much time left. He'd been percolating for over a year, long enough to almost forget what was coming. His hand, as if separate from him while his thoughts marched along, scribbled furiously on the yellow legal pad, the words so much a part of him now. An article for the *Chronicle*, his push for right and good, his white-collar self, he'd made his place in the world and it was to educate, facilitate, eradicate, communicate, and lead:

> *A nuclear power plant has no place in our county. The revenue it purports to bring is nothing compared to the great cost of its waste both in financial terms and danger to humans. The reactor rods have a life of two hundred and fifty thousand years! We do not need nuclear power. We need only to conserve.*

He paused. He'd said those same words before the state legislature and when he finished, reporters rushed to his side with their notepads, pencils poised. He loved it, loved the force, the power, the *permission* of power. He took it. It was his real self come to claim him. His past, his lawyer father and his aristocratic mother—if they could see him blossoming now. *He belonged.* He spoke everywhere—PTA meetings, grand jury appointments, churches, and it was because of him the issue went to referendum. Now the newspaper articles. And a proposal to teach conservation of energy at the local community college. Maybe a book.

His mother breathed at his side. He looked up in alarm. He'd only *felt* her presence, hadn't he? He'd never known her to butt into his business except when invited, which he did only once, when he was down and he thought she might have a clue, knowledge of some ancestral secret: *who was he like?* Not that he expected her to fix his problems, he'd just wanted to crack her New England staunchness a little, let her know everything wasn't exactly roses with him. *Why didn't she tell him his father was so ill?* He couldn't forgive her silence. Never even knew his father had a damaged heart. His mother wasn't unkind, just distant. And here she was now, at his side, with a shit load of things left unsaid. He was angry, but her placid face would just turn away if he shouted. Boys could raise themselves, she always said. He'd done what he was supposed to, hadn't he? All but the gravestone, and it was ordered. *Evelyn B.* next to *John G. So get back in there unless you have some answers.* He flailed his arms wildly. He was going mad listening to her breathing. Why didn't she ever say anything?

Specially designed quilted shades on the windows that face north eliminate drafts and cut down on the loss of heat through the glass. Our meals are enjoyed around the warmth and light of a kerosene lamp, where our children also do their homework.

He'd send the article to all the papers and if they didn't accept it, letters to the editors. Incorporate the cancer scare, hook that up with the power plants too. *We need to conserve.* He'd take on insecticides, pesticides—homicides, matricides, patricides, fratricides, suicide. Oh God.

And in the evening, we open the French doors to the living room to allow the heat from the woodstove to rise to the bedrooms above. There is no need to place additional logs in the woodstove, disrupting sleep. And while the thermostat is turned down as far as it will go, a small Christmas tree light set to a timer for the evening hours will prevent the thermostat from clicking on even during the coldest nights.

Somewhere in the last paragraph, she vanished. She was no longer next to him, taking something from him, depleting him. He was bereft. But not grieving *her*, exactly. Himself. He'd thought maybe it wouldn't happen this time. It was the first seed of self-doubt that told him, pushing forward, straining to flourish, just when there was so much to do—how much could he do?—before he was diminished.

Clock ticks like pinpricks. The hour chimes, offering nothing. I can change one thing and only one. I lift the heavy wooden case from the mantel over my head, now back, now follow the arc, around, down, against the bricks—an explosion, all its moments and movements used up in one cacophonous blast. Like me. Aaaagh!

Rosemary flies in, frightened. Bends to pick up the clock and weeps though she doesn't say a word, as if she knows some secret. Like my mother.

I hear myself say, "I don't want to drag you down with me, Babe."

"You won't," she says, standing, what's left of the clock in her hands, looking back at me with determination, not weeping now. "I don't understand, Justin. It's all bound up in itself and has a life of its own, dictating what you do. I don't think you get down because of this reason or that, although we could find a reason if we had to." She sets the silent clock back on the mantel, shattered glass at her feet.

I take her hand and rub my thumb into her palm, digging in as if to bury myself there. "I don't know, but if I had a gun, I'd use it."

She shakes her head and says, "Justin, it will pass. It always does."

"It gets worse each time. It's definitely getting worse." He hated to admit anything.

"How about going to a doctor?"

"Nope. Did that. Didn't tell you. A waste. There's nothing to talk about. They ask questions. 'What was your mother like?' I say she did the best she could. Talking doesn't do a damn thing. Waste of money."

She pulls her hand away and stoops to pick up the glass. I watch her try to set things right and after a while she returns to the kitchen to stir the soup. Loyal and dull, she is the constant from which I spin out onto some indefinable tract.

Michael had a job after school on the farm next to theirs checking tractor engines for oil and gas and cleaning up the workhouse. He was glad he beat his father home evenings so he could throw extra wood in the stove and turn up the dining room light, for if the house was warm, his father complained but he wouldn't open the doors and waste the heat. The dining room light was another matter. Bright lights annoyed him and he'd stride toward the dimmer switch as soon as he took off his work boots. Michael could count on it.

The smell of roast chicken mingled with the smell of burning wood. Supper was on the table when his father came in and Michael watched him wash up at the kitchen sink, turning his hands over and over in the cold water, hunching his back as if shielding his day from them.

"What's for dinner?" he said finally, and without waiting for an answer, headed for the dimmer switch, then struck a match to light the kerosene lamp.

"Aw, c'mon, Dad. We can't see nothing." Davey glanced at Michael for support.

"You mean anything. You'll get used to it," his father said.

Silence, as heads sank down toward plates. His father sat in his chair.

"Dad, they're starting another Gun Safety class next week. Can I go?"

"Do you have to have your own gun?"

"No, they loan you one."

"All right then. Because I don't want any guns in this house."

"Well, I just figured I'd like to hunt sometime, and a gun would be good to have around in case a possum comes for the chickens or something."

Justin stopped chewing and looked at Michael. "I said no. Too dangerous. Too tempting. Never know when somebody might fool around with it."

"Aw, Dad, that's not going to happen." As soon as he said it he knew it sounded dumb. His mother stared across the table.

"I'm not riding bus seven anymore, Mom," he said. "Can you drop me off on your way tomorrow?"

"How come?" she said, though her eyes never left his father's face.

"The bus driver stopped the bus today to quiet down the kids and he opened the door and told everybody they could walk if they didn't settle down. Well, Donnell Wongus, that big kid from across the field? He runs off the bus and grabs a chunk of dirt and starts throwing it at the bus and then two more kids run off and start getting chunks and they run back on the bus and the driver is yelling at them to get back off with the dirt clods and they start throwing them around." He watched her growing dismay, her eyebrows pulled up on her forehead, her eyes yellow like they got when she was reminded how she never wanted to come here in the first place.

"I hate riding the bus," he added, sorry now he'd said anything about gun safety or the school bus, wishing he'd forged his father's signature on the permission slip and hitched a ride to school.

"What didja do?" Davey asked. "I'm driving when I'm sixteen, or riding the back fields on my dirt bike. You want to borrow it, Michael? Ten dollars a week?" He grinned.

Michael said, "I ran all the way home across two fields. It happened up by Staley's Mill. I'm not going if I have to take the bus. Man, I can't wait till I have enough to buy a car." Silence. Forks scraped.

He went on, timid now, with mashed potatoes on his fork for comfort before the expected answer to his next question, "I've been thinking, though, maybe I could fix up the old Chevy. I mean it's just sitting there and I figure it was running a year ago. Might not take much to get it going again. Can I, Dad?"

"Huh? What? What's that?"

"The Chevy. Can I fix it up? I need a car bad."

"What's wrong with the bus?" His father was staring past him again to a space beyond, although he seemed to be peering at him intently, furrowed lines on his forehead, eyebrows inching toward each other.

"You never listen!" Michael exploded.

His father shrugged and headed for his vibrating chair. After he dug against its back and spread the footrest out into the living room, he pushed *Heat* and *Vibrate High* and dozed. The house shook. All evening, during the washing up, algebra, English essays, and TV sitcoms, Michael felt the tremors till he could stand it no more and turned to Davey.

"Let's make a fire down by the pond—bring the skates—get Annie," he said in a low voice. He left the house with his mother starting another pot of soup from the chicken carcass for tomorrow, and gathered branches for kindling as he ran down to the pond. When he got the fire going, Davey appeared. "Nobody even noticed we were gone," he said, his face white in the light of a half-moon. They tried racing each other in and out of moon shadows, but Davey never caught up. Michael flew over the ice, his speed buffering him against unforeseeable hazards, the power in his legs reassuring him that nothing bad could touch him.

OUT FROM THE COLD

The wind stirred branches all afternoon. By dusk, the windows had begun their direful complaint and the house swayed and shuddered all the way to its heart. The beds rocked. Branch shadows cast by the moon trembled across the white quilt where Rosemary, rubbing her feet together, lay listening. Once when they'd been sailing, Justin said the wind held a memory of the land, a thought that intrigued her now. There was little to remember here. Over land uninterrupted by even so much as a wrinkle, the wind flailed itself across the north fields and rammed into the house unforgivingly. Would it remember them as it passed? Rise and dip after the woods, be kinder to the old shacks along the railroad track?

The windows whined like a row of sick cats. She clenched her teeth and sandwiched her head between two pillows for respite. Her feet stopped trying to warm each other. Pulling her head out from under the pillows for a breath of air, she saw the moon, brilliant and white as bone china. Maybe if she stared hard enough, she could appeal to some superior wisdom to allow this house to raise anchor and set sail along the fields rippled with last summer's corn stubble, float past the meager shacks of the blacks, past the school, past Pucam, past the marshes to the river, the bay and the ocean beyond.

The bed trembled. She lifted her head and glared at the mound of snoring husband rising clifflike over the Sea of Tranquillity between them.

The cliff, impermeable, unyielding; the sea, tranquil because she put up with everything. She hated her wakefulness, his beastly, tremulous intakes of air—his peacefulness at her expense, a peace that waxed by night and waned by day.

Underneath the quilt, she was clad in a heavy-duty orange quilted hunting undergarment, including feet, ordered from Sears by her husband of twenty years. She wanted to laugh. The absurdity of what she had become for him! Despite the orange quilted underwear and the foiled camping sheet which was supposed to reflect her body heat, despite all his cockamamy ideas, she was still goosesfleshed and shivery. And virginally conserved as well. The metallic sheet like cracking ice beneath her, she leaned over, careful not to touch Justin's shoulder, and studied him in the strange white light, hoping moonlight would offer a revelation that studying his face across the kitchen table had not. There were the same straying strands of gray hair, the white whirls of his ear, the mole on his cheek that he continually tore when he shaved, his long nose with a shadow of its own against the pillowcase, and his breath rising to greet the frigid room. That was all.

And because he was, in this moonlight, some semblance of the man she'd married and not one of the many someones he could be by day against whom she needed to guard herself, she left the Sea and pushed one orange quilted foot to the floor. Compelled to put her scissors away in the sewing box and the knife that she'd probably left out on the kitchen counter because she didn't know what could happen in her sleep when her anger might leak into vengeful acts, that is, if she could ever get to sleep in this cold—her nerves pulled taut by the ceaseless moans of the wind—she caught sight of her reflection in the mirror, incongruously masquerading in hunter's orange.

Downstairs, she poked at the woodstove's ashes, reviving a tiny flare of sparks, and through the high old window eyed the rationed wood stacked on the porch, and beyond the porch as well, filling the woodshed and the side shed and running along for sixty feet in a waist-high wall from the edge of the lawn to the entrance of the woods and beyond, meandering like the Great Wall of China. And he kept cutting more. She looked at the small yellow light saved out of the Christmas ornaments, and then down at her fluorescent-orange-covered body as though it belonged to someone else. Pulling on one sleeve, she covered her hand with it and reached up to twist the lightbulb a barely perceptible counterclockwise turn till it went out. And while she was at it, she pushed the thermostat half an inch to the right, till she heard the familiar click and rumble of the furnace below, matching the same in her heart. She'd have a cup of tea. And put away the knife. The wind was quieter down here.

In the kitchen she put the kettle on to boil and watched the flame, rubbing her hands together in front of the stove. Justin had changed again, and like all the changes in him, it came gradually and unannounced, as silent and odorless as a carbon monoxide leak. She'd been proud of him as he spoke before the State Legislature against the proposed nuclear plant, proud as she watched him in his tweed jacket and tie, face flushed, his words clearly enunciated, sure of himself again. She had thought this time things would be different, reminiscent of their life in the city years ago when he had maneuvered his way through up-and-coming computer firms. But that was another Justin, another time. Even if his latest whim had not brought a paycheck, if he could at least have found himself as watchdog of the social conscience, the concerned citizen and community leader, she wouldn't have complained. But he'd stopped trying altogether, his newfound confidence gone. Now there was only his compulsion and anger. And her anger. There was no one moment to notice, no turning point, only a slow quietening until one day he stared at the floor, unable to decide what to have for breakfast.

"Tell me," he'd said, looking up at her from his chair with eyes that cared about nothing, "Tell me what to have."

"How 'bout sunnyside-ups and bacon?" she said. He picked up his hand from the arm of the chair and waved it slowly in the air, letting it drop in his lap. "Surprise me," he mumbled, chewing on his bottom lip. Soon after, the woodcutting began.

She rubbed her arms briskly. The kettle began to steam. As she reached for a cup, she caught sight of the kitchen windows covered with the yellow quilted gingham shades she'd made at Justin's request. She hated them and hated herself for making them, for humoring him, hated how they blocked out the sun and the sight of the chickens pecking their way across the yard. Everything was wrong, beginning with the cold, the unnecessary cold *inside* the house.

Things were often clearer at night. In the absence of clamor, she could think and take stock like some traveler stopping for the night and checking the map. But she and Justin were in a place with no maps, no roads. Her mother once said, "Men! Who can figure? As long as he's not fooling around, Rosemary, not drinking, not hitting you, you can put up with it, right?" But she never told her mother or anyone how they lived now. What lay beneath the words frightened her.

"Drink your tea, Rosemary," her mother would tell her. "Everything will look better in the morning." Sitting now on the couch with the tea mug warming her hands, she thought, to be fair, men must get tired. They must, at times, want to pull away from their families knowing their dreams were just dreams, their moment in the sun was never coming. Was it her fault? The children coming without his permission? Did he feel swallowed up by them? As for her, she didn't think about moments in the sun. For her the long journey in the sun was the family. Beyond that, she dared not think.

Her legs ached from holding her body tense against the cold. Tense against more than that. He was cutting wood incessantly. They had more than they could ever use. He went out each morning with the chain saw pulling on one arm and the gasoline can sloshing in the other. Each afternoon there would be fresh piles of split wood waiting for the boys to stack. Only now he insisted on stacking the logs at the end of the path himself and then turned to cut more. It was as if his life depended on cutting, splitting, and stacking wood, a decisionless occupation that somehow restored equilibrium to a brain out of kilter, the rhythms carrying his body to another dimension, giving him purpose, saving him. She sensed that without this physical challenge he would perish. Maybe he had already perished, his body performing the rhythms on its own, disciplined to wait for him to return. But would he? Yes, of course he would. He did the last time he was like this, didn't he? And the time before that?

The empty cup in her hand still warmed her. She studied the chicken coop shadow across the barren garden beds. She'd plant purple salvia this year, coreopsis and daisies. Her world lay about her bleached and eerie in the moonlight. Black shadows stretched across the yard. How long? She knew, although there was no one to tell. About a year. Maybe less. He'd be like this for a time and then he'd be someone else again. Committee members and reporters could call but they wouldn't find the man who led them. This downturn would probably end when the salvia bloomed, she told herself, and he'd be there for her for a brief time, maybe a few weeks before the upturn—the great surge of creative energy that gathered itself like a huge swell in the ocean. Then what? Then the new Justin, the new career, the new projects that would carry him into the early morning hours tapping his feet, drumming his fingers, looking past them again. Meanwhile, the trees danced and branches snapped and flew along the corn furrows. The tin roof of the tractor shed flapped at its north corner. The new saplings, ready for planting, stood in buckets by the hand pump blowing like spring rye. *Black locusts, Babe. They'll grow so fast they'll be ready for cutting in ten years.* Only the woodpiles lay firm, the cut ends gleaming in a white and stalwart mosaic wall. The log splitter, still bolted to the rear axle of the tractor, glinted like a diamond needle.

Covering herself with the afghan, she listened to the wind as if it could send her a message. Eyes closed, hands warm, she thought about their first summer at the farm. They woke one morning in July to the sound of migrant workers singing as they picked tomatoes, harvest of the benevolent earth. The workers waited to be paid at the end of the rows where the crew leader recorded the numbers painted on the sides of the full buckets. She remembered the heat and the miles of green vines and red tomatoes that surrounded the house, the blue-yellow-red-purple-shirted backs of the workers rising and falling, rising and falling like breaths, Justin's breath and hers quintessentially together as they listened to the workers. It was happiness she remembered, the day bursting upon them, the gathering heat releasing the smell of tomatoes, the chorus of rich, deep voices, and her husband smiling at her side. She had felt alive and conscious of the fullness of life—an empathy with people who labored, an aspect of their lives she wouldn't have known if she'd lived anywhere else. The smell of tomatoes made her conscious of her own breathing, of her own insignificant life taking in knowledge and making it her own, of the windows open to the resplendence and generosity of summer. Weighed against that moment in July, the present ceased to exist; she was not alive in it. The wind had stopped. She realized an absence, like the stillness beyond the walls, within herself.

Morning, soon. She rose from the couch and scuffed to the thermostat. Dutifully, she pushed the lever back to fifty, and twisted the small bulb, her fingers lingering to cup the light, savoring the delicious heat to carry upstairs. He had moved over to her side, thrown off the quilt and spread his thin body as far as it would go, filling her space. She nudged him; he rolled over.

"Christ, it's hot!" he said, and rose without further word to check the woodstove, the thermostat, the small Christmas light. She settled in the warmth his body had left. She was not marooned on this ship that sailed with no compass. He *was* there beside her. What would happen to him if she swam ashore? And what would happen to her if she stayed? And the children? If they could choose . . . Oh, where was morning?

"That sheet works wonders, eh?" he said, slipping back to bed.

"It's coming off in the morning," she said, fearing its virtues would be extolled in the next article for the *Chronicle*.

"What are you complaining about? I'm the one who's uncomfortable. Christ, I'm roasting!"

The sheet crackled as he grew more and more restless. Finally he got up, slammed drawers, pulled on jeans. He would make coffee, lug the saplings and the spade to the northeast field and begin planting. Then he would cut more wood. She closed her eyes. The moon left her its peace; Justin, his warm place in the bed. Yet in that hour when dreams encompass worries and are more easily remembered than those in the density of night, she dreamed her body was weighted down into something fearful, dark as water, where she must save herself. She was pulling the orange quilted top over her head now, sparking strands of hair, and she was kicking off the foolish orange feet parts, and pushing down the orange quilted pants so she could see the whole of her squandered and unheeded body that even she had not inhabited for so long. She was pulling on her best white nightgown, smoothing it over her hips till it swung petal soft at her ankles, and walking now, barefooted between the corn rows to the north side of the woods, as the wind tugged the skirt of her gown. She was bending down to strike a match, and, protecting the infant flame from the wind, igniting the leaves curled at her feet, and stepping back, she was watching them now scatter toward the woods like torches carried by unseen creatures, lighting the trees, the wall of firewood, the woodshed, and finally the house in one grand extravagance of heat, freeing her, freeing Justin, freeing the windows as they fell with their mournful sounds.

Through her sleep, Anne heard the chain saw far off in the distance, droning like a killer bee. She ducked and brushed her arms, fending off the bee, knowing all the while her father was working in the woods again. Once awake, she watched the first rays of the sun sneak through the trees and the shuddering dance of one of the treetops just before the tree was felled, marking the spot where he worked. A stream of sun slanted to the racing numbers tacked to her wall. She focused on Number Eighteen—last Sunday's number, when she had raced Lacy, her newly acquired Appaloosa, and felt the sharp turn of the horse around the barrel, the near fall and the clench of her knees to hold on as the horse dipped low, then the horse steady beneath her, regaining. First place, that day.

A school morning. She doubted that school had to do with anything. It was like the barrels—a series of obstacles, easy enough to skirt. The trick was to do it quickly and drive onto the next. Real life was in the creak of saddle leather underneath her and the morning sun to herself whenever she wanted. Like now. She had time for at least an hour's ride before school.

As she passed her parents' bedroom she saw her mother rolling up the camping sheet into a cylinder. "Didn't work, huh, Mom?" she said into the chilly air. Without looking at her, her mother laughed, but it was a tired, bitter string of sounds. It said: *I'm busy. I'll just sweep away this child's play. I keep the wheels turning, the house humming. I have to fill the lunch boxes, get ready for school, paint on my smile, start the oatmeal, wake up your brothers, scrape the windshield on the car and leave by seven forty-five. Out of my way.* But all she said was, "Take your watch with you if you're going riding. I won't have time to drive you if you're late getting back."

Out the window Anne could see another tree begin its final dance. Neither her father nor her mother ever lifted their heads from work, but she was excused. "Go on," her mother always said at supper's end. "I'll wash up.

You go on. The time will never come again when you'll be this free." And Anne did. She not only rode before and after school, but often after dinner as well. There were a hundred miles of trails in the woods to explore.

In the freezing morning air, she pushed the zipper of her jacket to her neck. The soft old leather jacket, torn front and back by briars and patched many times with black electrician's tape, was given to her by her friend Mr. Lucian, owner of two horse trailers and her chaperone to all the barrel races. Retired now, Mr. Lucian told her stories of horse-and-buggy days in Pucam and of the old days on his farm. He came by for her on Saturdays with the double horse trailer behind his pickup and off they'd go, Lacy and Mr. Lucian's horse, Starlette, swishing tails out the back. Once he called her *Sweetheart*. That's what she thought he said. But no, *My sweetheart* was what he said, and leaned over and kissed her on the cheek. After that she was hesitant about going places with him, not sure if it was right. But he was old and, on occasion, foolish and easily forgiven. He forgot to wipe his mouth free of ketchup sometimes, but he cared about her horse. Clapped her on the back whenever she got a ribbon. Taught her everything she knew about riding. Made her feel beautiful on horseback, confident in handling any situation that came her way. Loving horses, he understood the mysteries of wildness and the taming of it. He was like a grandfather coaching her. The jacket was branded with his history, all the years she never tired of hearing about—when he drove the team in the fields at haying time and when his old goat jumped up on the chicken coop roof and leaped onto the roof of his Ford at the sight of company coming into the yard, and when the barn burned into the night while he led the cows to pasture, *ever one, Annie*. The jacket was the warmest thing she had.

She led Lacy to the post next to the saddle shed, the horse snorting steam in the cold. Slipping the bit into Lacy's mouth, she thought about braiding her mane for Saturday's race. Lacy's hoof clopped the ground, impatient to race the icy sunrise to full day like her own Pegasus ready to follow the flashing swords of sunlight that break through the bare branches and lay the world wide open. Yet, if you really looked hard and allowed the world to enter you, let yourself feel everything, it could consume you, might even kill you, draw you to its glare like the bright lights of oncoming cars that pulled you to the wrong side of the road. *Really seeing* was only for the very brave. Like Van Gogh who was not afraid to feel the intensity of energy swirling through the sky. You could pretend not to see it. Most people she knew slept life away, or looked down at the circle made by their own arms and never looked up to see the sun slash the night in two. She did, as if she had been appointed in some way. She and her father. Wasn't he out in the early morning, too? Stealing time? Living magnificently? Taking one minute and enlarging it until it hurt? Letting it fan out—starting from a blade of grass and staring and staring at it until the twisted edges of it hurt, the wrangled roots lay visible through the earth, its one single bladey life telling you all that you could possibly know about greenness, and reaching, and patience, and will?

Somehow she had gotten on the horse and was riding in the thick of the woods. Funny how your body went on without your mind. When they caught up with each other, though, it could hurt. Tree branches whipped across her face in the cold. Through the trees she saw her father's blue jacket, the chain saw on the ground. She reined Lacy in and stopped to the rustle of leaves. *Dad!* she wanted to call out but hesitated at the sight of him with his head in his hands, crouched on the log of the tree he'd just finished cutting.

He looked up. "Hey," he said. "Keep going, Annie. I'm okay. Don't ride here. I'm going to do one more before I go back to the house."

She waved in answer. She'd leave the woods and ride on the road. She knew what he felt. Knew from the curve of his back and his fingers that pressed into his head. Every day she felt the same, something coming down on her, raw edges that knifed her. She was different from other people, except for one other person and he was there in the woods. Behind her was the house, its clocks ticking away the sunrise, its cupboards opened, its bowls filled with steaming oatmeal, its familiar vibrations as lulling as the womb. She still had time before she had to go back.

Should he tell his mother? She was busy putting oatmeal into bowls, making it come out even for him and his brother. Davey scribbled on a piece of loose-leaf paper and stared into the open algebra book. Michael came into the kitchen and his mother said, "I'll drive you to school and

I'll call the bus driver, too. Wait for me after school, just for today, till I can get something worked out."

Michael said, "Mom, I can't find my shoes. I know I left them around here somewhere."

"By the pantry door? Probably were in Dad's way," said Davey. "He threw mine out the back door yesterday. Said he tripped over 'em. Glad it wasn't raining. They're the only ones that fit me."

Michael looked out the backdoor window. "What'd he do that for? There they are! Jesus! I'll do it to him, see how he likes it."

"Just get the shoes, Michael, and put them in the oven for a few minutes," said his mother, but she spoke to a slamming door.

He had to tell her now. Mr. Johnston might call today. Davey held his breath every time the phone rang last night. Maybe nothing would happen. But then maybe it would. There was no winning this one. Either he would get in trouble or Anne would.

He said, "Mom, Mr. Johnston said he'd call you."

"Now what?"

"He thinks I did something, but I didn't."

"Like?" Everything about her said *Hurry up, I'm late,* as she slammed cabinet doors and swept toast crumbs from the counter.

"There was this centerfold picture from *Playboy*? Somebody taped it to his map of Europe? And that somebody told us to ask lots of questions about World War II and get Mr. Johnston to show us on the map which cities were bombed the most? And when he pulled down the map he never looked at it and started pointing—he hates to take his eyes off us even for a second—and where he was pointing was at her crotch." He couldn't help it. He started giggling, turning his eyes away from his mother. It was worth it, worth the phone call home just to see old Johnston turn purple when he finally looked because everybody started snickering.

He watched her. She was going to laugh. Her laughs always started up around her eyes. Her cheeks got lighter; her whole face lifted, and there it was—the sound that set things right.

"So?"

"He thinks I did it, Mom."

"Did you?"

"I swear to God, it wasn't me. But I know who—it was Annie. She's got History right before me. She told me to get everybody to ask questions about Europe. Please don't tell her I told. Just tell Johnston it wasn't me, okay?"

She only said, "You want to ride with Michael and me? You'll be there a little early . . ." and glanced out the window to see if Anne was coming. She chewed on her top lip. He knew she was figuring how late she could possibly leave for work. Finally she scribbled a note to his father and left it on the kitchen table. It said, *Anne not back. Check on her.*

At four-fifteen, Rosemary left her classroom. The day of teaching had absorbed and calmed her. All that was right with the world was reflected in the honest exuberance of a classroom of five-year-olds. Teaching came naturally to her, an extension of herself. She rarely thought of home when she was with the children and she never thought of school when she was home. Just now, in the afterglow of a day with children, the woman with bothersome dreams and moonlit fears was nowhere in sight.

The winter sun was already slipping behind the trees, but as she turned the car toward home, she realized the darkness over the trees was not late winter afternoon darkness. Smoke billowed in a black arch from the direction of the house. She pressed down on the gas pedal. Justin. Had his growing impatience erupted in violence against himself? His compulsion beyond his control? Was he in the fire, laughing with his head thrown back, accomplishing a final protest and release? She was way past the speed limit.

Drawing near, she saw that the core of flames was higher than the house. The smell of smoke seeped into the car even though the windows were closed. Feeling foolish, she saw the fire was beyond their woods in the section belonging to the paper company that had harvested trees weeks before. Justin was in the driveway, smiling with his hands folded across his chest, his jeans baggy at the knees and the sleeves of his flannel shirt rolled up. "I'd open the windows and capture the heat, but the smoke goes with it," he joked as she pulled in. He was okay. She'd been dramatizing again. She would go mad with anxiety.

Michael. She'd forgotten to pick up Michael at school. She stayed in the car with the motor running. Justin went on.

"They're just burning the debris from the pines they harvested. Glad I got as much of the hardwood out of there as I did. You'll have enough for a few years."

"What do you mean, *I'll* have enough? *We'll* have enough for ten years, Justin."

He looked down. "Yeah."

"I have to pick up Michael," she said through the open car window. But that wasn't what she wanted to say. She wanted to reach up and kiss him for still being around. She wanted to ask him if he would see a doctor, the one he went to without telling her, or someone else, a counselor—anyone. But he would refuse. She rolled up the window, the glass between them an invisible wall through which they could hear each other's words but couldn't touch. All they could do was wait. He'd come back to his old self around June. There would be enough wood by then for fifteen years. There'd be a maze of firewood around the house. They could plant corn where their woods now stood.

Later, when she and Michael came back, the others were not home. Anne was probably riding, and Davey with his father somewhere. The kitchen was cold and smelled of smoke. "Michael, please light the wood-stove while I get dinner," she said into the arctic air. Out the window a scattering of flames flared at the base of a few remaining trees in what had been forest. The deliberate fire of her dream the night before haunted her as she stirred at the kitchen stove. Soon Anne came in wearing Mr. Lucian's jacket, the electrician's tape shining in the kitchen light like Band-Aids. Rosemary hadn't given her one single thought since morning. Life was like those fitful flares in the woods.

Tonight the snow was driving sideways across the windows. On the eleven o'clock news they said it would get down to six below. Everyone went to bed early except Michael and Davey, since it was Friday. They popped some corn and Michael said wouldn't it be neat if they got to go camping in the summer when he got the Chevy fixed. He said he'd take Davey to the mountains.

"I want to get off these flat fields," he said, "and look at rocks and boulders. I want to be up so high I can look down for miles into valleys and lakes and watch cloud shadows move. Maybe even run into a bear or two. We got to figure a way to cover our food."

"I think you're supposed to hang it in trees," Davey said, not that Michael ever listened to what he said. Then they heard the front door open and the wind rattle the downstairs doors. Michael stopped chewing popcorn for a second and turned his head but didn't get up—they both had their quilts wrapped around them and neither one wanted to unwrap. The fire in the woodstove was almost out. Davey got up and was about to close the front door when he saw Annie, barefoot and in her pajamas, run out in the snow. She was sobbing—it was hard to tell at first whether it was her or the wind. The snow was deep, the drifts past her knees. That slowed her down a little. When he got to her she sank down and screamed, "Leave me alone! Leave me!" Davey started to pull at her arms, then he tried to pick her up with his hands under her armpits but could only drag her a little way, and all the while she was screaming, "No, leave me!" He looked down at the pink flowers on her pajamas and watched them get buried one by one in the snow as she burrowed down. He yelled for Michael. "She's too heavy, Michael, Michael!" He didn't have to yell long because Michael was right behind him and threw a quilt over her and picked her up even though she was kicking and screaming—that is until she saw Mom in the doorway and went limp—his mother alone in the doorway with her eyes popped out and her mouth open, saying in her usual way, "What's going on?" and his father sleeping through everything in his usual way.

But it was Annie's face that got to him out in the snow. She pressed it together with her hands and in that minute she was stronger than he'd thought—pressing and squeezing her face in, just like that picture she sketched of herself with two clamps on either side of her head making her face go all out of shape till it was all cheeks and lips and her eyes were gone. It was the opposite of laughing. It was way past crying. Her eyes were gone. She was gone. And did she leave the door open because she wanted them to find her or did the wind push the door open? Because what if she'd kept on going? What if nobody knew she ran out in the snow like that? At school, everybody liked her. "You her brother?" they'd say. "She's funny. How does she think up that stuff so fast?"

After his father threw their shoes out the door, she tied his work boots together with a two-inch-thick knot and he laughed. Just sat down on the kitchen chair and threw his head back and laughed. That made them all laugh, as if it was catching. Michael loved the way she'd gotten him. And their father understood he'd been had. But it was okay, coming from her.

She wouldn't say what was upsetting her and not even Mom's arms around her, pleading with her to say what was wrong, could get anything out of her. She balled up her fists tight and stiff like she was going to punch somebody and cried some more. Mom just held her, not bothering to wipe the tears that slid down her own cheeks.

In March the whistling swans gathered in the fields before migrating. Justin and Rosemary went for a walk on a day that surely held the last of the icy wind. As they approached a flock pitched in the rye, the birds began to move away from them. The closest birds began to run and a ripple of motion ran through the rest of them until the nearest birds took flight, followed by the rest in a giant wave of white and gray, mottling the pewter-gray sky.

"Justin! Listen to that whistle. Why are they whistling—I mean, is it their call or is the sound coming from their wings?"

"It's just because they forgot the words," he said dryly. His eyes waited for hers to meet his. She laughed, caught in the pleasure of his joke and the graceful motion of the birds. He was coming back, earlier than expected. He was definitely better. The tide was turning. Just in time for spring.

That night was different from other nights. When they went to bed, he closed the door to their room quietly. There was no anger in the closing, no force, no demand, not even expectancy, only asking, and hunger born of months of isolation and darkness. "Thank you," he whispered in her ear, "for waiting and not giving up on me, for holding down the fort." He held her for a long time and slowly, slowly his hand traveled up and down her body as though he hadn't seen her for a long time. It was his homecoming, the Justin she'd married, and they were in the moonlight watching their shadows on the lawn, flowing easily past time and trouble except that he was flesh and she was flesh and yes, they were coming together now but first he was gentle, and whispering to her again and she who had waited was impatient, and came now too soon, and then he and then she again and they lay for a long time flowing into and out of sleeping and gently finding places again that were still waiting, wanting, receiving—and wanting more.

The woodcutting stopped. Hopelessness left him for no reason except it was time. Or was it the settlement of Evelyn's estate? With the money, he was able to pay off the farm mortgage and there was now a collection of stock certificates made out to Justin Williams in the safe deposit. He talked about getting a teaching degree, finding a job in the local high school. They were always looking for people with science backgrounds. Besides he and Rosemary would have long summer vacations together, like the old days down at Sulley's Point.

"I'm tired of grunt work," he said. "I'll wear a suit again."

She waited for a good time to talk to him—when he wasn't angry, or low, or so high he couldn't hear her—then she said, "It's something with a name, Justin. People take medication for it. You could be Lincoln or Churchill, and it could still happen. It's not your fault."

He made an appointment for the end of April.

When he returned, Rosemary, at the kitchen window, watched him get out of the truck. He'd lost the spring in his step again. Minutes later, he stood in the kitchen with tears in his eyes and his hands in his pockets, staring at her for a long time before saying anything.

"What, Justin? What is it?" She went toward him meaning to put her arms around him but he backed up. With his tan jacket zipped halfway up his chest and his collar open, he looked casual enough but strained.

"Doctor said it's a textbook case," he said finally. "I got pills."

She stopped breathing. Something slammed shut within her with a *no wonder* finality that didn't bring acceptance. She felt as if she'd been duped. "Well, at least we know," she said, in an outward show of wifeliness. "At least we can do something about it."

"Just when I was starting to feel good," he said. "Just when I was getting to the part I look forward to—the part that gets me through the other, I've got to take pills to dull it, take the cape off Superman." He shifted his weight and smacked the bottle of pills down on the counter. "If I'm a textbook case, why didn't any of the other doctors know? How come I had to go through all that stuff about my mother? Assholes! A pill. A goddamn pill! Can you believe it! It's been hell—all those years—I'd start something and never be able to finish. I'd just fold up—lose it—my whole life down the tubes. *Because I'm flawed!*"

If Justin's faith in himself was shattered, Rosemary's faith grew. He'd be okay now. Everything would settle down. He'd find work and stick with it. Medication would lower the highs, raise the lows, level their lives. Even keel, that's what they said. She'd read up on it.

He took the pills for one week. He was angrier than ever.

"You be home at nine o'clock, Michael, or you'll pay me a dollar for every minute past that." He didn't shout. He spoke in a quiet, steely band of words that made them all uneasy. Michael flinched. He'd worked in the fields hoeing watermelon vines at a dollar an hour after school. He had a crush on a girl who lived down on Dillon's Neck Road, seven miles away. Lisa. Every evening in the long dusk after work he rode his bike along the narrow roads to see her. "She's real pretty," he told Rosemary. "And she's not like any of the girls around here. She comes from Vermont."

Rosemary worried about Michael cycling along the dark road at night, but he'd always been careful, level-headed. There was never any traffic on that road anyway. With reflectors he'd be all right. However, Justin, waiting for nine o'clock to ambush Michael, was another matter. In the kitchen, Justin filled his glass with ice cubes and turned to look at the clock. Just nine. The hands of the clock stuck out like the wind telltale on the catamaran, sharp and black. She did not want those hands to move. "Did you plant beans today?" she said to his back. Justin was almost gleeful when he turned to her.

"Five rows. Peas, too."

Michael arrived ten minutes after the hour. Rosemary watched him stand on one pedal, ready to leap off the bike as he rode in. He threw the bike against the shed and ran toward the house. Wordlessly, Justin held his hand out, palm up.

Michael glanced at him, at the clock, and back. "Aw, Dad," he said. "It's only ten minutes."

"That's right. Only ten bucks."

Michael charged to his room in fury, adding this new anger to rage he already harbored. In his absence, she said, "Justin, that's a bit much, don't you think? I mean, he did try to get home on time. It's a seven-mile ride."

"What do you want?" Justin sneered. "You want me to handle it, don't you?"

"Not like that. Have a heart, will you?"

"Stay out of it, goddamn it!"

The flush on Michael's cheeks, the wall of his top lip, his glare at his father's outstretched hand, the way he refused to look his father in the eye as he swung around the kitchen door frame on the way to his room—Rosemary knew she would see that hatred again and again. She heard Michael stomp to his room and imagined him taking the envelope that held his pay out of the nightstand drawer, the money for parts for the Chevy spread on the bed, him picking out a ten. When he came back down he lay the money in his father's hand and shrugged his shoulders, looking to the side, not at either of them, his face blank in the stark fluorescence of the kitchen light.

"Are you taking the pills?" Rosemary asked Justin the next morning, stirring coffee, her leg swinging under the table.

He glared at her, stopping in the middle of his egg. "What kind of question is that? What right have you? Telling me what to do? Taking charge? Laying down rules?" He half-sobbed out the words, "It's my body. Got it? You don't have any right to tell me what to do with it. Lay off, hear me?" He shot up and pounded the wall with his fist. The wallboard buckled. "Stuff makes me sick, do you hear me? I'm nauseous every minute I'm awake. How would you like to go around like that? Go around tasting a mouthful of salt?" He was over at the silverware drawer now. "How would you like to be told you're nuts? That's what it is, you know. Loony. Where's the goddamn can opener? Well, where is it? Aw, fuck it." He pulled the drawer all the way out and turned it over. The clatter of silverware seemed to satisfy him. He dumped the drawer on top of the pile on the floor and turned to leave, kicking open the storm door. The wind caught it and made a wide berth for him to exit.

She had hoped for too much. "What about me?" she screamed into dead space. "I've been holding you up, buddy! If you don't take the pills for yourself, how about taking them for me and the kids?"

She picked up the forks and spoons and knives and put them back in their compartments, laying the smooth round cups of the spoons against each other. As she slid the drawer back in its place, her heart matched the slam of wood against wood. She couldn't deny it—more than the drawer had been shut.

Mr. Lucian had a stroke. Her mother drove her out to his farm, and when she entered his room, she realized by the way he stared past her that he didn't know who she was. Half sitting up in bed, he played nervously with the sheet with his stubby old hands. It frightened her to see him like that. At first he didn't even look at her. His red, pocked nose had turned pale like a plant without enough light. "Whoa! Whoa!" he said over and over. His hands fiddled with the sheet until he held a pleat between each finger. The long folds ran down to his toes like reins—he was driving the team at haying time. She could see him as he saw himself—high up on the wagon with the sun beating down on him. Once he stopped and looked at her and called her Lily, someone he knew before he married Elizabeth. For God sakes, he said, Lily, sit down. Sit closer, girl!

They didn't stay long although Miss Elizabeth assured them it was all right to stop in anytime they wanted. "Some days he's better," she said, looking at him fondly and patting his hand.

In the car going home, Anne jabbered about school, about horses, about anything—just to keep on talking—to hold back the flood of fear about Mr. Lucian—and herself—what a jumbled mess she was. She couldn't help it when she got like this—she just couldn't help it. Her mom said quietly, "I know how bad you must feel about Mr. Lucian, Annie. He probably isn't going to be well enough to go to races anymore." But that wasn't it and there was no way to tell her mother how odd she felt. There was a change; it came in spurts. Right now, she was going faster and faster as if she were riding downhill on her bike when she didn't need to pedal— her feet turning much faster than the wheels—until she was actually fly- ing—way ahead of everyone. She knew it wouldn't last. She'd only have to wait, and then she'd feel better after a while, but she didn't know what she might do in the meantime. She felt as though she was flying toward the sun—might even burn up in it—she had so much energy—she couldn't stop—couldn't stop. When they got home she jumped out of the car and ran up to her room and took the penny jar from its place on the bookcase and threw it against the mirror which shattered like she was shattering— and she couldn't stop herself from doing it—or stop herself from smashing and smashing her fist into the pillow—crying to let some of it out— trapped inside a whirlwind—and her spinning around and around—till all she could do was scream and scream—and see her mother at the door—stooping to pick up glass and pennies scattered everywhere—hear her fear—hear her shriek, *Annie, are you all right? Are you hurt?* And, *What is it?* Then, *Stop it! Do you hear me? Stop it right now!*—as if she could stop. Her mother looked at her so horrified she knew she was a hor- rible, wild monster and she leaped at her mother across the broken glass hitting and hitting to keep her from watching—to shut her up—shut her up—*your feet, your feet,* she said—so what if she cut her feet to shreds— so what—she didn't care because she was strong—stronger than anyone— could kill if she wanted to and the killing would not make her sorry—did- n't care who got in her way—not even her mother—till finally, the screaming and crying and blood and broken glass and pennies and her mother's grip on her arms so fierce shaking her till she was dizzy and bro- ken and still and wanting not to remember.

It was beyond reason. Or was it grief over Mr. Lucian? Was it just teenage hysteria, raging hormones? Justin looked in on Anne that night, and came out of her room shrugging his shoulders. Anne cried until she fell asleep, exhausted. Harrowing as the incident was, she seemed okay in the morning. In fact, there were no more upsets. In the spring, she became queen of the Rodeo Riders and rode in the May Parade in Pucam. Mr. Lucian sat in a wheelchair on one of the front porches on Main Street with Miss Elizabeth and waved at Anne who sat pale and tense under a cowgirl hat, her dark hair in strings at her shoulders, the yellow ribbon across her chest fluttering in the wind. *Queen,* it said.

Michael had the Chevy running. He'd sanded down the old blue paint to make the car ready for a new coat. A few more afternoons of hoeing and he'd have enough for the paint. Light blue, he said. He'd earned his license, and bought a rifle from a friend after the Gun Safety class was over.

They got through, thought Rosemary as she took down the quilted covers on the north windows and filled the sills with seed pots. They'd slipped into regular life calmed by the first heat of May billowing through the open windows. Justin, too, was changing pace. He was onto something, he said, some kind of financial advisor business but he was vague about the details. People called him and left messages on the new answering machine. He had files of customers' names and addresses and free giveaways as well as presentations to prepare. Rosemary offered her help in getting papers into folders and keeping track of appointments. "Don't touch that answering machine," he bellowed one afternoon when she listened to the messages. "That's none of your business."

This afternoon they'd be driving to the mall in two cars, he told her, as he had a meeting later in the evening. He needed her to help him pick out slacks to go with his new blazer. He was agitated. He snapped his fingers and cracked his knuckles in a continuous drumroll as he waited for her to shut the windows in case of rain. His ears were dark red and he talked louder than he needed to. "Are you ready? How come you're not ready yet?"

"Go on, then," she said. "I'll meet you by the fountain in the mall."

He sped down the lane. Only two months ago he'd coasted down that same lane to save gas. "Don't accelerate before you get to the mailbox, Rosemary," he'd said as the car rolled at five miles an hour. But now, the blue Honda disappeared beyond a plume of dust.

At the mall, the sound of rushing water at the fountain always pleased her, but now there was another sound—a chain saw whining above a gathering crowd. She strained to see. A huge log stood on end as a young man pressed the saw around its middle. He was sculpting, chips flying everywhere. A huge pile of them lay at the base of the log. His sleeves were rolled up to his elbows, the movements of his arms and hands quick, sure. He swung the chain saw as if it were a sword. Digging into the bark with brief jabs, the saw buzzed steadily like on cold mornings when Justin worked in the woods, only now the saw was roaring in her ears. She could not get her eyes off the log, the cut-away bark, the exposed yellow-white wood and the evolving shape. Justin was at her elbow.

"There you are! Come on!"

"Wait a minute," she said. "Let's see what he does."

The cuts in the wood were short, jagged, furlike. Miraculously, ears appeared and the shape of a head, then a face, fur-lined. A snout. Maybe it was a bear—a bear leaping out of the log. The sculptor sprang from side to side as he worked on opposite sides of the bear at once, work boots rocking unsteadily on the growing pile of wood chips. His hands never paused. Hands like Justin's. Now there was a cream-colored bear, its mouth open and teeth bared, ready to charge. The man, the strap of his goggles across the back of his head pinning down the wildness of his dirty-blond hair, his beard trembling with the force of the chain saw, his effort beautiful in the face of the effortless crowd, this man having released the bear from the wood quieted the chain saw and pulled off his goggles. He looked straight at Rosemary and smiled. The crowd applauded. How could a simple smile bring her to tears? She wanted to be held by someone. That's all. Just held. She was shaken, but she would be all right in a minute. Just let me walk in the footsteps of the shuffling crowd again, she thought. Let me hang onto a shopping bag or two. She would get her bearings again.

Justin was gone. She had no idea when he had slipped from her side. But in reality, he'd left ages ago. Before the chain saw, before the planting of a thousand black locust trees, before the laying of the Great Wall of China, before the speech in Annapolis. Maybe he'd never really been there at all.

Oh, he'd come back for a day or two. But he was only passing through, flying headlong, pell-mell into the great upsurge, the big ascent up—up— and up that he loved. He felt so good, he said. Gone was the doubt, the rhythmic absorption to stay alive, the inability to decide. He was magnificent. A new career, another crack at making his mark. He would make the most of his short-lived glory. Who would he be this time?

She searched for the next two hours, all the men's stores, the shoe stores, the four big department stores. She waited till the mall closed and the security guard approached.

"Ma'am? The doors are all locked but one. If you're waiting for someone, you'll have to wait outside." His dark mustache was stiff and trim.

When they left, Justin's Honda was not in the parking lot.

She lay on the bed in her best white nightgown in case he should come home. The moon was full again, a blue moon. May had a blue moon. Once in a blue moon. It crept through the clumps of leaves in the red maple outside her window, sending its pale light across her and the sheet and the wicker dressing table. Then the whippoorwill began. Every May he was back in the same tree outside their bedroom, staking his territory and calling for a mate in his piercing, shrill way. As soon as she turned off the light, he began his continuous round, often stopping on *whip*—while she lay tense and annoyed, waiting—*poorwill!* She sandwiched her head between two pillows so she couldn't hear it. A bird not visible by day and making its presence known by sending out its perpetual, insistent, unheeded call now, made sleep an impossibility and filled her with contempt. She had no idea what a whippoorwill looked like, but knew it was ugly. Some longings were never fulfilled. Were hers? In the end, did it matter?

Michael stomped down the hall. "Want me to get him, Mom? Before he drives us all nuts?"

"The best you can do is scare him off, Michael."

The gunshot rang through the woods and echoed. The bird stopped, but they were all wide awake now. Davey and Anne ran from their beds as Michael trudged upstairs with the gun. "I think I got him for you, Mom."

Silence fell around them and restored the house to its place among the trees, sons and daughter and sheets fluttering down again to dreams. But in the distant deep woods, Rosemary heard again, faint but distinct, *whippoorwill, whip*—and missed Justin breathing next to her. For the first time, Rosemary knew she was alone. This was neither good nor bad; she would just have to think about it.

The boys were quiet at breakfast. Anne was combing down her horse.

"Where do you think he is, Mom?" Davey asked.

"I don't know. Maybe he's still trapped in the mall. Maybe he fell asleep in a movie."

"Or maybe he's showering in the fountain or trying out a new vibrating chair."

She smiled at him. "Are you riding with me or taking the bus this morning?" She needed Davey's constancy. Watching him stir his cornflakes helped. Listening to Davey's feet tapping softly on the kitchen floor, to his fingers drumming the table, she tried to match the rhythm to something she knew.

"What song is that?" she asked.

"Don't know yet, but I can hear it. Comes out a different way every time." He looked up at her, his mouth grinding cornflakes.

Rushing home after school, Rosemary told herself she'd see the Honda in the driveway. The fields lay freshly plowed; seagulls settled on the brown earth behind the grinding tractors. It was a good day to work in the garden, dividing the old coreopsis and Shasta daisies, maybe plant some seeds.

Justin's car was nowhere in sight. Michael was under the Chevy. His work boots stuck out so Rosemary spoke to them.

"What are you doing home this early?"

"Didn't need me today. Dad was here and drove off as I came up the lane."

In the dining room, she dropped her briefcase on the table and climbed the stairs to their bedroom looking for a note along the way. The louvred door to Justin's side of the closet was open and suddenly she was staring at the back wall, disbelieving its emptiness. On the floor lay the camping sheet.

This was new. The new Justin. She only needed to wait, of course. He would come back when he came diving down. He would need her then. Yet there was finality written in the newness of his leaving. She could sense it in the scent of charred wood borne by the afternoon breeze and in the silence of the long, brown seed rows that began below the bedroom window and ran singular and solitary, forever parallel, on and on and on. That they converged somewhere in the distance was only an illusion.

He had brought them here to backwoods country, to this house at the end of the corn rows, and left them. The clothes on her side of the closet were crammed. She slipped her hands among them so she could take an armful and spread them, still on their hangers, to Justin's side — things she hadn't worn in years.

Part Four

TORNADO YEARS

THOSE FUNNEL-SHAPED CLOUDS

The children's bright paintings lined the walls in bursts of red, blue, and yellow, each with suns like flowers, petals radiating, pure and dependable. In this room she was the best she could ever hope to be, the children in her heart, her purpose single-minded. There wasn't a problem she couldn't solve. And oh, how she loved the faces turned to her like sunflowers. *Miss Williams! Miss Williams! I need the paste! He hit me! My tooth is loose. Can I be the leader?*

Yet, she was two selves: one functioning, the other, remembering the sight of that empty closet, its back wall marked with scuffs from tossed shoes. Hearing, *I spilled my paint! He spilled his paint on my shoe! Isn't my picture beautiful? Do you like it?* she saw Justin's head on the pillow, his back to her. He snored beneath a child's words—*What does this word say, Miss Williams? How many numbers in one hundred?* He filled the constant iced tea glass, the one with the orange and yellow stripes, the ice cubes chinking as he made his way to his workbench. *Is this fourteen or forty-one? Miss Williams? How many more days till summer?* Across the breakfast table, he peered at the thermometer outside the window, his silence accentuated by his drumming knee.

She felt a small hand on her back work its way to her neck, like Justin's hand on the back of her neck, rubbing his thumb back and forth. When was the last time he'd done that, looked at her, held her hand, put his arms around her as she stood at the sink washing dishes? Each action with its own last time. The small hand paused. "Samantha," she said. "You have a long name. You still need to put t-h-a." Turning her head, she said, "Who hit first? Chris, put your tooth in this envelope and save it for the tooth fairy." And to B.J., "I already have a leader, thank you." Her anger funneled toward Steven, who stood with his hands behind his back watching purple paint drip off the table. "Don't just stand there and watch it drip! Get the sponge!" Quieter, sweeter, "I love your picture and so will your mom." Pause. "That says, 'round and round.'" They went round and round in a kaleidoscope, the colors breaking into new arrangements. In her turmoil, she was only sure of the large red bow in Samantha's hair.

Then Jason, his face screwed up, bawled outrage at Teddy, who punched him again and again with fists drawn like a prizefighter. *I walk through minefields,* she thought, calling out, "Excuse me! Teddy, Jason — stop it!" They never heard her. Teddy's face beamed with satisfaction. Rosemary reacted with a violence rooted in long ago, which overtook good sense and everything she'd learned since. Grabbing Teddy's fists, she stopped the blows midair, and held the wrists too tight as she knelt down, glaring into his face.

"Why?" she asked, but not just him. She asked Justin, God, the world, her mother, her aunts, her own children, herself and the bright yellow suns on the wall, "Why?"

Teddy pulled back. She held tighter. She spit out words in a half whisper. "Don't you ever do that again. Do you hear me? Don't you ever, ever, ever —"

He glared at her, waiting for her to let go. "We don't hit people in here, do you understand? Say you're sorry. Say it." Silence. "I'm waiting, Teddy." More silence. Teddy stared at the wall in back of her. The other children stood quietly around them. She let go of the small wrists. To her dismay, there were red marks like bracelets.

She led the children down the hall to lunch. The red bracelets swung back and forth, back and forth. They passed Ed Hagerty, the principal. He stood in the hallway, hands folded across his chest, staring out the window with eyes that disappeared behind the reflections on his glasses. He was thinking of his golf game, which meant they could pass like ghosts and he'd never notice the red marks of her unraveling. He knew nothing about her, least of all that she would injure a child. She wished she could tell him. Tell someone.

Tell what? That Justin left? That he was so far out of his head he was a total stranger? That he had become many different people over the years? That she had tried to become whatever person he needed for who-ever he became? That as she faced the walls of her classroom, she no longer knew who she was? If she told Hagerty, he would look at her in dis-belief, for she had an excellent reputation, and then he'd look for evidence that would enable him to fill out the evaluation form, translate her into educational terminology. He would write in his precise letter-perfect hand, *Needs improvement in classroom management and educationally acceptable standard practices for behavior control.* He'd sign his name and hand her the pen. Now, the sun glanced off his watch with its wristband of flying mallards and shone in the rectangle of light where he'd planted his Docksiders. What did he know of minefields? When his eyes met hers, he nodded at the quiet passing of five-year-olds in a straight line, and because he smiled, she wanted to strangle him. His blissful power over her. His cool. His detachment from the real work, the down-in-the-trench-es labor she'd always done for Justin, for her kids, for her students.

Jason stopped to tie his shoe and Teddy tripped over him. J.R. belted Teddy with his lunch box, which spilled out on the floor. She had always done what she should. Her life had not been hers. She was a puppet on strings moving to someone else's pull. Every eye turned to see what she would do. She wanted to hit them—those expectant faces, especially J.R.'s, feigning innocence as he turned to her with his wide-eyed explana-tion, "It was a accident."

She stopped in the patch of sun in which Hagerty stood. She looked into hazel eyes made small by the thick glasses, surrounded by a pool of hippopotamus skin. He'd retire soon, which was why he waited by the front door warming himself in the sun.

"Ed," she said. "I don't feel well. I need to go home. Think you can get someone for half a day?"

He blinked, nodded *yes.* The mallards on his wrist flew up from his khakis and he rubbed his chin. "Yes, of course. Hope you feel better. We'll call a substitute."

She continued down the hall. J.R. retrieved his raisin box and sandwich wrapped in plastic. She thought about clutching her chest and staggering into Hagerty's office, gasping, *Call an ambulance, will you?* Collapsing at his feet, she'd hear him say, *What is it? Can you tell me? Hold on! You'll be all right. Help is coming!*

On the drive home, the scent of honeysuckle along the edge of the woods soothed her. Now the fields, like patchwork. Watermelon vines burgeoning into indistinguishable rows. Now the ripening rye, turning gold, and corn, leaves clicking, pointing. Asparagus, feathery. Now the mailbox at the end of their long lane. The crunch of black shale under the tires. Now the pasture, Lacy prancing along the fence, agitated for some inexplicable reason. The dog, jumping on her, the heavy paws on her hip, the heat of the sun emanating from the broad brown back. "Down," she said, but the dog jumped on her again and again—"Down, down!" Now the doorknob, the familiar shush as the door shut out May warmth and May light. Justin's boots in the pantry, mud caked at the soles, laces trailing. This time yesterday, he'd still been here. Collecting clothes. Forgetting boots. Looking through the mail. Leaving bills. Leaving. Without a word.

Upstairs, she lay down on Anne's bed, in the room overlooking a sea of rye that rippled toward Pucam, to houses with couples in them and unbroken families. She lay listening to the empty house to see if she could stand it. He'll come back, she told herself.

There was comfort in Annie's room, in her sketches and paintings of the farm and the surrounding landscape. She had recorded the permanence of things, the primal wild Eden the farm had become—the old trees, the depth of woods, the fruit trees around the pond, the wide sky over the corn. The paintings held promise of technique to come and revealed Annie's observant, sensitive eye. Even the pitted road to Pucam had its moment in her hands. But it was Anne's renditions of the sky that held Rosemary. Dappled with varying shades of pink, violet, blue and even red, churning with energy, they were an exploration of depth, spaces where you could lose yourself. Staring into one of them, Rosemary fell asleep.

Doors slammed. Wind tore the trees. Groggy, she glanced at the clock on the dresser. Two-thirty—too dark for afternoon and not dark enough for night. Out the window she saw a purple wall of storm cloud so menacing she knew it was no ordinary squall. Lacy reared along the gate to the pasture. Rosemary would have to bring her to the shed, something she'd never done before. An agitated horse led by someone unaccustomed to the task—she wished Anne was home. She ran downstairs, stepped into Justin's boots, and clodhoppered out.

The dog cowered under the car. Rain pelted the dusty lane. In the pasture, Lacy reared again and again. The latch on the gate was stubborn. Not able to budge the crossbar, Rosemary kicked the gate with strength she didn't know she had. The latch broke; the gate swung open hitting Lacy on the rump. She galloped across the pasture, turned sharply and galloped toward Rosemary, nostrils flaring, her mane driven in spikes along her neck by the rain. She slowed down, thank God. *Hey girl, hey, okay, hey, okay*, said Rosemary, slapping the wet hide and grabbing the halter. Miraculously, Lacy tossed her head and pranced beside her, becoming Rosemary's anchor in the wind. On the other side of the yard, a tree, over a foot in diameter, snapped at the trunk, leaving shards of wood on the lawn.

Rosemary clung to the horse's halter as if it were a lifeline. Once in the shed, Lacy put her great soft nose into the feed bucket. The sound of grinding corn and oats steadied Rosemary but even when Lacy tossed her head again and again, wrenching her arm, her hand stayed frozen to the blue strap. With her other arm she toweled down the wet hide, the oily, horse-smell hide, the short hairs pasted slick to the horse-smell skin. With the terrifying wind howling around them, Lacy's hooves stamped the straw too close to her feet. She concentrated on keeping them out of the way, and on the sound of grinding corn, the black eye above her, the white eyelashes, the gray-white hide, the hairs inside Lacy's ears. Yet even when the rain lessened and the wind weakened, her hand clenched the strap.

She peered out the half door of the shed at the stirred-up yard, the twisted grass, the cosmos face down in the mud along the driveway, the scattered branches, half-grown tomato plants pulled up by the roots. The toolshed door hung by one hinge. Two roofing shingles sat on the back step. Yet she was all right, the house still stood, and she'd gotten the horse in the shed on her own. Water gushed from the drainpipes, the sound reminding her of water pouring down the stairs years ago, when Justin waited on the landing. Justin. Would memory forevermore be an unwelcome guest?

The next day, the *Chronicle* said two tornadoes had ripped through the area. Aerial photographs showed felled trees lying like pick-up sticks in the woods. A Mr. Otis Abbott was killed sitting in his living room in Pucam as he read the paper; a two-by-four had rammed through the wall and hit him in the head. However, the school bus brought the kids home on schedule that afternoon. They reported a splattered chicken in the parking lot at school, corrugated tin roofs littering the road, and cardboard boxes and wooden pallets clinging to telephone poles. The last tornado in the area had occurred sixty years before.

Grocery shopping on Friday night, women from isolated farmhouses and small towns shared news with their elbows leaning on loaded carts. In the cereal aisle, Rosemary met Ali, the mother of one of her students. Thin as a marsh reed, her narrow shoulders hidden by long, straight black hair, Ali swung her youngest into a shopping cart and greeted Rosemary. Sean, her middle child, hadn't been in school for two days. They were checking him out in Northern General for a blow to his head, Ali said. He'd been in the Buick with her when the tornado hit. They were directly in its path.

"They say it sounds like a train, and it did. I heard the sound before I realized anything, like I was parked on the track and the train was coming towards me. Next thing I know the car was picked up in the air and I was screaming for Sean to get under the dash as we went over the telephone wires. The car landed in the middle of the field. I was sucked out the window so I got a few bruises and scratches. That's all, though. I was lucky. Stunned, you know. And then came the rain. I guess that's what woke me up. I saw Debbie—you know her? Lives across the field in that white bungalow? She came crawling on her hands and knees like she was holding onto the rye to keep from being blown away. I yelled to her to go to the car to find Sean—make sure he was all right. She found him still under the dash. It was a time," she said with a shake of her head.

"You were sucked out of the car window?" said Rosemary.

Ignoring her, caught up in her story, Ali said, "Sean bumped his head when the car landed—on all four wheels, hubcaps flying. I remember watching those hubcaps roll down the rows and thinking Tommy, my husband, wasn't going to like those fifty-dollar hubcaps missing. Funny, the things you think of when you can't take in what's really happening." She smiled. The purple bruise on her cheek buckled; her eyes stayed wide, still scared. "A whole lot of things could have happened. The car could have landed on me, Sean could have fallen out. Debbie could have got swept up crawling across the field like that. Whole lot of things. Really makes you stop and think."

Incredible. *Woman rides tornado and lives to tell about it. Sent round and round the tornado's spiral like a speck going down the drain only in reverse. Up—pulled up into tornado fury. Then dropped. Discarded. Her rag doll body plummets down, smacks the earth, mouth fills with mud, grit between her teeth.*

Ali backed up and tossed her hair from her shoulder with her hand. She glanced at the child in the shopping cart and put her other hand on his knee. "I don't remember anything about landing in the field," she said. "When they came to get me, I was talking out of my head. I'm not driving yet. Tommy had to drive me here. He's out in the car, waiting."

Carried on a prevailing wind and finding herself dumped in the middle of a field, too, Rosemary was comforted to see the affirmation of catastrophe in another woman's face, and feel a victimish sisterhood.

"I'm glad you're okay, Ali," she said. "Sean, too. The class will celebrate when he gets back."

One afternoon weeks later, Justin came home. He walked in as if he'd never left, lifted the cover of the Tupperware container expecting chocolate cake. Finding it, he cut a piece and poured himself a glass of milk. His blue-and-white-striped sport shirt, unbuttoned to the waist, revealed a gold medallion hanging from a chain around his neck, and his heels clicked on the kitchen linoleum. Snapping his fingers, he strutted through the downstairs rooms, breathing arrogance, ready to spring. She hated him, hated the snapping fingers and center-of-the-universe assumption he'd undertaken. Who the hell did he think he was? An apparition, crossed wires of the man she'd married, whose children she had carried. He had the same features and height and build—he *looked* like Justin—but no, he wasn't, not in the eyes. There blazed intensity, rage and frenzy, demands, and cruelty. What had she done to provoke this? As if she were that powerful. As if she had any say in anything at all. She would be left with the responsibilities he chose to leave her with—the bills, the goddamn farm with its back against the woods, a whole way of life she'd not asked for and had consented to with her silence. Her compromising. She could not say any of this, and now it was too late. He would not hear her anyway. She was as significant to him as a fly on the wall.

"Where's my mail?" he said.

It didn't feel like he was coming to stay even though it felt like he'd never left. He propped his feet on the coffee table and dug into the cake. Unable to deal with the shock over who he was now, she was still trying to bring him to his senses.

"I've found somebody else," he said. She didn't know if the floor was firm enough—she might slip between the boards to the cellar below. Disappear. Dissolve. To tears. She fought them back. He was Enemy—from husband to Enemy in so brief a time. He was ill—surely he was—and she'd been expecting normalcy, reason.

"You should too," he was saying around a mouthful of cake. "Nothing like it." He scraped the plate clean and set it on the coffee table. The fork clattered to the floor but he ignored it. His eyes jumped from chair to chair, to the wall, but not to her. He folded his arms across his chest and pulled his feet from the coffee table. She waited and watched as he leaned his elbows on his knees. The medallion swung away from his chest when he leaned forward and, rising from the couch, glanced at her coldly, then looked away. "I'll be back for my mail." Her eyes never left his face, detesting him, fearing him. "Where are you staying?" she asked, although she didn't expect an answer. He ignored the question and turned as if he would come towards her. For a second there was a flicker of recognition; the green eyes blinked. But no. He sidestepped her. "You can do it," he said to the wall.

"Wait a minute," she said. "Just like that? That's it? More than half a lifetime and that's it? Stop it," she shrieked. "Think! Come back, wherever you are. You're lost! Don't you understand? Justin, this is me! This is our life!" He shrugged. Brushing her aside, he clicked his heels on the linoleum again. She followed him. When he pushed open the door without looking at her, it was as if he'd sucked all the breath out of her.

She watched him run down the steps and wave to Davey standing at the shop door. He climbed into the Honda. Nothing here concerned him anymore. The medallion flashed. She watched Davey move toward the car, heard him call to his father, "Hey, Dad, wait a minute!" but the car door slammed and the engine revved. Davey looked toward the house and saw her at the window. His look said, *What did you say to make him go?* and Rosemary looked back, Davey's face blurred by her tears. "Davey, Davey, I'm so sorry, Davey," she said under her breath.

Smooth. Like I'd always done it. "Lookin' for somebody?" I said. Oldest line in the world. Couldn't believe it'd be so easy—her sitting at the bar, blonde hair puffed out like cotton candy, chin on the heel of her hand, swaying her shoulders like she wanted to dance, rhythm rippling down to her hips. She parted those legs for me two hours later. Wide. With her kids sleeping in the other room.

Little kids. I always did like little kids. My own are teenagers, rebels, pains in the ass. I don't like big people much. Hard to close a deal. But little kids trust you and look up expecting something good. Like she did, that bleached hair sticking out from her scalp, caught in a black velvet bow, teased a bit but smooth, in place.

Is that it, or isn't it? Well, it's the whole shtick. Everybody's doing it. Everybody except Rosemary—Rosemary, her legs locked when she comes to bed, if she comes at all—her damned stony stares when I feel so alive— bursting through my skin. Hard. Always hard. Just looking at women in the mall makes me hard. I've never looked better, felt better—coming into my own after years of being on the outside looking in, trying to make a million, watching chances slip away. It's possible now. I know it. A change in the wind, a turn in the tide, an eclipse of the moon.

She's a good luck piece, this happy-go-lucky freebird. She doesn't belong having kids or a drunk for a husband. She's ready to bite off success, like me. Always did believe a good-looking woman made a man, made him believe in himself, smoothed out the rough edges, pumped him up. Blonde. Jesus, she looks like a million, the smile line under those plump cheeks swelling out from under her shorts like the line that spreads beneath her breasts where they rub against her ribcage. I can feel that fold whenever I please and fuck and fuck and fuck some more and she comes and comes and comes. Jesus. I coulda died without knowing what that feels like!

Rosemary—always cold. Feet like blocks of ice, toes sharp as icicles. Talk to me, she says. Nothing to talk about, I say. How do you feel about it, she says. So I feel her and she pushes me away. Doesn't that count, I ask her? Not in front of the kids, she says. Serves her right. Her face all swollen. Crying. You'll get over it, I tell her. You can do it, I tell her. Quit leaning on me. Off my back. The whole stinking farm. Leaking pipes—termites—peeling paint—kids out of control—wife taking over—my life sucked away. Through with that. Hear? Through. I don't get mad, I just get even. Her silence. Her stony stares. She'll hear some silence now all right.

She wants the car window up. Says she's cold. I need air, I tell her. It's suffocating in here. She rolls the goddamn window up. Says it's April and raining. I lean across and put the window all the way down. Mine too. You got a problem with that? I tell her.

Sexy as the kitchen table. What's the matter with you, she says, and sends me off to the shrink. Are you taking your pills, she says? Rod up her ass. Looking down on me. Like telling me I'm crazy. Fuck her. Think I want to miss this part? Miss *this lady*—this blonde dynamite? Think I'd bypass this flight to the moon? You're the one that's nuts, Rosemary. You just don't know. I'm blasting off. Flying high. I wouldn't miss this for the world. See you later. Hear?

I'm changing worlds. Me. Willy Nobody down on the farm. No job in five years. I gotta ride this, don't you see? Make the most of it before I crash. If I could only tell you so you'd understand. But you just lie there with your legs locked, shivering. Lips sealed. The martyr. Stiff and superior. Thinking you have me by the balls. You got another think coming. Babe. Used to be, Babe. You coulda had it all if you'd just come with me. But you're stuck.

You're doing it all, you tell me. So now you can have it all. Adios.

Jesus. I'm doing eighty. Cops'll be riding my tail. Windows open all the way. *Got that, Rosemary? Wide open. Somebody's waitin' for me who's wide open.*

He was gone. Dropped out of sight as if he'd died. She waited for him, expecting to see him march in one day and call her Skinny Annie again.

Weeks passed. Finally, a letter, *A. W. Ellison, Esq.* on the letterhead. Peering over her mother's shoulder, she read, *advise you to seek counsel, unfortunate marital situation, commence negotiations.* Her mother's face turned white as she folded the letter.

"Come on, Ma," she said as if coaxing a horse to its feet. "Let's clear that piece between the house and the pond. We can at least make a path." Encouraged by heavy spring rains, vines had crept toward the house. She used to see the pond from the kitchen, the ducks and herons on still mornings, now hidden by a wall of green. The south field, too, lay tall with weeds. Annie remembered the day her father swung a sickle out there when the tractor quit, suddenly throwing it to the ground where it stayed for weeks. "I can't do this," he said, chewing his lip. She'd never heard those words from him before.

"Come on, Ma," she said again.

"How will I manage alone?" she said, the words slow and plodding.

"You've been managing alone for years." Bizarre, wasn't it, that her mother thought she'd been dependent on her father when he hadn't been *present* for a long time now? She still saw him as he *used* to be, if he ever did exist as her mother believed. Now he was out somewhere getting a new family. Tara, at school, had seen him down at the cottage at Sulley's Point, his arm around a blonde woman with two little kids. Did he think he could switch? Trade them off like a new herd? And Tara at school, gossiping about it with her round flat face slit in the middle by a wide smile, stupid Tara who looked like one of those dancing grapes on TV, telling it as if she was talking about the lunch menu — *by the way, saw your old man all over this blonde.* How gross of her to say that when she wasn't even what you would call a friend. "Oh, shut up," Anne had said, realizing her words would whip past Tara and the news would be repeated in Pucam, at the Food City, the post office, the firehouse, the drugstore, along the narrow streets, and across the sputtering telephone wires. God, she hated Pucam, the road to Pucam, the mind-set of Pucam, the morality of its white steeples and the mortality of its empty storefronts, the inevitability permeating Pucam that could only be relieved by half-truths and spicy tidbits.

She told Michael what Tara said. Michael went down to the Point to check things out. He was super quiet and serious when he came back. He went into Dad's shop and didn't come out for a long time.

"Come on, Ma."

"Right now?"

"Yeah. I'll get the ax and pruning shears." Distract her. Make her walk to the edge of the lawn and start a project, she thought, as she watched her mother pin the letter to the bulletin board on the kitchen wall where she always put business on hold—sticky business she had no idea what to do about, that might even resolve itself or diminish in importance.

Together they peered into the dense jungle of vines and puzzled at the impenetrable strength of the green wall, a tangle of briars, blackberry vines, honeysuckle, young locusts with leaves in sprays of flat, round disks that hid thorns inches long. She watched her mother pull one small branch and clip it off, then handfuls, and hurl them to a pile for burning later. Anne chopped at the shallow runner roots with the ax, but the sound made her think of her father and the giant tree root, his hands and the sorrow in his face. Did his leaving begin then?

Anne chopped away, but the ax sprang back. They needed the chain saw. Dad had been the only one to use it; she'd watched him a million times. She could do it. Her mother pulled at a long rope of honeysuckle with the weight of her whole body. When the rope gave way, she fell back on her rump, feet sprawled. A shriek, then laughter. Anne imagined the sound spreading across the pond and into the woods to the boundaries of their land, claiming her territory. "You okay?" she asked and reached out her hand.

"It's too much," her mother said. "We can't do it ourselves."

"What about the chain saw?"

Still sitting, her mother nodded an unsure yes and gazed through the bramble as though realizing finally how survivors must take what was passed to them, how they were alone in the task. She said, "Think between the two of us we could remember how he did it?"

"I'll do it," Anne said.

"No, Annie. If I get hurt that's one thing. But not you." She got to her feet. "You know, I keep thinking what it would mean to have the land in my name, my own spot on this earth. I feel as if I've never owned anything outright before, you know?"

"I'll get the chain saw," said Anne. If her mother could manage, she might leave. Her father would get in touch with her. She could live with him or be out on her own. The farm oppressed her. She had no friends here, hated school, hated the isolation. That's why she painted roads, the road east toward the ocean, the road west to the bay, even the dirt road where she rode Lacy, and the worst road of all with nothing but cornfields to the right and left and a single dotted line you could trace to that nowheresville, Pucam. She hated the long flat fields, the terrible distance between houses, and the people flat as the landscape. Her father had escaped all that, and the steady onslaught of woods, the hopelessness of the old house, its crusted pipes and complaining windows. But had he really meant to leave *them*?

It wasn't as if it was a real farm, handed down like most. By comparison, her family was rootless, brought here on a whim, each playing at fitting in: her mother and her jugs of root beer fermenting on the kitchen floor and her father's maniacal harvesting of firewood. They rented the tillable land to Mr. Taylor, their only neighbor, who made all the decisions about what to plant and when to harvest. Her family merely watched while the landscape was scraped and plowed and planted and combined as they waited for colors to change on the fields outside their windows. They didn't own enough land to support them. They only held the deed, the land on loan for the brief duration of their presence. Everything needed mending, the sheds, the furnace, the lane. With drought last summer and the neighboring irrigation systems running constantly, the well had run dry. The trees were overgrown and the paths to the house were choked. She saw her father in a different light now: fighting to keep the woods at bay. Clearing his place on earth had drained his energy. That's why he left. She didn't blame him. Only the way he did it. The sudden disappearance. The silence. Punishing them all. The taint of sadness he'd left in his wake would engulf her too if she stayed.

In the shop she found the black vinyl case that held the chain saw.

She remembered him lugging it back to the shop, his hands leaving oily imprints on the case. She loved the memory of her father working with his hands, his careful, big hands grasping a tool, the steadiness of his gaze, the curve of his neck as he looked down absorbed in something he was shaping. When he was his truest self.

Damn him. She loaded the chain saw in the wheelbarrow along with the gas can and oil she'd seen him use. She held his safety goggles up to her eyes. What was it he saw through them? Like a horse with blinds, she could only see what was just before her. The now. She understood. His leaving was an impulse. A face-to-the-wind kind of thing. They could read blame and suppose reasons forever and still not get at the heart of it.

She would never depend on a man for anything. A man hated strength in a woman, hated competition from them. Didn't Michael detest it when she got higher grades or figured things out quicker than he? Didn't her father hate it when her mother had a job and he didn't? It could keep a woman in hiding, scared to admit even to herself her importance and how capable she was. It seemed to Anne that women could love more fiercely than men, and that made all the difference. They could stick to something and keep fixing, keep trying with a passion beyond reason. Maybe that was their downfall. Men were rickety, feeble by comparison. There was some kind of tug-of-war between male and female. If a man felt even the slightest tug on the female side, he'd give up. He'd walk away. It's not worth it, he'd say. His eye was the same as a deer's. Any movement, any challenge in the forest and he was gone. Yet what he thought of himself seemed to depend on a woman. She'd never let her opinion of herself depend on a man. Never.

In the grove, her mother pulled the saw from its case, checked the chain, poured in the gas and oil, and laid her veiny hand over her father's handprints on the handle.

"Remember to angle it away from you, Mom. Don't get it stuck in the tree, although I think it'll cut off by itself if you do." When her mother yanked at the starter cord, she opened her eyes wide at the roar. Anne held up the goggles; her mother cocked her head so she could slip them on. The saw was heavy; her mother could barely hold it, cheeks fluttering as though a demon had hold of her. Nonetheless, her other hand held the top handle and chips began to fly. Anne worried one quick flick of the wrist and the chain saw could whip into flesh. Rip through the bone. Do bones bleed? Chips of bone mixed with chips of wood. Then everything would be one swift river of pain. Then peace. There were different kinds of pain, some that had nothing at all to do with physical pain, but not separate either. She wondered about pain's onset in the unexplained whirlwind, the precise moment of its beginning in the middle of exhilaration, turning wonderful into torment. She'd never tell. Least of all her unsuspecting mother. She could never describe it anyway, the reckless, mindless stampede across the plains where her father was right now. He'd wake up one day and wonder. He'd always be wondering after that, shocked at what he'd done, dismayed at how much rope he'd given up in the tug-of-war.

Her mother stopped the saw and lay it down. "How 'bout that, huh?" she said, tearing off the goggles, eyeing the trees that lay on the ground, the undersides of leaves turned up. She appeared taller as she stood with her hands on her hips owning things, counting the trees she would tackle. Didn't she see that to love anything was to lose it? A double-edged sword. Life so tenuous. Anne had never thought of her mother as tenuous, yet here she was, stooped on the ground again, her head bowed over the chain saw, with silver in her hair—the surprise of so much silver.

Michael drove to the Point, window open, elbow out, the Rolling Stones on the radio as he turned the corner toward the cottage wishing he were home with nothing more on his mind than waxing the car, bringing her hood to an even more stunningly flawless shine. Maybe check under her hood—study her. She was one thing he could understand. No one showed him; he'd figured it out, partly by reading stuff and partly by his own intuition.

What he couldn't understand was how quickly things got turned around. Any other time he'd be looking forward to driving down to the cottage to fish, but today he was going to see if his dad was there or had been by, if there really was someone else in his father's life, and he felt weird, like he was the father and his dad was the kid. He wanted to say, "Get on home now. I mean *right now*, or you owe me a buck for every minute you're late!" Yeah, right. Anyway, he brought bait, just in case.

When he pulled in the drive, his was the only car. The river was calm and welcoming; *Greenfly* waited. He didn't think about his father again. After turning the boat right side up, he pushed it down to the water, leaving enough of the bow on the beach to keep it from drifting. But when he entered the house to get the motor, he knew there'd been another presence, a faint but invasive perfume. Not wanting to take it in, he held his breath against it and picked up the motor, which he swung easily over the doorstep and down to the boat. In two minutes he was off, bait in his bucket and seagulls hovering around the ninth buoy.

He no sooner had the hook in the water when he felt the first tug. He yanked on the rod, released the line slightly but kept the pressure on, then yanked again and released. Still there. A weight and vibration. He held to the pressure with his heart thumping, listening to the slap of the water against the boat and the laughter of gulls, and peered into the water as if he could see something, all the while feeling the pull of the rod, a mystery soon to be revealed as he'd pull it—whatever it was—out of the deep. He reeled in steadily, and when the fish appeared just below the water's surface, it was thirty-two inches, easy. The oversized scales like a plate of armor glinted in the sun as he pulled the fish into the boat, excited by the way it jerked and fought for life. Quickly, he hit the head with the broad end of the oar to stun it so he could remove the hook, and watched himself as though he was watching a movie of a man with a fish. He couldn't believe how easily he'd caught it when everything else in his life was so hard. Must be a good sign. He studied the fish. There was nothing more to do now that the best part was over—the action, the pull on his rod— and he thought how satisfied he was and a little sad because anticipation was the best part of anything, and that was over, too. The boat dipped and rose. He turned the fish over and poked at the fins. Good thing fish eyes didn't blink or he'd never be able to take a knife to it, the fish having been free so long, escaping catastrophes. Another time he might let a fish go as ransom for this fish but just now he needed a victory and he thought how he might need a good-sized fish to begin a conversation if his father showed up, and how pleased his mother would be.

As he eased the boat into their harbor, the fish lying still in the bottom, his old man appeared around the corner of the house as though he wondered who the hell was interrupting him. Michael felt a tightening in the pit of his stomach at the sight of a young blonde woman in a blue bathing suit following him. She seemed satisfied that it was only a kid, some teenage kid, and she turned and stared beyond him out at the water like she owned the place as she came up to his father from behind and slouched with her arm perched on his father's shoulder, owning him, too.

"Hey, Dad!" He tried to sound casual.

"How come you didn't cut the grass?" his father yelled. "I mean I hope that's what you're here for."

"Not this time. I'll do it later—tomorrow. I didn't bring the mower."

"Why the hell not? That's your job, isn't it? Think this place is an easy ride for you? Something you don't have to work for?"

He held up the fish as though it was explanation enough, but his father ignored it. How he could ignore a thirty-two-inch rockfish was more than Michael could understand.

"Cut the grass, you hear me?"

He nodded. No introduction. No "Meet my son, Michael. Michael, meet—" The woman looked him up and down. There was some kind of weird blue, iridescent and snakelike, along her eyelids. He heard shouts from the house. Two kids came to the door and held it open, gaping at him and letting the flies in. What astonished him more than anything was those kids holding the door open and his father not saying anything to them about it. He turned to his father and his words tumbled out with a will of their own. "Dad, what about Mom?"

"What about her? She can come down here to swim anytime she likes. Tell her that. Yeah, tell her. I'd like her to do that." He spit out the words, wanting them to hurt. It wasn't a real invitation. "And so can you, but cut the goddamn grass first, got it?"

He turned and there was Pete across the road, watching. He was embarrassed in front of Pete's rock solid existence and turned back to see his father spring toward the catamaran, the blonde attempting to be helpful but fluttering next to the boat like a butterfly. "Watch your feet, Lisa," said his father, laughing, giving her a name and the place where his mother should have been.

Without a word, Michael took care of the motor, put away his rod, wrapped the fish in newspaper, overturned *Greenfly*—the sequence freeing him to think about how his head ached, how bad he felt. Minutes later, his foot heavier on the pedal than it should have been, the engine screamed, an extension of himself. Strange he should feel responsible, but as the oldest, he guessed he was supposed to do something. He should tell his mother where his father was. He drove the back roads, taking the long way home. After much deliberation he arrived in his own yard—he did not want to look any of them in the eye, least of all his mother—and lifted the hood of the car, tinkering for a while with his wrenches spread on the ground, cleaning oily spots, and tightening bolts till he knew what to do.

He found his mother in the kitchen. "He's at the cottage, not living down there, just been by is all," he said. She nodded, saying nothing, waiting. "He's real high, Mom," he added. "Dancing around while he talks. He told me to tell you to come down anytime, that it's okay if you want to go for a swim or something." What he left out and hoped she couldn't read on his face was that he was hiding something, the fact that someone was with his dad. His mother searched his face, and he held up the fish to distract her.

She said, "Oh really? He said to come on down for a swim?" For a moment her expression softened and she said, "My God, what a fish, Michael!" but she wasn't all that distracted because the next thing she did was shove three dead bolts across the kitchen table at him. "Put these on all the doors for me, will you?"

He nodded and tried not to think. His father's chuckle at the blonde—his mother's tears at his leaving—and he, Michael, what was he supposed to do? Was he responsible for his father's hatred of them? Had he provoked him? He must have been a bad son, ungrateful, slovenly. A real pig. Dull by his father's standards. In the yard, he scaled the fish on the picnic table and cut off the head. He slit the belly, cut away the entrails and threw them in the bucket, then cut away the backbone and filleted the pink-white meat. He scraped the innards into the bucket too, with a nagging feeling of injustice done to the fish, then eyed the fillets seeing there would be plenty for the four of them. His life was full of contradictions.

After putting away the knife, he washed up and went into the shop to find a shovel to bury the fish scraps. When he was younger, he'd been chased out of his father's shop. "You don't give a damn, do you?" his father had said. "You never put tools back. Get out of here and stay out." But now the shop was empty of shouting as well as the sawing and pounding. Tools lay heaped and scattered. Scraps of wood and metal littered the floor. Sawdust covered the band saw. He'd surprise his father if he ever came back—show him he *could* take care of tools. But what if his father saw the shop wasn't like he'd left it, and that made him so mad he turned around and left again?

He wandered through the machinery for a while, tears stinging, but once he began cleaning up, he felt easier in his purpose and began to work frantically as if he would be caught any minute. He sized the wrenches, rubbed them with one of his father's old T-shirts thinking he'd rub away his handprints and replace them with his own, then thought better of it and wrapped the cloth around them before he touched the handles and positioned them on the pegboard. Hammers, rubbed with a bit of oil and shined, he put in size places too. Laying out the other tools, the level, T-square, drills, dropping the bits out of their cases, he placed them in size places on the workbench. Electric cords wrapped from hand to elbow he tied and hung in size places according to length, down the poles. He swept off each piece of machinery, polished every last bit until all of it was spot-less. Even after he swept the floor and had gone over it again with the Shop-Vac, he went back to dust the machinery, the band saw, the table saw, the power hammer which stood louder in its silence than when his father worked here, when he told Michael to get out, get out and don't come back—*don't touch the tools Michael until you learn some responsi-bility—and stay out, Michael*—yelling, lips quivering, eyes narrowed. Did he dare turn the machines on without permission? Would Dad come back and show him? Look over his shoulder and tell him how? He was ready now. He'd show his father he was trying, and his father would be pleased.

He'd keep everything in order. But against his hope was the fact that right now he had to get the drill and the screwdriver, the large one on the end, the one with the handle worn down by his father's hand, and use it to keep his father out. With a motion weighted with lead, he pulled the drill down from the pegboard so he could put on the dead bolts for his mother.

When he was finished, he went down into the trees on the other side of the pond where the wood duck nest sat on a pole in the shallow end. He watched the sun set through the trees, the shadows long and vague. Then he searched the closest tree at the base, studied the frieze of jagged brown islands on the bark, on up to the spread of branches, up to the tree-top, a storm gathering inside him that tied him in knots so strong he felt bound to the tree, this one loblolly. He pressed his forehead against it. "Aaaaagh," he called again and again, louder each time as he beat on the tree with his fists as though it were the tree's fault. For who was there to blame and who could name the awful anger that blew through him? It was beyond his will, uncontrollable, with or without cause—how was he to know? How was he to get through? His cries penetrated the peace of the forest and what seemed to him its terrible mysteries and he felt so crazy and just beginning—everything before him—confusion maddening him, strife like a field of muck through which he must wade. His head felt tight; it was ready to burst, the veins in his neck pumping venom through his heart as if he'd been poisoned, welts on his arms rising. He would never make it. He stumbled back to the house, the way dark now, the lights from the kitchen pulling him home.

His mother glanced up when he opened the door. The smell of baking fish only made him feel hollow. She rushed toward him. "Michael! Was that you yelling in the woods? Tell me, what is it! For heaven's sake!" she said as she searched his face. "*What is wrong with you?*"

SEPARATE WAYS

From the kitchen door, Rosemary caught sight of Michael walking down to the pond with a rope. He was either up to some foolishness or desperation, his moods like the weather vane on the roof of the shop swinging crazily before a storm. Despite her intention to saunter, Rosemary's steps quickened.

"What are you doing, Michael?"

"Just having fun, Mom. You'll see."

"What are you talking about?"

"I'm going to tie one end to this tree and the other end to a tree across the pond."

"What for?"

"So we can climb the rope to the other side."

"Climb it?"

"You know, legs, hands—kind of shimmy across. See if we can make it."

"Who's 'we'?"

"Anne and Davey and me—when they get home."

"If you fall in, the water will be chilly. It hasn't had time to warm yet."

"Aw, Mom. It'll be okay. It's just something to do, that's all." He was smiling. He had the rope slung over his shoulder as he legged up the first branch of an oak, his T-shirt snagging on another branch and revealing his not-yet-sunburned back, reminding her of how white and skinny he used to be when he was little.

"Michael, don't you have anything better to do?" she chided.

He ignored her.

Still doubtful, she watched as he climbed, and when he was seven or eight feet up and knotted one end of the rope to the branch with a strength and a grunt that befitted a man, she was reminded of time passing and how she had held his small baby body in wonder, worrying only about the onslaught of fever, teething, and ear aches. Now there was more than she could give voice to.

He aimed the loops of rope over the deep end of the pond where it was narrowest, and because everything he did he managed with grace and precision, the rope caught in a tree at his first try. She felt relief creep over her. Despite everything, Michael knew how to have fun. What they wouldn't dream up, any one of those three! Justin always said he hoped they'd never lose their playfulness, and they didn't. How about the time they went sledding on an old car hood? And skiing with water skis over the snow as Michael pulled them with the Chevy? Took Holly for a swim in the pond one hot summer day?

Now he walked around the pond to secure the other end of the rope, and she with him. Aware that he might think she was monitoring him, she chatted—he'd better change to his jeans so his legs wouldn't get rope burn and did he see how huge some of those tadpoles were? and how the leaves had come to fullness in just the last few days? She loved the new greens. How many different shades of green there were. He nodded. Again, he climbed the rope-bearing tree with ease and secured the rope. When he was finished, he tested it with his full weight, legs dancing as he struggled to grab the tree again.

"Aren't you going to try it now?" she asked, surprised when he climbed down.

"I'm going to wait for Anne and Davey to get home—'less you want to try it."

She laughed. "Think I'll pass on that one, Michael," she said and walked toward the house, glancing back once at the line across the pond waiting like a tightrope before the assembly of the circus, danger reduced to the slap and chill of May water, admonishing herself for her foolishness, *silly me*.

"That's my rope! You took it and didn't even ask!"

"Aw, come on, Annie. I only borrowed it. You can have it back. Anyway, I went across and it's easy—just take your time." His voice was gentle, coaxing. It didn't fool her. Nothing he ever suggested was in her interest.

"You did? When?"

"A little while ago, just before you got here. It's easy to make it across. Just keep focused. Five bucks says you'll make it. If I can do it so can you."

"You got that right."

"Okay?"

"You're a little too eager."

"Oh, forget it then." He shrugged and turned away from her.

"No, I'll do it. I can do it."

He could get her to do anything, especially if he told her *he* could do it. She did most things better than he anyhow, and he kept looking for ways to beat her. It was hard for her to resist the chance to walk away self-satisfied and superior. Showing *him*. She suspected there were times he hated her, and that was all right with her. Then they were even.

She shed her shoes. Trees were no challenge to her. She grabbed the rope with two hands, catching her reflection in the water below and that of the trees bending over the pond, bullfrogs sitting on the steep bank, bright green and still. She dangled for a second, then pulled her legs up to embrace the rope, which sagged at her weight.

"Don't laugh, Annie. It's important not to laugh," he called out to her, aiming his camera.

Of course, she did. A giggle to relieve the tension and the narrow edge of doubt under her belt. She was maybe ten feet over the water now and her hands and legs burned, her body straining to pull along her lower half, her head hanging down for a minute to rest and view the world the way she loved it most, the sky on the bottom as though she could just step into it and float away. Only her reflection in the water righted everything—if it could be believed, that surface demarcation beyond which lay all the things that took so long to see.

"Don't laugh, Annie."

And then she saw herself. Her hair straight out from her scalp, her eyes bulging, heard herself laugh—the impossibility of it—how he got her to do it. She shouted. "Damn you! You never did this, did you? You couldn't do it, could you?" And she laughed harder at her absurdity, her straining and straining and the burning in her muscles and the fact that she was in a spot, in a pickle, had been duped, *damn his hide!* and she on the brink of going in, she believed it now, and she laughed and laughed, laughing against the sounds of his laughter until she couldn't hold on any longer and with one final shriek had to let go.

It was time then, she knew, down in the dark waters with her feet in the early slime which emitted bacteria and algae and beginnings, to let go the old competition. This would be the last time Michael would get her because they would go their own separate ways now; this was the last chapter of their growing up, she resolved, shrieking at the cold, swimming with her confident, powerful arms toward the edge of the pond, frogs leaping off the bank as she rose out of the water and Michael doubled over, laughing. What hurt was it was her rope, her own goddamn rope.

"I got it on film," Michael said. "The whole thing."

"Yeah? Well let me take pictures of you," she said, shivering. "You limp dick."

"What? You were willing. Nobody forced you. You were laughing!"

"At least I tried. Untie the rope, Michael. I want it back," she said with her hands on her hips knowing he'd never take the rope down. It would be up to her. He took and didn't give back, the price she had to pay for being smarter. In a way she felt sorry for him. But she'd never let on, one way or the other. Her anger or the feeling sorry for. Distance was all she could manage, a closing in with nothing showing but the shell of the turtle. It was a different kind of graduation than the one from high school.

Midsummer, Rosemary hired a tree man, Len Shenton, to clear the rest of the woods between the house and the pond. Len arrived in his red pickup, *God's Chosen Tree Service* handwritten on the driver's side, a pack of Marlboros tucked in the rolled-up sleeve of his T-shirt. His cheeks were pockmarked and clean-shaven; he kept his eyes on the trees as she talked and nodded, glancing at her quickly through round, gold-rimmed glasses. Later, she remembered thinking she'd never seen eyes as blue as his.

Anne's dedication to clearing bramble grew with Len climbing the trees. Within the span of one morning, he thinned the locusts and underbrush while Anne watched, quietly clipping and raking. Soon they were laughing. Anne helped him stack wood, her eyes brushing ghost fingers through his blond hair, Rosemary could tell. There was a lot of sizing up, a lot of watching through the shaded limbs as Len quickly skirted trees, pruned and conquered, wielding the chain saw. In the days following, they raked and burned the debris together and came up to the house for Cokes, smiling. With the land cleared, the path to the pond was canopied and spacious. With the trees manicured, some even bloomed clusters of fragrant white flowers like wisteria. Rosemary had never noticed them before. The sight of the pond from the back door made her pause and begin planning a purchase of two hundred King Alfred daffodil bulbs to plant in the fall.

Len seemed in no hurry to finish, though he'd been there a week. One day when the afternoon sank into its own heat, he and Anne headed out to the cottage for a swim and a sail. Then Justin appeared, Anne said.

"It was awful," she told Rosemary. "Much as I wanted to see him, there was this blonde woman with him and two little kids. I just couldn't go up to him and say, 'Hi, Dad.' He's so secret and strange, such a *chameleon.* He doesn't even walk like he used to. I told Len to keep on going, just drive by. Dad looked at the truck but didn't see me, at least he didn't wave, and I was too stunned to do anything but stare. I wonder who she is."

"It doesn't matter," Rosemary told her. The woman wasn't real, something she didn't allow herself to think about. What mattered was he could do this so cruelly, without a look back. She knew less and less of him, could not think of him without crying, yet when she looked in the mirror after a shower, she was astonished that she'd lost so much weight her stomach was gone and her waist was as small as it used to be. She was still young. Was it grief that made one say a self-willed and unconscionable *yes* to life? Made one want things one hadn't intended?

From the living room, she heard Davey tune his guitar. Each day he practiced runs he heard on recordings, playing until he understood them and could add his own, runs so beautiful Rosemary, distracted from whatever she was doing, had to stop to listen. Soon her feet moved side to side, her shoulders lifted and she began to dance. Eyes closed, she lost herself in the music, never realizing Davey had stopped playing along with the tape. She froze when she heard him step into the kitchen. He pretended not to notice, and said, "Those new earrings? You got your ears pierced, didn't you?" He opened a Pepsi, the guitar swinging on his hip, and smiled at her. "You look ten years younger, Ma. You look all sparkly—come to life."

She needed someone to talk to. She and Hannah had drifted apart, Hannah tucked away in safe suburbia on the Western Shore with a husband who was steady and providing, opportunity on every street corner, doctors who kept up with things, friends who were like her and Garrett, sons who followed their father in his business. She'd never once admitted to Hannah the isolation she felt in moving here. When she told Hannah that Justin had left, Hannah said, "He'll be back. He knows where he's got it good. It's only temporary." Rosemary saw how far she had come when she thought of Hannah. How could Hannah possibly understand singularity? Or craziness? It would only be a story to Hannah, facts to repeat to someone Rosemary once knew—did you hear about Rosemary? Did you know Justin left her out there in the wilds? He went off the deep end, really, you know—crazy? Thank God the kids are old enough it won't affect them too much.

No, she couldn't confide. She was as alone as a doe in an open field, and even stranger, she did not know this new single self very well.

Nothing bad was going to happen today. Len was coming to get her and they'd go to Assateague and smoke—bring a blanket, sandwiches. She wouldn't eat, she told herself. Well, maybe a little. Seems like once she started, she couldn't stop. Didn't matter. She'd burn it off. Because fire was her companion, spontaneity her trademark. Until exertion became her jailer, the dancing wire that fed everything hitting the ground like one grand firecracker, showering sparks, hurling barbs, hurting her fragile core, that self-conscious, embarrassed, that having-been-crazy and who-am-I-now feeling, that heart-quickening fear.

Smoking eased her some. Only Davey knew. She had one on him, though. Grass behind the eaves. Even had a Gro-light. Where the roof sloped down and cut into his room, he'd slid out the paneling and in the dead space he was growing some. So if he ever told, he'd be dead meat. She was different. She could get there without the smoke. All by herself.

Hey, Len said, like he didn't have to use her name, like she could be just anybody. But she knew different. He *saw* her. He looked at her hard through those wire-rimmed glasses, those blue eyes drilling her till she had to tell him things, more than she wanted to, and then his face looked like one of those Greek tragedy masks, only with him it wasn't a mask. He kept his mouth shut. But in the dark sometimes with just a little bit of light, she saw what she was in the outline of his face as he hung over her, inside her and around her, his weight on her. She sensed his sadness for her, like there was nothing she needed to tell him. He already knew.

When she was really outrageous, he took it, laughed a little and rubbed her back with his thick, wide hands. *Stop,* he said. *Motor mouth. Women always gotta talk, but you—you don't shut up. Funny, though. Your saving grace, Annie, funny as hell.* She wished she could stop. She got so tired, couldn't sleep—days and nights—all mixed up, blurred into one long crazy—but she wouldn't let it happen today. She'd concentrate. Make herself presentable. Easy. Quiet. Because if she couldn't stop, there might be only one way out. So she'd see. They'd go to the beach and smoke and she'd see.

At home, it was different. Michael cried all the time. She was calm compared to him. Mom said, *I'm worried about Michael. You, I can always count on, Annie. You're strong. So strong. And steady. Vivacious.*

For her mother, she was. But her mother didn't notice things. She did-n't know half of it. Take that grass. Growing right under her roof. Oblivious, that was what her mother was, which was okay. As for Anne, she was two people, one she let her mother see, and the mess she really was. She could take care of things herself, though. Michael saw the counselor at school, who told him he needed to get rid of his anger. He told Michael to hit a wet towel against the trunk of a tree so Michael took an old rag towel down to the pond and dropped it in and dove after it. She waited for him to come up and thought, *What will I do if he doesn't?* Then she heard him crying and yelling back in the woods, heard that towel smack a tree — womp, womp. She just wanted to shake him stupid sometimes.

Michael, why? Mom said. Then she cried in the kitchen over the dishes and shook her head and when he came back, she said, *Michael, why?* His eyes were half-closed and murderous and she said, *What can I do, Michael, what can I do for you — maybe if you quit working after school, maybe it's too much pressure, maybe if you just get through this term —* and he said, *What will I do? I don't know what to* be! And she said, *Maybe if you could pursue your art — you always were good at drawing. Remember? Or maybe you need to study to be an archeologist. You could say that word in kindergarten, I want to be an archeologist, you'd say. Remember? So bright. Teachers were always telling me what a bright kid.*

She'd heard this conversation before. What her mother always left out was the *but.* Bright but not working up to ability. Creative but not applying himself. Michael couldn't hide. Everything hung out in his face. But she could hide. Despite everything, she never cracked a book. All A's. Never told anybody anything. Michael told all. That was why Mom said, *I'm worried about Michael. But you, Annie, I can count on you.*

From Len's pickup, she watched cornfields and peach orchards skim by along Route 50. Signs, pitched in the sandy soil, announced *corn, 'lopes, cukes.* Farm stands cascaded yellows, reds, and greens in profusion. The sun steamed everything equally, the willows along the drainage ditches, the macadam, the red hood of the truck as it sped toward the beach, the black vinyl seat where she sat staring into the rearview mirror, Len's thigh rock hard against hers.

He was her friend. She had few friends, maybe only one friend. She could *be* a friend, she thought. Maybe if she could've gotten off the shore, lived in a different place, she might've met girls who could be friends, but here she never felt part of things. She liked boys better anyhow. They were far more interesting.

Her stomach flivered and flopped. She was hungry. But maybe she wasn't. It was difficult to tell. Sometimes her stomach sat rigid and fragile as a glass ball in her middle, a secret like the other secrets she covered with her skin. She had a hard edge. She kept bumping into it. Not like her mother, which was the trouble with her mother—no hard edges. You need one. Anything well defined has a hard edge, the door of the truck, the dashboard, Len's gold-framed glasses, the line of gravel at the edge of the road, but not her mother.

Len had a hard edge, too. Something about him was unyielding. It was what she liked in him, that strange combination of tough guy and compassionate listener. But hey, she didn't need compassion. She only needed someone to laugh with, smoke with, have a good time. Soften the edges. Len's right hand left the steering wheel and found her knee. She watched the stubby fingers knead it and felt tears well up. Her neck muscles tightened.

"You okay?" he said, dipping his head to look in the rearview mirror so he could pass. She wanted to scare him, she had to admit. Make somebody pay attention to the storm she was in, at least remark about the darkness, how things spiraled in, how her brain swerved off to the edges of the spiral and how hard she tried to will herself into its center, so she could carry on conversations, pretend she was fine.

"If I got off this roller coaster," she said to him suddenly, "would you remember me?" In the rearview mirror, she watched his eyes grow big, eyes blue as cornflowers, rimmed in those round metal frames. He has an old face, she thought. Lines etched down his cheeks already. What she felt just now was not tenderness. She wanted to push him away. Tell him not to look. See the back of his neck where black hair lay underneath the blond? Silky blond hair on the top of his head and on the sides and back, thick, wiry, curly hair like pubic hair around his ears, down his neck. A dark undercurrent, full of incongruities. Like her.

His hand patted her thigh. "Of course I'll remember you. What're you talkin' like that for? But don't get off the ride. Only sissies want off," he said, watching the traffic. She shrugged and pulled her knee away from the sweat of his hand, feeling a few seconds of sweet cool.

On the beach, he lay propped up on one elbow under the umbrella, staring out to sea. She lay her head in his lap, watching the reflection of the umbrella's rainbow stripes in his mirrored sunglasses. They both had mellowed with each puff of the stuff. He was sweet. Hadn't he been her mirror? Let her know when she was off? Treated her with gentleness? She didn't have to tell him anything now that his eyes were shielded from her. It was better this way.

They stayed like that for a while, silent. Then she said, "Know what I did once? I kissed my first boyfriend on this beach, only I had a sand crab in my mouth and when we kissed, I passed it to him." Len laughed. "You would." He shook his head.

But now the strings that held her together were coming undone, loose ends brushed just under her skin. Messages. She had to listen because they argued and contradicted each other: do something, get up, stay, stand, scream, catch a wave, kick him, spray sand across his face, lose yourself in a wave, let the water fold over you, tumble you in its fury. Out loud she said, "Think I'll go for a swim." When she got up, he glanced in her direction, nodded and resumed staring at the ocean.

"My friend, George, has a shrimp boat in Florida. Think I'll go down and help him out for a few months. Beats climbing trees in this heat."

"Yeah," she said. "Good idea. Make some decent money," then ran from him toward the water, feeling his eyes on her back. She broke into a run along the edge of the water, splashing in the licks of the waves on the sand, and ran until she was out of breath. Entering the water, she faced an oncoming wave square on, wanting to be swallowed, to listen to the water isolate her, bubble around her, let her go, purge her. She tumbled and slammed into the sandy bottom. Struggling to get her bearings, she got up quickly, pushed the hair from her face just in time to catch the next wave, and dove under its curling, smooth cascade of water. She could do it if she had to. She could suffocate in water. It would be easy. She would hold her breath, feel veins burst, muscles cramp, air bubble out and water force its way in. All pain, then no pain. She would become the ocean's flow.

He would suffer a little, but only a little. She reached out with long, sweeping strokes. She could swim to England. She could swim for years or for as long as it took her arms and legs to fall away, and she was, finally, nothing but a glass ball, smoothed down and polished. *I am worn down and tireless all at once*, she thought.

Sometime later, she remembered the current. She was a long way from the crowds and the rainbow-striped beach umbrella and the boyfriend, if he could be called that. She listened— although it seemed she'd heard it for a while now—to the far-off shriek of the lifeguard's whistle. *We are so eager to save each other without knowing why.*

She headed toward the beach riding the roller coaster waves and when she could, put her feet on the tenuous shore. The water pulled at her, trying to reclaim her, but she walked as if she were without choice, in fact, wasn't even present, as if she watched herself from afar—two selves, one contemplating her demise with terror and one who watched coldly. How alone she was, alone among the crowds, which was okay—people wore her out. She burst into a run, a gallop, a canter, a spin and a dance, foolishly, people-watching foolish, people-grinning-at-her foolishness, people wishing they could do what she was doing on a summer day like this. But maybe they never felt the energy, the air moving, particles swirling and reflecting light, light, everywhere—too much light. A paradox, seeing and not seeing. She knew she must keep moving to relieve herself of the whirlwind that took hold. She must spend it, all of it, and find peace in its absence, yet wait with a longing like hunger for it to come again. This was the dilemma—her longing for the rush, and her terror of the exhaustion it held, the downwind that sucked her crashing to the ground, when there was a great possibility she would hurt herself. It couldn't be helped, Mother dear. She was sure she was living beyond the borders of ordinary life, off into the white ends of the spectrum, living before alpha and beyond omega.

Len strode toward her, his face white despite the afternoon sun. His arm shook as he slipped it around her and asked, "Why, why did you do this? You've been gone two fucking hours. I thought you were—never mind. God, never mind. You crazy girl—crazy bitch. Stop and think for a minute for chrissakes, will you? Think about how you scare somebody! Goddamn!"

He would be gone soon, and she tried to believe it wouldn't matter. He was planning a trip south to get on a shrimp boat. She'd never admit she needed him for anything. Still, his arm was around her, a weight that steadied her, slowed her heart, her breathing, her terror.

The blonde was long gone. That last time she'd been at the cottage for almost a week. Left her kids with the husband and came on a Friday, purring and clutching her little pink gym bag. By Wednesday she went out the door crying and screeching, her underwear trailing out that same bag. She must be made like me, he thought, fitful as the wind. Anyway, she was gone. Easy come, easy go. There were plenty of others. One he saw now looked a lot like Rosemary, come to think of it.

The geese had arrived. They'd settled on the opposite shore in flocks of thousands, honking into the wind. And with them, chilly mornings, and thoughts he couldn't keep away. He called Anne to see if she'd stay with him.

She came on a Friday afternoon and set up her easel in front of the big window, but after trying to squeeze some oil paint on her palette, she said, "It's too cold in here, Dad. I brought the thermometer inside. It's only fifty degrees!"

"Well, close the drape," he told her. "Heat's escaping through the glass."

"But that takes away the light," she protested. He pulled the dark, green drapes closed anyway, and then showed her how he put the saucepan half-filled with water on the kerosene stove for two and a half minutes exactly, and how he simultaneously kept the tea mug warm as well. He baked a whole bag of potatoes and then fried them as needed to save electricity, he explained. Her eyes narrowed. "I thought Grandma left you a lot of money," she said. He laughed.

"Has to last me the rest of my life. If it doesn't, your old dad will be a bag man. Sent seventy-two résumés so far and nothing. Zippo."

He shared his potatoes, lettuce, and tofu with her. She laughed at his jokes and read the article he'd just finished writing on middle-aged men who had talent and wisdom to offer society but couldn't find a job. "I'm on a campaign," he told her, "no issue too big or too small escapes my watchful eye—like the narrowness of the road down at Watkin's Corner that was painted with a dotted line down the middle leaving lanes three feet wide—I measured them. Here's the letter to the editor." She smiled up at him.

"Dad," she said, "that's not a new issue."

His life was uncomplicated. He loved calling attention to injustice, the careless thinking and incivilities of this backward, wild place he'd chosen. He could still make his mark. He had begun to run. *See, Anne? Look at this pile of T-shirts, one for each 10K race, and look at these running shoes—the best you can buy.*

He talked too much. She stayed the night, curled up in a sleeping bag on her old bed, her head tucked down inside. When he checked on her later that night, she'd left nothing exposed to the open air, not even a lock of hair. In the morning, she looked sad when she said, "Sorry, Daddy, it's just too cold for me to paint here, though I'd like to keep you company."

That was okay. His life was orderly and he wanted it to stay that way. Ah. He'd had so many hopes, such big dreams. With a little bit of luck, who knows what might have been? His opinions used to become everyone's opinions; he'd been unendingly quotable. But for too many days recently his thinking had been muddied and now it seemed he was willing to compromise with an indifferent world. He was only a little low, back on pills, although the doctor said he wasn't taking enough to be of "therapeutic value" but hey, seven of those suckers a day were just too many. Just one, maybe every other day, he decided. Running made him feel good. He was high when he finished. And there were all those women in T-shirts and shorts, numbers pinned to their chests, eyeing him. He never considered himself handsome, but he could charm. No one turned away from a good laugh.

"That's a lot of races," Rosemary said when she dropped by the following Monday. He was surprised at how good she looked. "You look good," he said to her. She had long hair now, like he'd always wanted. That was the trouble with her. She never gave in to him about anything and now he was detached, impervious. She noticed the racing numbers he tacked to the wall to mark his time and prove his effort. "Yeah," he told her. "Lots of people race who are just like me, looking for high gear, stuck in low. Never thought I could do it, though."

"You always did love racing. Remember the race around Manhattan in that little ten-foot racing boat you built? You were the only one to finish, the water was so rough that day? That big trophy? I think it's in the barn somewhere." Her eyes began to tear. He couldn't think why. That was another thing about her. She cried easily. The last thing he wanted to do was remember anything. He had failed. No matter how hard he worked, how many good intentions he had had, he had failed. Still. It wasn't too late.

"I'm changing the résumé again," he said. "It's like that old joke: Bernie, the clothing salesman, says, *Irving, the customer wants a green coat so turn on the green light.* I turn on whatever color they want."

"You can do anything, Justin," she said. "Anything. I always said."

"Yeah. Of course I'm careful not to tell them everything I've done. Spread things out a few years and leave out some of the in-between jobs."

"How are you doing, anyway?" she asked. "Are you getting enough to eat?" As if he couldn't take care of himself.

"Hell, yeah. Tofu and lettuce are saving my life. Never did eat right. You know how early my father died. Grandfather, too. I've lived longer than either of them, me—the one who doesn't give a damn—I've lived too long."

"Justin! You're only forty-four!" Maybe she didn't realize the contradiction. He was fighting for his life, for health. It was the old him he wanted to bury. That's why when she started telling him about the furnace at the farm acting up, and the well running dry, and the toilet that wouldn't flush on rainy days, he looked away. But when she told him about Michael, "He's going through those anxiety attacks again where he just bursts out crying in a rage and starts punching anything in sight," he began to block her out, her goddamn need to talk everything over. He just wanted life to go smoothly. No problems. But she couldn't stop. "I mean, he's seeing a psychologist who told him he needed to get rid of his anger, but—"

He interrupted her with, "How about some cappuccino?" He brought her one, his hand around the cup, the handle turned toward her and when he looked at her, tears had spilled down her cheeks. He waited for her to finish the cappuccino and leave. She made a few more stabs at conversation—did he see the ad in the paper for a computer programmer in Salisbury and was he warm enough? Yeah, yeah.

He was finished. Worn out. He walked her to the door and noticed dark circles where her mascara had run. She never used to wear it. As for him, he was pleased to be here in the cottage alone, the house he built back when he believed in everything. A house could be many things, a status symbol, a cocoon, a coffin. This one was his refuge—the one ship that came in and the only thing he hadn't lost. If he counted losses, he'd anguish over them. Anger was easier. The goddamn road crew painted a centerline right over a dead squirrel. Nobody gave a damn anymore. About anything.

Never mind. His running shoes sat by the cottage door, two rows of them. They were his only extravagance. He wrote today's time and distance on a Post-It and stuck it to the wall. The race was everything. He had ads to answer, personal and employment, and he had miles to run, one foot in front of the other.

The blacksmith, John Stanton, came in the afternoon on a Tuesday and began firing his portable forge under the chestnut tree near the pony shed, a scene reminiscent of a painting Anne had seen many times, reminding her that horses and riding might be as much in the past for her as the horseshoes she'd collected, vessels of luck spilled out and nailed to the weathered boards, although she couldn't say what kind of luck it was she'd had, but whatever it was—that set of peculiarities that made up a family, or where she lived or those who walked in and out of her days— the parts of her life over which she had no control, that too was finished. *The rest is up to me*, she thought, as she watched John heat the metal and begin pounding, the ring sharp and loud in her ears. His hair, caught in a ponytail, was wispy, his beard black intermingled with gray. He'd been doing this a long time, he said, and he liked the life. When he smiled, she noticed he had a tooth missing, and she thought it might be evidence of the price he'd had to pay for his freedom. Yet he seemed a satisfied man with an aura of peace about him, his requirements simple. Unpacking his tools, he handled them as though they were to be caressed.

He lived in Pennsylvania, he said, and traveled between there and Florida in the winter months, shoeing along the way, his map dotted with the locations of farms he visited, horses he knew, kickers and mean-tempered ones marked in his brain, although he could calm any horse and eventually get it to tolerate him and the shoeing. Take Lacy now, a beauty, and well behaved. Must be what you whispered in her ear, Annie. He smiled at her, and she envied his freedom, his living hauled in the back of the pickup along with his sleeping bag, as she held the harness and peered into the black crystal ball of Lacy's eye as if it could unfold the secrets to her future. For her future was held in part by Lacy's future. Exactly how, she couldn't be sure, but there'd been a mutual consent they'd settled during the hundreds of trails they explored, an understanding she'd had to establish, the one place in her life where she was in charge. She'd learned a lot from Lacy, because underneath Anne's turbulence, there always remained something she mustn't let go of and that was the command of the horse and her responsibility.

She stroked Lacy's nose, that sweet, velvety place, now hers but not for long. Her first introduction to horses, when she was around three and still in her mother's arms, was her mother reaching out to pet a pony on a farm they visited. "Pet him right there on his soft nose, Annie, like this," she said. When Anne tried, the pony nipped her. She remembered the shock of it and her mother exclaiming, "Oh, Annie, I'm so sorry! I should never have—thank God, he didn't break the skin!" The bite didn't squelch her desire to go back again, and later, when she was seven, she pleaded with her mother to cancel ballet and let her take riding lessons. The mystery of horses' slender legs and powerful bodies, their beauty on the run, contained the dichotomy of something unbridled and free on the one hand, and the call to mastery by human hands on the other. It was amazing her interest had not come to an end with that first encounter, but it was as if her love of horses was already deeply part of her, impossible to deter. In the ensuing years, that love became a discipline, as though she was cultivating something larger within herself, a greater strength on which she could always draw. That's what she thought now as the blacksmith raised a hoof onto his leather apron and began to nail the shoe. The truth was, this love affair was not easy to give up—yet who was to say she would have to give it up forever? She tried to comfort herself with the words *just temporarily.*

Because she had to trade the horse for her freedom, whereas before Lacy *was* her freedom. She saw that, although to say it out loud would only bring tears. She would have to do it quickly, like ripping off a Band-Aid. Oh God. All those times she had raced Lacy away from the house and her brothers, through the woods, in April winds or summer sweat or with the bite of a winter morning on her face, galloping through her childhood, her release—she must leave it behind now. Could she? She'd go on to better. That's what strength was, and determination, progress. She hoped.

John was saying something to her; she answered as though she pushed the words out, because between the last breath and this, she had made a decision that pained her; and all the while she paid him and watched him pack his gear and took in the sweet molasses smell of Lacy's feed as she filled her bucket, she'd been hanging on his words—praise for the horse she had trained and the care she'd taken and his announcement that he'd be by in six months on his way back through to see if she needed him— making her envision the reality of a future in which she saw herself as horseless—while he invited her to catch a burger with him down at Murphy's, was that the place? Right there in Pucam? But she said no, thanks. She had stuff to take care of, but thanks anyway, and watched him drive off down the lane knowing she would do the same and not come back for a long time.

Having to take care of Lacy was a bother, Anne announced one morning after combing her down. "It's time to sell her, Mom," she said. Rosemary listened to Anne dictate an ad for the classifieds over the telephone, amazed at her stoicism. Anne would be leaving soon, which was what the sale of Lacy was all about. "I'd keep her for you, love," said Rosemary, wiping the kitchen table, "but you know how I am with horses."

"I don't expect you to take care of her, Mom. There won't be time to ride anyhow, between college and work." Two days later, a black pickup pulling a horse trailer rolled into the yard, and a man in riding boots and his young daughter jumped out. Rosemary was reminded of Anne at that age, the same slender frame, the red-brown hair, the same eagerness to fall in love, already in love the minute she saw Holly, reaching out for the velvety nose. Anne led Lacy to the pasture and put her through her paces, and after she'd inquired what kind of place they had to keep Lacy, a fenced pasture, a barn, she heard Anne say, "How old are you—thirteen? Fourteen?" And to the girl's shy reply, "Thirteen," she said, "A good stage in a woman's life to wrap herself around a horse." A lot of wisdom in that, thought Rosemary.

A week later, Anne got a job waiting tables, rented a room near the community college and began taking classes, a chain of events so swift and final Rosemary was stunned, despite telling herself this is what kids do, grow up and move away.

Michael applied to merchant marine school. Once accepted, his mind seemed to latch onto worries and hold them tenaciously. Now it was the fact that he was color-blind and he was sure he would fail the tests for boiler room operation since they were based on a color-coded system. What if they found out he was color-blind? What if he turned the wrong dial or pushed the wrong lever? Her answers, that he could ask for help or that he might not be as color-blind as he thought because he was only blind to certain tones of a color, did not seem to pacify him. When he was a child he asked her over and over what he should do if there was a fire in the house. Who should he save? He was never satisfied when she told him to save himself and whoever was nearest to him if he could and that he was not responsible for them all, knowing the questions went far deeper than the situations he posed. Now he talked of nothing but his fear of failure, like a fly buzzing around the same piece of meat, until it was time for him to leave for Baltimore. When she walked him to his room at school, he turned to her and said, "Just go, Mom, will you? I'm okay."

"Of course," she said, wanting to believe peace of mind would come to him as soon as he put his underwear in the drawer, noting at the same time there was no dresser in the room, just an olive-colored metal locker. She heard its door clang as she turned to leave. The sound marked his resolve. *That's good*, she thought. *Work will distract him, give him confidence.*

Only Davey still lived at home. He played for a band called The Lug Nuts, and Rosemary went to hear him in a small bar two towns away. She was shy about entering a bar that first night but it seemed justified with Davey playing. "That's my kid on lead guitar," she'd say to anyone who'd listen as her toes tapped to the music. "He's good. That kid is incredibly fast with his fingers," a man with horned-rimmed glasses told her as they sat together at the bar.

"He's a great kid, too," Rosemary said. The guy was probably a regular. She could tell by the way his arms encircled his drink like it was the most important thing in the world. However, he was listening to her, or seemed to be, nodding and looking into her eyes. Encouraged, she went on.

"We have this huge TV antenna with a motor that had stopped working. I didn't really notice because I don't watch TV that much, but I did see a fishing rod leaning by the back door. I asked Davey to put it away several times and he kept ignoring me but finally he said, 'Mom, I can't.' 'Come on, Davey, get it out of here,' I said. Then he said, 'Mom, you didn't even notice the TV antenna was fixed, didja? Well, I cast the line up there and when I want to change the direction on the antenna, I just reel it in.'"

"Ha, ha. That's pretty good. I like that," said the man with the horn-rimmed glasses. But then he looked away.

Rosemary stared down at her glass of white wine and wiped the base of the glass with her thumb. Her feet felt swollen and heavy as they hung from the bar stool, and she felt out of place but as she watched Davey on stage with the spotlight on him as he performed his solos, she suddenly felt a strong hope for her youngest. He'd be all right. He'd already found something to love. She was lost in the music, carried along by the wailing, improvised notes she'd heard in her own living room and on occasion through the night when Davey was practicing, when Justin came in. Alone, he waved to Davey on stage and looked around for a familiar face. When he noticed Rosemary, he came directly to her, and she welcomed him.

"Want to dance?" he said and held out his hand. She slid off the bar stool. The hand that curled around hers was so familiar her eyes teared instantly. Once on the dance floor, she studied his face, the deep lines on his cheeks, his turned-down mouth, his shaded eyes that seemed to emphasize eye sockets hollow as a skull's. In time with the beat, he jumped from side to side, and punched the air like a prizefighter. In the strobe light, the effect was that of a man in a stilted, solitary frenzy, a puppet connected to strings he wanted to break. Rosemary called out to break the spell, *Justin, Justin,* but he never heard her, the music so loud and driving and hurting her ears. He glared at his feet or up at the ceiling, never acknowledging her presence as she danced before him, as he fought his way against the strings, his steps wooden, his desperation amplified.

Rosemary looked up at Davey on stage. She focused on his smile with an extravagance of pleasure. Davey, the happy one. She silently prayed, *please God, please let him stay that way.*

He watched them from his place on the stage, fleetingly, jerked back to the music by the chord changes slipping off his fingers. He wished he didn't know the older couple among the kids on the dance floor, trying to *be* kids, which they weren't. He wanted them to go home and act like parents.

He turned his amp up. Angelo turned it down. Okay, okay. So he had no right, but someday—Angelo told him he was the fastest thing on strings he'd ever seen, and pretty much let him take lead. He was listening, all the time listening, picking up runs and chords, and practicing body moves. No matter what they played, he could add something. Take off on his own. He tried to look cool. Not grin. But it burst out of him. His fingers ran ahead of everybody. He laughed; Angelo laughed. They *paid* him to do this, man!

Music filled the room and he had little to do but enter, as if the sounds collected themselves. *Notes,* his piano teacher had called them, but they weren't notes, little black droplets on a white page forever qualified by their position on a line. He couldn't read them anyway. The sounds he heard had no notation at all. They were here for a second and then gone, part of some greater mystery. It was as if he closed a door to the visual world—ahead of him formations of sound like cumulus clouds building up in a great blue space—the million droplets of sounds he'd collected all his life. There was enough to fill a sky. He'd never run out. His mother at the bar, on a bar stool—he wanted his old mom back. No, he didn't either. He liked his freedom—no one paying attention. He could be inside the sounds, keep on playing, and be any one of a million places. None of them home. It was okay.

They ripped through "Cocaine." He had seen his father walk over to his mother, and he'd thought at the moment that was a good sign. Maybe they'd go back to the house together. But now, they were on the dance floor moving to "Cocaine," and the sight of them dancing but not looking at each other hurt him. They looked silly, trying to be something other than what they were. If they listened to the words of the song, they'd hate it. They'd know they should be out of there. They were stray notes, a broken string boinging into the amp and jarring the air. *Delete them. Pay attention. Listen to the music. Follow that.*

His playing was not as clean as he would have liked. He was distracted. He wished they'd go away. Imagine him connected to that stranger out there, the one battling the air with his fists, calling it dancing. Imagine his father taking him to a movie or something. Or talking to him—about anything. Imagine that. He couldn't. Didn't matter. He had his own thing. Out of it he'd make a life. He caught his mother's eye. She smiled at him and he smiled back. He was good. He knew it. In the same way Michael was when he skated.

"Rosemary? How are you doing?" Len's voice sounded polite but urgent through the telephone. "Think you'd have time in your busy schedule to go out to dinner?"

"How nice!" she said, though puzzled. He and Anne had broken up a while ago. Anne didn't talk about it, saying only that Len went away. What began with promise seemed to fizzle before it went anywhere. Now that Len was back maybe he wanted to see Anne again and didn't know how to approach her. Maybe he just wanted to talk. Conversation flowed easily between him and Rosemary when he'd been around the house. But dinner? Well, why not? She was a free woman, wasn't she?

"Can you pick me up at my house?" he said. "I'd hate to take a lady out in my rusty heap."

Thursday evening, she drove along River Road, peering at the names on the occasional mailboxes. Soon she saw a figure crouched next to a mailbox. Beyond was a lighted farmhouse, gabled in front, with a narrow front porch nearly hidden by overgrown cedars. A denim jacket thrown over one shoulder, and those gold-rimmed round glasses catching the beam of her headlights, Len rose to meet her.

Oddly, they began talking about books. "Saw you reading Virginia Woolf one time when I was there. Ever try Elizabeth Jolley?" She didn't know he read. There are all kinds of tree men in this world, she thought. After dinner and over coffee he made his purpose clear. He didn't want to tell her over the phone. He knew things she should know. He wasn't sure how to begin. Taking his time, he looked at her with eyes she could be half in love with if she were younger, if this were a date.

"I'm not sure you know this—but maybe you do—it isn't something I wanted to just blurt out over the telephone. It's about Anne. We broke up—I'm not sure why, but nonetheless, she's not well and I find myself thinking about her. I mean—I hope she's okay, but I know she doesn't let on much, does she?" He hesitated; she waited.

He put his elbows on the table and leaned forward. "We went to the beach and she talked about suicide on the way and then disappeared for two hours when we got there. I got pretty rattled. I thought of telling you then—and didn't, though I should have, I guess. It's bothered me ever since. Maybe it's stupid to tell you so long after the fact. Maybe it was just a passing thing—I feel lousy, like I'm telling tales behind her back." He waited for an answer.

She should say something. Whose mother was she? Michael's. Davey's. But not Anne's. Anne was more like a sister. Anne was the one she counted on. Coached her in her new single life. *You can do it, Mom. Hell with him—old Justin wants to act like that?—You'd be surprised who you can live without!* Annie made her laugh. Annie, the strong one.

He put his arm on her arm, his hand wide, thick, rough, calloused. He was a hard worker with an honesty about him you could trust, she thought. Why would he lie? She didn't believe him. And she did. He sat back and studied her.

She was thinking of a night a few years ago when they couldn't find Anne. As far as anyone knew she was home, had been doing her homework at the dining room table. At bedtime, they called and called, but Annie was gone. Thinking she might have gone horseback riding, they'd checked the stable. Lacy was there. She, Michael, and Davey took flashlights and walked the woods and fields surrounding the house, calling *Anne, hey Annie.* Hours later, panicked and tearful, Rosemary called the sheriff and reported her missing. She remembered the sheriff entering the house, the Right of him, the rules firmly packed in his head and in his pressed uniform, the badge, the holstered gun, his unmuddied view of infractions great and small. He questioned her and the reason for the belt casually placed on the chair by one of the boys, the way it must have looked to him, the belt a piece of evidence, a supposition. Then Davey shouted he'd found Anne curled up in a dark corner of the stall, not sleeping, listening to their calls, looking up at the horse—*what had she been thinking?* Later, when asked why, she said she was angry, and after that grew stubbornly silent. And now again, Rosemary's child living away from home, out of reach with some great trouble looming—who knew the reasons for the storms that blew?—still harbored the same thoughts of disappearing.

Rosemary made it to the parking lot. Under the streetlight she had trouble with her collar stuck inside her jacket. She reached up to pull it out but her hands flew to her face instead, to hide the tears and stifle her fear for everything she hadn't acknowledged and knew all along. Len put his arms around her, and she hung on to him, just stood there under the streetlight holding on to someone who felt like a good, strong tree.

"Where you from?" His roommate's brown eyes and handshake opened spaces between them. Michael liked Anthony immediately. There was something essential, primal, in the way he swaggered, arms hanging out and down from his body as though he had everything under control.

"Eastern Shore," said Michael.

"Cornfields. Tomatoes. Crabs. Log canoes. Canada geese. Jeez, it must be paradise."

"And you?"

"Philly. My parents split and I live with my grandmother. She packed me a box of food like nobody's business. Cheese. Bread. Cookies. Want some?" He held out a tin.

That first day, with visitors coming down the hall where the showers were, Anthony managed to lock himself out of the room with nothing but a towel around him. He darted through the halls, downstairs, and across the playing field to find Michael. "Got your keys, man?" he said, with his bottom lip drooped and eyes half-closed. "Here," said Michael, throwing them. With only one arm on the towel so he could catch the keys, Anthony was vulnerable—an opportunity Michael couldn't pass up. He grabbed the towel; Anthony tackled, white legs and buns exposed. They both went down, pounding. In the end Anthony laughed, a low rumble of a laugh like he was pleased at the kind of attention he'd sorely missed. He had an older brother, he said, who tackled him regularly. "Just once," said Anthony, "I'd like to beat his ass—one good one. I'll practice on you, okay?" He said it without malice.

Anthony was all right and so was school, thought Michael, though he dreaded math, which he'd never been good at. The meaningless numbers jumped around the page transfixing themselves into inevitable piles of crossed-out scribbles. He panicked and broke a few pencils. Anthony showed him and showed him, his thick hands writing decisive, dark numbers that not only stayed on the page but left an impression on the next. Slowly, Michael began to understand.

And Anthony began to understand, Michael thought. Only once did Michael punch the wall hard enough to put a hole in it. It wasn't because of any one thing, he just came into the room and felt like punching something out. "Hey, man, let's get a beer," said Anthony and stepped up to him as if he'd tackle him again. The black hole in the wall gaped like a mouth, which they both ignored until Michael painted a tongue hanging down from the hole and bright red lips along the broken edge. "Meet Mick," he said and Anthony laughed.

First semester they were assigned to the lab, a room where the ceiling rose for three stories. It housed an immense green and silver diesel engine polished as a show horse, a model of the ones at the heart of the container ships where he'd eventually work. The smell of oil and fuel overwhelmed him at first, but he could feel the odor fulfill a longing in him so deep it went all the way back to his father's shop. Steel, frictionless and lustrous, parts churning and repeating and thundering in his ears—this was the life he was meant for, he knew. He put in earplugs like he was told to and stood taking it all in, embracing the engine's precision as though it were a religion, his heart matching the beat of the engine. He thought it was the first time in his life he was truly happy—no, the second—the first being when he skated on the pond back home.

Their first six-week assignment on a container ship, Michael stood on deck and watched the land slip away with all its troubling ties. He and Anthony were off to great adventures, or as much as could be had from the boiler room, thought Michael, the queasiness in his stomach beginning vaguely.

Two days out and somewhere in the round of sleeping on the bottom bunk in a narrow puke-green room and the hissing heat of the boiler room, Michael began what Anthony named the Royal Panic, which was somewhat like the Royal Pain. He was that, he knew—as he lay on his bunk in fetal position, sweating till the sheets were as wet as the aftermath of some of his dreams, the world swirling about him. He wandered dizzily through narrow halls of escape, losing his way, claustrophobia sending him into turmoil. "Take some Dramamine," said Anthony.

But it was the buttons—color-coded as hell, confusing in class and now crucial on board ship—and switches and gauges, matching dials and levers, things shutting down and starting back up and humming, all depending on colors, and he, likely to touch the wrong one with Anthony behind him checking and his supervisor watching every move and he faking it and lying and smiling and sweating without breathing, unable to concentrate, though Anthony said, pay attention, learn the position of the red, remember what I told you, on top is the red, push left to blue to decrease pressure, or something like that, till he ran in a mad dash—"Hey, where're you going?" yelled Anthony, "You can't do that, don't do that, man—it'll be it for you!"—as he leaped up the steps without breathing, lungs bursting, choking, chest caving in now and water pouring out through his pores, running to the deck and—heave. Oh. Head in arms, cradled, he wished he were dead—his mind in shackles, the ship his prison, the ocean a vast moat. If he could get through this he would be a man, he thought, realizing he would always be apart, his path more treacherous than most.

He feigned seasickness, although that was only part of it. With nothing but the supreme will to do so, he returned to the boiler room in two days, where Anthony wrote R for red and G for green in chalk in strategic places at the end of his shift, which Michael erased with his sleeve at the end of his. "You owe me big time," said Anthony good-naturedly.

By the next change in shift schedule, Michael had the gauge and lever positions memorized, and had become accustomed to the suffocating heat of the boiler room. He spent as much time as he could on deck water-watching, as Anthony put it. Sunsets, stars, moon risings, dolphins, clouds—he began sketching in a small black notebook a collection of things real and surreal: monsters with wings and creatures that poured out of the clouds. The faces of demons that stole him in the night. And turning the page, the turbulent order of the boiler room, the broad, dark angles, the contours of the engines and maze of pipes and ducts, the constant heat, the sweating men running, tending—he sketched those too as he sat on his bunk, which is how he managed to lessen the confinement of his cramped room. He wrote no letters, never thought of home. Each shift in the engine room was an episode in his metamorphosis, and he climbed the stairs out of the hellish heat to the brisk open air on deck with a sense of conquest and an immense gratitude for being alive. It was a daily wash, like the waves over the deck in a storm. He felt toughened in the way he imagined his grandfather and father had been, his grandfather having spent his youth at sea and his father building the seawall, a feat he still thought magnificent. He recognized moments of peace as he stared out over the ocean, lamenting how little of it he'd had, but the hard line of the horizon on clear days gave him courage, a parameter for his imaginings past which he tried not to stray.

Then they headed for port and a return to school.

"Michael. Mari," Anthony said. The simplicity of some things astounded Michael. They were in a tiny bar along one of the narrow streets in Baltimore where many of their classmates hung out after classes, although Mari wasn't one of them. Lean, self-assured, smooth black hair tied back from her face, she had gray eyes that peered at him as though her next words would be, "Buzz off." But she was too nice for that, the sinews along her throat emptying into that sunken spot just above her collarbones as she tilted her head to look up at him. Skin so white. After about an hour and a few beers, he stopped glancing back at Anthony to see how he was doing and actually started talking to her.

She was not beautiful, he decided, in the way movie stars were beautiful, but pearly—that was it—the way she smoothed out his attempts at conversation, glossed his murkiest thoughts with clarity, an alabaster precision to her speech, her even teeth enunciating every syllable clearly. She smiled a lot. She said "Serendipitous," with a smile that made him forget what they'd been talking about as he watched the word leave her teeth and lips. In his confusion he folded, unfolded, and refolded the napkin before him, pausing to watch the pale moons of her nails in a slow dance before him. The longer he watched, the more they seemed to direct her speech and him, wiping out all traces of the frenzy he felt when he first sat down in front of her.

Could he have her phone number? Right on this napkin? He had a pen. Yes, she said, yes, told him yes though he didn't know why, nodded yes through the last call for alcohol, and was there before him still listening, nodding yes as the ghastly fluorescent lights threw pallor over them, with the napkin folded now and in his chest pocket. He couldn't believe it.

After that, they went out a few times, he with his arm around her and she looking up at him and laughing. They strolled along Inner Harbor and stopped to watch the ships and smaller boats with their spectral lights shining across the water. But it was her he saw, her hair so thick he could lose his hands in it. There was nowhere they could go unless they rented a motel room. She, too, lived in a dorm with a roommate. Yes. So he held her in the car and kissed that sunken hollow at her throat and on down, whereupon she said quietly and succinctly that she was going on a trip with a girlfriend during semester break to California, and she'd call, yes, of course, when she got back, in a week she thought, and buttoned her coat again.

He knew it. He'd blown it. For some vague reason. He was slime, basically. He dared not touch her again. In his agitation, he'd forgotten the motor was running and shuddered at the grating sound when he turned the key in the ignition, causing a rush of dismay for what he'd probably done to his car. The lightness in his stomach from which his weakness emanated panicked him. Not this again. She was pure; he was tainted. He didn't deserve her. He was contemptible, putrid, and unmanly. She could see that. But she was just going on a trip for God's sakes. No, she'd never come back, he knew. It was just an excuse. She never wanted to see him again, he was sure. He dropped her off in front of her dorm, watching as she turned to go, the heavy veil of her hair like the dark side of the moon. In a second she slipped inside the door, "I'll call" on her lips.

He went back to the harbor and glared at the water. Few walkers now. It was late. The water was inky black as he stared down trying to read its message, his hands fidgeting in his pockets. While the small waves swished against the seawall, he cried for what he never had and never would have, for the vacancies in his life. He dug his nails into his cheeks and dragged them down his face leaving stripes like whip marks.

When he got in, Anthony was in bed, but awake enough to say, "Boy, you missed it—some party down at the bar—where the hell were you, anyhow? How come you're all cut up? A fight? What?"

He couldn't answer at first. Dumbfounded when he looked in the mirror, he felt sick at his own discrepancies. "Forget it," he bit into the air. "I'm not worth it."

"What're you sayin', for chrissakes? Cut it out, Michael! What's the matter with you? What the fuck?"

The chaos in his head was maddening. He jabbed at the metal locker. A sound exploded. Then he stood with his forehead pressed against the cool metal and punched again and again and again. The locker resounded. Anthony grabbed him from behind and locked his arms. "Jesus, Michael, guys are sleepin'!" Michael wrenched his arms free and went out the door, turning to say, "Don't come after me. I'll kill you if you do."

He went to classes the next day but lay on his bed the rest of the time staring at the ceiling. "It's something," said Anthony. "I've got a brother at home just like you. The family's pretty worried about him. Why don't you go to a shrink? Although, I don't know. Lotta times that ain't much help either."

Sometimes he cried. Sometimes he broke out in a sweat and picked at the scabs on his face. She called midweek, on Wednesday. Anthony got him. "It's for you," he said. "C'mon Mick, it's for you."

He couldn't help it. In the phone booth in the hall he sat with his face to the wall and cried, choking on the answers to her questions, trying to ask her how the weather was out there, her voice the beacon that would save him.

In the middle of the night Rosemary woke up listening. She heard someone crying, a sound that gave voice to the undercurrent of worry that ruled her life. Stirring covers and moving soundlessly as she could toward the open window, she realized the cry was Davey's, and then she saw him sitting on top of the picnic table with his feet on the seat, his head in his hands. She slipped quietly downstairs, opened the kitchen door and entered the night, the moonless night with its litter of stars and black trees and owl hoots from the woods and her son, head bowed.

"Davey, what is it?"

"Don't know—don't know—don't know." He continued crying. She climbed up on the table and sat with him, arm around his shoulders, her mind leaping around for reasons, causes, solutions. She tried to contain her fears as she waited.

"I don't want to but I feel like I might. I might do it. Don't let me do it," he cried out.

"What? Do what?"

He shook his head. "I want to live!" he screamed out. "But I'm afraid I might do something!"

"Davey, we have to get help—talk to someone."

"I *am* talking to someone. I don't want to talk to a doctor. What's he going to do? What's he fucking going to do?" His screams echoed from the woods.

"Come inside, Davey." She would coax him, beg him, soothe him. She'd protect him from himself, from all harm. She'd watch him, save him, get help somehow. She must not have done anything right as a mother. This was what became of the innocent babies she had delivered into the world; she'd ruined everything. She and Justin. But she was the mother. She must have done most of it.

They sat there till the sun splayed rays through the trees, till the storm inside Davey played itself out. There didn't seem to be a specific reason, although he hated school, he said. "Everyone expects too much from me."

He drove the old family car, a tinny station wagon in which he could fit his equipment for gigs. Saturday morning, he got out the Turtle Wax. "I'll do your car too, Mom, when you get back," he said. When she returned from some errands in town, she found herself staring at a sheet of jagged metal leaning against the garage door. Dumbfounded, she recognized the gray metal as the roof of the station wagon. Thinking there might have been an accident, she ran into the garage and found Davey sitting in his new convertible, grinning.

"What will you do when it rains, Davey?" she said, the words oscillating between relief and anger. It's a script for a comedy, she thought. A goddamn movie that would sell millions of tickets at the box office. The set was sitting in her garage. Canned laughter followed her as she walked to the house. Couldn't she see the humor in it? Was it craziness or unconventionality? Lunacy or teenage foolishness? The line vague and foreboding.

It rained that night during his gig at Jimmy Joe's. The inside of the car got soaked. It didn't seem to matter. Davey borrowed a towel and sat on that.

Rosemary called a counselor. If Davey wouldn't go, she'd go. She chose the minister of a church twenty-five miles away. She was cautious about seeing anyone locally. In small towns, word always seemed to get around.

The picture of Jesus was the same that had hung in her Sunday School room when she was a child. Reverend Schroeder was stern-looking, though his words flowed easily as if he'd been practicing them for a long time. When she started to cry, he looked vaguely disgusted and asked her what her birth order had been and what her husband's was. What did that matter, she wanted to know, blowing and weeping into the tissue, when the kids were all miserable and suffering and her husband was, you know, in *exile,* and *separated* from her and the kids were wringing their hands at life and she felt so helpless, so hopeless for their futures and was it a reaction to their father leaving or what? And what was she to do—they were in such a mad turmoil, every one of them, though the oldest was off at sea now and she supposed he was okay but he was so angry, violent at times, and her daughter might be suicidal, she didn't know for sure—she said she wasn't—and the youngest doing strange things—cutting the tops off cars—she suspected drugs.

He interrupted the outpouring with, "How did you raise your kids? What kind of upbringing did they have?"

Rosemary paused. "Well, I encouraged them to be creative, I guess—think their own thoughts—we both did, their father and I—and we encouraged them to express their feelings I suppose—you know—we weren't real strict, like the way I was brought up."

He tapped his pencil on the legal pad. "Well then," he cleared his throat, "you got what you asked for." Pause. "We'll set you up for another appointment."

Like hell. She dried her tears. Having heard the Judgment, she *did* feel better. Anger was easier than hurt and she was blind with anger.

Six weeks before high school graduation, Davey had a fight with his girlfriend and wanted to leave school. "You can't mean it—so close to graduation! What is it?" she said. "Don't you think you're overreacting? You can't do this!"

His hysteria came as a shock. His face purple with screaming, he stormed through the house in a rage. Hours later, he came to her as she sat reading in the living room. "Mom, I took some aspirin," he said.

"Got a headache?" She spoke without looking up, her eyes anchored to the page.

"A whole bottle."

"My God! Davey! When?" There he was looming over her like a giant, the weight of his trouble in her lap as he stood thumbs hooked in his jeans pockets, eyes swollen and red. If only she had looked earlier, much earlier.

"Three hours ago," he said.

She called Poison Control. The voice on the telephone said firmly and calmly, "Get him to an Emergency Room." She called Justin at the cottage for help. "Just come with me, Justin, please."

"I'm too tired," he said.

Not understanding how he could refuse, she persisted. "I need you," she said. "Please—we have to get Davey to the hospital."

"I'm going to bed," he said, and hung up.

It was fury at Justin that carried her through the drive to the hospital, the inquiry, her fright, her guilt in not getting help sooner, her shame at the questions fired at her from a clipboard through the bowed head of the doctor. Her answers came from her dream, directed by her fantasy where life was as it should be. "We *are*," she said emphatically, "a close, caring family," while Davey was having his stomach pumped.

"Just go, Davey. Just go one time to the doctor you met in the hospital."

"Forget it," he said. "I'm gonna graduate, okay?" Later, he relented, obedient as a five-year-old. She simply packed him in the car and told him where they were going. Then, as if suddenly awakening to the hold she still had on him, he blurted out, "I'll never forgive you for this."

Soon after Justin called. "How is he?"

"He's home and seems to be fine," she answered. He sounded beaten down, his voice barely audible when he said, "Want to go see him play next Saturday?" Like a date. Like twenty-five years ago with a little flavoring in between. It might help Davey to see them together.

They didn't dance. They sat, he with a beer and she with a glass of wine while Davey seemed to disassociate himself from the both of them After a few sips, watching the surface of the table and wiping up imaginary crumbs with his napkin, Justin got up and said, "Let's go."

They sat in the car at the farmhouse looking down the cleared path to the pond. "Well," said Rosemary, her hand on the door handle.

His lips moved. He said something. It sounded like "coming home."

"What?" she said.

"All I can think about is coming home."

She knew she would probably regret what she would say, but to welcome him was unthinkable. "Just like that?" she hissed. "After all the pain? Disappearing? Not a single word? Running off with God knows who? Knocking the wind out of your kids? Not helping with Davey? Will you go to counseling with me? Will you? Will you get a job? Take your meds? Will you help me or do you just want to be *taken care of?*" When he didn't answer, she got out of the car and enjoyed slamming the door.

CREEDMORE

~∢~

She had chosen to be alone, she guessed. The choice had been made with the slam of the car door. After he pulled away, there was nothing but the night silence of the woods, and no light but that of the moon, so bright she could see the keyhole in the door. The house had never been as quiet as this, the air heavy with the newness of nobody in it.

In the dining room were the five unmatched oak chairs she'd collected at auctions long ago. She ran her fingers lightly across the designs etched along the spindled backs. She had scraped off the varnish, worked the paint remover in between the intricate designs with a toothbrush and picked out the old varnish with a nail file. She'd been so careful in the details that make a home. Rocking side to side as if there were a baby in her arms, she clung to the desire to nurture, the only thing she knew how to do.

The doctor she'd met yesterday was grandmotherly, unpretentious and kind; the folds of her blouse draped softly over full breasts, her short reddish hair in gentle waves around her face. She spoke with her glasses in hand and looked at Rosemary with a concern that caught in Rosemary's throat. Davey, she was saying, was fragile. She allowed a long silence, giving Rosemary time.

Beyond the closed blinds, traffic hummed. After her outpouring, Rosemary was finally out of words and tears. On the wall behind the doctor hung a painting of bright red poppies and blue strawflowers. Unsentimental, the composition was disproportionate, the flowers seeming to leap off the table on which they sat, the red and blue dominating, glorious and harmonious where nothing else in the painting was—like a memory, that subconscious choice of what to remember—the flowers, the beautiful flowers and little else.

Because Dr. Vincent had acknowledged her worry, she'd no longer have to think about everything alone. Answers neatly defined the trouble. Suddenly, there was tangibility, containment, and eradication in sight. And exoneration.

"You mustn't blame yourself for anything," Dr. Vincent said.

Wanting to believe it, Rosemary smiled. Yet, the rages in the middle of the night, the smashed mirrors, cupboards, walls, the cries to end a life just barely begun had left her bewildered, making connections she fought against. She believed in living robustly, in her children's willingness to take risks, and cherished the sensitivity that allowed them to see beyond what most people had the capacity for, their talent for feeling deeply. But the other side of the story frightened her and she had spent a lifetime keeping it at bay. Silence meant more than the absence of others, it meant an absence of self, *madness.*

Now, the silence of the house brought her back to that awful, overbearing quiet in her mother's house when she was a child. She was not usually left alone, but because her mother found a part-time job for a brief period, Rosemary had to enter the house after school without her mother's presence. She hated it. The key to the back door hanging from a shoelace around her neck worried her all day in school, thumping her chest whenever she stood to answer. She might lose the key. The lock might stick, as it sometimes did, and what would she do then? Once inside, she would find cookies on the counter, a vacuous presence of her mother. There'd be the lonesome, crinkle sound of the radiators, and the way the door shut with a heaviness she never felt when her mother was home, and the fear of things that happened only when she was alone.

In the living room and after the cookies, she played Solitaire with her mother's cards, and waited for the hands on the clock to move. After Solitaire, she placed the kings, queens, and jacks down in a swirl on the dark, velvety-quiet rug. Talking to them, she turned the cards face down, placing the repeated finely scrolled designs in a spiral, a garden path she could walk slowly down, down to the center. Somewhere between putting her left brown oxford in the spiral and stepping with her right, the silence snatched her mind away. Her heart raced and her pretending froze and her self *left*. That's the only way she could think of it. She could never tell anyone. The self that was her—her thoughts—her spirit—her will—hung over the spiral she had made like a feather afloat, teased her as to which way it would go, but escaped her. She was empty, going down the long, dark, velvety spiral space between the cards—deeper—deeper—diminishing. She tried to scream but no sound came out. She knew her body could do anything it wanted to without her mind to tell it not to. Fear vapored up from the dark velvet. And paralysis. And death. She couldn't tell how long she was gone, like sleep, but it seemed to be a very long time.

Then the radiator crinkled again—and her mind jumped back. Just like that. She knew in the way children know things that she'd been *out of her mind*. She knew too it would happen again and it did—twice more, always when she was alone in the house. If anyone ever found out she could wind up in Creedmore, the state hospital, two blocks away.

If you did something stupid or if someone didn't agree with you, they would say, *You belong in Creedmore!* Kids at school said it all the time. Her father said it to her mother lots of times. But if someone really did lose their mind, that was where they put them till their mind came back. She could never give the feeling a name. Many shadows hung over her young years, but the darkest had to do with the fear of losing her mind. It was, in all the ghoulish imaginings of childhood, the most terrifying. She knew it could happen. She'd heard the screams of the men when she and her mother, on their way to the park, walked along the march of high, black iron fence that surrounded Creedmore. The yellow brick buildings, three stories high, were set back from the fence and separated by green lawns and cement walks, their mysterious arched terraces filled with shadows. Along these terraces the men reached out from the iron bars as they waited for their minds to come back. They screamed because they didn't have minds to tell them not to. There was no telling what they might do. But, as her mother pointed out, they were far from the fence. They were up on the terraces behind iron bars, just getting a breath of fresh air. Like recess. Despite her optimism, her mother tightened her hand on Rosemary's. She quickened her steps and said, *Don't look at them, Rosemary. Don't stare.*

Whenever her mother took her to the wading pool in the park just across the avenue from Creedmore, they would see passengers from the city coming off the Q-43 bus, hurrying toward the gates of the hospital. Some carried shopping bags and valises, others clutched bundles of bread and peaches and rolled-up bits of clothing, and some, carrying nothing, held onto the arm of a companion, but they all walked with their heads down as though they didn't expect anything good to ever happen.

Don't look at them, Rosemary. Don't stare. She tried not to. She kept her eyes down, but she wanted to look into the faces to see if she could tell which ones had lost their mind. She remembered the heat, the sidewalk sparkling with the tiniest chips of glass in the cement, the cracks filled with dandelions and gum wrappers as she watched her feet swing in front of her in rhythm to her mother's steps.

Once, a couple passed them. The woman spoke to her husband in a quiet voice. He plodded along beside her, then stopped.

"Come on now, Horace," she said.

He was one, Rosemary was sure. He seemed to look without seeing. When he wouldn't move, his wife said, "What would you like, Horace, out of the bag?" She spoke as if what she'd been worrying about was now going to happen. She set the shopping bag between them on the sidewalk, its cord handles spread open, the word, *Macy's*, wrinkled along its side. He began to pull out a straw hat and a pair of blue plaid pajamas. His belt disappeared under his belly as he bent over.

"Don't stare. Don't look at them, Rosemary," her mother whispered.

"Now, you know you don't need the pajamas this minute. Just the hat, Horace," the woman said and reached for his hand. People streamed by. The man searched the passing faces, slowly putting the hat on his head. In a flash his mind came back, Rosemary knew, because he threw his hat on the ground, his hair wet with perspiration, and threw his arms around his wife, sobbing. He sank down in the grass and shook his head, pleading, *no—no—no—no—no.* Two guards appeared and carried him off. "C'mon now, mon," said one of them in an Irish brogue.

Her mother yanked Rosemary's arm, two dark circles showing in the armpits of her dress. She kept her eyes straight ahead.

"Why is he with her and not inside?" Rosemary asked.

"They go home for visits once in a while if they're not too bad," she said.

"But not Julia?" Rosemary said. Her father's cousin, Uncle Gene, was married to Julia.

"Not ever, Julia."

Across the avenue were the iron gates of the park entrance. She could hear the water spray and the other children as they splashed in and out of the fountain, calling and laughing. They walked toward the gates as if they held a safe haven. Soon she watched her mother settle herself on the park bench and check her watch. "We have until three-thirty," she announced, while Rosemary shed her sundress and scratched places where her swimsuit itched. Her mother reached for the dress and carefully placed it on the bench beside her, then pulled blue wool from her knitting bag, ready to twine the wool around her index finger. "Go on now, Rosemary. Why don't you get in the water?"

But Rosemary, feeling white and bony and shivery in the shade of the high old trees, ran instead to the fence and pressed her face against the bars, toward the yellow brick buildings. This was how it felt to look out from one of the arches, to feel chilly in the shade and never stand in the sun, to wait for something to come back to you that was yours. That was *you*. Rosemary turned around quickly to see if her mother was still behind her on the bench, to make sure she hadn't been snatched away, but her mother was still there, her knitting in her hands—a blue sweater for Rosemary—blue like her dress with the bird buttons, blue like her eyes. Rosemary ran back to her.

"Don't you want to splash in the pool, Rosemary?" she said, smiling, putting her arms around her, wanting to keep her safe.

Don't stare, Rosemary. Don't look at them. Don't see. Stay safe.

In the safety of her own house, Rosemary was looking through the bars again. Safety was a mother's illusion. There was nothing she could do to keep her children safe from the very thing that had haunted her over the years. How strange that this fear of hers should surface so many years later, find her, touch her family, and curl its insidious way through their lives. They had struggled with its complexities without recognizing what it was. A cruel trick had been played.

She knew she was being far too dramatic. People could be helped now, but could they count on pills and what would it mean, taking them over a lifetime? What were the choices? And the most difficult of all: Justin, coming home, not on medication—did she want to live like that again? Did she have the patience to pour herself in that mold again? Life, like the suit salesman joke Justin loved so much, *He wants a green suit, Murray, so turn on the green light,* for her had become a series of disparate roles, invisible when he was high, carrying the load when he was down. Yet, what was love but a willingness to tolerate—a view that rested on self-lessness and imprisonment? As a child she read it in her mother's fingers that turned gritty potatoes round and round, the knife leaving a trail of potato skin curling off into the newspaper spread on the counter. She read it in her mother's soft cheek half hidden under dark hair as she leaned over to dig in the bag for another potato, and waited for her blue eyes, round and sad, to look at her though they seemed only to talk to the potato, "Hear those locusts? They only do that on the hottest days. God, I hate the heat! Stop picking that scab, will you? Let's see, we can't go to the movies on Tuesday because that's the day Uncle Gene comes, and Wednesday we'll go to the Bronx to see Grandma but maybe Friday. Okay? *Pinocchio's* playing. I think you'll like that. We'll be home in plenty of time for supper at five."

Despite the sun and summer sounds streaming in, fear filtered through her mother's small kitchen. Her mother did the best she could. She tried and tried to make the world safe. Don't all mothers? Diligence and patience and sacrifice came with the thick slice of raw potato her mother slipped her as she made plans for the week. And so did fear. Everything depended on having supper on the table by five, on meeting her father's demands. When the Good Humor bells rang on the next block and Rosemary looked up at her mother, she said, "Don't even ask, Rosemary. I've got just enough for the bread man and the movies. Want another slice of potato?"

Now in the silent farmhouse, Rosemary found herself staring out the window at the few scattered streetlights from Pucam. She would make herself a pot of tea. Turn on the radio. Dance a few steps. Soon she'd feel better. But in the end, what she did was climb the stairs and wander in and out of the bedrooms. Once more she sat on Annie's bed and looked across the moonlit, shadowless field that stretched to Pucam. Silent Pucam. A different kind of silence, felt in the way that misunderstandings and prejudice are, in the way being disconnected from community is silent. And stigma is silent. And so is the need for silence in the face of it.

And then there was the silence surrounding Julia, Uncle Gene's wife. Uncle Gene came for coffee every Tuesday afternoon after visiting Julia in Creedmore. Rosemary remembered searching for clues to Julia's mystery in a small picture Uncle Gene produced from his wallet. She was a pretty, dark-haired woman, with her head cocked to one side, who might have said just before the picture was taken, "Is this all right?" She'd been *put away* in Creedmore for most of their marriage, twenty-one years, so her mother said.

Uncle Gene was a pleasant oddity in Rosemary's life, a man who wore high-buttoned shoes and whose gray eyes looked like big jimmy marbles until he took off his glasses, which he did whenever he talked about Julia, dabbing his eyes with a pocket handkerchief while her mother politely poured coffee. Then he took the handkerchief and wiped the glasses, his thumb and forefinger chasing each other around the lens. "So strong, so healthy," he'd say shaking his head. "Not a thing wrong with her body, but"—and here he would blow his nose— "she's out of her mind."

Sometimes when the five o'clock whistle blew and it wasn't five o'clock, it meant that one of the patients had escaped Creedmore. Whenever she heard the whistle, Rosemary wondered if Julia was coming to find Uncle Gene. From the sound of it, Julia was strong enough to climb that high fence and run like the wind. Visions of her sudden appearance filled Rosemary with fear. And sadness. She couldn't imagine how awful it would be to be *put away*.

"I don't want Gene in this house," her father once barked, "always looking for handouts just because he had a little bad luck. He wants more from you than meets the eye."

"But there's nothing to it," her mother said, wiping her eyes with the hem of her apron. "He just wants someone to talk to." Then Rosemary understood that Uncle Gene's visits were never to be mentioned, like the scratch under the doily on the coffee table. They had their secrets, she and her mother. Uncle Gene would ask Rosemary to sit on his knee and she did, hoping he didn't notice how uncomfortable she was. She never sat on her father's lap. She always felt like crying when Uncle Gene asked her, though she wasn't afraid of him. "Rosemary, Rosemary," he'd sigh and begin to croon a song in her ear. His gray eyes peered out at her and his bushy eyebrows danced up and down. She both loved and hated it, and looked over at her mother, who sat there with her arms crossed over her apron, smiling.

Once, Uncle Gene said Julia had to have shock treatments and that both her arms were broken. By way of excusing the orange spots all over his white shirt and tie, he said he had to feed her, which he'd done that afternoon.

"Florence," he said to her mother, "we won't talk about it now, but I—"

"Rosemary, go out and play," her mother said.

On the way out, Rosemary imagined it was Julia she saw on the terrace the last time she walked past Creedmore, that woman wearing a yellow sweater who waved at her and watched her for a long time. Even when Rosemary had walked so far past the terrace she could no longer see the woman, she saw her arm waving and waving through the bars.

The next time Uncle Gene came, he didn't take Rosemary on his knee. He came in with a big box like the coat boxes from S. Klein, tied with string and done up with a wood and wire handle. He handed the box to her mother and she tried to undo the knots to save the string but finally had to use her paring knife to cut it. Inside were folds and folds of white tissue paper. Her mother's face lit up and her voice dropped to a whisper. "Oh, Gene?" she said, his name ending like a question.

"It's a bedspread," he said, and his hand covered hers as he tried to help her pull it out of the box. A white shower of snowflakes drifted to the floor, the designs crocheted with millions of tiny stitches.

"It's exquisite," said her mother. She busied herself with trying to get it back into the box the way it was. Maybe she knew what Uncle Gene was going to say.

"Julia finished it just before she went in. I want you to have it, Florence, for listening to me all these years."

"Gene," her mother said softly. "Are you sure? She will look for it when—"

"She isn't ever coming out—hasn't known me for years. I won't be coming by anymore, I don't think," he said. He took off his glasses and began wiping them while his face hung bare over his lap. Her mother sent Rosemary out to play. The word *divorce* hung in the air as she slipped out the door.

"What is divorce?" she asked her mother later.

"It's when people who are married decide not to be married any-more."

"But Julia didn't decide, did she?"

"No, she can't. So Uncle Gene had to decide."

"Is that why he's so sad? He doesn't really want to?"

"No, he doesn't, I suppose. But there's nothing else to do."

Divorce. The syllables had a violence to them. For a long time after Justin left she couldn't say the word, didn't want to think about it. There was more to the story. There always was. She had to think through to the end this time. The end was important. If only she could get to it. She had looked out this same window across the same fields the day after Justin left and thought about her freedom, yet she still wore the house like an old coat she couldn't part with, her freedom an illusion. Confusion and doubt had become her own form of madness.

"Is divorce very bad?" she had asked her mother long ago.

"Yes," she said, "but not if your wife or husband is sick and can't come back to live with you."

"Then you and Daddy aren't going to get divorced?"

"Well, what kind of question is that? Hurry up, now!" she said and pulled Rosemary along. "Your father will be home soon and I've got to get dinner on the table."

Dinner was on time that night and the next, but not Friday, when her mother took her to see *Pinocchio*. They heard the five o'clock whistle just as they walked past St. Gregory's and by the time they got home, the car was already in the garage. Her father paced the kitchen, his hands rolled up in fists.

"Where the hell have you been?" he yelled.

"I told you I was taking Rosemary to the movies this afternoon. Supper's ready—all I have to do is put a light under the soup and we'll eat in five minutes," her mother said and hurried to get bowls out of the cupboard.

"If you think I've got money to burn on movies in the middle of the day and wait for supper too, you belong in Creedmore," he yelled, and banged his fist on the table.

Maybe Rosemary would have felt better if she'd liked the movie, but she hadn't. It frightened her when Pinocchio got swallowed by the whale and the whale's open mouth looked like the arches at Creedmore. All she could think about were the people who never get out of the darkness. In the movies she looked up at her mother and her face was blue-white and far away as she watched the tiny flame of the match going out inside the whale's mouth. They were in darkness, she and her mother, like islands, staring at the screen as if they'd been swallowed too. The light showed her themselves, small and afraid. Rosemary buried her head in her mother's lap.

"That's all right, Rosemary. Don't look if it scares you," her mother said and shielded Rosemary's head with her hand.

But there was nothing to shield them from her father's words or his fist which might explode, or shield Rosemary from the sight of her mother's tears which were on the rims of her eyes, or the droop of her shoulders as she leaned over the soup, stirring. Were there different kinds of madness? Only some you got put away for? Was a person crazy when you never knew what they might do? A look, a dangerous turn, an infliction like the snap of a whip that you could feel forever, because you expected understanding where there was none? Could you dismiss it all by saying, they were *out of their mind?* Did madness have its own right?

Then, with her father's words tearing through the air, she ran to her parents' bedroom and dropped to her knees. She reached under their bed to pull out the box from Uncle Gene but the box was bigger and heavier than she thought it would be. She tugged but it was jammed against the bedboards. Peering down into the shadows she tore open the side of the box and pulled out the spread. When she gathered it in her arms, she took great care not to step on it, yet slipped and tripped and banged her head on the dresser anyway—felt the sting of what was sure to come, hurrying now—wanting to wrap the spread around her mother to keep her from hearing any more angry words—wanting her to hear only the silence of the snowflakes. But what she heard was her father spitting out, "What's that? Where did that come from?" and saw his eyes wild and her mother trapped and herself with her hands in midair, heart still, body suspended down that long, empty hall, mind gone—and nothing, no one, to call her back.

Now, forty years later as she looked out over the fields from the high window she saw the captives—her mother, Julia, and Uncle Gene as he wiped his glasses—herself, Justin, her children—they were all captive. Anger was better than sorrow. Swifter, familiar, stronger, and self-propelled. Raising the sash and leaning far out, she felt a madness of her own begin as determined as the eye of a hurricane. In the bedroom she once shared with Justin, she tore their wedding picture off the wall and ran back to the open window. She flung the picture as far as she could, and listened for the crash of splintering glass. Satisfied, she ran through the house and gathered as much in her arms as she could—wedding crystal, wine glasses, vases, Hummels—out, smashed, the framed wedding invitation with the watercolor rose—out into the clear, hard horizon, the crystal bedside lamps—over and down, brass candlesticks—out. Mad madness hovered, heaved, spit, stomped, screamed obscenities to all the chains that ever were. Now *I'm* the one who is mad, she thought, watching herself from afar, astonished.

RESPITE

~✦~

When she was a kid, her mother would thump her between the shoulder blades and say, "Straighten up!" The gift of armor. One had to make one's own opportunity, Rosemary said to herself, pulling in her stomach and pouring on Loving Care. Her first ventures alone on Friday nights seemed daring, but it became easy to enter the dim lounge at the Days Inn on Singles Night, the bar at Sammy's when the band was good, or the VFW once in a while. She watched the bodies moving like agitators in a washing machine and began to dance herself into a frenzy—wild, expansive movements—she *was* every note, every beat. On occasion, when the dance floor emptied, she jumped up with the nerve of someone she couldn't imagine, setting off into spins and gyrations of unnamed desire, feet that couldn't be stopped, arms that formed a fluid flame around her body. She felt wonderful—and young again. She imagined myriad possibilities in the eyes of the lonesome men who watched her. Even though her clothes were soaked with perspiration and smoke, her partners held her during the slow songs and said, "You're a terrific dancer." Women stopped her in the Ladies, dipping and turning their heads at different angles before the smoky mirrors, and said, "I love to watch you dance. You're good."

The music told her what to do. She had only to listen and respond. Dancing became an obsession, the key to her transcendence. Strange, in all the turbulence of sound, to feel such tranquillity within. It was lovely being someone else. *I'm a dancer*, she said to herself, as if that was explanation enough. *It's what I've always wanted to be.*

One night on the dance floor with a blur of a man—she could not even remember his name—she happened to look toward the bar where, reflecting the restless strobe light like two small beacons, were the unmistakable round lenses of his glasses. She was conscious of being watched, more conscious than ever of the reason for her dancing. When the set was over, Len walked toward her.

They left together and walked along the tree-lined streets, the collar of his denim jacket turned up against the cold, his corn silk hair glowing under the street lamp. She liked the way his cigarette smelled when he first lit up, and the way he asked her about herself, not her kids, not her husband. "How are *you* doing?" he said. He studied her when he asked a question as if the answer was important to him. "What are you reading these days?"

Soon after, she lay with him and it made no difference, it was that easy. The rest of her world was as it was but the window that had opened saved her. Kindness saved her. Blue eyes piercing, saved her. He said he loved her, and that saved her. "How do you know?" she said. "Because it's a real deep feeling," he said and left it at that.

When he held her breast that first time, she said, "We have to use some common sense about this. I'm a lot older than you."

"It's too late," he said. And so when he, laying the round, gold-rimmed glasses down on the dashboard, down on the blanket, down before the fireplace, down in the grass, down on the nightstand beside her bed, down among the sand dunes, down in his rented room in the farmhouse, down among her trees, down under the stars, she willingly went. It was strange, she thought, that her desire now ruled everything. Her needs were answered over and over. The paradox was, the more they were answered the more she needed. She was a stranger to herself yet she could do what she was supposed to now, even sit in the empty house and listen to the silence. They never mentioned Anne, or Michael, or Davey, or Justin. They never talked about what came before or what could never be, but only about the present, rich and poignant. Secret. It was the secret, however, seductive and at times burdensome, that imprisoned her in a different way: *Would Anne, if she knew, feel betrayed?*

Meanwhile there was his hand over hers, the calloused palm gentle against her skin. When it left, he always squeezed her hand to let her know that leaving could be tender, and not a tearing apart. It was one of the things she loved about him. She felt cradled. Comforted. She no longer needed to dance so much, or cry. The whirlwind her life had become slowed, and for the moment, she thought she knew what love was. They decided to go away for a few days to the Poconos, to a cabin in the woods surrounded by blueberries that held the sun's heat in them, growing on bushes so tall and thick they could hide inside them as they picked. It seemed as if they had God's favor for one whole week: words, a fire in the fireplace each night, books, the darkened room, soft sighs, the lighted end of his cigarette.

"Will you come with me to get a beer?" he would ask in the evenings after dinner. Once, walking along the road, the Big Dipper close to the horizon and pouring luck into the trees, she picked up a small, smooth rock that had been split in two but fit back together so perfectly in her hands she could hardly see the split, defining the way she was with him. And later, the only ones at the bar, they danced in the semidarkness with their arms wrapped around each other, their shuffled steps close and inti-mate. He just happened, and she breathed him in, the rich smoke filling her lungs like a long-awaited answer.

By day, the leaves outside the kitchen window of their cabin turned yellow, dripping with the late August rain. They read *The Great Gatsby* out loud. It took all day. Neither of them stirred from the table, hour after hour, satiated by the words, other lives passing before them, becoming their own, and intertwined with theirs. Everything they were and were not came into each separate moment, his eyes on her, her eyes from the page to his eyes, so blue, filling her for a lifetime.

You read, he said. *I love to watch you taste the words.* So she read to him before the words could crush her, every motion in the stillness becoming significant. Even his lighting a cigarette was filled with mean-ing, the tiny flame short-lived and then again, the brief smoke measuring the moments with pleasure she never could have had were it not for him, the flow of spoken words like music, the room so bare yet opulent because of him, the old chrome and vinyl chairs, the small red table, so meager, so immaterial, it hurt to know how misguided she'd been for most of her life.

He had no right to love her like this, and she had no right, no family, no mind, no will, only life pushing her toward him so she could touch his face and know before she did what that would feel like, what that would do to her and there she was being held, cradled, considered, her thoughts almost read out loud as she looked at him because he was looking back. She was herself, her deepest self, walking toward him.

She was with him and he with her. The word was *with*, and it was the first time since she'd left her mother's womb she'd been with anyone.

Part Five

COMING AND GOING

THE VISIT, 1982

He bought the dog in Florida the day he auditioned for the band. Saw the ad in the paper the same time he saw the ad for lead guitar. A Great Dane. Biggest damn dog he'd ever seen. The guy who sold it to him said he got a job playing on a cruise ship and he couldn't take the dog along. The soulful brown eyes in that gigantic head—Davey couldn't walk by him. Not only that but the dog chose to jump on his lap when he sat down on the guy's couch, pinning him down as if to say, *Take me, I'm yours, all one hundred and fifty-nine pounds.*

His name was Taxi because his paws were checkered, two white pads and three black. The rest of him was gray with black spots, as if he'd gotten stained with raindrops. He was majestic the way he sat, exposing massive shoulders and chest—even when he was on somebody's lap, which always got Davey laughing—and he had a careless elegance when he sprinted, too, his long legs dancing like a canine Gene Kelly. Davey thought the leader of the band, Damon, was as impressed with the dog as he was with Davey's guitar runs that first meeting, and from then on, Taxi was the band dog, everybody slipping him treats, giving that big head and those silky ears a good rub.

The band was on the move, from south Florida to Georgia—Disney World, New Orleans, Jacksonville. Any long break in the gigs and Davey went home, like now, but this time they had a long tour ahead of them so he decided to bring the dog home, and here he was, on the road again, heading for Jacksonville, staring into the long beam of his headlights, thinking about the dog, the house, the cedar shingles rough as tree bark, dormers like sleepy eyes, chimneys that seemed to lean more each time he went home, and his mother in the driveway fighting to hold back Taxi, her thin arm high over her head waving good-bye as he drove down the long lane, still waving as he turned past the mailbox, yanking the dog's collar and still waving through the long shadows of the woods till the dark, looming trees shot between them.

Everything he owned was packed in the VW—the two huge Pevey amps, three guitars and the banjo, his grandfather's leather suitcase he'd found in the attic, carton boxes of cords, pedals, hookups, tools. Home to Maryland, back to Florida, again and again—his life had a rhythm of its own, a need that tugged at his sleeve until he went in either direction, fleeing or returning—a condition that often found him speeding into the night, like now, feeling as if he was in control of his destiny, something he never felt in the light of day.

Mostly he drove alone, all seventeen hours, but this time there was Vance, the bass man, who looked cramped with his feet on a box of tapes, knees pulled up to his chin. There wasn't much Davey could do about the lack of room. The trip up from Florida the week before was bad with Taxi looming from behind and slobbering over their shoulders. Right this minute, Taxi was probably stretched out in the front hall of the farmhouse, his gray coat rising and falling with each long, deep breath, rib cage as big as a full-grown buck's.

"You need to stretch?" he said to Vance.

"Yeah, man. Soon. Just thinking about that dog of yours, you know? You did the right thing—he's too big to drag around to gigs. That farm is the place for him. Dog like that just don't belong sleeping in smoky bars or waiting in the band bus."

"He's a great conversation starter. You see how many times girls come over and start talking about the dog?"

"As if you needed a conversation starter. Women are always hanging around, throwing it at you."

Yeah. More important, something big was waiting for him in Florida.

He could feel it. He wanted to run—just dump the car and run all the way, feet flying, nose to the wind.

"Oh, man!" Vance peered out the side window. "Moon's following us. Never could figure out why it looks like it follows you. Yeah, let's stop."

"Okay. Next chance we get."

"You know there's a dog star?" Vance could always come up with something. Any conversation, he'd come up with stuff nobody else knew.

"Yeah? Where is it?"

"I don't know right now." Vance leaned forward and peered through the top of the windshield, his long plaits trailing on his shoulders. "Can't see a thing with those headlights and that moon. We can look when we stop. There's a whole group of stars called Canis Major. The brightest one is Sirius, watchdog of the Egyptians. In the spring, when they saw it in the early morning sky just before dawn, they knew the Nile would overflow its banks."

Overflow. Overburden. Overlap, overpower, override, overdrive, overdrawn, overgrown. Overabundance. Deluge. Overwhelm, overthrow, overturn. Overalls. Overwrought. Overstrung. Maybe. Megalomania. Spell it. Now use it in a sentence. Major—Canis. Davey laughed. The thought of Taxi stuck in his throat for a minute as he, Davey, sped away from him at seventy miles an hour for twelve hours now.

He watched for an exit; he'd had enough of the broken white line, his link to the farm, to the one place where he always knew what to expect, every small thing in its place when he got there. Motels and hotels for the rest of it. Sometimes a girlfriend would take him in and he'd have an address for a few months, *in care of* written on the letters his mother sent. He'd pretend his life was like anybody else's, but that got too tight in short order. The farm was some sort of baseline. Each time he came home his mother would check out the changes in him. This time it was, "I don't remember your hair being so blond, Davey, except when you were little, when you would get so brown and your hair would bleach out white— those summers at Sulley's Point."

Sulley's Point. The very name brought a stab. His father living there alone, a recluse. But before that, when summers belonged to Michael,

Annie and him, his father would put up the mast to the catamaran and take him for a sail the whole afternoon. His job was to hook the lines and place a centerboard in each hull as his father pushed the boat to deeper water. He was hardly able to move his head in the red, white, and blue–striped life jacket. With his father pulling hard on the sheet and swinging the tiller to free the boat from the bulkhead, the first gust of wind vibrated the lines like a song. His father would call out, "Lean out on the opposite side, Davey!" The tameless wind filled the black and orange sail like a grand cloak, playing with the two of them as they skimmed over the water. They were a speck on the pall of the river, together for only a second in the span of time.

"That farm needs some life," Davey said. "It's been too quiet since my dad left and we all went off on our own."

"Your dad left?"

"Yeah, he flipped out. He flipped out a lot before he left. It got so you didn't know who he was. A real roller coaster ride."

"Ever been to Jacksonville?" Vance said.

"No, but I got a great-aunt there, on my mother's side. Mom gave me her number. When does this gig start? Tuesday? Maybe I'll call her Monday."

He was curious to meet Aunt Anna, his grandfather's sister. The grandfather on his mother's side, that was, who died when Davey was a baby. The fact that Davey's first name, William, was the same as his grandfather's had brought the elder William a lot of satisfaction, his mother told him. "He always wanted boys, Davey. Women seemed to infuriate him," she said. Davey saw a picture of his grandfather holding him as an infant, looking proudly into the camera. "He died of a heart attack while washing his car," his mother said, "which seemed appropriate—he cared for *things* a great deal. But I think that was because he'd been very poor as a child. His possessions owned him. Funny, I always had the feeling that he really wanted to be elsewhere, out to sea maybe, like when he was young."

Davey stared into the dark. He wanted to know who else was among his forebears. Shed some light. Some other connection. When he'd walked into the waiting room on the day of the family session at Dr. Vincent's, the door slipped out of his hand and crashed into the wall. Bam! It got everybody's attention. There was his father, laughing in the old way, making jokes about Davey's grand entrance and his ponytail. Michael and Anne were there too, a kind of magnetic field touching the four of them. His mother sat looking out the window. She glanced at the faces of the other people in the waiting room, her fingers pressed into the palms of her hands as if embarrassed at the clatter they made. During the session, his father looked directly at him and said, "Maybe Davey is more like me than anybody," and Davey remembered saying, "Aw, shut up," laughing as he said it but with more vehemence than he meant. Green eyes exactly like his own stared back at him, the lines along his father's hollowed cheeks deeper than he remembered. They were ganging up on their father, saying, "You've got to take the pills to ward off the demons. Davey, too."

What demons? He felt great and played like Hendrix. Davey stopped seeing the doctor after that. "Don't want anything more to do with it," he told his mother. And that was that.

Suddenly, he steered the car off the road. "Man," he said, "I gotta get out of this car—now!" And pounded the dashboard.

"Wait, Davey. Calm down. Let's get off the interstate and find a back road somewhere. Some place dark so we can see the stars," Vance said, so he kept going, and finally pulled off where a sign said Pine Marsh, and pointed toward what he guessed were swamps along the edge of a forest of scrub pines, toward mosquito heaven, trying to keep his mind on that one task, finding enough darkness. He was good at darkness. It liked him. Bright sunlight drove him crazy. Fluorescent lights killed him. But darkness was a haven. This morning at the farm was the last morning light he'd see for a while, roosters crowing, doors banging, the smell of bacon and coffee, and Taxi barking from a hole he'd dug in the field while the tractors ground down the rows. Now it would be smoky darkness in the clubs till the band packed the equipment around four in the morning. They'd crash around five and waken to room-darkening shades sometime in mid-afternoon. They lived like moles. Band houses with cots and motels with cooties.

Off the main road, he and Vance stopped on a farm road closed off with a rail gate. Vance looked up the minute he stepped from the car. "Moon's down. Which way's north?"

In answer, Davey sent a stream into the gully on the side of the field.

"Okay. Got it," said Vance, turning his head. "Should be around five o'clock, close to the horizon. See those three stars close together? That's Orion's belt. Follow that down—the belt points to Canis Major—that bright one?—that's Sirius. It's about eight point eight light years away."

Davey stared up at the stars, suddenly orderly, and then down at his friend who only reached his shoulder. Vance was good-humored, steady. His face was dark as the night itself, his gold earring the only thing Davey could position for sure. And now the stuff about the stars.

"You know, this time we're going to make it big, Vance. This band is going to move," he said as they leaned against the gate. "I can feel it coming."

"It don't matter, man. We're just getting through. Don't hope for more than that, otherwise you get your teeth knocked out. We're doing good. We get to different places, the girls go nuts over us, all we can drink, play like crazy—that ain't bad, you know."

"Yeah, but we're on the edge of something, I just know." Davey jogged in place, his legs like springs while his hands grasped the gate rail. In another instant, he was up and over the gate, sprinting down the dirt road, eyes on the stars. Damn, he felt good. There wasn't anything he couldn't do—create, accomplish, determine, make, perform, take on. Burn up. If he didn't, he'd explode.

He kept on running. The woods towered on either side and the sky was one thick slice, littered with stars. Bejeweled. Bothered and bewildered. His head was filled with trivia. Circuits crossed and zapped all over the place, sending sparks, shooting stars. There goes one! Across the sliver of sky. A sign. He was marked. Inspired. Exalted, exhilarated, exuberant, explosive, excessive, exaggerated, exonerated. Exclusive.

Once he heard his mother say to his father, "You're burning the candle at both ends." Maybe he *was* like his old man. He'd wear out before he was thirty. Didn't matter. He kept running through the cutaway of trees, the night soft and alive around him, crickets almost deafening.

He heard a long, low whistle. Vance. He'd forgotten him. Probably scared of the woods. A city boy. Davey stopped and gasped as he bent over his toes. The white stars of his tennis shoes leaped out at him. Man, he was in no kind of shape. He turned back, working up to speed in a few seconds.

Vance was smoking. "Have yourself some sweet stuff?" he said in that mellow gold voice of his. "Smooth out a few kinks?"

"You'll see, Vance," he said, ignoring the offer. "We'll get back and work on that tape, get it polished enough to send around to a few radio stations. Something's gonna fly."

"It's not in our hands, Davey. Depends on luck." Vance passed him a joint and stared into the stars again.

"How can you look up there and not feel hopeful? The whole damn thing is one big accident. The fact that we're here at all trying to understand mysteries is some kind of fluke. Who gives a crap about whether or not we make it? We do, that's why we will. Nothing going against it. The *why* side's getting weaker and the *why not* side's getting stronger. Besides, there's a message dropping into my brain right this very minute—something's up." Uproar, upset, upheaval, upmost. Uppermost.

"Dropping in from where?" Vance was laughing at him.

"From that star, that bright one, what's its name?"

"Sirius."

"Yeah." Serious, delirious. Tide's gonna overflow. Everything was good and getting better. Somebody might spot him. Offer him a contract. He'd take Vance with him, if he could. They did their real talking up on stage, he and Vance. Damn good bass man.

A star shot across the sky. "I've counted eight of those since I'm sitting here," Vance said. "If you look away for a second, you miss 'em, they're that quick."

"That's the way it'll be with me, too," Davey said, sitting down, tension easing. He was calm enough now to look for the Big Dipper. That was one he knew. Something else. It was part of a bear, Ursa Major, though he could never find the head. "I mean, I'm not up for longevity. One super colossal streak, then I'm outta here."

"What's that supposed to mean?"

"Just what you think it means. My life, man. You know I never stay in one place too long." He probably shouldn't have said that out loud, but it was what he believed sure as he was sitting under Georgia skies with Vance right now, smoking, looking up, watching for the gossamer thread of the next shooting star. He could accept his fate looking into that great dark space, the stars like stepping stones to mark his way, accept it with a clarity that brought him peace.

"You don't know that," said Vance. "It don't have to be like that. You'll be making big bucks—wouldn't want to leave that now, would you? Big house with a hot tub in the yard? Corvette in the driveway?"

"When you're planning a short stay, you don't need much. I'll leave it to my mother so she'll never have to work again, and to my brother and sister so they can keep doing what they're doing and never have to worry. I don't need anything. I got it all right here." He held out his hands before him, the long fingers ready to curl around the neck of his guitar, the calloused tips ready to worry the strings.

"Figures. You like being out of the mainstream. No license, no insurance, no taxes. Bet you don't have a Social Security number either. Right? You're just an angel dropped down here for safekeeping, or a ghost nobody can pin down. Right? Look up, screwball. See them stars? Every one's got a name and a story. And you're no different. Music's here and now but then it's gone. A noisy vapor. Turns into memory real quick, and half the time it's so elusive you can't get it back. Not like something you can hold in your hand. But you, Jack, you're living and breathing. You got no reason to cut anything short. You got everything, man. Looks, talent." Vance shook his head and glared at him. Davey had never seen him so upset, cool-headed Vance, nerves of steel. Comes of having a white mother and a black father who nearly killed each other and him, too. Left home at twelve and been roaming ever since. Vance could handle anything, get along with anybody. Even had a legal driver's license.

He shouldn't have told him. It was a weight he had no right to lay on his friend. "Hey," he said, "don't worry about it. It's just something I know, nothing I'm planning. Aren't there some things you just know without anybody telling you?"

"Jesus, Davey. You scare me," Vance said, staring at the space between his shoes.

They hit Jacksonville around three-thirty in the morning. After a few wrong turns, they searched along darkened streets for the band house and finally saw the van, *Raven's Flight* scrolled on its side, parked next to a stucco cottage. The bedrooms were filled. No one stirred. Davey threw his suitcase and carton of tapes on the floor, jerked an ironing board out of the way, scooped a set of earphones and a Doritos bag along with three beer cans off the couch as Vance rolled out his sleeping bag. Davey closed his eyes and listened to Vance's breathing on the other side of the room for what seemed like a long time. Once he dozed off and reached out for Taxi though that only woke him up enough to remember he'd left the dog home. He tucked his arm under his chest, but it was no good trying to sleep. He got up and made his way through the maze of Peveys and leather boots to the door, to the brick walk, to the early morning sky that glowed through the yellow haze of Jacksonville. Already traffic was humming, colors coming back to the roofs and shapes of houses, crowding him with details. Soon every shingle, every flower, every leaf, every shape, color, and sound would come to life, drowning him in its glory, drawing him to its single-mindedness. He squinted as he looked to the southwest sky, but even Sirius was gone, stolen by the morning.

He called his great-aunt the next day, just before rehearsal. Vance was fooling around on the drums so he had to shout into the phone.

Davey heard a faint hello, slow and questioning, as if the ringing of the phone was an unusual phenomenon.

"Aunt Anna? You'll never guess who this is!"

"No, I wouldn't, I guess," she crackled out of the phone. He motioned to Vance to pipe down.

"I'm Davey, your brother's grandson."

"What? I know there's a Michael and a William."

"That's me, William. My first name's William."

"Where are you?" she said. "Is everything all right?"

Vance tossed the drumsticks into the air and missed.

"Not too far from you, I think. Off Mandarin Drive." She said something else. Was it about dinner?

"What?"

She went on. "I fix something nice for you. You like German food?"

It was the accent that startled him. Of course she'd have an accent—he'd forgotten he was related to someone from another country. "You go down Mandarin and look for the sign for Mandarin Estates. Number 204 by the entrance. Five o'clock is good?"

"Yeah," he said and turned around. The guys were setting up. This place made his stomach queasy. Purple carpeting extended up the walls as if the floor and walls were interchangeable, making him think of a shipwreck from a tidal wave. *Poseidon* would have been a better name than *The Blue Diamond.* Lines ran everywhere, from Peveys to mikes to guitars and banjos to pedals to lights to sound boards and keyboards and back again. Damon stuck his fingers in his mouth and whistled for everybody to assemble but nobody paid any attention at first. Then slowly weaving in and out of club chairs and tables, they meandered toward the stage holding drinks and cigarettes—four guys in T-shirts and Sue, singer Sue, with more moves sideways than forward to get where she was going.

He began tuning the guitar, then warmed up with a few scales, his fingers barely landing on the strings, every note blurred. He had to slow down but wires ran across his shoulders and up and down his arms, vibrating, breaking away. No—slow—slow down—slow down, but the notes tripped over each other, blurred at first, then clearer and clearer, every step, then every half step, then the notes broke free of the scale and sang out for a while in their own combinations, reassembled on the steps, orderly, finally blurring into one raucous sound.

"Hey man, you okay?" Vance tried to step between him and his wires. He felt Vance's arm heavy around his shoulders and then his hand on top of his head, turning it, making him look in Vance's eyes. Who the hell was he? Some kind of brother's keeper? Davey flung his head free, hair splayed over his face. He slapped it away. Tight. Man, he was tight.

"Yeah, yeah. I'm okay. Let's go," he said, lips clenched.

Tuesday's performance was a zinger for a Tuesday. The girls who followed the band came early. Ladies' night. Drinks half-price, shooters free. Mostly wives from the nearby Air Force base and temporarily husbandless for one reason or another, they hung in groups of three or four, dressed in body suits and short cling skirts, hair with body and strength enough to stand out as if they were in constant flight. They had an air of expectancy—

life owed *them* as they sat smoking clouds and sipping drinks, legs crossed. From their midst came explosions of laughter in attention-getting gales. They were ready for the chains of love and Davey loved them. They called to him and he nodded back. They believed in frenzy, the mania of a good time, in the loudest, the fastest and the best. They began to scream the minute Damon jumped on stage with his baggy pants and bare chest, his silver-studded leather jewelry and thick, curly hair that hung six inches below his shoulders. His saxophone swung from his neck like an oversized medallion. Husbands and boyfriends couldn't even come close. They were doomed. But the band guys now—they made out pretty good in the illusions packaged in the flickering spotlights. This was it, man. They could be all their dreams told them, their attention funneled by the paralyzing sound into a common mind, a faith as right as religion, although the difference between them and Davey was that he would play even if there was no one to listen.

He backed up Damon like a willing servant, but truth was, Davey was lead guitar and nobody could beat him. Sister Sue, buxom, same hair as Damon, at the keyboard in spandex black, winked at him. He couldn't contact Ty, rhythm guitar, who was shy and hid behind hair that completely covered his face. Davey glanced around to Ken, the rap man and drummer whose head bobbed along with the drumsticks. Davey bobbed back, then bowed. Vance was at his side; he aimed the neck of his guitar at him. Bam! Vance, buddy, cover me, man. He stepped on the pedal that released smoke, which wafted now across the stage and encircled his chosen family.

They'd rehearsed the steps so many times they were on automatic pilot now, but he still kept his eye on Damon to make sure he was in sync and not too fast. To the side, forward, back, heads swinging in a forward circle, hair sweeping in blue and red circles in the stage lights, the ducks-in-a-row motion releasing the tension. Then it was his run. Damon tapped his foot and waited on the side for him to finish. The notes screamed past, ripped through the air like the nose of a jet; sweat streamed under his black leather hat and vest. The girls screeched and applauded with hands high over their heads, hips swaying. Down on his knees, hips on heels, his fingers skimmed over the frets, barely staying long enough to make contact. He stood up and backed away. Damon smiled and put the sax to his lips and the guitar and sax played like butterflies in a mimosa tree.

Every song was a dance, five hours of aerobics a night. It all passed by in a blur except for "Midnight Blue," his own piece. Alone on stage, the blue light bathed him and he was lost in his lament, as if he were out in the snow and there was Annie again, down at his feet and barefoot. Would he ever get over it? What made him think of her whenever he played this? Why didn't she feel the snow? *Michael help me! Get a blanket! She's too heavy. Michael!*

Sing it sweet. High notes arced and brought in the angels. His fingers were blue; they didn't belong to him, went beyond anything he could do. The guitar was separate from him and an extension of him, a place to pour his fear. He swung around and faced the deserted drum kit, his back to the girls, and when he turned to the audience again the music was as mellow as he could make it.

Then the rhythm picked up. Vance jumped on stage and played the frets on Davey's guitar with his left hand while Davey strummed near the bridge with his right, his other arm around Vance. They strutted across the stage together, Siamese twins joined at the guitar. The girls screamed. Even the bartenders let out a whoop. Ken was back on the drums; Ty— that moving mountain of hair—bent over the keyboard and the sound man increased the volume for the last set. Couples clung on the dance floor. Glasses stood empty, ashtrays full.

Davey was wired tighter than the treble G-string. Not even the constant draining of beer glasses helped. They quit around two-thirty, dawdled and flirted and reset equipment until almost four. Then Davey, a beer in each hand, pushed one toward Vance. "Aw, man. What you trying to do to me?" said Vance, yanking at the bandanna.

"You got anything better?" said Davey. Hoping. He was out. And broke. But Vance might try to pull that brother's keeper shit again.

"Only grass," said Vance. "C'mon."

"Nothin' on you?"

"You kidding? You know Damon. Showtime you go without or you're out. He catches it on you, that's it."

They smoked in the woods behind the band house and a little while

later walked through the streets. Once they came upon an empty lot and
lay down in the bracken staring up at the stars again, but Davey couldn't
concentrate. There was a bridge just ahead. Maybe they could see the stars
better from there, he told Vance. He had to walk fast. Maybe Vance had a
hard time keeping up because this whole time he was quiet and breathing
hard. But not Davey. Diarrhea of the mouth. Just kept jabbering. God
knows what he was saying, what he told Vance already and he, Davey, kept
laughing, which helped. Christ, man. These assholes that think they can
play. Haven't got a clue what it's all about. What it takes. Your soul, man.
Your very life. Hendrix knew. Davey knew everything about Hendrix there
was to know, just by listening to him play. All his life, practicing at the farm,
every breath he took was toward one goal. To play better than anybody. Play
like Hendrix. That was all he ever wanted. And he was gonna make it.
Maybe even surpass him. Guy like Hendrix—he got breaks. Davey's break
was still coming. But take his family. They knew the stuff of life. Knew how
far a body had to go to live with heart. They were all special. Apart. People
always saying so much talent in one family. Damn, he was proud of them.

Maybe that was it with his dad. He'd never found something to love.

He was up on the parapet seeing if he could keep his balance, keep
the same distance between him and the blackened water below, that water
that seduced him like one of those band followers. Nothing would happen. And if it did, it would be a good time to go out. Feeling so good. It
was only that look on Vance's face—scared shitless—that made him laugh
crazylike to the cushion of air that held things in place and then think—
how Vance would take it to be his fault—never forgive himself for not
grabbing his feet and holding on so he wouldn't go over—it was only that
look that made him jump down beside Vance and put his arm around his
bony shoulder and say, "Hey, Bro! Lighten up, will ya?"

Death had to be a solo.

Wednesday, he found his great-aunt's place in a development of garden apartments, the kind where every blade of grass stood at attention. His
eyes teared and burned in the glaring sunlight as he squinted at the high
walls of beige cement studded with seashells. He felt closed in before he
ever entered the garden gate.

Okay. So he knew what it would be like before he came, from her first breath over the phone. Maybe he should have gone to the beach today, taken a couple of six-packs. He'd make this as brief as he could. There was an old pair of spotless, faded tennis shoes half his size in the center of a fold-ed towel beside the door. He lifted his feet to check for mud or sand or worse and smoothed back his hair. The door opened before he could knock.

"Hey there!" he said. She was small, just coming up to his chest. "So—this is Davey!" she said. Her hug was faint; he thought of sparrow wings. She pushed back her glasses and smiled up at him, hair frizzled in a white cloud around her head.

"You know, William I like better. Your grandfather's name was William. We called him Willie. And what is this in your ear? One earring is not enough; you have to have three?" She laughed and wrinkled up her nose like a sixteen-year-old. He wondered if he was clean enough to sit down. Little crocheted doilies lay under bowls. Not a sock or a newspaper in sight. What had she been doing when he knocked? Even the birdcage had a mat under it to protect the rug from a stray seed. The blinds were closed against the hot Florida afternoon; she was probably worried about the rug or furniture fading. She lived like she would leave no mark. Tightness spread across his shoulders, through his neck.

"You like a drink? Some Pepsi or ginger ale?" She said *chincher* ale and pulled open the refrigerator door while a small mop of a dog sniffed at his feet. Taxi would have finished him off in one gulp. "No, no, Licky. Come in the kitchen with Mama. You don't walk on the rug. Come! Come!" She handed him a Pepsi and a glass of ice, saying, "So, you're playing your guitar?"

Licky sat dutifully at the kitchen threshold, his brown eyes vigilant. Taxi, now, even when he was being ridiculous, had majesty. Black spots on gray floated by. He could see him bounding across the rye in five-foot leaps, stopping to jerk his head around, ears flapping, lips quivering. When Taxi was on a leash, Davey had to lean away with his whole weight to hold him back. He loved the sight of him as he sniffed along the macadam on a hunt for even so insignificant a thing as a fly. When he found one, his head traced its path, the fleshy lips flapping down the sides of his jowls and his jaws snapping again and again—head jerked around between his legs for the fly, body whipped this way and that, the leash wrapping around Davey's legs.

What time was it? Better not forget to pick up Les Paul strings. Six G's. Need them for tonight. Always break those G's. Down to one guitar.

"Yup, playing guitar," he said, still watching Licky.

"And you stay here in Jacksonville?"

"Well, for a while, two weeks, playing at The Blue Diamond."

"Oh. A night club. Where you go after here?"

"Down to Orlando, then to Savannah."

"You like it?"

"Well, yeah. Sometimes I get tired and just want a dresser drawer I can call my own. But this band is doing some original stuff and we're going to record in September so I'm going to hang in there."

"Yah. Some kind of life. Bet you don't eat regular."

This morning's dream came back to him. He'd been trying to remember it all day because the feeling stayed with him, a heaviness that pulled at him underneath everything he had to do. In the dream he was small enough to climb up on his mother's lap. She bent down low—he could smell the rose water—and he whispered in her ear, "I'm tired. I don't want to play guitar anymore." Why? Was he telling her what she wanted to hear? Wasn't he to be trusted with his own life? He was scared sometimes, he had to admit. Like in December when he signed himself in to that hospital, afraid what he might do. The doctor took notes on a clipboard— what did he know? Give me something, damn it. I'm losing it! I'm slipping away! Don't think about it. Vance knew. Vance looked out for him. Cover me, Vance. Good name for a song, "The Roller Coaster Star."

"How is your mother?" Aunt Anna smoothed the skirt over her knees.

"She's doing good, busy all the time, keeping things straight." She always looked the same, said the same things. How are you feeling, Davey? Are you taking your pills? Yes, yes, yes, although they were all still in the bottle in his gym bag. Kept them in case. Hated 'em. Salty as hell—mouth always dry—made him nauseous. Play better without. Forgot to buy dog food. Should have told her Taxi likes Gravy Train.

"I got this big dog. He's a Great Dane. I figured the farm would be the best place for him so I took him home. His name's Taxi. Told Mom she's gonna look pretty silly standing in the middle of a cornfield calling for a taxi."

She looked a lot younger when she laughed. "You know," she said, "your grandfather played guitar, too."

"Yeah?" Why hadn't he known that?

"He taught himself to play. For a fact, when we was kids, he earned enough money doing errands for violin lessons but he didn't have no violin and the teacher saw he wasn't practicing and so he said to him, 'William, you must practice more.'" She shook her finger in the air. "Finally, it came out that he didn't have a violin and the teacher said, 'Well, no more lessons.' Then, after a while, he taught himself mandolin and on the ships he played harmonica. He played by ear. He just had to hear it once and he could play it."

"I never took guitar lessons," he found himself telling her. "We had a blizzard when I was fourteen and we couldn't get down to the mailbox or to the state road for six days. Had no electricity and the generator was strictly for the well pump and the furnace, so we couldn't watch TV. Mom had a guitar then and I asked her to show me what she knew, which was three chords. I played those three chords till we got dug out, played till my fingers bled."

He saw again his reflection in the high old windows of the living room at home, as he practiced the stance with his guitar on his pelvis, making the moves. He'd learned the music by playing along with the tapes of Hendrix, which grew scratched and staticky; doors slammed throughout the house, but he played through the night, not able to stop. Where the hell could that license be, the one he pinched? What shirt did he wear yesterday?

He had to get up, walk around. He never told anybody the next thing. Why did he want to tell her now?

"You know, I did have piano lessons when I was seven or eight but I never learned to read the notes. When I got home from lessons, I would ask Mom to play the new piece and I'd remember it. No one ever guessed I couldn't read music." He still couldn't.

She said, "You must be hungry. I fix a steak quick. I don't cook much now with Uncle Franz gone, but I did make you an apple kuchen."

That was okay with him.

"Maybe you like to see some pictures while I fix supper?" She pulled out a brown scrapbook from the shelf under the coffee table, its black pages soft and fragile. Black corners held the pictures; fancy scrolls framed the snapshots. A clear hand had long ago printed in white ink: *Brooklyn, 1929, Atlantic City, 1931, Wildwood, N.J. August,* and people his own age smiled back at him. There was his grandfather, he guessed, with dark curls hanging down his forehead, round horn-rimmed glasses, holding a mandolin. He sat on a tree stump, his legs crossed and his head thrown back, singing. What would it have been like to play together, some old plink, plunky tune—dull as marsh mud, man. Do musicians ever meet across the eons somewhere? Surprise, man. I'm your grandson and this is what *I* play.

He lay the open album on the floor and paced, hands jutted in his pockets. He yanked them out, cracked his knuckles, stretched those rubber bands in his fingers, one by one. Should be practicing or running, lifting weights, lying out at the beach. Glass door. Yard about eight feet square. Got to get out, smell the air. Got to get those strings on the way back. Left one package home on the piano. Bird feeder on the ground, broken. He poked his head in the door and said, "If you have a hammer and some nails, I'll fix the bird feeder."

"Oh, Davey. That's nice. Thank you," she said coming toward him, drying red hands with her apron. Solitary women killed him. They were helpless with their growing collection of broken things. Each time he went home his mother had a list of things for him to tend to. He'd go into his father's shop and feel again the silence of rust growing on the tools. Down to five bucks. Probably can get only one set of strings. If that. Might not have enough with tax. Damon promised pay on Friday.

In the garage he found some nails and a bag of birdseed. Yeah. Home, sweet home. Fixing bird feeders with steak cooking in the kitchen. He hung the feeder under the eaves outside the kitchen window, and took in the sweet smell of fried onions. Steak must be almost ready. In the bathroom off the kitchen he washed his hands. The only towels were little fancy ones. He wiped his hands on his T-shirt.

Sitting down at the table in her tiny kitchen, she seemed to be scrutinizing him for some sign of her brother. She must be disappointed. As far as he could tell, they looked nothing alike. He began tapping his heel; his knee vibrated under the table.

"I want to tell you stories, Davey," she said, "because all the others are gone, Willie, Franz, all the old ones from the other side, all gone, and I am eighty-three this year. I have pictures you should have. But later—now you eat."

"Tell me how it was when you came over."

"I tell you so you know how easy you have it," she said, putting a baked potato on his plate and sliding onions over his steak. "How lucky for you we came here." It sounded accusing, as if his life was frivolous. Maybe it was. It was certainly easier than doing something he didn't want to do, like computer programming or marketing or any other vague slipping away of his life that had been suggested to him. "Keep your music as a hobby," his father told him once. "Get a skill you can use." How could he explain? There was no deciding really, no standing back and saying, "Hmmm, what shall I be?" from his first tenuous press of the wires against the frets and the resonating pluck in his ears and heart.

She was droning like a queen bee, setting down the rules of the hive. Hard work. Determination. First her mother, his great-grandmother, came over and worked as a housekeeper to save money for her children's passage. She sent for Anna when Anna was sixteen and got a job for her in a pocketbook factory in New York. "It was a first-class passage," she said, laying down her fork as if to let the importance of this sink in. "Mama didn't want me down below, traveling alone. I was a pretty little thing then— thick red hair and not a word of English."

He worried that this would take all night, because he could see she was swept up in her story. She was not looking at him any longer, but playing with her napkin, folding and unfolding the starched corners, laying it on the table and lining the edges up with the table edge, running her fingers along the fold, smoothing the cloth as if her hand was an iron. He watched, mesmerized by the carefulness of her fingers. For a moment, the motor in his legs quieted.

His grandfather came over as a stowaway, which had been arranged by his great-grandmother. Letters arrived from Germany of how Willie, then fourteen, was beaten by the uncle he'd been staying with, how he was often hungry, how he tied newspaper around his feet to walk in the snow and do the chores. Aunt Anna looked at Davey, her eyes red around the edges, like wounds in the folds of thin, white skin. "I don't know why I'm crying now," she said. "I never did before. But I got first-class passage and he got stowaway. We had only each other when we lived in Germany, never been separated. And then we were together only one year after we left Germany, the year he came home and we would go camping in New Jersey. That's when the pictures were taken. For years he couldn't come in the country so he went on the ships, starting as a mess boy, never home until he got typhoid and almost died. For years, he wandered around at sea."

How was it easier, he wanted to know. Different, maybe. But not easier. His grandfather and he, nomads. He wasn't complaining though. Bet his grandfather didn't complain either. Davey scraped his empty plate and scooped up the last bit of juice from the steak with his knife. Might be the last good meal till Friday.

"Ach!" she said. "I can't believe it! Willie cleaned his plate the same way!" She clasped her hands together, satisfied. She was so easy to please he had to grin. He wanted to say, *Jesus H. Christ,* but instead drummed his heel on the floor again, shifting sideways in the chair so his knee wouldn't hit the table. He should be playing now, or walking Taxi, running with him down through Mandarin Drive, the dog galloping ahead, quick as a deer.

"I wished I could go to sea, too," she went on. "Your grandfather had all the adventures. One time he cooked for William Beebe when he went to the South Seas and he would tell stories about the strange fish they found." Then came the moral. He knew there'd be one. "Then he settled down. He went to Canada and lived, then entered the country legally. Got a good job with the gas company, got married, had children. He had his chance to see the world. And you, too. You'll get this out of your system. But don't wait too long."

His need for escape was becoming urgent. Did she feel his urgency or did she have her own kind of urgency to pass on the stories? He thought there was something in this unexpected corner of the family to save him, to let him know his fate was not sealed. But Jesus if he didn't get out of here soon—it was becoming urgent that he play tonight because he knew he would be really good, really good they would tell him later, never heard anyone do those runs as fast as you, Davey—were you born with a guitar in your hands? How do you *do* that, man? They were always telling him that. His fingers itched, no—ached, itched and ached—rub your knees with your hands, he told himself, calm down will ya, calm down, goddamn it. He wished he could say, "I'm outta here, see ya!" Soon though. His heart might jump out of his chest. She hadn't even begun to eat.

He got up from the table and stretched. His knuckles cracked against the patient ticking of her cuckoo clock. He stared at it and then looked down at her. "Aren't you going to eat?"

"Ach! Don't feel like it. I give you the other steak. Come, I get you some pictures," she said, moving toward the couch. "I can't part with all these yet, but here—this one is yours, and this, and this." She handed him the pictures with a slight tremble of her hand. There was his grandfather dressed in a double-breasted suit, leaning with one arm on his Ford coupe, one foot on the running board. What would it have been like to ride in that car with his grandfather, chugging along some country road, telling jokes, watching his hands grip the steering wheel? His grandfather would have had a strong heart, with no disappearing acts. In another picture, he was leaning on an oil drum on the deck of a tanker, and in the last . . .

"This is my favorite," she said. "We always had fun when he played and we would sing, all those times at Wildwood. When he came back from the ships, I couldn't believe how handsome he got, how he could play the music. It was the best time. After that, when he married your grandmother, he never seemed to be so happy again." She looked up at him. The man with the mandolin was still singing, and she grew serious suddenly. "I can still hear him," she said. "Thank God I can still hear him. Funny thing, no? To hear a sound that isn't there no more?"

He stood up.

"Oh, wait," she said. "I wrap up the steak and the apple kuchen for you. You take it."

His arms held his guitar in the air and he ran his fingers along the neck, the wild notes spinning through his head as she walked toward the kitchen. In a few minutes she returned and handed him a brown paper bag, saying, "You should get out of this crazy business. It isn't good for you. I think it makes you jumpy, nervous. You should find a nice girl and settle down. Eat three meals a day and sleep all night. Get a good job with benefits. Play your guitar for a hobby; play for your family. You don't believe it, but you won't be young forever."

He knew she meant well. The whole goddamn world meant well. Yes, yes, yes, he told her. "Someday," he said, bending down to kiss her on the cheek. The door closed behind him. It was only then he thought about how her story had been more important than food to her. If he could have pointed that out, she might have understood about the music. But it wasn't her fault. Lots of people existed on food and lived through stories, never bothering to understand the significance of that.

Once outside the garden wall, he breathed deep again, eyes open wide to the night. Just ahead near the horizon he could see a bright star, the only one he could name. Sirius. Taxi! Here, boy! That your star? He could feel the dog beside him, leaning on his thigh, pointing. Yeah, that's it. River's gonna overflow. Fill his cup. Tell his story.

He made it back just in time. The smell of smoke engulfed him, permeated his clothes and the pores of his skin. The crowd was already drifting to tables and settling on bar stools. Perfumed and sprayed, they lit Marlboros and Slims, sized each other up and watched the door for newcomers. The band members withdrew to the stage and arranged beer mugs and mikes. Ty, Sue, and Vance were hooking up to the sound system as they looked over their shoulders for him. He leapt on stage and pulled at his fingers to loosen them up, then set them free in a flurry of pantomime positions. There was the familiar grip of his guitar, his lifeline, steadying him. His lathe and his wings.

He played the opener as though it were the last he'd ever play on this earth. Sweat poured down his legs into his socks, down into his leather boots. He glanced over at a brown-skinned arm, pounding bass, but avoided the eyes he knew were on him. *Just leave me be, man.*

They were in the middle of the first set when he spotted her, a pocketbook swinging from the crook of her arm, her small, thin frame struggling to pull the chair away from a table near the stage, her glasses glinting in the candlelight. He watched her sit down, clasp her hands in her lap, the pocketbook still on her arm. Her mouth hung open as she stared at each of them in the band. The waitress bent low to take her order, but she motioned her away. She waved at him with fluttering fingers.

Was that his grandfather at her side? His dark, curly hair contrasting with her white halo, his eyeglasses shining with hers, like stars in a sea of darkness? He listened to something that came from his fingers but wasn't his—all the things he couldn't help that had come back to haunt him. He heard the sweet sounds of his grandfather's harmonica and the whine of the catamaran's guy wires, his father's chipping away at the tree root and Annie's wail out in the snow, all of which was separate from him and insistent like a story passed on, things said louder between the lines and notes than he ever intended, but there nonetheless. And then a new triad, a blues minor that came out of nowhere that just occurred to him, that he followed blindly to wherever it would lead. He could see plainly, just like he could see the moon in a stretch of black space, space upon space that fanned itself out into myriad possibilities that called out to him, unknown to him now and waiting to be revealed but *out there.* His faith was vast.

He saw his grandfather nod, the eyeglasses glitter. Now he was with him in the first car of the roller coaster. His grandfather gripped the bar with thick, stubby fingers. His hair was swept away from the pale skin of his forehead and his lips were pulled back as if his face had already left him in the rush downhill. Davey could feel the misplaced gut, the great shudder on his brain and jaw from steel wheels on unrelenting track, the plummet of his vertebrae slammed against the seat and then the ride he came for—the upsurge swing—the grand ascent—inching now—to the peak ahead—the cresting wave—toward the stars—and beyond—up and up—the ride up—such a gift—no one knows—how alone—he'll be the best—among the stars—the glasses nod—play it—Davey—play it—play it—play it—

HOUSE OF CARDS

～

The telephone rang. The sound slashed through Justin's letter:
"Painting a white line down the center of the road along Sulley's Point
where the road isn't even three feet on either side of the line proves the
Roads Department is wasting taxpayers' mon—,"—his finger slipped on
the keys at the ring—another ring—that beautiful heart-stopping jab—he
let it ring again—that was three—four—he better pick it up but he loved
the sound which said urgency and persistence and *want to talk to you*. It
filled the empty spaces of which he had many, he never realized how
many until now when the wind's wail was punctuated by the ringing.

"Hello?"

"Justin, is that you?" A coquettish voice broke through the static. "Do
you remember me? Justin, can you hear me? This is Michelle."

"Michelle?"

"Yeah! That's right! This connection is bad so I'll hang up and call you
right back, okay?"

He hung up and leaped to shut off the radio and glanced around. He
clicked off the fan switch on the heater and stood watching the telephone
on the wall. It rang again.

"Justin? Is this better?"

"Yes it is, much better, uh huh. But—I just can't seem to place you."

"Oh, you remember. I met you at the singles bar at the Sheraton last
weekend? I'm the one with the long, dark hair?"

He rubbed his thigh with his palm. "Well—"

"Don't you remember? You said I had great tits." Male laughter exploded through the phone. "Gotcha! Dad?"

"Michael, you son of a bitch!" If he was kidding around with his old man, maybe Michael didn't judge him as much as he feared. But what was all this talk about Michael's anger? Anxiety attacks, Rosemary said. But she was always a worrier, embellishing things, dissecting, analyzing. Anxious, my foot. Kept his sense of humor, that boy did. Had a little bit of the old salt in him. Did Michael good living away from home, taking up with Mari.

"How ya doing, Dad?"

"Okay, I guess."

"Going to Christmas dinner at the farm?"

"Guess so. Your mother invited me. But I won't be staying long. You can always come down here. Bring Mari. Do some fishing. Rockfish are still running. Been a warm fall." He wondered what Michael thought of him. If he could, he would say, *See Michael, if I were to tell you why I left—I don't think I even know why anymore, but I suspect it had to do with life slipping away, and the last hurrah, one long dark tunnel leading to another dark tunnel where I just wanted to get a glimpse of the blue sky again, and when the blue sky came, I went bananas.* Out loud he said, "Hear you and Mari set a date."

"June. June 17th."

"Puttin' on shackles, eh? Look out for them. Me, I'm free now. Cures a whole lotta things." He meant it to sound light. Just man talk.

Michael said, "Well, look. I'm heading out. By the way, what would you like me to tell Michelle for you?" He listened to his son laugh. It was a bit forced. Did he detect derision? Michael went on, "Dad? Listen. I want to ask you something." He hesitated, then, "Think I could use some of your tools? I'm going to start my own carpentry business, maybe do some carving on the side." He sounded like he hated to ask, which made Justin say, "Take anything you want. I'm through with them. Thought you were going out to sea, though."

"It's not for me, Dad. I hate being away from home for long periods of time."

"Thing is—if you find something you like to do, stick with it. That's the only word of advice you'll ever get from your old man." He hung up and glanced around the cottage at the cedar walls, at the collage of photos of his kids on water skis, in the boat, fishing, diving off the pier, hanging onto the tractor tire tube. Those were the days. He missed them, the squeak of the screen door as they darted into the cottage with dripping bathing suits and tousled, drenched hair, calling him, "Dad! Can we go out in the boat now, Dad? Can we? When can we?" They'd gang up on him, the scamps, and they'd follow him anywhere. If he could measure his life by that, he'd done okay.

If he could.

He took the teapot from the kerosene stove and put it on the front burner of the electric stove, setting the timer for two and a half minutes. He could hold out forever—make his mother's money last a lifetime, all he had to do was live that long. He tilted his head back and laughed, a shriek that could have broken glass. He heard it, his own frightening laugh—a crazy's hoot. It sobered him. Too bad, Michael. Sometimes God spits on us.

The long strands of Christmas lights lay jumbled on the lawn. Michael worked on untangling them. He couldn't believe he was back home again, lighting the same old pine in the front yard, doing exactly what he was doing last Christmas, but then he believed for a few seconds that with everyone coming home it could be like the family portrait on the piano, and so he was inspired to drive his pickup on the lawn as close as he could to the pine, place the stepladder on the bed, and loop the first string over the broom so he could reach the top of the tree in the bitter wind.

It was all pretense, he thought, illusions of togetherness, hope for reunion, remembering things he didn't want to remember. It pained him to think of his father living alone at Sulley's Point. What must he be thinking as he lay beneath the huge log trusses with the wind driving its way through the boards? A different person altogether, the bravado gone, the dad-authority eaten away by his own hand. Put in his place? *No,* Michael thought, *broken. He is broken now, and I'll go see him even though the thought of the dark house, the wind, the tragedy of him tortures me and makes me think of fate.*

He said as much to his mother—"That's what's ahead of me, that's where I'm going. I know it." Her mouth hung open like the thought had never occurred to her. She shook her head and almost shouted, "No. No, Michael. You are your own person. You're you. You're not *like* anybody. Besides, it's different for you. You know how to help yourself. Your father wasn't that fortunate."

So she thought of him as fortunate. No, he wasn't like his father. For him there was no euphoria, no high to live for, only a long, torturous winding path. Imagine the hell of living a long life. He never once thought of himself as fortunate, except maybe for Mari. It amazed him that she loved him.

Inside his work gloves, his fingers had grown stiff. Looking back at the house he could see the moving shapes of people he loved. He plugged in the tree. For them he'd pretend, but thoughts of the cottage in winter and his father's isolation weighed him down and the tree with its small lights paled by the sun lent no brightness, none at all.

A while later, he knocked on the door of the cottage thinking how strange, a recognition that this was his father's house and not his own or the family's any longer, how decisively ownership had been delineated by his father's lonely presence where before its sharing had been taken for granted. But the man who opened the door was hardly his father, as Michael stood staring at a shriveled version of him, dry as a stalk of October corn, only the eyes familiar, with skin crinkling at the edges, glad-to-see-him-warm—actually warm.

He stepped inside as if entering for the first time, although the fishing poles still stood in racks to his right and the king-size shell of a crab he'd marked *1973* hung in its place on the wall. The beige floor echoed his footsteps and the screen door snapped behind him like always. His old man, the old geezer, the old fart, builder of the great seawall, controller of the heat, the inventor, master carpenter, and racing demon, was taking him in with "Heeeey, Michael!" on his lips and smiling.

Michael was stunned at the sight of him.

He sat on the couch like a guest while his father offered him a beer.

The ceaseless wind gnawed its way in: Michael watched the dark drapes stir. He said, "How're you making out, Dad?"

"Fine, just fine. Got my little projects, you might say. Keeps me going."

"You still going to a shrink?"

"Don't see where that's any business of yours."

"Just wondering, that's all. What do you do when you get real low?"

"Run a lot. Get real busy."

"What happens when you let yourself get so low it takes a lot of stuff to get you out? Why don't you just stay on the meds, even out the score?"

"Forget it, Michael. I've already had the fifty-cent lecture dozens of times. What you don't know is, I *am* the highs. That's where I live, in a kind of forever. The best me there is. The rest is four in the morning when I have to pay the band."

"Your choice." Michael shrugged his shoulders.

"My choice," echoed his old man, the lines along his cheeks pronounced. "Come down, anytime," he was saying. "Catch us a fish. I'll cook."

There was so much Michael wanted to say. He was torn between feeling sorry for him and rage so great he was afraid he couldn't contain it if he talked anymore.

"See you on Christmas," Michael said although he dreaded Christmas, dreaded everyone being together in the same tedious way even though he'd thought that was what he'd wanted, the family back together, that great myth of inseparable loyalty.

Christmas is the turnstile we have to go through to get to the new year, thought Rosemary as she drove up the lane, the backseat of the car lined with grocery bags. Still, it would do them good to be together. Some things forgiven, some things forgotten, there was never a better time for Justin to become more fatherly, maybe even come back into the family.

Davey had arrived home the evening before with Melinda, a girl he'd met in Florida. Besides the immediate family, Justin's brother, George, and his wife, Maude, were coming Christmas Day, with their two sons, Parker and Thomas, who'd be properly clipped, tucked in, and belted.

They always had an air of expectancy of future six-figure incomes about them. How did George and Maude manage it? The frozen turkey swung from Rosemary's hand in its plastic grocery bag as she jumped from one island to another toward the house. The driveway was a sea of mud in the downpour. In a fit of holiday frenzy she had tied red bows around the necks of a few of the Canada goose decoys that Michael had carved for her. Now the rain ran blood-red down their necks and breasts like a bad omen.

Set by the kitchen door to catch the rain was a small, potted tree given to her the day before by Joshua, one of her students. "Here," he'd said, red-cheeked and serious as he plunked it down on her desk, silver trumpets and bells swinging from needles sprayed with white foamy plastic snow. Christmas. He brought it in and—if there was a vote—would probably win for the True Meaning Of and The Way It Was S'posed to Be. But Christmas was a test of realities, she decided as she dropped the turkey down on the kitchen counter on the word *test*. The turkey sat like a boulder dressed in blue plastic. The counter was as clean as she'd left it, proof that Davey and his girlfriend, Melinda, were still out this morning, visiting some of Davey's friends.

She must keep steady. They were all in new and strange territory—her foot stomped on the first stair to her bedroom—as they pushed forward through changes, new relationships. At least Justin's leaving hadn't splintered the family. They would stay together—maybe Justin would have a change of heart, see his responsibilities, and things would right themselves. She had never known such confidence, such fierceness of purpose, as she puffed her way to the top of the stairs. She didn't know about that Melinda though, with her hair stiff and bleached, her eyebrows carefully penciled in and blood-red fingernails. Melinda had a way of stomping her high heels on the kitchen linoleum and pitting it mercilessly. Another way of saying, that girl would leave her mark.

With a stab she thought of Len. He was with his own family for the holidays, a large gathering of brothers and sisters, nieces and nephews. She envied him being part of a family when he wanted to be, yet separate from them as he needed. Her life *was* her family. Time spent with Len was the only time she could be a person without a role, without expectancies to fill. She thought of him as a respite. For the time being. If she could be two people, the *second* one would stay with him. But nothing could thrive under those conditions, she knew. Nothing could be fair. It is as if I am waiting on the shore again, she thought, waiting for the catamaran to right itself, looking through binoculars over Len's shoulder, feeling the support of his arms, his warmth, but watching for what is central to my life to stay afloat, to go back to the way it was.

From the upstairs window, she saw Davey's VW pull in. Door slams. Melinda ran from the car and Davey followed, his head bowed against the rain. He'd been a kid who was undemanding, and who smiled easily. Yet now in the rain he looked burdened, the round of his back—her youngest—so old.

The kitchen door slammed. It was a relief to hear laughter exploding in the house. He would be all right. He—they—were all more aware. They'd been educated. She stood motionless and strong-willed in her hope, and called downstairs, "Bring the rest of the groceries in from the car, will you please?"

Christmas Eve, the colored lights on the huge pine outside the living room windows brought a sunsetlike softness to the room. Poinsettia beside the fireplace hearth, the gas log lit and fluttering, a choir singing from the tape deck, and Davey began shouting. He made little sense at first.

"What's the matter?" she said as Davey hovered in the doorway, his tension cutting through the coziness like a knife into warm bread.

"It's hot in here, stuffy. I'm going. Me and Melinda are taking off."

"We can't open presents without you, Davey."

"Okay, okay, what about right now? I got a few minutes. Let's get everybody out here."

Michael said, "What, *now?* You want to open presents *now?* It's too early. We haven't even had dinner yet. What's the rush? Nah, I don't want to open them now. What'll we do tomorrow? Imagine sitting around tomorrow with no presents to open."

"And besides," said Anne, "I haven't got mine wrapped yet."

"What the fuck. You two ganging up on me now? Making me look like the bad guy?" Davey tried to sound like he was kidding, his lips jerking nervously, but his voice was full of static like some of his runs on the guitar when the notes were too fast.

"All right, all right, all right," said Rosemary, conscious of Mari's wide eyes as she sat next to Michael on the couch watching Davey. "Forget it. It's not that important. Go do your thing, Davey. We'll open them tomorrow."

Davey bounded upstairs to get Melinda hurried along. After a few minutes he followed her pizzicato heels into the dining room where they had all assembled, Melinda's arm straight out and fingers spread, her hand parting curtains and leading the way as she shrieked, "Ooooooh, I never thought he'd do it but he did. Oh my God, he actually did it, AAAAGH!" On her fourth finger sat a diamond—small, but definitely a diamond.

Rosemary set down a platter of potato salad (Davey's favorite) on the table set for six, the hope of a peaceful Christmas Eve supper slipping away, when she heard Michael say, "What about your car payments, Davey? Plus your insurance, plus the five hundred you owe me? Where the hell did you get the money, huh, Davey? Huh?"

"None of your fucking business. Leave me alone, you mother fucker!" Davey punched at the kitchen cabinet. "Keep your nose out of it, asshole."

Rosemary decided not to look up at the cabinet, refusing to acknowledge the loud crack she'd heard. Instead, she said gently, "Does this mean you're engaged now? That we'll have another wedding to think about?"

Davey, face flushed, cracked his knuckles and said, "No, Mom. It doesn't mean anything. Only that I love her, you know? Gotta go!" and he swept Melinda toward the door which flew open and banged against the house, his nylon jacket filling with wind.

When she allowed herself to look at the cabinet, the door had been split from the top hinge to the bottom panel, which held by some small miracle, leaving the bottom hinge intact. She looked away, as if violence to the house were just another inconvenient but tolerable fissure on life's road. It could have been worse, she thought. It could have been Michael's jaw. Davey wanted out. He wanted to get away from all of them, from the whole idea of predetermined fissures over which he had no control. He wanted to break the house, break the pattern, free himself from the God-awful mold.

"Well," she managed. "Let's have a bite."

Michael looked away from her and, with teeth clenched, mumbled, "I'd like to wring his goddamn neck. You can't pin him down about anything, not even something as important as an engagement ring. Where is he?" ranted Michael. "Every time we try to find out, he slips away again."

"It's okay, Michael," she said. "No harm done, except for the kitchen cabinet. Nothing a little glue can't fix," feigning calm when beneath the surface, she was as frightened as an eight-year-old.

Things looked better in the morning. Her hands greased with lard, Rosemary patted the damp, cold goose-bumped skin of the turkey. She looked up to gaze out the window and thought of other Christmas mornings when the kids were underfoot and Justin called her to come for God sakes, leave the bird alone and open presents. Now there was only the bird.

She wondered about the deer. She'd seen them yesterday, five of them as close as the chicken coop. They'd headed for last summer's patch of zucchini where a few squash still lay like leathery blimps, brown-yellow from frost. She had stood at the window and clapped her hands. The startled deer leaped into the trees, tails high.

At the edge of the woods she had begun to tame wildness, keeping the honeysuckle vines trimmed and pulling up loblolly seedlings. The trees were being cared for now—Len saw to that—and she'd spent many hours after school outdoors, moving truckfuls of topsoil, building a stone wall to landscape a section of the yard, and had even begun a rose garden, which stood now, burlapped against the winter. She had great hopes for spring, and the work soothed her. Their mild winter, she decided, was a good time to garden, get the soil ready, plan and prepare new beds. She'd been totally absorbed in this, although it was nothing she could put in a Christmas newsletter such as the one she'd received from Hannah, which stunned her by the contrast between Hannah's family and her own. Giles was setting up branches of his company in France; they'd bought a waterfront home on the shores of the Chesapeake last summer after they'd traveled to China last spring (to see the Great Wall) and were planning a skiing trip to Utah for the holidays. The children were doing marvelously well, the oldest now the Vice President in Giles's company, and their daughter, a straight-A student at Virginia Polytech, was majoring in aviation, and the youngest had just received a $16,000 scholarship upon graduation from high school. As for Hannah herself, she had opened her own business designing specialty items for women from hand-loomed wool, and it was flourishing. They'd been blessed by the Lord, Hannah ended her letter, and wished their friends an equally happy and successful (underlined) New Year.

As she stood watching for the deer again, Rosemary composed a letter in her head for Hannah.

Dear Hannah,

In the spring the well ran dry and I had a new one put in. Then the furnace gave out so we have a new one of those too. We also have a broken kitchen cabinet door, and instead of getting it fixed, I've decided not to look at it. Michael had to drop out of school, Anne painted her car pink and Davey acquired a convertible which he junked for $25. As for me, I'm having a lurid love affair while Justin is in exile at the cottage and setting the world right with his essays.

We are continually amazed at how many ways there are to mess up. The only way we can go from here is up.

Yet what was happening to them seemed merely extraordinary now instead of hopeless. Everything had a chance of turning out all right. She would no longer have to harbor fears. Even the extremes she suspected in herself could now be brought to light, as if it were safe at last to admit her own failings, as well as her sorrow for the loss of the old Justin and for Justin-the-textbook-case, and her guilt for the unwillingness to live with the down-side of the bargain.

When she hung out the window and clapped her hands at the deer with such vehemence, it wasn't the deer she wanted to chase. But one had to do *something*. She put the bird in the oven.

He decided to run to the farm. This morning, with the kerosene stove turned on high because it was Christmas and the comfort of a cup of coffee in his hands as he looked out on the cold, blue river, he knew he could do it, though the cold might bother his breathing. And when he got to the farm he could go up the lane without the usual vise on his temples and ball bearings in his stomach. He'd be too tired to feel anything. Besides that, he'd save on gas and gifts. He'd show them—her—he was fine. Hell, yeah, could run ten miles and be on time for dinner.

At twelve-fifteen he did his leg stretches by the warmth of the stove. Resting his hands on his bent knee (he loved feeling those rock-hard quadriceps) he stretched his other leg behind him, perfectly balanced. He was in terrific shape though his left knee still bothered him. He hoped he could do what the hypnotic tape said, tell himself not to hurt and will his senses to a level beyond pain. He loved this new body; there was half the flesh on him there used to be. No more scrapple and eggs and fried potatoes for breakfast. Yegh. The garbage he used to eat.

The wind off the river this morning was strong enough to blow him to the farm. He tugged on his gloves, zipped up his jacket, checked his watch, and began his journey. The road sparkled. He was fresh and eager and his impulse was to run as if each step were an explosion. He knew better. He'd hold off the high, the trip to the moon he lived for, that divine, limitless, breathless expectancy he loved. Nothing like it. He had paid his dues—the lows that exhausted him. He'd endured, eyes on the prize. He caught sight of the bursts of fluff on tall marsh reeds out of the corner of his eye; they stirred the sky. Cold air bit his cheeks, rushed in and out of his throat cleansing any germs he might have picked up which was why he was never sick. His thoughts were as crisp, pure, and decisive as the day, punctuated by the *pad, pad* of his running shoes on the side of the road. Life was good, so good he couldn't believe it.

He began to breathe through his mouth. Later his teeth would ache with the cold, but he couldn't help that now. Each blade of grass was his, each tree that reached its truth into the blue was his, the branches that snapped and tapped against the cold wind—they were his, too. He was here to witness them instead of seeing the world filtered through a windshield. In tune with the world's energy, he moved like the wind in the trees and loved the biting cold on his face. The day felt like a baptism. He held his arms open as he ran along the distances of newly planted rye rolling out to the horizon like an emerald carpet promising spring even against the rusts and gray-browns of December woods, which were his too, those woods he once feared on the mornings he went out to cut wood, where he could meet his end if he slipped, just once, with the chain saw or his thoughts. He knew what the woods held. But he made it through. If Rosemary only knew what he knew, what he never told her, she would have been more forgiving. But it wasn't sympathy he wanted. Anyway, he answered to no one, took up little space, consumed little, owed nothing—and was free. That was the way to live.

His feet drummed the macadam. He could measure himself by the distance he'd come and how much he could endure. He knew who he was. His feet told him. Sweat dripped off his nose; he wiped it off with his sleeve. He'd found steadiness. And comfort. Decision-free, driving comfort that would keep him alive. So simple. Run—run for your life. He would push back death, illness, pain, hysteria, convention, failure, loneliness, guilt, all into the currents of air that parted for him. *Look out*, his feet said, *here we come.*

He was numb now. His body needed nothing but motion to cure it of its excess energy, the thoughts that raced like small birds in flight over a vast ocean. Today he was safe. He was a runner. Streamlined. Unencumbered. Ah, the geese flew in a huge check mark directly overhead. An affirmation from God. He could feel it. Life was stupendous, miraculous.

> *Sally the screw is out getting lumber*
> *Want to talk? Leave your number.*

He laughed out loud. His jingles drove Rosemary crazy. He put them on the answering machine and half the county called, mainly kids after school. Word had gotten around. A new jingle every day. On the tape, Rosemary heard giggles, snickers, clicks, over and over. She called the telephone company about the harassment. The local manager told her they'd been aware of the messages on the machine. "Kids listen to them. We're planning to investigate this. Listen to your tape, ma'am. Someone's fooled with it. You're a teacher, aren't you? Out Pucam way?"

When she heard Justin's falsetto Mae West voice on the tape, she was furious and threatened to throw the answering machine in the pond. As time went by, however, it was one of her favorite stories. He laughed again.

There was Pucam's skyline, the fortress of granary silos that announced the town was as impenetrable as ever. He couldn't say he and Rosemary ever had any friends here, yet everyone knew who they were, at the hardware store, the Shore Stop, the post office, and certainly at the drugstore, where he'd hated getting his prescriptions filled. In small towns, it was no sooner done than said he always told Rosemary and she'd laugh, every time. She used to laugh a lot. Whatever happened to that silvery laugh of hers?

After a few nauseated starts, he'd stopped taking meds. Didn't need them. Ran instead. But people didn't run in Pucam. Once he was on his way to a race and stopped for gas at the Exxon station. Quincy Taylor was pumping then. When Justin got out of the car, Quincy eyed his fuchsia shorts and headband and his eyes narrowed. "I didn't know you were like one of them California people!" he said and turned away. It didn't matter, of course. Hell with 'em.

He ran under the glittering Christmas angels tied to each telephone pole on Main Street. The town was twenty angels long. He counted. Large for an Eastern Shore town and run down, as if anyone with serious purpose in life had long since gone. It felt like the last town on earth, the end of a road. He passed the elementary school, which was for sale, and the locked gates of Jackson's Demolition with its stacks of derelict cars, and the Nativity scene outside the Presbyterian Church with its cracked plastic Virgin and wise old infant Jesus, hand raised to bless the poor of Pucam who forgot to look. There was no one, no sign of life to relieve the town of its ghostliness, not even at the Shore Stop, which advertised chicken wings, moist and crispy, and gas for ninety-nine cents. Closed for Christmas. The rows of Pepsi machines stood sentinel, bearing explosions of red, white, blue like uniforms.

He saw everything out of the corner of his eye, half out of memory, as he stared straight ahead. Pucam epitomized his failure, the move to the Shore his inglorious undoing. Along the black, sparkling ribbon that was Main Street, he tried to ignore the odd collection of rambling, unsteady houses, the torn, upholstered easy chairs relegated to front porches, the gashed screens, the peeling gingerbread designs along the gables, patches of unmatched roofing, sunken front steps and moss-laden shingles, mowers left to rust in front yards, pink plastic Big Wheels left on the broken sidewalks, the down-to-bare-wood house trim, the boarded windows of the shop on the corner—*Mabel's Marvels, Antiques* printed on the cracked glass— the sunken roof of the old movie theater, the broken bricks of its facade, the gnarled, dead halves of ancient maples, overgrown cedars and English ivy clutching foam cups from the Shore Stop—everything colorless and ugly in the hard, cold, unrelenting sunshine. The angels glittered. They depressed him. How had he ended up here?

He was a long way from home. Oh, not the home he had with Rosemary, but his first home, on Long Island, with the father who'd been a lawyer and the mother who adored her husband, and the life of golf games and expensive cars and the exuberant and substantial house in Hewlett, where his father was a pillar of the community and his mother the gracious hostess. For a moment he was there, back in the dining room with the gleaming silver and the elegant china, not that he gave a damn about that except that it was class. They had class, and he was expected to do great things.

At the edge of Pucam where yards widened into fields, houses appeared in the distance, tiny against the far-off woods. He could see the farmhouse, turned sideways, the front door facing an abandoned road that receded into a path in the woods. On the nearby field, Taylor's steel supports for a new irrigation system lay bottom up on the ground, like the keels of skeletal Viking ships that had lost their way.

In the driveway were his children's cars, Michael's old Datsun pickup with the rusted fenders, Anne's pink Nova—she tied the hood down with rope—and Davey's red, white and blue–striped VW. Not a company car among them; he was proud. They'd kept a sense of humor, a thumb-to-the-nose attitude toward the world, followed their own drumbeat. Like him.

He slowed down. Tree shadows crisscrossed the cars. Soon his own shadow ran across them, as it had crossed the faces of his offspring. Maybe he should never have fathered them. It was the first time that idea ever crossed his mind, and it shocked him, negated his life with regret so strong he felt powerless. He could smell turkey, hear laughter and someone on the piano. He bent over, gasped deep into the driveway stones, trying to catch his breath, and straightened, still gasping for breath while he took in all of it, the pond, the black locust grove manicured and tamed, the shingles on the house that had come loose and curled in the wind, and the small, potted, pathetic Christmas tree by the door. Sweat trickled. He shook his head like a dog, and his skin tingled and jumped under the running suit, his breath coming in raucous gasps. He hoped he wouldn't at this moment drop dead at her door and make her think he'd come home with his last dying breath.

The sound of his gasps brought Rosemary to the kitchen door with a dish towel in her fist and that worried look in her eyes that he always hated, *What crazy thing are you up to now?* unspoken on her lips. He waved her away. He did the run, and the pain he'd endured was private. None of her business. His lungs would burst while his family laughed, clung together, and spit him out, like Pucam, like the companies he once worked for. He was on the outside looking in again, because he was on a different path, his own man, like one of them California people. He grinned. What the hell. He raised his foot to the bottom step and looked up at the door. Though it was open, he no longer hoped for anything.

They held hands around the table, "like the roots of trees that reach for water and meet each other," said Michael. He could be poetic when he wanted to, and fatherly. He ended with, "Glad everybody made it."

Justin snickered and looked up. A small stuffed angel made from a stocking swung from the chandelier as if disturbed by an unseen force, its fetus face round and pinched and its hobble feet pigeon-toed. "Anne made it. Isn't it cute?" said Rosemary, her face red from the morning's cooking. Justin sat in his old place at the table and looked across at her. She presided over her kingdom. Well, let her have it. Her eyes turned from him, unsmiling. The silence between them was temporarily abated by Maude and her tale about Dr. Phedis, the pediatrician she worked for who put newborn babies on the metal scale and who fussed if Maude laid a paper towel on it first. No need to waste toweling, he had said, which Maude found horrifying, so cold for a newborn that it set every one of them wailing. She helped herself to a mound of mashed potatoes. Anyway, he fired her but she was glad to leave and found a job at a rest

home where elderly patients recuperated from major surgery — bowel sections and lung cancer operations, for example — Justin interrupted her
with please spare us the bloody details, will you — whereupon she dug
deep into the potatoes with her spoon to make a well for the gravy, her eyes
saying to hell with it anyhow, this is Christmas and I'm entitled after all
the carrot sticks I've eaten all year and not one ounce off. Pass the cauliflower murmured Parker and the meat please said Thomas while Justin
covered his navel with his hands and waited.

There he is, sighed Rosemary, like a boulder in the middle of the
road. The cruelest thing about him is his silence. She fingered her earring
and remembered that even silence with Len was filled with *something*, a
glance or a touch, a feeling, and her heart pounded as she spooned
creamed onions onto her plate because she had not remembered touching ever being so enjoyable although it had been years ago with the other
Justin, the one she married. Now he only stared at her, those green eyes
boring holes, his face without tenderness, scowling. She remembered
when he'd shouted at her, "Sex is my conjugal right!" She shivered. What
a relief, what happiness to have sex separate from responsibility and duty.
She would have to be strong, not let feelings of sadness overpower her, she
resolved, as she watched Davey cut his turkey and mix his potatoes, broc-
coli, cauliflower, and stuffing in a mountain of baby food on his plate — I
am either-or, I am between and straddled: there is the ghost husband who
sits in his place and the ghost children who laugh and eat around this
table and there is the real husband who is in exile and the real children
who live a tormented inner life and the ghost me, who passes gravy and
nods and smiles and dares to sit at this table living another life elsewhere.
No wonder we are such puzzles to one another. And no one lets on. No
one dares break the allegiance. Except Justin. Poor Justin. If only she
could run her hand across his back, reassure him in some way, but she did
not want to touch him or allow him to touch her. Amazing how everything
could be stripped down to that simple truth. But if he did, if he did reach
across, hold her hand, tell her he loved her, reassure her, she would fold,
she knew. She wanted to hear him say, "Let's try to work things out." But
she could trust him not to. It simply wasn't something he could do. Maybe
he truly hated her. She would never know. That was why she couldn't say,

Just come on home, Justin. Come on home, though the words were on her tongue. Without his meds, there was no chance. Meanwhile, there were Len's hands rubbing her back, her arms, against all reason and against all right. It was peaceful in that place next to Len, though peace fled when she returned to her life. The choices were hard, either castle built on sand, neither one an answer. There was only herself. Her wavering self, existing in some vague interim, neither completely here nor there.

Michael leaned across his plate and said to Andrew, Anne's new boyfriend, "How much do you make anyway?"—to which Andrew blushed and laughed uneasily and glanced at Anne. Everyone laughed, which only encouraged Michael to add, "So what do you see in Anne, anyway?"—which brought more laughter and a murderous look from Anne but caused Maude to say, "More than he'll ever tell you about, dear heart." George glanced at Justin to see if he was listening as he began a joke, "Did you hear the one about—?" and laughed at the punch line himself, though he watched Justin for a sign of appreciation. There was none, only that accusing stare at Rosemary.

How can you do this to me, it said, which of course he had no right to say, having been the one who left. He did her a favor by leaving. She could never have left him, though she was leaving him now, she thought, as her eyes skimmed past him to George, now diminished and keeping his eyes on his plate. Maude went on that the boys had been sick, and Thomas, though he was eighteen and graduating this summer, succumbed to his mother's hand on his forehead now and nodded at her command that he retire to one of the bedrooms right after dinner with two aspirins, while Parker helped himself to a pile of mashed potatoes too big to finish. Cheeks puffed out like a frog, he kept mouthfuls for a long time.

Swallowing that much mashed potato must be painful, thought Michael, eyeing the nearly empty bowl. Kid always was nervy, invasive. Caught him snooping in his parents' night table on one of their visits to the farm when Parker was ten and Michael was fourteen. Found him upstairs opening drawers while the grown-ups were downstairs, fingering stuff he had no business getting into, stuff Michael didn't know about, which made him even madder because Parker was younger. Michael knew about chickens though. While Parker and Thomas stood around with their hands in their pockets he explained, *See, you measure the distance between the breastbone and the pelvic bone. If it's big enough for three fingers, she's ready for laying. Four fingers means a real good layer. Then you better have nesting boxes ready or they'll lay in the garden and the dog'll get the eggs. She sucks them out, boy. Nothing like a nice warm egg to a dog.* He ran after his favorite hen, a barred rock, and put his hands along her sides and lifted her up. He petted and crooned to soothe her and the hen allowed him to nuzzle his nose in her neck feathers. He loved the smell, like pillows and hay and fresh eggs mixed together. Then he turned the chicken around, her head under his arm, and held her legs together. With his other hand he measured three fingers under her downy bottom and felt the hardness of her bones. *Want to try it?* he asked them, but they both backed up, smirks on their faces. They must have had a good laugh on the way home. Maybe we were weird from the get go, he thought. But he didn't really think so. Everything was neat and tidy for Thomas and Parker, like their L. L. Beans and shaved necks. Michael looked around the table, at similarities in noses, eyes, and hairlines, at right-handedness and left-handedness, and thought about who got what. Life's a crapshoot, he said to himself.

His father still stared across the table at his mother. Who knew what it meant? Was his father sorry he left? Michael was haunted by the lines down his father's cheeks. "Can I pass you more turkey, Dad?" he said, and felt the intensity of his father's stare, his reluctance to look away from his mother and her deliberate disregard—a vacancy so loud the table rocked with it. Michael's thoughts flew round and round and fluttered down to astonishment at the broken circle around this table. He pushed his plate away. Leaning toward Mari, he put his arm around her. She turned to him with a sweetness that spelled forever. They'd make their own circle.

After dinner, Davey passed Anne a Thanksgiving card. He'd crossed out *Thanksgiving* and scratched in *Christmas* in several places. The cards were on sale, a nickel apiece, he said, at McCrory's in Pucam. He'd been drinking, Anne could tell. Baby brother. He gave her a tape of his original pieces, unwrapped but a present all the same. He'd meant to make more copies of the tape but so far got only two made, one for Mom and the other for you, Annie, my favorite, Annie, my dear, across the miles, Happy

Christmas, Merry Thanksgiving, whatever. He didn't care, Davey didn't. Not at all. That's why he so astounded everyone but her. He was everything she expected, while everyone else puzzled and shook their heads. Aunt Maude was probably thinking, *Thank God he's not mine, in those sweatpants from Goodwill and earrings riding up his earlobe.*

Music was the only expectation he had of himself. In the last few days he'd completed four pieces: a piano solo, guitar and piano duet—where he'd recorded himself playing piano and played along with the taped recording on the guitar—and two guitar solos. Finished. Now that was astonishing. He'd never been able to listen to a whole song on the radio never mind play one all the way through, his concentration being the broken, fretful thing it was. Anne hooked her arm around his neck, Davey baby, let's hear it, man. He called the tape *Hope and Patience.* Five consecutive notes down the scale on the piano, *da, da, da, da, dum,* over and over, in varying octaves while the bass notes rolled arpeggios in and around the recurring theme. The guitar broke in, lonesome as a coyote, and the notes wailed through the rooms. The family listened: Aunt Maude took a breather and hiked a leg up on one knee till you could see way past her knee-high stockings and Dad nodded to himself as he stared out the window. Uncle George pulled on his bottom lip, absorbing the punch Parker playfully delivered to his father's arm. Melinda sat alone on the couch picking at her fingernails, leg swinging; Michael whispered into Mari's ear and Davey held on to Annie. He drummed his fingers on her back, playing it all again, this time with his eyes closed. She'd not seen him this calm in years.

"See, Davey, you take the meds and you can *do.* You can concentrate and produce, man. This is great, Davey."

"No," he said, "it's not great. I did finish it, but that's all. It's not great. I'm only great when I'm lost out there, desperate to find my way back but not in any hurry to *get* back. You know?"

"With me, I can't do a thing till I'm calm," Anne said.

"Yeah, but that's you. Pills reduce me. I'm less than half what I can be otherwise. Look at you. You paint way-out stuff when you're crazy. You take that shit and you do nice little scenes, vase and flowers shit. Flatwork."

"Take it, Davey, just take it. It'll all pan out. When you're feeling right, good stuff can happen. It'll flow through you. Otherwise it's just a free-for-all."

"I like the free-for-all. It's pure and extraordinary. I don't wanta be ordinary. Ordinary would kill me."

"Just like you know who."

"Yeah. Just like our old man. Look at him. Now don't you think he's extraordinary?"

"Yeah, but no fun, Davey. No fun at all."

"Leave me be, Annie Laurie. Just leave me be. As for you, I love you just the way you are, fearsome or flatworked. But listen, that painting you did? Your face squeezed narrow in that clamp? That says something I can feel. Feeling is everything."

"Yeah, but if you don't know how it feels, you can only say, *Too bad. Too bad for you and how weird.* It's a freak show. It isn't art, Davey. It isn't the best I can do. It has no color, or composition, or endurance. It isn't anything anybody wants to look at for long. It's hype, Davey—pure sensation."

The fourth piece was static guitar, jumbled notes, noise, confusion, wild stuff. She couldn't tell him that. What she said was, "Your fingers are just a-flyin', Davey man. You got to be the fastest draw there ever was."

He grinned. He got all the looks, Davey did. Taller than any of them, blonder, leaner, deep dimples in his cheeks, eyes deep sea green, so pink around the edges—they always teared up easily. He's so physically perfect it must be hard for him to accept wrenches thrown at him, she thought.

"Let's get out of here," he was saying, "take a hike in the woods. Andrew, too, if he dares to get his feet muddy. He's okay. Not good enough for you but okay. Maybe we can get Melinda to go."

"You got to take care of yourself, Davey," she said, though they were wasted words. Did they use words? Sounds maybe, expressions, eye contact, that's what they were good at. Without speaking he answered, Yeah. I am, I am. Let's go. He rummaged in the pantry for his father's boots, which had been left there some time ago.

The kids had been gone for a while when Justin, George, Maude, and Rosemary put on their coats to go for a walk. Rosemary wanted to talk to George so she said, "Be right there," to Maude and Justin—"George can you help me with something?" while Michael and Mari cleaned up the kitchen as if they were playing house, giggling, him sneaking up behind her and grabbing her around the waist so she'd squeal. They didn't mind doing dishes or anything else right then.

Rosemary said softly to George, "You know when I told you Justin was diagnosed, George?" George shrugged like he always did and looked uncomfortable, blushing a little as he glanced out the window at Maude waiting with her scarf around her head and knotted under her fleshy chins and Justin staring off into the woods with the dog prancing around him in the cold. "George," she said, "was there anyone else in the family who was like that?" George shrugged again and she said it out loud but not loud enough for Michael or Mari to hear, "Well, I'm worried about the kids, George. I just thought you ought to know in case signs ever show up in Thomas or Parker. We have a good doctor," she told him and hoped she sounded upbeat and capable and coping well while George just watched her and blushed some more, then shrugged again.

"I don't know," he said, "I don't know. I never heard of anything like that before," and he looked helpless and kindly with the lines around his eyes deepening before he said, "Here—let me help you with your coat. Let's go before the sun starts going down," and he reached for the door-knob as if she'd been telling secrets and he was implicated simply because he'd listened.

The four of them walked down the road while Maude talked about the price of outfits at Zayre's and knit pants, a rust-color pair to go with her new blazer which she got there also at the pre-Christmas sale which ended Christmas Eve but which would probably be marked down again come the new year so she should have waited. Maude nattered, George listened, and Rosemary worried while Justin drifted to the side, not speaking to any-one but moving his hands around as though conversing with an invisible friend. His lips moved and he watched his feet. Once he moved close to Rosemary and said, "You should hear me laugh now, just like Mozart in the movie *Amadeus*—a real crazy laugh, high-pitched,"—and his eyes looked frightened. He turned away quickly, astonished at his own confes-sion, and he watched the ground again while Rosemary remembered the Queen Anne's lace that had grown along here in the summer. In its place was a flower skeleton curling itself into a small, dried bird nest which she picked, keeping her bewilderment to herself. She was a hundred years old, each year leadened with regret, but she couldn't give in. She had to breathe. She said quietly in an aside to Justin, "Let's get some help, Justin."

He broke into a run. "Thanks for dinner," he said, running, running away from her, glad to escape. "Take care of all the fledglings," he said and laughed, leaving her with the bird nest in her hand as his skin-and-bones figure trotted down the road never looking back. He reached his hand up over his head to wave a good-bye at the sky—leaving again, glad to be leaving, couldn't get away fast enough leaving, down the road as Maude paused for a breath and began reciting sales at K-Mart this time and George looked at Rosemary and shrugged as Rosemary watched Justin's diminishing figure beyond the first field of winter rye—running and running and leaving and fooling her because in his running she saw the choice had not been hers to make and now that it was no longer a choice she wanted to say something to his back and felt the pull again, the part of her he pulled toward him as he ran, gladly ran, and left her. Again.

By the time they got back, dark had settled on the woods and they were bathed in the rosy glow of sunset. Like a fortress, the house stood silhouetted against the sky, every window lit. Christmas tree lights twinkled through the front door. Yet he was running into the dark, running toward the cottage which lay cold and vulnerable to icy winds off the river with no one he could call family.

"Where's Dad?" said Anne, when they came in the kitchen door.

"He headed back," Rosemary told her.

"Oh," said Anne, "I was going to drive him back so he could take his presents."

Michael snapped the dish towel on Parker's chest and said, "Christ, how'd you get so tall, Parker? I'm the oldest and the goddamn shortest."

"And the strongest," said Parker. "The one who plugs away and perseveres."

"What say you, perspires? Persists? Persnicks? Perpetrates? Perpetuates? Perceives? Percolates?"

"Perhaps."

"Smart ass." Parker was okay, but he was one dimension. He probably never doubted, screamed, or cried. Why should he? Or anyone, for that matter, within a cozy circle, with questions as finite as the indications on a thermometer and answers as definite as a couple of aspirins.

A SPECIAL VULNERABILITY

Davey was back in Florida, Michael back in school, Anne in her own apartment, Justin at the cottage. Rosemary, at the farm, was not alone on this winter workday morning when the first rays of the sun splashed through frosted windows. Len stirred. Threw his arm over her waist. Mumbled, "Our own ice palace."

She looked at him with an overwhelming feeling of tenderness—he was so completely hers in this moment, his eyes so direct without glasses, squints of sky-blue looking back at her, making her believe in forever, in things working out—whatever that meant—in the oasis they shared. Being with him was monumental in her life. Her first big, daring choice. Which is where I live now, she thought. Loving luck. Relishing fantasy. Looking forward. She knew she loved him. The first time she loved anyone beyond family. Her family. She pushed them away. She'd worry later. Today at lunch. On the drive to work. But not now.

She buried her face in his shoulder.

Last night at PTA, parents wandered through her classroom. She mingled, chatting briefly with them about their children. She looked up to see the back of his denim jacket as he studied a child's painting, the primary colors in thick, wide bands across the paper, pretending he was a parent carefully guarding and appreciating the world of his progeny. With his presence came sweet acknowledgment, and in his turning to face her, a smile of rapport, as if everything he saw held reasons to love her. He was as pure as the innocent paintings behind him.

And now, they'd drive to where he'd parked the truck last night away from the farm and she'd climb in beside him as he started her car, the cold biting, both of them squinting in the dazzling light, he to go climb trees and she to the classroom of primary colors and uncomplicated words. Wrapped in wool hats and scarves and mittens like children, they held hands in the cold believing in their luck and love and warmth and light and the amazing right that still was alive in the world. Like revisiting a first love that had been lost somewhere in the ruins, she said to herself. No, better. This time she was visible. This time she felt loved, and loved him back easily, the balance in loving a balm to her soul.

She'd worry about the family later. She was tired of duty, looking out at the frozen fields, which was easy to think armored by Len's hand warming hers, resting, pushing away the dream she'd lived in all night, the one about Justin, smiling and joking, holding her. In the dream, they planned what they would do to the house, maybe make a sunroom out of the porch.

She looked across at Len, and leaned over to kiss his cheek, the craggy honesty of his face, the moment frozen in time, in her time. Loving him was separate from her hope that she and Justin would be together again someday. When he was better. Guilty now as she watched Len, she thought she'd write Justin. Perhaps he'd be open to seeing Dr. Vincent now. Yesterday she called to see how he was, and a woman had answered.

"Hello?" the woman said. "What do you want him for?"

It was a good question, not that anyone had a right to ask. And despite the warmth of Len's hand in hers and the calm, icy morning, she felt an agitation, a quivering leaf she couldn't find in her field of vision, the reason for not answering the question for herself. What *did* she want Justin for, other than to answer a sense of duty, and was there still duty in her shattered life? And what, in God's name, was it? In her head, she began to write, *Dear Justin, I'm sorry about everything. I remember how hard you worked on the house. I see your hands everywhere, placing ceiling tiles and smoothing down walls. It was a colossal task. I love the house you made for us. In my dreams you never left it.*

Oh, the weight her heart had become. Her life was a series of separate chambers. She kidded herself that she could enter one and forget the others. What would it all come to? Len was searching her face now and she leaned toward him, feeling he was real, and all the rest, ghosts in her head and hopes she had to let go of. While she grappled, something had opened, something beyond pain and disappointment and sorrow. Maybe it was love. Not only for another. For self. Had it begun with the return of glances and touches? Her cup filling up?

Concentration was more than Anne could handle. Sitting in class was agony. People talked to her but she was not sure she'd seen them before, although they seemed to seek her out, and walked away laughing. She was always teasing, always poking fun, making her microcosmic observations—the best of which often culminated in bizarre imitations. The class clown. Which was why there was an endless supply of male attention, though mostly brotherly. One weekend she painted her car lemon-lime green, and spanned brightly colored flowers across the fenders and doors—a harbinger of spring, and change. Before midterms, she dropped out of school and took an apartment in Baltimore. She tended bar at night, saving her daylight hours for the good light that poured across her canvases through the high, old windows of her apartment. She painted with an unexplained restlessness she knew as well as the wall beyond her bed, which she studied after work when she couldn't sleep, her eyes following cracks in the plaster and landing on patched holes where former pictures had hung, isolated moments of other haphazard lives and other cubicled views passing through apartment life, temporary and ephemeral as her own. These city walls. How anonymous they were!

The paintings were experimental she liked to say down at the gym where she worked out, or at the club where she tended bar, but the truth was she flung the paint with impatience, quick, long dashes that sometimes ended in a particular detail she labored over for hours. Never right. Never quite it. She painted over these, aware of the paint she wasted, or was not wasting, depending on your view, each canvas an education, a practice as searching and diligent as Davey and his stringed runs through the long, starry nights. Sometimes the shapes of former paintings showed through on the next painting like the ghosts that had once adorned the patched walls, other views and other choices. It was all a muddle, but out of it—came something, albeit too slowly.

Was her restlessness mere moodiness? Or was it the seeking, and not quite finding, that plagued her, the journey she must take alone?—she and the brush and the canvas, that white plane on which she would pour herself and which she would send off one day into the world, and then to begin again, to work through doubt, and never to quite finish.

Finally, the painting before her, yellow ochre on top of yellow gold, the blue clashing, softening for a while under the brush, mellowed now, and then muddied. She looked at the still life of last April's daffodils in the blue pitcher set on a blue checkered tablecloth and admitted she'd lost their essence in the intervening months. She could tell mediocrity, that was one thing. And she wasn't afraid to admit defeat. Another paint-over. But not now. A drive home would do her good, where there was amazing yellow, the sun pouring through the dining room on forsythia her mother was sure to have brought into the house to force into bloom. She'd take the easel.

She hadn't planned to go home when she got up, but now that she found herself on the way, slipping down the hills toward Annapolis with the woods sloping gently on either side, she felt it was a good way to spend an early spring morning. There was no reason to go home except, of course, to see her mother and the fact that she woke up this morning longing to see the limitless sky uninterrupted by storefronts and row houses. She needed space around her, a good distance between her and anyone or anything else.

On the other side of the Bay Bridge, everything simplified, a scattering of strip malls, the first of myriad antique shops with outside displays of painted furniture in various stages of peel, a roadside cemetery and pier-laden creeks leading out to rivers dotted by slow-moving sailboats. Anne breathed easier and deeper, the landscape lulling her until she came upon the neatly combed fields surrounding Pucam. Soon there was the large cemetery on the outskirts of town, its history and Mr. Lucian's now too etched in its stones, its stories silent under the grass, and then Pucam, unyielding, unchanged except for the recently installed public telephone outside the post office and the new brass door handle on the old, chipped post office door. Anne noticed. *How could I not?* she thought, and smiled as off in the distance the farmhouse appeared at the other end of a sea of green.

The farm itself was another matter. The trees made her anxious the way they leaned over with rotted trunks. Shrubbery darkened the house, having grown high enough to cover the downstairs windows, although her mother never seemed to notice. But then, Anne thought, you need to be away from something to really see it. Like her mother's kitchen and the comfort of the kettle on the stove and her mother's glasses on the table along with notes to herself and jokes cut out from the *New Yorker* on the refrigerator, snapshots of her brothers and her everywhere and every card she'd ever given her mother saved on the dining room buffet. Her mother kept her place for her when she got lost. Not that she was lost now. She was okay.   •

She grabbed her purse from the car and entered the kitchen door. "Ma?" she called out. "Ma?"

Mozart trilled through the rooms; curtains flowed spiritlike and lazy around sun-filled windows; and yes, the vase on the table held forsythia branches with swollen buds and the first timid, single, yellow blossom. A collection of short stories by Elizabeth Jolley lay open, pages down on the couch—there was only one person who would tell her mother about Elizabeth Jolley. With a stab, she called out, "Mom?"

And then uneasiness returned to her, danced around her teasingly, caught between her teeth as she remembered the time she came home and her mother was going out on a date, dressed up in a new black jump-suit, earrings swinging—her dancing clothes, she said. At first Anne felt a kind of relief at the new Mom. It meant she was okay. "He's not picking you up?" she had asked. "No," her mother said without looking at her. "I'm meeting him."

She remembered thinking at the time, who's *him?* Her mother shared no details, but Anne wanted them. Not about her date, but Anne had never had her questions answered—like who had told her mother about her desperation, her really bad time, whether or not it was Davey.

So she asked. "How did you find out?" Her daring startled her.

"Len told me," was the answer. "He asked me out to dinner and told me. He meant well, Annie. Don't be angry at him. But I wish you'd told me how bad you felt."

She hated people talking behind her back, hated admitting anything to her mother. She was, after all, the one her mother didn't worry about. "I didn't think it was anybody's business."

"I understand that, Annie. But I feel bad—you needed help." Her mother's face was crestfallen. She'd been cheated of her mother act. But Anne didn't need it. She could take care of herself. She hated Len for telling on her, that scum of the earth.

"Mom? Where are you?"

Slowly it occurred to her that the signs were there, but she had avoided reading them. There had probably been more than just one dinner—the two of them with their heads together, a rapport and an empathy unrivaled. She could see it. If ever there were two people who could reach out to each other and be comforted it would be the two of them. There was a sadness in Len that underlined everything, and the same with her mother, an embrace of life's tragedies because they brought depth and awareness. Theirs was a special vulnerability. In a way, they were well suited.

Nonetheless, churning began, and anger, a quick rage. The thought of them together made her sick. Was it possible? Her kind, patient motherly mother? It felt incestuous. No. It couldn't be. She wouldn't.

"Mom—I'm home!" No, she thought, there was no home, no mother any longer. It was all in some distant, naïve past.

The bathroom door opened. "Oh, Annie!" she said, wrapped in a towel as she stepped out of the steam, dark curls pasted down along her neck, her arm clutching the towel over her breasts. What was that written on her face behind that motherly smile? Guilt. Anne saw guilt behind the mask. And someone she no longer knew. *She was seeing him.*

"Are you?" she said, the words giving birth to a misty shape that had lurked in the back of her head for weeks.

"Am I what?" her mother said, her eyes in fake puzzlement. All of her was fake right now. *Mom. Where's my Mom?* She wanted to shake her—that phony stare—*she knows what I'm talking about. I can tell by the turn of her head.*

"Are you seeing Len?"

"Well, I guess if you're ready to ask the question, you must be ready to hear the answer," she said as if she had the words stamped across her brain for a long time now. "Yes," she breathed out, her face all mushy, pain pouring out at Anne through her eyes.

"I mean—sleeping with him," Anne heard herself scream, wanting to see everything plainly as on a rare day when the ocean was so clear she could see her feet on the bottom. Her mother's eyes said yes and her breathing ceased, held in as though she had no right to the space she took up.

And she didn't have—any right—*an*-y-right—Anne kept time, saying the words with her fists—an-y-right-an-y-right—feeling the sting, hearing her mother gasp as she swung at her over and over, hitting the soft part of her shoulder and hitting and hitting, aiming for her face which was covered with her hands letting go the towel and there was her mother standing bare-ass naked which she'd never seen, never knew her breasts were so white or that she had scars on her stomach and she kept hitting while her mother yelled, *get out, get out,* and she said the one word she knew was deadly because her mother was so saintly and motherly and patient all the time she couldn't stand it and she screamed at her, "Whore! You whore!" through the blur of arms and hair and skin and scars and tears enough to make an ocean, aware suddenly her mother never once hit back. It must be she believed it too, and when she bent down to get the towel to cover herself, Anne saw the red birthmark splattered on her mother's breast which she hadn't seen since she was a kid when her mother nursed Davey.

Which made her stop.

Mother. Backing off, she ran through the rooms and from the house—never to go back—couldn't breathe with the hate and the hurt—she might do it again—she might! Oh God—next time, kill on the spot without a thought—she could, she knew she could, my God, her own mother. No matter what, how could she? But how could her mother—no mother of hers.

Daffodil buds swelling, forsythia, pussy willow—those were the usual signs, but they were never the first. End of February the frogs began singing, so loud you could hear them through the walls, louder with the opening of the side door, deafening as you walked toward the pond. The low places in the woods were filled with them though you could never see them and their tenor stopped as soon as you approached, their silence leaving such a void that you depended on them beginning again. Like the thrill of the first of anything—first baby, first leaves, first sip of coffee in the morning, first plucks on an acoustic guitar—the first vibrations of the frogs were something to celebrate. Spring was breathing, and from the sun-warmed back steps, Rosemary sat and listened, in her hand the deed to the farm. In her name.

So easy. Things divided right down the middle. He, the summer cottage, she, the farm. He, the river, the tides, the sunsets. She, the land, the trees, the seasons. Divorce was only a word, division only paper, but more painful than death she was sure, her life with Justin beginning so early, lasting through births and deaths and accumulations and relocations and a million looks and sighs and laughs and putting their feet on the floor in the morning. First love. In the beginning they'd had a luxury of days that were good, memory that could never be divided. Her name on this piece of paper only meant *from now on* as she moved through time. She stared at the name, *Rosemary Williams*. So singular.

On her way to the pond, her feet kicking up soil, the frogs stopped. But the silence was not dreadful, she noticed, it was filled with presence and expectancy. Hope. She laughed out loud. Then standing still as a tree, she waited. Ah, yes. They began again. Yes.

She listened until she couldn't anymore. The constant scream reminded her of other screams, and Anne. She began walking toward the house. She'd deserved the blows. That's not what hurt. It was that Anne *could* hit her. She looked again at the name on the deed. It was a good name. Some of it borrowed, some of it given. But hers. The farm, too. And all the mistakes? Hers too, and love for Len connected to everything because she'd allowed it. She tried to imagine not allowing anything that had happened. It made her laugh, the frogs still screaming, the patient, determined willingness of spring.

"Michael's getting married in June," she told Len. "Here. There'll be a crescent-shaped garden under the mimosa trees and a live band."

To help her get ready, he came and worked on the trees one day in

May although he wouldn't take any money. "If I gave you a bouquet of roses you wouldn't think of paying me. Think of this as a bouquet of roses," he said. Afterward, he sat with her on the porch, quietly smoking, and looked out over the lawn shaded by high lilacs and rose of Sharon.

"Sometimes I think I should sell," said Rosemary. "Old house—all this peeling paint—new well, new furnace this winter—I had to take out a loan—I can't do it all."

"I can't imagine you anywhere else," he said, and reached for her hand. She couldn't either. Not in this season, the full swell of summer almost upon them, the purple irises and Shasta daisies along the path to the pond, the smell of honeysuckle and wisteria from the woods beyond.

In the dusk, she watched the lighted end of his cigarette. She had tried to give him up. There were weeks at a time when she didn't see him, telling him over the phone, "No, I can't, it isn't right," but there was always something she wanted to tell him, a vacancy at her side she had to dispel. When she did see him, it was as if he gave her pieces of herself. For days afterward, she was happier than she'd ever been. He acknowledged what she loved and what she was. More than that we really can't do for one another, she thought.

WEDDING

"The wedding should take place in God's house," said Reverend Tomlin over the phone from Bible Baptist. "Well, I should think God's house could include a canopy of trees down by the pond," said Rosemary. After the fifth call, which exhausted all the churches in Pucam, Brother Shain from the Open Community Gathering consented to marry Michael and Mari at the farm. He appeared one afternoon with an Indian arrowhead and a wooden cross hanging from a leather necklace. Would they be interested in an Indian Sweat Lodge gathering the night before? Rosemary said she thought not, but thanked him anyway.

Meanwhile, she dug a new garden down by the pond and planted seedlings she'd raised in peat pots along the windowsills. She bought white paint for the garage doors, gray for the porch floor, and barn red for the chicken coop. Mari's mother and father were coming from Baltimore to lend a hand with the painting and Michael and Davey had just finished hammering down the loose porch boards and replacing torn screening when Anne called. Rosemary held her breath. "Annie, oh Annie—thank you. It's so good to hear your voice! Where are you?"

Anne said, "Need help with the sprucing up, Mom? Michael told me to show up on Saturday morning. That okay?"

Later, when she stepped out of Andrew's car, she pushed a bouquet of wildflowers toward Rosemary and said, "Here. Got a vase big enough, or an empty pail?" She looked Rosemary right in the eye, her face open as a sunflower. Reaching out to hold her, Rosemary said, "How're you doing?" and Annie—my God, Annie hugged back.

The morning of the wedding broke with storm clouds along the horizon. Undaunted, Mari, Anne, and Rosemary left at six to pick wildflowers and returned just before the clouds burst with the trunk of the car full of Queen Anne's lace, daisies, tiger lilies, and butterfly weed. "We need a bit of blue in all that orange and white," said Anne and went back into the rain for some chicory she remembered seeing at Poke's Corner. In the kitchen, as they waited for the rain to end, they ate jelly doughnuts and drank coffee, listening to the rain shush down the drainpipes.

"I hope it lets up soon," said Mari. Rosemary rubbed her feet together and thought about her own wedding day and the promises. I do, she had said. I will. In sickness and health, death do us . . . Justin appeared, still limping from the last marathon and a torn ligament in his right leg. "Came in second," he said to whoever would listen. "But it's easier in the over-fifty slot." Along came Mari's three sisters and two brothers. They filled the kitchen and spilled into the dining room and living room, munching doughnuts, laughing.

When the rain ended, Anne and Rosemary filled every bucket they could find with flowers, saving the smallest of the Queen Anne's lace for Mari's bouquet, and placed the buckets to form a path to the garden. Chairs arrived, the folding wooden kind from church basements and tent revivals, delivered by two volunteer firemen from Pucam who trod carefully along the lane of flower buckets as they set up chairs on either side. Mari's parents came, her mother, Lillian, dark-haired as her daughter, carrying a basket full of birdseed packets wrapped in netting and tied with pink bows, and Ted, Mari's father, lugging a carton of champagne through soggy grass.

Michael and Davey appeared in white short-sleeved shirts, gray jeans with suspenders and white tennis shoes.

"That's what you're wearing?" said Rosemary.

"Why not? This is a crab feast, remember?" said Michael, teasing Mari. "Somebody tie up that dog, okay?"

At full speed, Taxi was nothing short of magnificent—but excessive, like everything else in this family, thought Rosemary as she watched him leap over the flower buckets and lope amongst the chairs, nudging people who turned to see this Goliath of a dog that made them start as he lifted his huge nose at some faraway scent.

"Davey," she called. "Do something with that dog, okay?" When he got home, Davey said, "A good dog's better than a girlfriend." He meant Melinda, of course, who'd stomped away and kept the diamond. Davey shrugged when he told it, and watched Taxi drop down in the field after pawing a nest in the soft earth, and stretch out in the sun, daring the tractor to work around him. "Man, this is his *territory!*" laughed Davey. Caught now, Taxi sat motionless at the end of the chain eyeing the women from the Ladies' Auxiliary who had just arrived with platters of ham and potato salad, sliced tomatoes, and coleslaw.

Rosemary took a seat next to Justin in the front row. He kept his eyes averted. "Justin?" she said. "Hmmmm?" he said from a great distance. Quickly she put her hand on his as they lay folded in his lap. He looked away. She removed her hand and wished it could be otherwise, especially now.

Davey, as best man, took his place with his guitar in hand, and began strumming "Morning Has Broken." The dog sighed and sank down on his front paws; the chairs sank into the muddy lawn and the sun streamed down on the garden where bees hummed on the impatiens and petunias. Mari walked down the bucket-lined path, back straight as a rod, her thick hair in an upsweep, pale skin delicate as a calla lily. Her eyes stayed on Michael.

Brother Shain brushed his hand through his red-brown chest hairs, clutched the arrowhead and cross necklaces, looked off into the trees, cleared his throat and began. Rosemary stole a glance at Justin, who stared at the top of the tall pine behind Brother Shain, his mouth turned down at the corners. "Where'd you find *him?*" he said, loud enough to set Davey smiling.

Soon Michael mumbled oaths and Mari answered distinctly and surely; Davey played a few triumphant chords and it was done. Taxi howled a long, lonely, deep-throated cry that sounded as though it blew in from ancient plains. Laughter, a loosening from the bonds of all those sticky words and chairs, allowed people to rise and mingle and wish well and rush into the house to change into shorts and T-shirts. Tables appeared, soon covered by long rolls of brown wrapping paper to welcome the heaps of steamed crabs. There was Hannah bearing bread again—two overlapping circles like wedding bands—with questions on her lips Rosemary didn't want to answer, and Giles, looking rounder and older but jovial as ever, Anthony with a bunch of guys from school, Mari's friends from Baltimore, Maude and George quietly watching the dog, loose again, as he ran between people sniffing, jowls quivering. Everyone under the trees Len had shaped and cleared, everyone except Len, thought Rosemary, and wiped him away with a sweep of her hand across her brow. Her best friend and her truest self denied. No. Her truest self was here, mother of, mother-in-law of, hostess of, owner of, friend of. Imagine the ease of honesty and openness, her life under one roof, the state of things declared: lover of. The labor of lies over.

A path clearly defined, Brother Shain had said. A path on water was more like it. Unmarked before, traceless after. But all the hope here in this moment—that was something to hold on to. Her eyes rested on Michael, on his red curls and full red beard, on the shirtsleeves tight around the muscles of his arms, doing a normal and expected thing like anyone else. It was only a rough beginning he'd had. He was in good currents now and heading toward harbor. She watched as he signaled to the band. The music started.

I am Anne and she is Rosemary.

She turns to my father wanting more than she can have, and he relents this once. They walk together where Michael and Mari waltz, but they don't touch, are careful not to touch as they step into the sunlight before each other. I wonder how we were ever conceived.

Uncle George stares at his feet. He wants to dance, but wanting to isn't enough. "C'mon, Uncle George," I say. He looks panicked as he shrugs, but doesn't refuse. I dance around him. He follows, glances at Aunt Maude and looks down at his feet again, sweat beading under his nose. Aunt Maude waits, hips rocking. I pull more people out of the circle of watchers—some I don't even know. Rosemary prances by, arms open, motioning, "C'mon," inviting. The dance to her is everything, which is where Davey got it. And me.

Leaves flutter. A faint breeze I can't feel. People churn, this way, that. Red faces, dusty feet. Hannah steps lightly and pushes back her glasses, takes Giles's cigar from his mouth and leans into his chest. He grabs her elbows and they laugh, rocking in place. Togetherness for the longevity — is it a matter of luck? Being lucky, do they know it? Does anyone understand what is happening until it is long past?

Anthony, a beer can in each hand, turns his ankle on a tree root. He puts his swelling foot in the ice bucket and keeps on dancing. He's looking at me, beckoning. I don't want to. Drunk, he persists. I dance with him for a few seconds and go on. Rosemary floats by like a silk scarf. Davey, part of the band now, steps inside the music and closes the door. Michael's feet blur they move so fast. Brother Shain dances with one of Mari's girlfriends, one hand on his chest, his eyes on her chest. Andrew's shirt and belt become unraveled, his arms snap at the air, a smile up to his ears. He winks at me. Dad's in the air suspended by invisible threads. His feet shuffle back and forth, and Aunt Maude joins in, her small feet daintily released under her weight. Catcalls.

Yeah! Aunt Maude!

Mari, looking regal even as she lifts the skirt to her wedding dress, has her arms around her brother. They are in a chorus-line kick; Ted and Lillian are in an old-time Lindy. And me — weaving in and out of everybody — I loop my arm through a hundred arms and spin them around, whoever they are.

Shadows move around us but we beat them back, beat everything harsh and woeful back. We've learned how and now we're good at it. Breathless, I slow down and look around: no longer posing, people look at each other with faces believable and earnest.

We dance so hard all our fears leave us, roosting in the trees like a flock of challenged chickens. Uncle George is a wild man, Maude, his heavenly angel. Dad's hah haaaaa competes with the loudspeakers. The clouds sail; the corn inches; water pulses from the irrigation system and all of us sing and clap to "Pink Cadillac." We interrupt the scheme of things. We explode. I hope they hear us in Pucam, and on Mars. We love every-

thing, even the rusted wash pole by the chicken coop, the blood-red siding, the cypress tree, and all the bobbing heads.

A flash of white makes me look up. Is that Davey climbing out of a
bedroom window and onto the porch roof? I glance at the band. They go
on without him. The curtain follows him through the window and flows
back as he dances. He flings out his arms and throws kisses. Parker,
Thomas, and two others follow. Rosemary screams, *It won't hold!* They
can't hear her, of course. Davey slips, then catches himself as he sings to
the trees and the audience below. Someone throws the bridal bouquet and
blossoms scatter. Seeing Aunt Maude with her hands on her hips, Parker
and Thomas go back through the window.

Rosemary turns away and starts dancing again, and I dance with her,
as if Davey was doing the expected and it was just too much to contend
with anyway. Hey, she says with her arms curled around her and her shoulders rocking and her head thrown back, we're alive and well although
Davey may be for only a few more minutes if I get my hands on him—and
we laugh—we've been tenacious on this scrub of land—held the wagons
tight around the campfire for so long that it's our duty now to celebrate the
wide sky and craziness and life. Besides, she's paid the band good money
and "Honky Tonk Women" isn't over.

Suddenly, icy bullets rain down on us. Who turned on the hose?
Screams. Water pelts us and drills holes in the ground. We are drenched.
Shocked, everyone looks up to see that the irrigation system has been started by the neighboring farmer—the one detail we forgot to take care of—
and sprays us and what's left of the wedding cake. We laugh as we stand in
mud—steaming—disbelieving—cooler, yes, and calmer—a bit sheepish—
duly baptized. Subdued. Mari's family hold hands in a tight little group and
anxiously look up at the roof; Andrew is wringing out his shirt.

I am Anne and she is Rosemary, and the one who's shaking his head
is my dad, and that's Davey with his leg stuck in the porch roof. The one
who has his arm around Mari and looks stunned is Michael. We just got
him married off.

That's Taxi under the porch. He hates to get wet.

LAST TIMES

⌒

The last girlfriend—had no name—dark hair like Rosemary's—up and left. Anne gone, long ago. Davey ran away and Michael disappeared. Rosemary—dead. Along with the philodendron. Justin couldn't remember when he last watered it. He knew he ought to. Leaves curled, turned yellow, gasped. Yet it refused to die outright. Just sent strings sparsely leaved, as though conserving, waiting.

He had come alone. The car brought him—he didn't drive it. He walked through the automatic glass doors where the ambulance delivers, walked in and sat down. Found his head in his hands. That's it, he thought. That's all there is. He was crying, he knew, but he didn't care about that. He'd never cried before. Maybe he should have. Half of his life he didn't remember and the other half he didn't want to, while the tears rolled down his cheeks and blotted his T-shirt. He was an eggshell, his insides dried out. They could prick him and he'd crack. He'd had a life and he'd wasted it.

They were coming closer. He couldn't get up and run. It was too far. He couldn't explain. He'd just sit quiet and maybe they wouldn't notice.

Though the lights pained him. And whether or not he had to rise and give his name pained him and get out his medical card—he wouldn't be able to, he was sure.

He was inside a pocket of silence, a bubble beyond which there was movement, distortions. He didn't care. He was part of the chair. Immobile. He was—ready—to be released. He'd had—enough. The white flag—on the cot—he'd wave if he had the will to pick it up.

Steps. Feet. Voices. He only wanted to tell his heart to stop beating.

Can I help you? What's your name, sir? How did you get here? Mr.—?

Everyone was dead so who was talking? Because he was dead, he couldn't answer.

They called her at school. There was no emergency, and even though they'd been divorced, could she come down and sign papers? There seemed to be no one else they could call. He was all right, yes, physically that is. The doctor would be talking with her this evening.

On the wall in the hospital corridor was a photograph of two swans swimming past each other. She hesitated before going into his room as her eyes searched the perfect opposing symmetry of the swans, from which concentric ripples emanated in the dark blue water. Could she do anything? Probably not. Though when he needed to be taken care of she had been unwilling. Would she ever forgive herself? She breathed a long, slow sigh and entered.

He did not look at her. Foolishly, she started talking about the weather— how cool it is, Justin, for this time of year though there are a jillion stars out tonight, and did he want her to bring him some ice cream? He had always loved coffee ice cream. He would be all right now and coming here was a good thing to do and it showed he really did want to be well and he must remember that this would pass, like everything else, and did he want her to bring him anything? Till he said, *Stop, please* and the nurse came in and said, "Mrs. Williams, I don't think you should be here right now—who gave you permission?"

"I'm sorry," she said. "I thought—no one stopped me."

"Perhaps later," the nurse said, and smiled, and Justin raised his hand in a good-bye gesture without looking at her. There was no compromise. He either stared at her for hours at a time like at the Christmas table a year ago or he ignored her completely.

He was broken for the time being. Maybe now he'd get stabilized. Get well. Come back. Come back well.

Soon after, she lay with Len in a field under a night sky. Of all things, she said to herself—the simplest of pleasures. They'd been out riding—there were a hundred roads they could take without seeing another car—when they came on a break in the woods and a stretch of field planted with barley. A new moon hung in the trees. Len stopped the car and reached in the back-seat for an old quilt which he shook out and spread on the ground, patting it down in the lumpy places. He cradled her as she lay against him studying the configurations of stars.

Would this be the last time they'd lie together? She didn't know because in all of her thoughts about him she always left room for a time that would repeat itself, winding its way through and around her other life, but—was she deciding? Maybe. She thought of him as the thread that held her togeth-er, his touch the one her body had answered. *I want nothing more*, she thought, and realized how peaceful that was. They'd never discussed a future. There was only the fact of loving, and the memory of it.

Once, when she was eleven, a boy in the old neighborhood in Queens had given her a blue velvet rose for her hair. The gift was sudden, out of con-text—he was a kid she played stick ball with in the street after school. "Here," he'd said, presenting her with the small package loosely wrapped in tissue paper. It was a milestone, as if by that simple gift he'd managed a major shift in the way the world worked for her. For weeks the rose lay on her dresser to be worn for a special occasion, not that there were many in her regulated and sequestered life. One day, when a friend of her father's invited the family for a ride in his new boat, she foolishly wore it. When she leaned over the side of the boat, the rose slipped from her hair into the water. She remembered the blue of the rose turning green as the depth of water closed around it, her disbelief at its short-lived glory, and her own star-tled gasp, her helplessness as it sank.

This time, however, she was not helpless—she had a choice—but the heart-stopping dismay was the same when she realized something within her would be lost if she continued to see Len. She could, at will, bring back his face, the touch of his hand, the round wire-rimmed glasses and the shocking, intense blue of his eyes. As she stored up the feel of his body against hers and his thumb rubbing the back of her hand, she knew she would always recall this quiet, easy happiness. But there was her family, and she, still, its hopeful, watchful sentinel. She wondered about bliss, how in its midst was a small yet momentous place where love and guilt mingled, one indecipherable from the other, where worry and pain began.

Okay. Okay. His life depended on pills, he told himself as he stood over the toilet bowl emptying his gut. He got it. He didn't have a choice. He always believed in choices, in solving things his own way. Never let anyone tell him what to do. Maybe that's what did him in.

This was new—listening, obeying. Christ, he was the king of independence and self-reliance. That's what he hated about his old life, the confines of family, the chains of the farm, the duty, then, the final insult: Rosemary carrying the load. Why didn't he see it? He never let on. Never once broke down, never admitted defeat until now. He did hate a whiner. And then he always felt better and thought he could do it, all he needed to do was withstand the downers. What was he made of anyway? Couldn't he take a little rough spot now and then? *Couldn't he fix it himself?*

He'd fought back for a long time, he could see that now. All but the fear. What if in public, on a job, on the road running, he went berserk, and made a fool of himself—he didn't want to look crazy—which if that was the final act, the door he'd have to go through to die—that would be okay. Didn't have to worry then who he'd hurt, or how to support himself. But what if he didn't die, what if he kept on living? When everything was gone, if he had himself he could always make out. But when he didn't have himself—he couldn't live. Neither did he have the wherewithal to end it. There was no hell like that kind of hell.

Each time he tried to take the damn pills and felt sick, he hadn't been willing to compromise. Certainly not the highs. But the hills on the roller coaster were steeper now, the plunge and the ascension more than a body could stand. He'd been broken. Now he was broken in. An old shoe. So maybe he could be comfortable in this body sometime, not yet, but sometime. It was the beginning of faith. For now, he still couldn't concentrate. Like a three-day drunk. Doctor said, "We'll adjust the dosage. Hang in there." Poor choice of words.

A fly walked across the bathroom mirror. He watched, sharply aware of the fly's utter lack of self-consciousness, and for a second or two envied the goddamn fly. Behind the man in the mirror was another self, like an apparition, watching him with mournful demeanor.

HOME FIRES, 1986

The floor needed washing again. What was a white floor doing in an old farmhouse beleaguered by mud and weather? A bit of extravagance she hadn't expected. Water from the tap flowed into the bucket, foam rose to tiny flecks of color. She pulled the rag from the bottom of the bucket, wrung it out and plopped it on the floor. Gray squares outlined on a field of white, pink blossoms entwined along opposite corners of the squares, it was so much brighter than the old floor, that dull configuration of red, tessellate squares and rectangles, pockmarked and chipped, etched by kids with muddy feet and girlfriends with spiked heels.

Davey walked in the back door one night a month ago with his guitar in hand, tennis shoes worn through at the heels. Starred and striped, the shoes were remnants from a smoky stage presence in some Georgia bar, back when his hair was long and blond and his face lean. He had sent pictures of the band and although she could barely make him out in the dry ice mist, there he was, baggy pants and shirt opened to his waist, the guitar resting on his groin, and those red, white, and blue tennis shoes.

"Mom," he'd said before he even said a good hello, like he'd just come in from playing with the dog in the yard. "We got to give this kitchen a facelift." She hugged him, the bigger-than-he-ever-was him, and he just dropped his head down on her shoulder as if he'd been a long, long way and she didn't know the half of it. There'd been a few frightened, tearful calls late at night—hysterical—like he was hanging on by one slim thread—the thought of coming home. This time his car was dead and he had to tow it behind a U-Haul for which she'd sent him money, Western Union. "Thanks, Mom. God, thanks," his voice ached through the phone.

The squares on the floor stretched before her like opaque panes of glass. Down on her knees, she began wiping, her arm a pendulum sweeping from side to side, dissolving stains, clearing perplexity. She dropped the rag in the bucket. The remaining suds fizzed away. She thought of her mother who'd told her how she'd spent the night Rosemary's father died, how she'd held his hand in the antiseptic ambulance and for the brief time in the ER, and then heard the doctor's *I'm sorry.* "I went home without him, Rosemary, and washed the bathroom floor all night. Ten, twelve, fifteen times, I don't know—I didn't cry—just tried to wipe the strangeness away."

Rosemary knew little about Davey's life. There were only glimpses, like the night he spent in jail and his request for bail, the bar fight when he got his ear slashed, the call from the emergency room when he thought his leg was broken from some fight he'd been in, when he fought the X-rays because he didn't have the money to pay for them nor the taxi ride back to his room. There would be the collect call from some strange city, and then silence. For days, crazy with worry, she thought he was lost to them forever with never a way to reach him. Yet when she saw him, she was reassured. He sauntered around the kitchen as if he'd never been away, smiling and taking charge. "Make a list, Mom," he said, "of what you want done. I'll take care of it. We'll get some paint—pick out a color—take off the old wallpaper, get some new flooring, maybe even redo the cabinets."

His face was swollen as if he'd just awakened from a long sleep. His body, too, was swollen, which didn't go along with what he told her about being hungry most of the time he was away. He'd been on food stamps—he had one of the workers at the mission down there in Texas to thank for that, and visited soup kitchens regularly. Now he ate like someone who'd known hunger. Great mounds of food disappeared before she even began her own dinner. "Slow down," she told him. "There's plenty." But he didn't seem to taste anything or realize what he was doing. He looked at her as though he noticed her sitting there for the first time, an interruption to his thoughts.

One night, sitting at the kitchen table he did talk some. The band did well on the road, he said, but everybody was tired of the vagabond life. "Stuff just gets heaped in suitcases, stirred up till you can't find anything," he said shaking his head, "and each place looks like every other you've ever been to. Gets so you never see daylight, you just move from motels to clubs and back again." His eyes looked bloodshot and old.

"This guy had a lounge just outside Waco that wasn't doing too well so Damon made a deal with him. We'd play rent-free and give him part of the take. The place was huge. Twenty-four hundred square feet of old smoke. For weeks we painted, cleaned things up. We even ran the bar ourselves between sets, but the crowds just didn't happen. The other guys had wives to go home to, a restaurant business here, a hustle there," he said and stared down at his tennis shoes. "I spent most days on a cot in one corner of the club—didn't care if I ever got up again, didn't want to talk to anybody, see to things. I was glad the dog was with me this time. The only reason I got up was to feed him—couldn't stand to see him hungry."

She would always remember the floor as a gift: Davey, a pencil in his ear, measuring, thinking how he was going to do it. He managed by himself, although his father had done the same thing with the old floor, years ago. This one Davey didn't have to glue down. His father had laid a good enough foundation with the old one. He had to cut the flooring from one big sheet and secure it with the molding on the edges. He got a few nails caught under it and had to perform a little surgery, make a slit on the edge of one of the squares and fish the nail out, but you could hardly see the cut. He worked hard, moved out the stove and the refrigerator and carried the washer out the door as if it was an empty box. There wasn't anything he couldn't do. He said it himself and she believed it.

"Your new career, Mom," he said the night he'd finished it, "keeping a white floor clean," and laughed with those even teeth of his. She got to feeling hopeful about everything again, wanted to paint the yellowed woodwork in the hall and replace the carpet. Wanted to get rid of the feeling of hardscrabble about the place that hung around ever since Justin left, and before—well, from the first moment she'd stared down that long lane and looked at her fate. Huge white clouds sailing by and apple trees in bloom distracted her, but you come to a place like this and you don't leave easily. She and Justin had concentrated on restoring the house. They were young enough to be enthusiastic about it then. The forward motion of building had nothing to do with the treading-water feeling of staying. One sank to the other before she knew it.

There was the tear. Right in the middle of the floor, along the cabinet edge, six inches out. She thought if she kept the floor clean, the crack wouldn't show as much, but it was darkening even after a few weeks. She pretended not to notice and Davey never mentioned it. It would have been nice to have everything perfect. He was down on all fours cutting with the carpet knife, wanting to do it right but quickly too, to get on to something else, but doing it for her, wanting to be done with the whole damn thing, wondering what he would do when he was finished with the kitchen and whether or not he would stay or go back into the music and the life he left.

Was he giving up? He had only played once since he came home—set up the amp and the pedals, laid out a few picks, and kept the guitar on the couch most of the time with the cord hooked up as if it was leashing some tired old dog. He played a long, sweet, bluesy-type comfort of notes that sailed through the rooms letting the walls and corners know he was home. And that was that. She hoped it would be different this time, that he'd stay home for a while, get a job, let other things fall into place like a legal license and insurance—all the compromises he'd never been able to make.

He trimmed the steps and the new molding fit perfectly. The finished floor was a surprise for her when she got home from school. She sat at the kitchen table with her cup of tea and enjoyed the light bouncing off the shine, the white-gray and pink as she skimmed her stockinged feet over it, planning new curtains. He appeared around the door frame from the living room and smiled that million-dollar smile of his. She hugged him and said what a wonderful lift it was to have a new floor and thank you, love. He said, "Think it's okay, huh? Figure I could maybe do this—I mean fix up things, home-improvement-type stuff—for a while?"

She was glad to see him making plans. "For a while, then, maybe," he said. And then, because it was in him deeper than anything else, from a well chiseled out of hard ground, he said, "Then this summer, maybe I can get a couple of guys together and we can do some gigs around here."

In a way, she was relieved to hear that, despite the tennis shoes with the bottoms falling out and the illegal Florida license and the collection of worn-out T-shirts from Goodwill—all the trappings of that other life. Maybe he could have both the life of his soul and a practical one.

But practicality was never part of his plan. She only had to enter his bedroom to see that. It looked as though some giant hand had stirred its contents with a wooden spoon—the sheet knotted on the floor, the quilt looking as if it still contained his shape, keeping his place for him in the sea of spilled change, tangled clothes, cowboy boots, sweatbands, scattered guitar picks, keys, folded-down and muddied receipts, cassettes, T-shirts and underwear, dirty socks that marked trails through a map of orange rinds, the open guitar case splattered with paint, yawning at the chaos.

She'd only gone in there to see if he'd meant it when he said he was leaving for good. He snarled the words out with an anger she'd forgotten about. He seemed to change so suddenly. She tried to remember exactly what she'd said. Or was it the house where there were so many reminders of a fate that wouldn't let go? He'd left everything where it was except for the cashmere wool coat he got at Goodwill for three dollars. It had been raw in the evenings. *He'll be back*, she told herself. He'd left his guitar. And the dog.

Finishing the floor was the high point of his coming home. It held the purity of good intentions. Hope of change for the better. When he was little, he was the most gentle child, always taking pictures of clumps of wild-flowers he found around the farm. "Now it's the time of the tiger lilies and then it'll be the time of the black-eyed Susans," he'd say. Did it do any good to say he was fatherless? Of the three of them, he'd had the least of Justin. By the time he was ten his father's presence remained vague and noncommittal. Michael played father for a while, and got serious about his assumed role—walked around stooped with the weight of it. Davey just got more playful. He always laughed easily.

She didn't want to think about it now. Go down to the pond, she told herself, and visit the willows bursting green before any of the other trees. Clumps of green lawn, spurting unevenly like small fountains—clumps of daffodils—everything so eager in the spring.

Funny how life educates you even though you want to look the other way, she thought. It took a long time for her to see that Justin was tired, worn out from an illness that consumed him all those years, and for her to see that there might be a connection between Davey and Justin beyond the fact that Justin had not been there for much of his growing up. There might be, or not. If she'd learned nothing else about the human heart, it was that anytime you were sure of something, the opposite might be closer to the truth. In any case, there had to be forgiveness, which had to be reborn with each episode. Still, the changes would forever catch her off guard.

In the driveway, Taxi loped toward her, nudging her side with his huge head, which meant, "After you rub my back, we can go for a walk, yes?"

"Yes, old boy. In a little while," she told him and she rubbed the long, lean back that missed Davey's touch, and told herself Davey would not go off and leave his dog.

The tire tracks cut two long ruts into the earth; he had left last night in a great hurry. The truck lurched forward, spinning stones into the side of the house. She regretted lighting into him the way she did, but she took a stand finally and asked that he not build any more fires. It made her nervous, a fire every night in different directions from the house with the wind picking up as it did when the sun went down.

The first fire he set soon after he came home, and he asked her to sit out there with him and watch, but there was a hard freeze and she didn't want to sit out under those spooky black locust trees when she could sit with a book inside. Later, she looked out from the upstairs window and watched him staring into the fire, the dog curled up beside him. She wished then she had kept him company; he was so alone.

The next night when he asked her again, "It's so beautiful, Mom, you won't believe it!" and he got a lawn chair out from the shed, she couldn't refuse him. Though it was cold with the north wind at their backs, they sat faces burning while the flames danced before them—and it *was* beautiful. Every once in a while, a log would burst and send yellow stars toward the real ones sprawled above them. Davey pulled branch after branch that hadn't caught yet from the edge of the fire, and set them over the flames, nursing the fire as if it were a piece of music he was fiddling with, reshaping, redefining, keeping a close eye on the wood as it caved in.

At one point, he ran back to the house and brought back two cans of baked beans, opened, labels peeled off, and two foil-wrapped potatoes in the crook of his arm. He set the cans on a forked limb and the potatoes right down into the fire. In his jacket pockets he had cans of beer, one of which he passed to her, and then he stooped to rub Taxi's head. The dog lay close to the flames. She wanted to talk to him, ask him about his new job at the boatyard, if he would get medical benefits, what his plans were for the coming months, but everything she thought of asking seemed like an intrusion. Only this moment mattered to him, she sensed. He was still composing the fire, stirring the beans, stroking the dog. "Warm enough?" he said, bringing tears to her eyes. She nodded back and smiled up at him. His dark eyes reflected flames. "This is it, huh?" he said, laughing. "It's so goddamn simple, isn't it?" He was right. They were at the heart of everything, at peace and needing nothing. Primal. And it was February, the month of longings—and no promises.

They split the potatoes with his penknife, doused them with some of the beans and wrapped them again. He ran back to the house for forks while she held a hot potato in mittened hands. Davey dumped spoonfuls of beans on a paper plate for Taxi, and after they ate, with the dog sniffing the ground for more, Davey leaned against the nearest tree and dragged slowly on a cigarette. His eyes drifted from the fire to the trees and to the black space above.

"I remembered, the whole time I was away," he said, "that we could see the Milky Way from here. All the places I've been, I could never find it, but I used to think about coming home and that I would see it again soon."

They sat for a few hours, until she began to think about bed, and teaching tomorrow, while Davey continued to stoke the fire. She got up from the chair and caught him watching her. "Thanks, Davey," she said and put her arms around him, tearing up again because in all her worries about him, he was the most okay person she knew. Only the world, she thought, was not right for him. She left him still shaping the fire, raking up the smaller limbs and throwing them on, his jacket tied around his waist, the long sweeps of his arms blessing the fire and the night.

She had no idea how long he stayed out there. He was not up by the time she left for work the next morning though she tried to rouse him by knocking on his door. Once she opened it and called. He answered in a muffled "Yeah!" but never got up.

For weeks there was a fire every night, in a new place each time. He'd drag dead branches out of the woods and start splashing gasoline as soon as he got home. One day, he never went to work at all, and began to pile branches in the afternoon. He was dragging them from deep in the woods now. Looking out over the farm from the upstairs window in the morning, she could see black circles and charred logs dotting the paths, even out into the rye field. But when he began on the north side of the house one evening at dusk, burning the brush beneath the pines while the trees smoldered black around their bases, she rushed out with the shovel yelling, "No more fires, Davey. We'll lose the trees and maybe the house. No more, do you hear me?"

"You're driving me crazy," he screamed into the black sky. The beer can in his hand became a missile he launched into the brush and his face contorted. His voice, pushed to a pitch beyond his endurance, cracked. He leapt into his truck, leaving the fire, leaving her to heap soil around the base of the trees with the shovel, sorry she'd said anything, wondering how much was her, how much was him.

The wind picked up. She worried all night the fire would spread, and waited for him, unable to sleep. He never came home. Probably an all-night drunk, though this was the first time since the floor. Maybe he needed a change, maybe it was losing his job, maybe not fitting in, maybe not being able to care about the same things the rest of them did. Maybe he missed his music, his old life. Depression forced you to see life without any illusions, she thought. Everyone needed some illusions.

She filled the bucket from the outside spigot, and leaned against the warm shingles of the house that still miraculously contained the remnants of family, and defeated them as well. She hoped the same sun was beating down on him, warming him, bringing him to his senses—if he wasn't in a ditch somewhere.

WINGS

~✦~

Michael called her first. "Dad's selling the cottage. He got a job on the Western Shore, D.C. somewhere, I think. Says he bought a town house."

The news signified a definite end. Michael said, "I'm just glad he built the cottage when he did—when we were kids—when it meant the most. We were lucky to have enjoyed it for so long," although there was a tension in his voice, as if he were trying too hard to compensate for an immeasurable loss.

"How could he?" said Davey over the phone. "Places like that get handed down from generation to generation! Why don't we all put up some money and buy the cottage from him?"

"What money?" Rosemary asked.

Anne called to say, "He must be doing well, Mom. He got a job. Aren't you glad for him?"

And Rosemary was. She really was.

A few weeks later he called to tell her the cottage was sold, his voice gentle again; he called her "Babe." It was the old Justin, the one she'd married. Could that be possible? "I don't want any of the stuff, Babe. Sell the furniture if you can and keep the money," he said.

"I know this must be difficult for you," she managed to say.

"Yeah. Uh huh. But by the time I pay the mortgage on this place, there's nothing left. Know what I mean? And I won't get down there much anymore. I don't even think the kids go down there, do they?"

"Michael does. Fishing. All the time."

"Yeah. Uh huh. Well. Look, I've got a call waiting."

If he did, he was probably grateful. It wasn't like him to say he did when he didn't, but he was slippery if she reached out. She probably reminded him of a lot of things he wanted to forget. He was working for the first time in eight years and he was on a regular regimen of meds from what he said. He had new acquisitions: a girlfriend, medical insurance, a new house, and a new car. She'd been part of his illness and now he was on an even keel.

Part Six

❧

REQUIEM
FOR A SUMMER
COTTAGE

THE LANGUAGE OF TIDES, 1988

The martins gather on the telephone wires like they do in mid-August for the long flight south. She hears the chink of the halyards on the masts of the catamarans marking time against the flow of the river, and listens to the persistent lick of small waves on the beach. It is high tide. She enters the cottage and notices the threshold is as springy as a peat bog. Moss grows along the beams. And lichen. The log trusses overhead bear a bird's nest at one hollowed end. Where once the windows reflected sunsets, there are now jagged edges of glass. The feeling she has is that she is returning to reclaim the house, or maybe not the house so much as something pure, like innocence. The house goes on and on with diamond-shaped, impossible rooms and the roof gapes open to a clarity of blue. A deck on the second story faces the sun and overlooks a placid sea. A gull cries. She wanders through room after empty room and finally decides: the small back bedroom will be hers. It is bare and white. She will live here at the edge of a calm sea which somehow will always stay calm, and it will always be midday in midsummer in the middle of her life. Is it heaven?

In the distance, a dog barked. Tree branches scratched the window. Rosemary opened her eyes, dully recalling the room without a ceiling, the sun-drenched walls, her hope despite the softness of the moss-laden wood. Lately, she dreamed about houses every night. Sometimes the house burned while Justin was off on one of his long absences. Sometimes the house was on an inaccessible mountain surrounded by apple orchards

where they lived self-contained and reclusive; sometimes Justin built a
new house and she helped, bringing the level or the drill or nails as she
did in the old days and he would take them with his long, lean fingers,
turning from her to a point on the wall, the stub of a panatela in his teeth,
sweat running down his face while she held the ladder steady for him. But
he was nowhere in this morning's dream.

Swinging her legs over the side of the bed, she looked out at a faint gray
sky crisscrossed with red-bud maple branches, the dark gray of the barn siding, the trilliums poking their way through at the edge of the woods—the
things she could count on. And here she was still *being* counted on. She'd
allowed it. They'd divorced, but she was still picking up debris. For the last
time, she promised herself as she shook her head at the woman in the mirror. Blessed are they who divorce in anger and shut the door with a bang.
Blessed are they who become widowed and the door is shut for them,
though cruelly. But woe be to those who hold the door half-open.

She heard the pickup slow down for the turn at the mailbox, then skirr
its way up the lane. Michael was early. The picture of him on her dresser
was taken in front of the cottage when he was ten. He stood in the sun
holding up a twelve-inch rockfish, pleased with himself. He would help
her now as they cleaned out his father's house. The sale of the cottage was
probably harder on him than any of them. Michael loved Sulley's Point.
Just yesterday he had caught two large rockfish and held them up for her
to see, looking like a larger version of the kid in the picture except now his
hair was dark and his face bearded.

They would have to stop in town. She was out of trash bags. Sheer
idiocy to be buying something for the specific purpose of throwing it away,
Justin used to say.

"I don't know why *we* have to do this. It's his cottage," Michael was
saying a half-hour later as Rosemary pulled herself into the cab of the
truck and brushed aside empty Big Gulp cups, a smattering of pennies,
and a yellow extension cord that trailed to the floor. She didn't miss his
pledge of loyalty to her, the mother, injured by the father, in the accented *we*, but wasn't comforted. Long ago, she hoped for Justin's redemption
in Michael's eyes, but for now, she focused on Michael's hands encircling

the wheel—his arms strong and capable. He had steadiness, Michael did, a willingness to take care of things. He was staring out his side window.

"Not for long, Michael. Closing is tomorrow." There were the bedspreads and curtains she'd made, the picture collages of the kids cavorting on the beach. She'd retrieve them.

"Well?" she asked Michael, sharper than she intended. "Aren't you going to start this thing?"

He nodded toward the pond. "Look. Deer. Eight of them."

"I think they're closing in on me—wilderness closing in no matter how hard I try to beat it back." He glanced at her. He always heard every tremor in her voice. "Maybe sometime when you're not too busy, you could cut down some of those new trees and brush around the pond," she went on, trying to lighten up.

"You okay?" he said.

Sometimes he listened too carefully. "Fine," she said.

He turned the key and they listened to the engine whine. Michael slid off his cap and scratched his head, then maneuvered the cap back and forth on his forehead trying to find exactly the right spot. The truck jostled them down the lane onto the dirt road.

"By the way, I told your father what you said about having the cottage when you were a kid. I think he appreciated it."

"You're always protecting him. Always wanting things to be okay with everybody." And then, with his eyes on the road, he said, "It's not your fault, you know. You did everything you could."

And that made it worse. Because everything that had happened, all the events and denials, they had shared, she and Justin. Manic when he left, shirt unbuttoned to his waist, that gold medallion on his chest stating some other woman's claim—she hated him then. And when the tide turned and he wanted to be taken care of again, she could not bring herself to say yes. It grieved her still.

They passed acres of new rye. So green. As Michael shifted into third and the gears were released for a second, Rosemary relaxed her grip on the seat. In the side-view mirror she watched the cloud of dust they had raised, then the beginning of paved road, the centerline falling away as if they had left it there, the graceful arcs of the irrigation system, now large, now diminished, an open mailbox, dandelions at its foot. She was free to leave. Why didn't she?

But all she said was, "Don't forget to stop at the IGA."

The wind was picking up. The huge sugar maple stirred outside the old elementary school. A *For Sale* sign swung on one hinge. Beyond lay the crumpled cottages of what they still called colored town along the west end of Pucam's Main Street, and across the way, St. Mark's First Baptist Church, also for sale.

"How many towns have a school and a church for sale? Place is really going down the tubes," he said. He could only distract her. He could tell she was upset by the stony outline of her face, the way she pulled her chin forward, the sadness around her eyes.

He noticed clothes strung from tree to tree in Mabel Wright's front yard, rayon dresses in pinks and yellows, wool suits in browns and grays, ghosts suddenly brought to life by the fresh wind.

"This is Saturday—traffic in town—yard sales. Want to stop?" he asked her.

She cut her eyes at him. "Haven't we enough junk to clean up now?"

"Aw c'mon, Ma. It'll make you feel like you're a part of Pucam's culture." He tightened his neck and spoke from the back of his throat. "Buy a jacket for a quarter today and pass it on next week, sell it for fifty cent. How 'bout a par o' them thar pol-yester bell-bottoms, only a few snaggly threads hangin' from the seat—got caught on Mabel's picket fence las' Tuesdy chasin' 'em banties outen the yarrrd."

She smiled.

"Course them good wool pants o' Clem's—been dead ten years—kin you b'lieve it?—just come clean outen the closet, been wrapped up with mothballs all this time, but you shoulda seen them moths, my lan', none too happy without their balls, I might add." She was watching him and laughing, the life back in her.

Yard after yard crept by them, and tables laden with shirts and pants, glass doodads that sparkled in the sun, Parcheesi games and plastic tumblers, pictures with frames and without, mirrors with dark, imageless patches and high-heeled shoes with witch-point toes, plastic flower bouquets, tennis rackets. A full leg prosthesis swung from the limb of a dog-wood tree—"Now thar's a wind chime for ye!"

"Michael, the IGA. You just passed it."

He swung the truck around at the stoplight. Inside he felt hollow; the facade he put on for his mother evaded the persistent anguish at his core. *What's the use?* it said. He tried not to listen. The town was so full of life this morning, people looking for something they could use, making do— he wanted to cry. An old stick of a man yanked and yanked on the starter cord of a dead lawn mower; a stout woman rocking on stiff legs gathered up a curtain and held together the torn place with one hand as it billowed around her; a skinny blond kid tried on a pair of ice skates; the solitary hump of a man perched on a table with his arms crossed over his lap stared at the ground, the table before him filled with baskets made of Popsicle sticks—all that hope and momentum pushing forward out of the rubble—did they not see how useless it was? Some kind of wool over their eyes? They were happy, too, with reruns of *Roseanne* at four o'clock. They would always be happier than he. He was sure of that.

"One box of bags enough?" he said as the truck jumped the curb on his way into the parking lot. "I'll run in."

He was healthy. Not a pain or a twinge anywhere. He didn't appreci-ate every moment like he should. Time was finite. He should make every moment count, as if it were precious. All he could do was pretend. For Mari.

The truck was empty without him. Evidence of the things he thought about was all around her, receipts for wood and tools from Brooks' for his latest design, Pepsi containers for his morning fix, an oil rag to check the truck's consumption, a small grease-covered address book. But what else did he think about? He was too silent at times. He was all kindness to her, though. Bent on cheering her. Was she depending on him too much?

She supposed so. Funny time of life she was in, like those Christmas angels still clinging to the lampposts, their tinseled gowns and wings rustling in the April wind, trumpets poised, waiting with a patience par-ticular and exemplary to all things out of season.

Michael arrived with two Pepsis and a box of trash bags. She leaned over to push the truck door open for him, suddenly laughing as she did so. "What's so funny?" Michael asked.

"Mothballs," she said.

They made their way down Main Street, past the sagging front porches of the old Victorian houses in various stages of peel and posture, the crumbling railroad station and the city of grain silos at the outermost edge of town, then along Cemetery Road, on past the county dump with its ever-circling seagulls, past tractors pluming dust and painting dark brown ribbons over the fields, on past the uprooted oak at Poke's Corner and the decayed house folding behind it, past Heron Marsh and muskrat mounds, to the tall pines of Sulley's Point Road—every landmark in the flat landscape memorized. She could shut her eyes the whole way and know where she'd be at any given moment.

They were close to the teasing glimpse of the river sparkling between the pines. Yes, there it was—the sharp turn to the left onto the Point, and the single row of summer cottages strung out to meet the river like cultured pearls on a deep blue rug. Near the end, their cottage, just as they'd left it, with its low-pitched roof and weathered cedar, still strong, the windows whole. Stalwart.

In the thin, crisp air of April the washline swung gently and the bare limbs of rose of Sharon brushed the boys' bedroom window. There was the workbench on which they had piled crab pots and tongs, and the wooden platform Justin had built by the outside spigot for washing sandy feet. Michael walked ahead of her and turned the corner of the cottage toward the beach. She followed him into the chilly wind and pulled up the zipper to her jacket. The day was unusually clear, the horizon sharply defined. There were the waiting-to-be-raked bunches of feathers and marsh reeds that had washed up along the narrow beach through winter, the ducks flying in, the workboats—everything dependent on the river flowing on about its business, first in one direction then the other, swinging boats around, bringing storms and calms. Mother river.

Michael was silent as he looked out over the water, his profile like Justin's, long straight nose, bushy eyebrows, the slightly-hunched-over way he stood squinting at the water. She'd seen that stance a thousand times when Justin checked the wind before a sail. Impatient to be going. Edgy.

Suddenly Michael turned and said, "Haven't got all day. I'll go in and get started," though he stared at the house for a while as if he really didn't want to begin disassembling what was inside. Then with the same stoic determination she'd seen in him on the first day of school, he headed for the side door.

Alone, she listened for the peace and promise of that soft lick of water at her feet, mirroring those still mornings when her world was in its beginning, as if in the next moment the green aluminum rowboat would scrape the pebbly bottom and Michael would thunk the bait bucket between the seats. She could hear the tap of the fishing rods and the plop of the seat cushion on the wood, Davey and Anne splashing and calling, pushing the boat out a little as Michael shouted to them, "That's enough! Let me start the motor. Get back!"

Just like him to leave it all to her. The picking up after. Flicking the words out over the water, *You jerk,* she said, *You jerk, Justin.* How much was illness, how much was him? It kept her straddling the fence, unable to jump off either side. She turned her back to the river but glanced at it over her shoulder. The river just went on. Swollen now in the rush of tide and spring rains, harbinger of the first crops of nettles and crabs, new rockfish and blues—the river was life despite everything, life that promised renewal and was silent about loss.

Go on in there, she told herself. Go on in there and be done with it.

Inside was a bone-chilling dead kind of cold. Michael heard the familiar tick of the wood on the waterfront side of the house as the wind blew. Winters when he visited his father, the drapes never stopped stirring. It kept him awake nights worrying, wondering what could be so terrible about staying with them at the farm that his father was willing to endure the cold blowing in and around those dark, green drapes.

The house was meant to be open to the sea air and the sounds of seagulls and motors and waves washing the beach. He threw open the front door and began sliding back the long windows. The incoming air felt warmer than the chill of the cottage. Immediately the wind chimes began their hollow tinkle—the sound he fell asleep to many a night. He reached up but couldn't bring himself to take them down, their ring the essence of summer.

Everything was determined by the wind here. How do you stop listening for the wind? The new people would want to know when the wind picked up. The new people—they would clean up everything. Even the handprints on the exposed ceiling planks would be an annoyance to them. The oil from his father's hands had gathered grime over the years and now the handprints were as distinct as a signature. He liked to think of his father putting the boards in place, his head against blue sky, his words bending around the cigar in his teeth, though that image of his father pained him, too.

He walked toward the bedrooms. On the wall was the fighting dinosaurs picture he painted when he was seven or eight. He remembered the watercolor tablets stuck in a tray, the small brush he dipped in a glass of water to clean it, the water turning brown, the blood dripping down Brontosaurus's side, Tyrannosaurus Rex sinking his teeth into flesh. He wished he could as clearly see his enemy now. There was one—real as the day, silently creeping into every muscle, every thought.

He looked around for tangible evidences of his brother and sister, any small trace, but in the years his father lived alone, he'd filled the rooms with his things. Only the bunk beds with cowboys and broncos riding the range of bare beige mattresses remained, and the dinosaur picture.

Rosemary lingered in the front room, taking family photos off the wall and leaving pale rectangles on the wood—Justin looking over his shoulder and pulling on the jib of the catamaran; the boys, Michael and Davey, displaying their catch of rockfish lying like exclamation points on the newspaper; Anne, most of her hair out of her ponytail, sitting on the steps with a slice of watermelon.

Her eyes skimmed the room. There was nothing else she wanted. Certainly not the organ, though it stood grander than ever against the back wall like an oak dinosaur, crowned with spindles and cloaked in dark, scaly varnish. She had always planned to redo it, scrape off the old skin and reveal the golden glow of mellowed oak; she'd always found pleasure in seeing wood that lay in secret over the years suddenly brought to life, years bubbled up with the varnish remover and rolled off in long, curled shavings. Why hadn't she gotten around to it? She couldn't bear the thought of things left undone. It was too close to the feeling that she hadn't loved Justin enough.

She could hear Michael scraping furniture on the floor of the back bedroom.

"Coming, Ma?" he called.

"Just a second."

She remembered now, it was because of the decals she could never bring herself to tackle the organ, the gilded lilies and ribbons flowing over the mandolins on each of the side panels, a delicious little dash of decoration that made the organ different from any other she'd ever seen. She could have just removed the decals, of course, along with the old varnish, but that was like erasing an old song, one that could never be heard again. She couldn't let go of anything, she thought with disgust. Justin could. He could shut the door and never look back. He did it twice, damn him.

Michael appeared and raised one of the panel doors. He took out a small, yellow wooden shoe, his favorite marker from the Monopoly game. "One thing I could always count on," he mumbled, "this being here," and put it back where he'd always kept it. "What are you going to do with the organ?"

"I don't know, Michael. Send it to auction, I suppose."

They began hoisting furniture out the side door and onto the pickup. The bunk beds, the musty pillows, throw rugs, stained mattresses, faded curtains—only when the truck was filled did Rosemary think about where to send it. "Lutheran Mission Society?" she said to Michael.

"Well, if you don't care, there's a family down in Thomastown who lost everything in a fire," he said. "I'll head there first."

She nodded and stared at the truck with headboards and footboards sticking up at odd angles alongside mirrors and dressers. Would her life forever after be fragments trying to make a whole, missing pieces scattered over the landscape? What she needed, she suspected, was a lobotomy. She laughed softly to lessen the choke in her throat.

"What is it?" said Michael.

"I can't even begin to explain, Michael. Too many memories. Just go. I'll try to find out about the organ while you're gone."

"No. Tell me," he said softly. "All I can think about right now is bad stuff."

"Well, remember when your sister dove into that Styrofoam ring—

that life preserver? She ran toward the house but couldn't fit in the doorway? She was only about six, but so embarrassed."

"Yeah, I laughed at her," he said softly, wincing.

"And when you did, she tried to punch you but couldn't reach beyond the life preserver stuck around her middle. We were all laughing—it was hard not to."

"We shouldn't have laughed. None of us," he said angrily.

"I don't think it did her any permanent harm, Michael."

He turned away and yanked on a rope tied across the furniture in the truck until the maple headboards groaned.

Alton Gootie. That was his name. She'd been trying to think of the name of the man who'd come to look at the organ years ago. A young man in his twenties then, with a bush of blond hair caught up in a ponytail. She went inside now to phone him, leaving Michael standing on the bed of the truck.

Alton said right off, "Didn't I visit the organ a few years ago?" Not them. The organ. This was a man dedicated to organs. "Out at the place on the river? Sulley's Point? Yeah. You wanted it tuned."

"What do you think it may be worth? I'd like to put an ad in the paper, but don't know what to ask."

"Seen 'em go for as high as fifteen hundred. Sold one last month."

"Can I ask how much you sold it for?"

"Hundred and fifty. I sold it too cheap. Lady wanted it as is and I got eleven of them. Had to clean 'em out."

She saw him clearly. To look at the bellows, he had pushed the organ away from the wall with his massive shoulders. "Doesn't need anything but a good cleaning," he told her and poked and vacuumed and blew dust till the sounds came out pure and holy. Now he sounded as if years of that dust had lodged in his throat.

When she hung up, she said out loud, "Abbott's Auctions it is. Let them auction that baby off, and free my soul."

The truck loaded, he stood back and listened to the splashing of waves. Out of habit, he looked upriver for the boat whose wake was now hitting shore, but didn't see one. His thoughts raced again, like one of those cartoon figures in a flip book that you could make come alive, only pages in his flip book were all different—rain pouring off the roof, the bull lips in the bait bucket, geese flying in to settle across the river—night sounds, the halyards, the wheeze of the organ—the dread it held for him—the sound of his mother playing as they fell asleep in the back bedrooms—the terror he used to feel just before falling asleep as if he would be snatched up while his body lay limp—the terror that would wait for him each night—somehow the organ was part of it, coaxing him to sleep when he didn't want to. He was glad to get rid of the thing.

He walked toward the water. Though chilly, the air already seemed to carry the sound of bare feet hammering along the pier, the whoosh of the net down along the pole to get the doublers. He saw Davey's skinny brown back bent over a bucket of minnows as he tried to catch one with his bare hands. And the injured purple martin they'd found that sat on Davey's finger for most of the afternoon, iridescent black and sleek, blinking up—its eyelid on the bottom of its eye.

Mallards streamed out from under the pier and came toward him, eager for corn, softly quacking. A speckled feather floated on the skin of water.

"Aw, go on," he said, sweeping his arms. "Just go on." The ducks flared up, half-flying, half-swimming, splashing. Ice had pulled up some of the piling on Mr. Phillips's pier this past winter and it buckled upward, then tilted down toward the water, a bridge that went nowhere. It was covered with chalky white splotches which he remembered pointing out to that couple from Baltimore with the heavy-bellied dachshund who came to look at the cottage. That whole scene and the buckets in the middle of the living room floor for "roof leaks" were his own little bit of sabotage.

"Ducks come in here by the hundreds—man next door feeds them," he told them. "You can't even use your own beach or bulkhead without stepping in it." But they nodded as if they hadn't heard, already in love with the view of the river and the idea of hundreds of ducks. "What kind are they?" they wanted to know. He never imagined there were people who didn't know a mallard. Nests all over the place, too. One right down in the marsh grass next to the bulkhead. What if they cut the grass down that end? Probably would. They didn't know anything.

He skirted around the side of the house, past the kerosene tank up on spider legs and through the tall grass of the front lawn, around the sink-hole in the middle where the septic system had given way, past the split-rail fence that separated their yard from the road and Pete's Marina. The gulls, resting along the seawall that ran out toward open water, faced the same direction like wind worshippers. He could always come down to Pete's. That part wouldn't change.

He'd loved Pete from the first moment he called to him, "Hey, son, what's your name?" and he loved how Pete readjusted the cap on his head, looking down at him with a red face and eyes that stayed drawn up small against the sun. Michael took to doing the same thing with his own cap as he scouted the poles along Pete's pier checking for doublers. Soon he was help-ing customers gas up their cruisers and checking on the soft crabs in the peel-er tanks. He was eleven the summer Pete said, "How about going out with me some marning? You got to get up early, right smart, three A.M., and meet me out here on the pier, start my coffee in the caaabn." It didn't take Michael any time to start imitating Pete's way of talking, making fun of the drawl, but loving it too, and his dry humor matched with work so real you could smell it, feel it biting through your skin. His own father disappeared Monday morn-ings and entered a separate life, one of mystery as far as Michael was con-cerned, for which he dressed in a suit and carried a locked briefcase.

Afternoons, Pete sat on his porch with Michael, Anne, and Davey and told stories about the time he worked on the steamboat *that went on up to Ballmer,* and sailed a skipjack during the worst storms, grander than any-thing that squalled up since. Michael had come of age because of Pete. He had a job. The alarm went off for *him,* not that it needed to because most mornings he was wide awake, already listening for Pete's porch door to snap lightly—his signal to pull on his jeans and T-shirt, and hold the screen door in his hand so as not to waken Anne and Davey as he slipped out into the dark, excitement in his legs so great he'd always run, jumping into the boat before Pete could get there, and stand arms folded as if he'd been there all night. Pete mumbled, "All right, boy. Start that coffee 'fore I use you for bait on the trotliiiine." Later, Michael taught Anne and Davey how to say trotliiiine, tucking in his chin, and they'd say it over and over, giggling and falling into a heap on the front lawn.

Once they were out on the river, time went fast. Ten, fifteen bushels of crabs to show for a morning's work. Pete netted mostly, but once in a while he'd let Michael, and Michael missed very few as the crabs came out of the deep, hanging onto the line, mysterious, miniature monsters, their empty claws lashing out at anything nearby, spitting and bubbling. A never-ending source of fascination as he bent over the wooden baskets, they responded furiously to his teasing them with the net handle during Pete's coffee break.

There was a time he thought he'd go on the water himself. Still might, if things didn't work out with the carpentry. Either one suited him better than life on the bottom of a container ship, he'd decided. But being a waterman—well, he liked the hardness of it, and the solitude, the quiet of the water in early morning. Nothing like a good workboat purring under his feet to let a man know what he was about.

The workboats, moored along the network of piers, bobbed. There was the *Miss Linda* sitting low and broad and Pete's red cap swaying back and forth as he hosed his deck. The boat creaked and rubbed. Sea smells, stronger now from the boat. Pete, hip boots slick and forearms bursting from rolled-up shirtsleeves, greeted Michael as if he were still a boy of ten.

"Well, if it ain't the highlander come to visit." Pete chuckled at his old joke. He never forgot who wasn't a local boy. "I seen your pickup pull in and figured you was down here to fish till I seen Momma get outen the truck. Must be moving day. Where's your daddy? Your ma still doing the cleaning up?" He shook his head and touched the visor of his *Po Boys Yacht Club* cap.

It came out different the way Pete said it. Everything did from the moment his father suggested that Pete stop throwing beer cans into the river.

"What? You highlanders come down here and tell me my business?" Pete had yelled. "Fifty years on this goddamn river and you gonna tell me?" Years ago.

Michael was ready to change the subject. "When're you going to start crabbing?"

Pete put his foot up on the transom and crossed his arms on his knee, settling in for a long talk. "Don't know right yet. Still cleaning up after arsterin'. A sick year. Man can't make a living on the water no more. Not in the winter anyhow. Ninety percent of the arsters we thoed back. Sick.

Hoping we can make up for it crabbing. Not like when you was a kid. Never thought you'd do it, eleven year old, getting up at three coming across that road with the hood of your sweatshirt all drawn up jest to make my coffee and cull them crabs. Almost makes you a lowlander like us. Not your daddy though. He stayed a highlander. My God, when I seen him holding on to that blonde showing her off while he got a family settin' on the farm—I thought, that man's crazy. And he taking her kids sailing and when you show up starts yelling at you to cut the grass. Jest plum crazy. Don't make no sense. When them new people coming?" he said, as if coming up for air.

"Don't know exactly," said Michael. "Closing is tomorrow." He had to keep his hands in his pockets now, balled up in tight fists like they were. He wanted to grab Pete by the throat and knock his head off. He didn't know where the rage came from. It was the swift judgment, all of them standing naked, the word, *crazy.*

"Well, you can come down here and fish anytime you want. Just set yourself on the pier like the old days, when you was coming around with a bucket of minnows and a Band-Aid across your nose to keep the sun from burning it clean off."

He wanted to look Pete in the eye and tell him how much this place meant to him, turn his anger around. "I hate this," he blurted out. "I hate leaving here—it's the kind of place you should leave to your grandchildren."

"Aw, now boy. Only time a man should cry is if he lose a good woman, one of his kids, or a good dog. The rest don't matter. The rest can be replaced. Bet your daddy's crying though. If he ain't, he will be. He'll pay."

"Think he wants it like this? He doesn't, Pete. I swear to God—he's suffered. What's right or wrong has nothing to do with it." His voice grew loud and he was conscious of walking away. "Listen. I gotta go. Lot to do." He didn't want to say any more. He didn't want his voice to carry across the water, bounce off anybody else's ears, although it would be good for them to hear what he had to say. How do you goddamn tell what's right or wrong when your brain plays tricks on you and you can't see through the chaos, see through your own fractured existence—tossed between Superman and toad? Stay alive? How hard it was to keep away the question, "What for?" He saw how it would be so easy to give in, how you could walk in and out of fire and ice, fire and ice, and get lost. The part he couldn't forgive was his father's silence. His walking out and leaving it all up to him, Michael—the oldest—dealing with everything, deciding what to do, where to go with the stuff, cheering his mother along, while his old man just closed the door. How much do you forgive in the face of illness? And here was Pete, placid, hard, summing them up. He'd pound some understanding into the man. Let him see the way things were.

He dug the hard knots of his fury into his pockets. He couldn't trust himself. That he knew. He hated what he was, what he had been, even as a kid, hurting his sister, beating on Davey, blaming his father. There was no peace, man, just no peace. He wanted to be peaceful. Take a pill. Pop some peace.

His heart beat wildly, skipping beats. It would fly out his throat in another minute. Goddamn. Not even pills were enough. Dissolving his kidneys, repulsing his stomach, turning him into a pillar of salt. What he might do scared him. He was split down the middle. What he should do and what he was forbidden to do. But his body had its own course to follow and all he could do was admit his helplessness and call the doctor. He would call her. Only because of Mari. She was the only reason. But sometimes not even that was enough, as though Mari would be better off without him. But there was more to it now. The baby on the way. His kid. But maybe he wouldn't need to call the doctor. Maybe he'd come around once he got the truck started. Get to Pucam and get a Pepsi. Get the beds and stuff to Thomastown. Tears streamed and he wiped his face with his sleeve so that anybody looking would think he was just sweating. Sweating in the April breezes. Oh, how he hated beginnings, any kind of promise. Things would wind up like they always did, and there was no hope for the mess he had become.

He didn't so much as glance at the cottage as he climbed in the truck. He pounded the dashboard, just once, and looked down at a fist numbed by the blow and watched blood trickle. He never bothered to wipe it off. Just let it trickle, madden him further. He deserved it.

Macadam stretched before him, his truck consuming the snake of road. Trees with a tinge of green loomed and shot by him. Rivers of rye, patches of limed earth, plowed fields. Mailboxes. An unending flock of grackles swarmed in ribbons across the sky. Now rolling, doubling back on itself, the shape thickened as the birds angled in a new direction. Telephone poles marched along holding hands. He could just drift off the road into one. Not drift. Slam. Break connections. Telephones—silenced everywhere. Down at the post office, people dropping in for the morning mail would say, "Hear about that guy what carves them birds? Wrapped himself around a pole. Lines out for three hours. Probably on drugs."

The rear bumper of a Buick dropped into view just ahead of him, stopped to turn left. He hit the brake and swerved, barely missing it. Like his nightmares. A bright light. A flash. Maybe an explosion. Premonitions, night after night. In the end it would be an accident that would get him. Something engulfing him. Just make it to Thomastown. Just think about that. His life going. Where? Out of control. Would he spin out of control? Sweating now. Pressure in his gut. Nauseous. A cramp in his chest. Do one thing. Call Dr. Vincent. Just do that one thing.

He braked when he saw the flagpole outside the Thomastown Post Office. Flagless. Somebody forgot. He pulled in near the telephone; the booth door cracked along the glass. Door stuck—didn't matter so much as the cool metal frame in his fingers, as the phrase *dimensions with determinable edges* occurred to him. He repeated the words over and over as if they were some sort of mantra, spitting out the d's while he searched his wallet for the number, worrying about his own determinable edges and did he have any and what might he do if left to his own devices? Would he *go crazy?* Taking stuff that didn't work—what then?

"The doctor is not in. If this is an emergency, dial the emergency hot line number and leave your name and number. The doctor will contact you within fifteen minutes." He pushed the emergency buttons reading the number off the telephone, fearful of confusing the numbers as he often did. Across the road, an empty house, peeling paint. Green roof shingles worn down to the tar where tree branches hit. Looked like a bruise. Porch roof caved in. Everything breaking down. Should get off this goddamn Shore.

He waited in the truck and was just about to start the engine when the telephone in the booth rang. He bolted out of the truck. "Michael? Dr. Vincent. How are you doing?"

"Not great. Been taking what you gave me—it's not doing it."

"I'll call in something else. Can you get in to see me on Saturday? Nine-fifteen? Any problems, call."

The scales would tip the other way soon. Soon. He would detour to the drugstore and Sam would have that knowing look on his face and ask how he was and then he'd start jerking around and twist up his face. Set them all off in there. Not today, though. He couldn't manage it today. With great effort, he pulled himself into the truck and headed for Pucam and then Thomastown.

He heard about the fire at the gas station last week. Family burned out—four kids—all okay but one, burned pretty bad. He knew the mother, Mazie, from high school—Mazie and her easy laugh. He'd see her working at the Quick Stop, taking his money, her huge breasts in her way as she turned her whole body toward the cash register, laughing still with a light in her eyes that was hard not to be pulled into. She teased him about those Pepsis, "There you go again, Mickey, pumpin' yourself up for a day with them birds, huh?" But she hadn't been at the Quick Stop lately and he missed her.

Thomastown appeared suddenly from behind a clump of trees on the right, no bigger than a short city block of houses. And off on the left of the road, within sight of Taylor's Granary, was Bounds's cottage. Bounds died the year Michael graduated from high school, and was the only black farmer Michael knew about who owned land. He plowed with a mule until the day he died, and from the school bus Michael watched for the figure of the old man pulling back on the plow, coming from somewhere out of the history books right up the corn rows with his big-eared mule. As he drove, sweet-gum trees dotted the field, the woods advancing, the puny efforts of a man easily overgrown. Same with the stuff in the back of the truck. All that building and gathering. How fragile everything is, he thought.

Mazie now, coming out from behind the screen door and standing with her hands on her hips, laughed at the sight of him coming up the steps. Her smile flamed like a fire on a cold night and he just coming to warm his heart, said, "Can you use any of this?" He waved his arm at the truck, not sure if she'd take it as an insult.

"You betcha," she said. "Got three to a bed now. Be four when the other one gets out the hospital." Then, "How you doing? How's your wife? When is she due?"

"Another three, four weeks."

"First one. How about that. I don't know—I shoulda done what you did—waited a little. Maybe never get started on this." She waved her hand at the house and the kids who now sat on the front steps. "I coulda had a career singing. Got outta here, gone up to Baltimore. But seems like I couldn't wait to do what everybody else was doing. Still, I wouldn't take nothing for them. You'll see how it is. Life is never the same again."

It was nothing for Mazie to lift her end of the dressers, the maple one that had been his and Davey's and the small blue one that was Anne's. Together they hauled them onto the sagging floor.

"You kids take two drawers apiece," said Mazie. "Putcha clothes in 'em now while we get the beds. C'mon now, act right," she said as they tumbled into a pile of clothes in the corner of the bedroom, looking back at Michael with watchful eyes. The children looked all the same size to Michael, maybe a half-inch difference between them. Not like Anne and Davey and him, definite steps, clear-cut roles.

Mazie held the headboards while he joined the side boards and foot-boards and when they finished, the kids jumped on the mattresses, clamoring for first turn on the top bunk. Mazie laughed and said, "I'm getting the top bunk tonight. I ain't never slept in a top bunk and after I try it out, I'll let you know who's next."

"Better get me a few extra boards then to prop it up in the middle, Mazie," said Michael. "Any takers for the bottom bunk?" The kids looked up at him with serious faces.

Sudden fury at his father's walking out on them resurfaced, the cool, oblivious way he'd closed the door, leaving him, Michael, the oldest, to deal with the piece-by-piece disassembling. Free, his father still used them, trusting they'd pick up where he left off.

The screwdriver in his hand shook; he kept missing the slot on the head of the screw, rusted and black, refusing. He felt a small, brown hand on his arm like a star laid on his shirtsleeve. It was Mazie's youngest, boy or girl, Michael couldn't tell, hair wild as a bird's nest, face like a young Mazie with Mazie's knowingness about it, too, looking up at him with eyes that were pools of black, saying, "You want Mama to do that for you?"

Anger melted. "Well," he said. "I know your Mama can take care of anything that comes her way, but let me try one more time, okay?" Fighting back tears, he felt the hand pat him.

When he was about to go, he asked Mazie, "How's the one in the hospital?"

"Don't know yet. He got burned bad. They flew him up to John Hopkins by helicopter. His father up there with him now and I go tomorrow. Sixty percent of his body. I don't know sometime why things turn out like they do. Doesn't do any good to moan though. He the oldest, you know. He went in the house because he thought the others were in there, sleeping. But they were down the road at my sister's."

When he turned to go, he was shocked to see socks tacked to the door frame to keep out the cold. He was aware she might see him noticing so he quickly turned his head. He didn't have one thing to bellyache about. He didn't deserve to breathe. Out loud he said, "You need anything?"

"No. We were lucky to get this place after the fire. We're making out fine. Say a prayer for Sammy though, would you?" She raised her hand in a wave and said, "And thanks, hear? Let me know if I can do something for you sometime," the palm of her hand pink and vulnerable in the shadow of the door frame.

The telephone's ring made Rosemary jump. Abbott's Auctions, returning her call. He'd take the organ, though he'd have to charge her forty-five dollars to pick it up. He thought he could include it in next Saturday's auction.

So that was it then.

There was one more room to clean out. Walking into the bedroom Justin converted into a study, she surveyed what was left. His clothes still hung in the closet, his blue windbreaker, jeans, a few shirts, a cowboy hat, and his sailing cap with the cork sewn in the peak. Shoes. Stacks of cassettes. A large poster bearing the inscription *Poverty Sucks*. There were shelves of odd papers, files on job applications and rejection letters stapled with the ads he'd been answering, telephone books, his joke book with quips he collected over the years, water skis, running shoes, racing boat trophies, two cans of Desenex, a schedule of 10K races two years old. And a collection of yellowed singles ads stapled to a picture or two:

Check This Out! SWF, 44, evil, moody, opinionated, looking for sincerity. If so, you'll love the flip side! A dark-haired woman with heavy eyebrows looked out at her.

Fun Loving Mature Woman: DWF, 48, looking for DWM 45–60, must enjoy beach, boardwalks, movies, dancing, traveling. Want to spend quality time w/someone who knows who they are, where they're going. No picture.

Looking for Mr. Right: DWF, 37, looking for quiet, down to earth, sincere, honest, SWM for friendship. Only serious minded individuals need apply. Must love children. A woman in a bikini lay on a beach chair, smiling into the camera.

It was curious to think about what kind of woman he would choose. It had nothing to do with her, nothing to do with a lifetime of fixing coffee the way he liked it, hovering with a cup of tea when he had a cold, knowing when to balance the boat with only a nod from him. Nothing could replace her, nor him. Not even Len, with whom love had never been challenged by daily-ness, with whom love had remained unsullied by life. Nothing could replace the side-by-side education of twenty-five years.

When Michael came in she asked, "Can you use any of this? The jacket? Shirts?"

Michael shrugged. Peering in the closet, he found the stamp collection, stamps from all over the world carefully sorted into business envelopes and stacked in a shoe box—NIKE, Internationalist, size 11, *Best in Running Shoes.*

"I can't believe he left this. He's been collecting stamps his whole life," she said, blowing the dust off the box.

"Maybe we can sell them. Probably worth a good lick by now."

Exactly what Justin would have said. "Pardon the pun," she said. "No, Michael, I think I'll save that for him and that old plane which I'm sure belonged to his father." She wondered how Justin could walk out without the shoe box of stamps tucked under one arm and the plane in the other.

"What about these?" Michael found a box of tapes and began reading the titles, *You and Real Estate, How to Stop Smoking, How to Retire Rich, You and Your Money, Success in Career Changes.*

"Any music?" She busied herself with the T-shirts, unfolding them, judging sizes and making piles for Anne, Davey, Mari and Michael.

"Don't see any."

"Chuck 'em."

He had his back to her, a lumpy trash bag in his hand, emptying the closet. "I'm glad Grandma missed all this. Although if she hadn't died, he'd still be here, I bet."

"What do you mean?"

"I just don't think he would have pulled all this stuff with Grandma around. She was some sort of standard, just by the way she was."

"Michael, the seeds for everything that's happened were always there, only we didn't know it, of course. He was going to do great things, and he did. He was enormous fun."

Michael turned and faced her angrily. "Why do you say that? He wasn't fun by the time I was fourteen. He was mean and angry all the time. Remember when I had to pay him a dollar a minute for being late one night? It was either like that or he'd shut me out completely. And you too. You're better off without him."

"The color has gone out of my life, Michael." She was astonished at the words.

"The thing that gets me—what I keep asking myself—am I going to get just like him?"

Now she glared at him, denying, refusing, trying to infuse courage in him where there was none. "You are not your father. You are you. It's different now—a matter of monitoring. You're doing it, Michael."

"You have no idea—none at all—what it's like."

She didn't. She began to throw everything into the trash bag. Everything except the shoe box of stamps and the plane. Everything.

"See if you can get Pete to help you with the organ," his mother was saying. "I don't think I want to even try to lift it. But I figure if you can get it in the truck, then we won't have to pay the forty-five dollars for Abbott to pick it up. Okay?" Silence. "Okay, Michael?"

"I hear ya."

"Are you worried about something? You feel okay?"

"I'm okay. Got another prescription."

"Yeah, but did you take it?"

Nothing went by her. "Not yet, but I will." He had to work up to it some—might keep him awake at night, or nauseous, besides making him impotent but that was okay since Mari was not so inclined right now anyhow.

"Why don't you take it right now?" His silence made her say, "Well, you know what you have to do."

"That's right. My body—I decide." Maybe he had raised his voice because she looked alarmed, her yellow-brown eyes wider than usual. Then the lines around her mouth settled into place like they did when she was tired, when things over which she had no control persisted, when there was only the present moment to trust.

"It will pass, Michael. It always does," she said softly. "Look. We can forget this for today. I'll finish up tomorrow."

He shrugged. "We're almost there," he said. He pushed open the screen door and let it bang. His father would have tanned him for that when he was a kid. He would be different. He would never hit his kid.

He could see a child at his side, holding his hand, boy or girl, didn't matter. Horsing around, giggling, squealing, *Daddy!* He pictured showing whoever it was wonderful absurdities, like the toy his father brought back from one of his business trips when he and Anne were little. Wound up, it balanced a bicycle on the rope his father strung across his bedroom. He'd go to sleep watching the blue-coated clown nod his head and pedal the bicycle back and forth, back and forth. His father had watched with him, laughing himself into a helpless wheeze, *Aaah jeez.*

Pete was chopping eels on the block set up in his boat. The gulls circled overhead, waiting for him to throw a piece of fish in the water. Pete set the cleaver down, scooped up the chunks, and threw them in the barrel. His arm circling over the barrel in an easy motion that came down through centuries, he sprinkled them with salt.

"Hey, Pete? Got a minute?" The broad, round back shifted, then turned, a thick forearm reached up to tip his hat. "Help me move something?"

Pete pulled off his work gloves and put them on the block. They lay like a mold of his hands, stiff fingers curled like the teeth of a rake.

"Yeah. Want to talk to you anyhow." He lumbered from portside to pier like an old bear, and stood looking at Michael. "Didn't mean nothing about your daddy, Michael. I know blood's thicker than water."

"Yeah, well. You don't know how thick, Pete. You just don't know."

"Say no more about it then," he said, adjusting his cap. "What you needing?"

Once inside the cottage where he hadn't stepped a foot since the day he helped them twenty years before, Pete let out a long, low whistle. "I forgot what a beauty that bulkhead is," he said, looking out the front window. "Seems like whatever else you got to say about the man, he sure could work. Never seen a man build his own bulkhead before, nor will I again. Always did think your piece was the best one down here, with the beach in close to the house and a shoreline that swings out in a big curve like that. Meant he had four times the wall to build than if his land went straight across. Makes a nice little harbor." Then he turned toward the organ, and without looking at his mother, said, "Well, Miss Rosemary! Don't seem like it been five minutes since I helped you bring this thing in here."

After Pete had gone, the house felt like a coffin. He was glad to step outside while his mother swept up. He let the screen door bang as if the house contained nothing he wanted, everything he feared. The house held secrets while the river held constancy, and moods which he knew so well. How many times did the wide sweep of open water and sky welcome him, the motor pushing him far from the troublesome house? He didn't want to think about it now.

With the organ in the back of the pickup, his job was almost done. High in the bed of the truck, the mirror on the organ caught the sun and the world became a flash of light brighter than any he ever remembered, blinding him. Every day was a goddamn fight. Every day had a big black hole in it. How the hell did his old man stay alive? For most of his dad's life, there'd been no little green pill. Maybe he could ride this one out. Like Mari said, it was no good putting all that strange stuff in your body, freezing up your kidneys, turning your balls to jelly. If he'd just cut out the Pepsis, the sugar and caffeine. Maybe it was his fault he was like this after all. He wanted to believe it was his fault, so he could control his demons and make his father claim ownership for his, for all he'd done and not done. No excuses. Only way a man could be a man.

Yet, one memory pursued him. He'd never told anyone. Sometimes it crept into his dreams at night and he would wake with the knowledge that he was capable of everything his father was, and he understood the madness around which they had tiptoed for so long.

He had gone down to the river to fish and invited Shelly, the girl he was dating at the time, to meet him at the cottage around seven. He planned to have a rockfish by then, although fish for dinner was not all he had on his mind. He grabbed the wire crab net and went down to the pier. In the slack tide when wind and water were still, in the great gray silence of a rain-holding sky when even hushed voices carried themselves plain through the expectant air—his favorite time—the crabs clung to the poles in doubles, waiting. He snagged six in a few minutes, keeping the peelers in his bait bucket, and threw the hard shells into the crabfloat. Then he mounted the Evinrude on *Greenfly,* yanked at the starter line of the motor until the beginning roar, and listened for the toning down, the even purr of the motor. He glanced over his shoulder as he rounded the curve of the bulkhead, and headed out toward the red buoy—a sequence of actions he'd done a million times, a ritual that soothed whatever ailed him. He liked to think on it, the richness of simple, everyday doings he knew so well, and his mind rested in the memory as he stood on the steps of the cottage.

Rockfish were easy to catch then, and soon he pulled in a good-sized one, cleaned it on the bulkhead when he came in. Soon, too, the perfect evening unveiled itself: Shelly arrived, the champagne was chilled, the candles lit, fresh rockfish roasting, butter crackling in the pan. And afterwards, leading Shelly to the master bedroom with his hand around her waist, he took in the sweet scent of her perfume. He turned from her kiss for only a second to pull down the bedspread, and there, with a sickening wrench in his stomach, he saw written the fate of the family in the desecration of his mother's bed with drawings done in thick, black indelible marker, cartooned and dripping penises and breasts and dates of penetration and names of secret loves all over the white sheet.

Shelly gaped, then yanked away.

"This supposed to be funny?" she screamed. "Get the hell away from me! Do you think you're going to add me to the collection?"

In the end, he was glad she thought he did it. Better that than have another story about his father in circulation. She fairly flew out of there, her blonde silky hair flaring behind her.

Pretty funny if you thought about it—his old man, the stud with an insatiable ego. That is, if you didn't know how he'd been, like Superman in flight, arms up, cape flapping. How he would be bending over the bed, gleefully writing and drawing, laughing in that high screech of his, buck naked, face flushed, eyes crazed, answering the force that raged through him, alone in the night and not remembering in the light of day. Mad.

Michael stripped the bed and took the sheet down to the beach. It was a brief fire for so big an omen.

And now, with the shutting of the cottage door, he turned away, having released the beds where they all slept once in innocence, he and his brother and sister, mother and father, on long summer nights half listening for changes in the wind.

She swept the beige linoleum and the more she swept, the more there was to sweep. It took a long time. Until the sun threatened to set and the light grew dim. Michael hadn't returned, but he would soon.

Finally, she slipped on her jacket and sat on the bulkhead looking back at the house, thinking how the first time she saw it she couldn't take it all in. There were so many aspects and views and slants of light, walls and corners that took turns glowing. Favorite places her eye returned to while she pondered things, rooms branded in her brain she could rummage through forever. She couldn't remember her children's faces though she'd studied them for years, but she'd always remember the maple table at which they sat before the great window overlooking the water, the position of the knots in the wood on the wall, the log trusses overhead, the windows open to still summer mornings, the river so silent that even a sound as tiny as a pebble dropped in the shallows assumed a heightened significance. *Stay*, she silently pleaded to no one, *stay for a moment longer, as the tide pulls out and the boats face their mooring from the west, their reflections shimmering in the water, while peace echoes in from mid-river on the morning's catch—just a moment longer before the wind chimes sound again signaling a change and the curtains stir, until the voices are carried elsewhere, the flags billow, the boats swing to the opposite sides of poles. Before whitecaps.*

Ah, but the river never stayed put, did it?

The house, too, could be moody and full of contradiction as if it sailed the river though anchored to the shore. The wind was always slamming doors, creaking walls, blowing curtains, stirring up the water, and when it stopped, turning the water to silk and voices to echo, a motionless quiet took her breath away. She remembered standing inside that first time and feeling the cool calm of early June, sunlight streaming, promise flowing, a love for a place born in her like new knowledge. She had expected life would always shine with the same love and promise, but she was at the other end of always now, looking back at a time that contained the best of Justin and their life together. Had she ever told him, forgiven his silence enough to tell him what a great thing he'd done?

She waited for Michael a long time. Through sunset and first star. It wouldn't do any good to call as he was probably on the road. Buttoning her coat, she walked to the warmth of Pete's house to wait.

The organ delivered, he was on his way back to the cottage. The truck screamed while behind him a hazy, pink sky lingered as the sun lowered. He sped into shadows. High tide now. The river spilled over the macadam where marshland lay on either side of the road. Muskrat shelters among the reflections of sky and the islands of reeds and grasses. A heron stepped slowly, awaiting a fish or two, then flew off. He envied its unerring pursuits. Narrow strips of water widened to a creek over which stood an old wooden bridge. He was heading toward it when the road disappeared altogether, though he wasn't far from the bridge. He might be off the road now—it turned somewhere along here, and he dared it to not be there even when he'd lost traction and felt the truck leave solid ground.

He'd done all he could, hadn't he? But he hadn't slowed the truck— that was the only thing he hadn't done—though who's to say? He might have done far worse things. For he was his father's son, and he bore his father's blight, and it flourished, fighting with him every single minute. He was tired; the river sucked him in as the truck dove and he let it, welcomed it—didn't fight back—had no fight left. In a flash, water filled the truck and claimed his feet and knees and chest, rising, rising, it forgave where he could not forgive. He thought of no one—nothing but the river of which he was now a part, and in the last instant understood the blessed exoneration of leavings and sudden silences, *serendipitous* sent up with his last bubble of air.

She sat with a cup of tea warming her hands, talking to Pete, when the sheriff knocked on the door. She had taught his children. Sheriff Hunt. He asked Pete if Miz Williams was here—someone had said she was down to the Point. She knew what he was about to say as if she had waited in dread for a long time—maybe all of her life. She shivered.

"I'm sorry to tell you, Rosemary, there's been an accident," he said, his lips thick and precise around the words. "Your son's truck went off the road down by Harlin's Creek and he was trapped inside."

He did say accident. The other words took a long time to take in.

UNBROKEN CIRCLE

A baby girl was born early. For a while, she took the anger out of them. Maria.

When he got news of her birth, Davey disappeared, which was easy to do down at the ocean bars where the music was constant, loud and numbing. He picked up a gig or two, he wasn't sure and he couldn't remember where or when as the week spun itself out. He'd crawl into his truck in the wee hours and lie on a foam pad he kept in the bed, glad not to feel anything. Under the stars most nights. He was lucky about the lack of rain. On the seventh day—must have been—although he wasn't sure of that either, he showed up at the farm again, like an old dog coming in out of the weather. Nobody asked, "Where were you?" as if they already knew and he was glad because he didn't want to say.

When he walked in, Mari held the baby close, nursing her. Davey thought he'd never seen anything so beautiful in his life as Mari's white skin and long black hair hanging down over her shoulders, her hair and her arms making a circle with the baby inside. *How could Michael leave her?* It was beyond him.

Mari covered her breast and, without a word, put Maria in his arms. He'd never held a baby before. He wasn't clean enough—he was such a mess—for so pure and trusting a thing asleep now against his flannel shirt, the weight of her no more than that of a puppy. If only Michael—life—was not so hard. He held her, though it was himself he cradled, this tender bit of their lives he couldn't reconcile. He saw himself in Michael and Michael in him and the sorrow in Mari and the promise of the baby. A delicate thread of good as fragile as he. How connected they all were—failing and falling and succeeding and rising again in such paradoxes it made his heart break and his tears flow in the flood he'd managed to dam all week. But mostly he wept for Michael, for all that Michael would miss, for the Michael he missed, the vacancy where Michael should be.

"Davey," his mother said to him later, "you must take care of yourself. Promise me."

"I *am* taking care of myself, Mom," he said. "But I'm not taking pills. I don't think any of us have anything that can be cured by a pill. I'm telling you, I only need to learn how to cope. All of us do. We never learned how to talk to each other—I mean really talk. But I'm talking now—I'm telling you I choose to be fine. I *choose to be free of it,* whatever it is you think I inherited, you hear me?" He hadn't intended to raise his voice. He watched her bite her lip and turn away.

But one thing he could do for her. He'd keep his thoughts to himself about how Michael had died. She had said, "I will cling to that one fact, that it was an accident." For accidents are less preventable than will, a will that might have been changed from its awful fulfillment. *And I was the last to see him* left unspoken, though it was in her eyes.

So he swallowed what he knew and said nothing although he wondered how his mother could not know, though he didn't blame her. Some things were beyond anyone's doing, or undoing. But when he heard the words from his mother's lips: *Michael left us, Davey,* the meaning of which, knowing Michael, was that Michael couldn't cope with his darkness, Davey couldn't believe Michael was unable to get out of the truck unless he was knocked out which the coroner said he wasn't. Not Michael. The thought maddened and sickened Davey, which was no excuse. What an ass he'd been. He drank day and night through a blur of words and fistfights and heaves and shakes and a DWI arrest, and after the storm of his anger blew itself out, he knew he'd have to accept the meetings and the humility, pay homage to higher sources, things he wasn't sure about. But it was time to try.

Then Davey turned his attention to Mari and the baby, Maria, as they all did, for Mari did nothing but cry when she held Maria. Rosemary told her gently, "Come now, she will think that's all people do in this life," and Mari said, "She'll feel our tears and know her father," to which there was no answer but a nod for the plain-spoken truth. It was one of the things Rosemary liked about Mari.

Anne told them she'd felt Michael's presence so strong down by that bridge at Harlin's Creek she had to stop. She didn't have a thing with which to mark the place where he'd left the road. The tide was down; there wasn't even the smallest trace of catastrophe, the river having had the last word.

"So I got out my paints and started painting the last scene Michael saw—the bridge, the river, the marsh—there was even a heron out there on one of the islands. I kept wondering if Michael had seen it, and why it wasn't enough to pull him back, make him fight harder for his life, much as he loved birds—loved life—or whether the sight of the bird was his one last pleasure, a distraction in his final moment, or maybe—I found myself hoping—he was comforted by the assurance that life would go on. What, in God's name, *was* he thinking?" she suddenly gasped, seeing again that paper-thin wall between being and not being, the will to live grown fragile and the desire for release, strong. For Anne, Michael's absence held a deep, sharp pain. She wasn't sure it could be called love. Love, it seemed to her, was more of a dull ache.

Out loud, she said, "I think no life is wasted if there's love in it, and Michael loved the river." But she wasn't convinced. What about Mari and the baby and all that could have been? She was angry at Michael. She couldn't tell him off, bring him to his senses—save him. He had allowed something terrible to happen, taking a large piece of her with him, denting her convictions.

Maybe it *had* been an accident. Only then could she forgive him. Was it impulse, that meeting place of accident and design, an awaited and eventually seized opportunity? *We are not helpless, Michael,* she wanted to tell him. *We are responsible.*

"But we cannot blame," she remembered Dr. Vincent had once said. "One can only do the best one can do. The vigil is daily, and nothing short of heroic and admirable when balance is achieved."

The words quieted her now. Looking down at the baby, she smiled and, in answer, the baby cooed and focused as if she were saying, "I am here, and you are there."

Yes.

If he'd been silent before, Justin was what Rosemary would call wooden at Michael's funeral. He didn't stay long, excusing himself immediately after they'd gathered at the cemetery for Michael's memorial service. Briefly, and with a sense of duty, he sat next to Rosemary, staring out across the field where the wind played, trying to keep his eyes away from the wound in the earth before him. Once more he and Rosemary were together as mother and father. He felt sorry for her, sorrier for her than himself. He'd been out of the family circle, but Rosemary had depended on Michael. He'd put his hand over hers but it would only start her tears again. He would talk to her. But not now. Now they were each alone. He could no more have told Michael anything than Rosemary could have told *him* anything. Or Davey. No need to tell him anything either. Each had to run his own track. That's just the way it was. He was surprised he himself hadn't wound up like Michael. He felt an arm push its way through the crook of his. As in a spasm, he stiffened, but relaxed when he saw it was Annie. He leaned toward her, all of him grateful. So grateful it almost broke him.

Weeks later, on a night to be marked by a lunar eclipse, Rosemary was getting ready for bed, gathering her book and her glasses, the radio turned low, watching the clock so she wouldn't miss the eclipse. The moon dominated the sky, appearing larger than usual because of its closeness to the horizon, a huge copper ball nestled among the trees with an odd bright crescent now on its lower edge. She turned off the light so she could see clearly.

The telephone rang. She picked it up and went back to the window. There was no hello, only words beginning as though he was right there beside her.

"Can you see it?" he said. "Like an eye looking back?"

"Yes, I'm watching," she said softly.

The crescent slowly grew larger, an eye surprised. She was not surprised at all by the familiarity of the voice in her ear, which seemed to connect her with all of her life, a direct link to what she liked to think of as her soul. They were silent for a few moments, watching. She pictured him standing in the eerie light as she was, expectant, reverent. That he should choose this moment to call seemed significant, although she couldn't say why.

"Michael would love this," he said. Then he said, "How Michael loved natural things!—like chickens laying eggs, you know? He'd want to know all about it, exactly what happened. It was never enough to know that chickens lay eggs. He had to find out how."

She said, "Remember how he nailed a sign to the chicken coop door that said *Home?*" and she laughed for the first time since Michael died.

Justin went on, "He was a good son. I never worried about him handling *Greenfly* alone—how he loved to fish, remember, Rosemary? He'd come back with a bucketful—cleaned them all too, from the very beginning. He took—care of things," and there was a break in his voice.

Oh, yeah. Yeah. A good son, a responsible, sad, carry-the-weight-of-us son. Michael's eyes were suddenly before her, his curly hair so close she wanted to run her fingers through it, the underlying, unspoken anguish, *Could they have saved him?* floating in and around her words and Justin's.

Then finally they came to another silence, as though they'd simply run dry with grief at the heart of everything, drifting off where their own separate river of heartache began, where the words *if only I'd*—would remain unfathomable and seductive, lying in wait for weak moments the rest of their lives. Justin, turning to an easier flow of words, said, "Ran a 15K race this weekend. Still having a little trouble with my knee."

"How's your back?" she said.

"Running is good for it," he said. "Are you going to plant tomatoes this year?"

Yes, she would, of course she would, and peppers and lettuce. "The trees, Justin, the trees are producing beautiful apples now, finally," and as she listened and answered she realized it was no longer important what they said so much as the tone between them, gentle and low, the laughing deeper, the forgiveness in the words, the way he half-whispered, "Bye,

Rosemary." Her name sounded beautiful when he said it. She hadn't heard it in years, and she'd been living in its absence for so long.

When she thought to look back at the moon, it no longer looked astonished and confused, but shone full again, the circle complete, releasing her.

Word drifted back about the new owners down at Sulley's Point and what they planned to do. Renovate. Landscape. Did they know they must put up the purple martin house or the birds would circle the empty pole?

A check arrived from Abbott's Auctions. One hundred fourteen dollars. She tried not to dwell on the bitter knowledge that she had saved forty-five dollars and lost a son. She kept busy. Her attention focused on Mari, on the children at school, on such everyday things as the search for an antique dresser with a pink marble top for the baby. Sometimes it seemed to her an outrage that the world kept revolving.

She often took a ride on weekend afternoons, driving through the countryside along the network of back roads that connected everything in her heart, the wide landscape, the families of the children she'd taught, the houses, lonely and staunch, set back at the end of long lanes amid adjoining fields, the swells of tide along the marshes, the farm stands just opening with trays of timid seedlings. She often stopped the car at the woods' edge to stare into the tangle of trees, her eyes resting on honeysuckle, blueberry, blackberry, through them to one or two trees—dogwood, wild cherry—and through them to the next, refreshing herself on wisteria, sumac, beyond them to oak, maple, sweetgum, persimmon, and then to the thick, black strength of the high loblollies, the quiet greens that textured the depth, on and on, deeper and deeper—comfort as real as a hand on her shoulder while her mind searched the natural order of things. She no longer wept into her hands, *Poor Michael—poor, poor Michael*, but looked about her as if just waking up. Everything said, *You, Rosemary, are not that important, your losses not unique.*

One day, she found herself on a road with antique stores on three of the four corners of a crossroad. One was in an old church, one in a general store–gas station combination, and one in a long, high barn. She considered them for a minute, but the church had such an air of gloom and decay about it and the store seemed to have mostly glassware, so she chose the barn, the place with the furniture.

She picked her way around oak chests and headboards, bottomless oak chairs, and ran her fingers along the rich, pink-flecked marble of a washstand, perfect for the baby's room. And while she contemplated and planned and pressed her hand on the cool marble, she looked up to catch herself in the light of the old beveled mirror on the organ. Their organ. The same one, the mandolins softly gilded, the ribbons flowing through some evensong. Forgetting the washstand, she leapt to the organ and lifted the panel door. Her heart pounded. There was the small wooden yellow shoe from the Monopoly game. Michael's last connection with them, a way to return the five of them to their long, sweet summer dream, the boats gently slapping the water, flags stirring. Rosemary picked up the shoe as if she held a baby's hand. Michael. Her hand reached for her pocket, but instead she opened the panel door, pushed the small yellow shape into the dark corner of the shelf and closed the door.

She stared into the patch of blue sky caught in the mirror. Unguarded as in a dream, she watched as Justin dove into the river with the children following. An empty rowboat floated nearby and swimming toward them was a huge buck.

"Justin, look up! Justin, quick!" she whispered as if he could hear her. When he shot up through the riddle of water, hair splayed over his forehead, his body lustrous and slick in the spray, his old joyous aria was springing from his lips, "Hey! Hah haaaa," as he spotted the deer. Justin swimming, the children calling, herself standing on the shore—all, all was lost in the sound of his laughter which followed her to the open barn door as she left them, their faces clear as yesterday.

Photo by Cynthia Carmichael

A graduate of the M.F.A. Program at Vermont College, Barbara Lockhart has received Individual Artist Awards in Fiction from the Maryland State Arts Council for an excerpt from *Requiem for a Summer Cottage,* and for her short stories which have appeared in such venues as *Indiana Review, The Greensboro Review, Pleiades, Women's Words, Baltimore City Paper, Oceana Magazine,* and an anthology, *Generation to Generation.* She grew up in New York City and now lives on a twenty-two acre nature preserve she's planted with pines and dogwood on the Eastern Shore of Maryland.